She had given up on love, until he showed her the rich treasures hidden in her heart.

Praise for Kristin Hannah's previous
book,
A HANDFUL OF HEAVEN

"Reminiscent of LaVyrle Spencer ... A heart-warming love story that was a delight from start to finish."

JILL MARIE LANDIS

"A small treasure ... Hannah is a shining star on the horizon."

Romantic Times

"Light and entertaining."

Rendezvous

Also by Kristin Hannah
Published by Fawcett Books:

A HANDFUL OF HEAVEN

THE
ENCHANTMENT

Kristin Hannah

FAWCETT GOLD MEDAL • NEW YORK

A Fawcett Gold Medal Book
Published by Ballantine Books
Copyright © 1992 by Kristin Hannah

All rights reserved under International and Pan-American Copyright Conventions. Published in the United States by Ballantine Books, a division of Random House, Inc., New York, and simultaneously in Canada by Random House of Canada Limited, Toronto.

Library of Congress Catalog Card Number: 92-90149

ISBN 0-449-14773-8

Manufactured in the United States of America

First Edition: August 1992

*To my dad, for all the roads that needed to be explored.
You taught us to dream. To believe. And that has made
all the difference.*

And, of course, to Benjamin.

Special Thanks to . . .

Kathleen Gens for her invaluable assistance.
And Ken John, the storyteller who started it all.

Chapter One

Rain. Miserable, boring rain.

Emmaline Amanda Hatter stared out the mullioned window, trying to see Central Park through the gray haze that shrouded Eighth Avenue. Angry water drummed the thick glass, slashing downward in opaque, zigzagging streaks. A frigid postwinter wind rattled the pane. Cold seeped through the window and shivered across her fashionably bare shoulders.

Frowning, she let her gaze wander back to the men clustered in her parlor. Railroad tycoon Wilbur Jacobs stood hunched over the hors d'oeuvres table like a greedy rodent preparing for winter. With barely a pause to breathe, he rammed one elegant canapé after another into his already overstuffed mouth. His gray-whiskered cheeks worked feverishly to keep up.

Good God, she thought with a deepening frown. At the price of caviar, he could at least *chew*. There was nothing that irritated her more than spending her hard-earned money on fools.

She glanced at the elegantly clad man standing beside her. Tonight's horror was all *his* fault. "I can't believe

1

you talked me into hosting this disaster,'' she said to Michael Jameson through clenched teeth.

The president of Columbia College laughed softly. ''I saw you studying poor Wilbur. Should I fear for his health?''

Emma took a small sip of the ridiculously expensive champagne her cook had ordered. ''If you feel inclined to worry, try worrying about me. I should be examined by that German doctor from Vienna—what's his name? Freud? Only someone with a mental defect would host a fund-raiser in such financially uncertain times. I cannot imagine why I agreed.''

''You owed me,'' he said easily. ''Dr. Zinberg's patent made you a small fortune—and I could have taken him to Rockefeller.''

''Well after tonight that debt is paid in full, Michael. I refuse to—''

A boisterous pounding at the front door interrupted her. Emma's gaze cut to the salon's doorway. Long, tense minutes passed as she waited for someone to answer the door. No one did.

The hammering intensified until it echoed through the empty corridor and trembled beneath her feet. She thought about the dainty Meissen vase perched on the brass sconce beside the front door. That expensive knickknack represented her first big stock payoff, and it had cost her dearly. Like all her possessions, it was important to her—perhaps even more than most, because it was the first. If it fell because some stupid, unwanted guest didn't know how to knock like a gentleman . . .

No, she realized, no guest would be so rude. It had to be the butler she'd engaged for the evening. She glanced at the sterling-plated clock on her mantel and frowned.

He was more than an hour late. An hour!

Emmaline took a deep breath to quell her anger, and set down her Waterford goblet with exaggerated care. "Excuse me, Michael. It appears my butler has finally deigned to put in an appearance."

"Certainly."

With an almost imperceptible nod to Michael, she plucked up her heavy velvet skirts and exited the smoky, overcrowded room. The unseen man's hammer-hits reverberated through the walls, punctuating the rat-a-tat clicking of her elegant French heels on the walnut floorboards.

She crossed the marble foyer and reached the door. Prepared for battle, she flung it open, and immediately realized her mistake. Her gaze shot to the antique vase just as the door cracked against the wall. The Meissen wobbled precariously.

She surged forward but wasn't fast enough. The precious antique crashed to the floor. Porcelain shattered, flew everywhere. Eggshell-thin fragments scattered across the black and white marble tile like a pugilist's lost teeth.

She stared at the fragments in horror. The memory of the vase's purchase—and how much that day had meant—rushed to the forefront of her mind. Furious, she spun around. "Now look at what you've—"

One look at the intruder and her throat went dry. She stared, gape-mouthed, at the . . . thing in her doorway.

Tall, thin, wearing a hopelessly out-of-date black cape, it stood shadowed by the hallway's meager light. Beneath a sagging, slightly askew top hat was a dark void where a face should be.

She shook her head in disgust. This . . . creature . . . was no butler.

She reached for the door, prepared to slam it shut. Suddenly a hand snaked out from the sloshy black cape. Long, dripping wet fingers curled around the door, and a brown creedmore rain boot snuck through the opening and planted itself on her floor. "Is this the Hatter apartment?"

Even the voice sounded wet. Emmaline squeezed her eyes shut, briefly imagining herself strangling the biddy at the employment house. "Yes, but—"

"Great!" He shoved the door open and pushed his way through. Emmaline stumbled backward, crashing into the wall behind her with a resounding thud.

He limped across the threshold like some creature from a Grimm Brothers fairy tale. His uneven, wobbling gait gave him an odd, drunken appearance. Emma watched in horror as his muddy boots squished across the wooden floor and sank into the ivory wool of her Aubusson rug.

Water streamed off his ugly top hat and cloak in a thousand silver streams. He pushed a lock of dark brown hair off his forehead. It immediately plopped back in front of his eyes. Shrugging, as if to say, *I tried*, he flashed her an eager grin and extended his right hand. "How do you—"

She charged him. Halfway there, a spray of water hit her in the face. The world turned into a watery blur. She came to a sputtering halt. It took a moment for her vision to clear.

The hulk was shaking like a freshly bathed dog!

Emmaline flung her pointed finger toward the open door. "Get out!"

His already oversize grin expanded—although Emma

would have sworn such a thing was physically impossible. "What?"

"Get out."

"Just a second." He rammed his flattened palm against his ear. At the contact, more water flew from his head and clothes.

"*Get* . . ." Emma's teeth came together with a snap when she realized she was screaming like one of the fishwives she'd known in her youth. An acrid memory of old Mrs. Hopcoat sitting on the tenement's decaying stoop slammed through her mind. The woman's shrill, biting voice assailed her. *Whitefish . . . day-old whitefish . . . two cents a pound . . .*

The unexpected remembrance brought an involuntary shudder. With a ruthlessness born of practice, she forced the memory from her mind. "Get out," she repeated with considerably more control.

He smacked his ear again. "What was that?"

Deaf. She stared at him in disbelief. They had sent her a deaf butler.

Marching forward, she snapped her chin up to look at him. Bright, intelligent green eyes peered intently into her own. He smiled suddenly, and her breath caught for an instant. She came to a dead stop. In his eyes was something she hadn't seen for a very long time in her own: happiness. The bright and shining emotion was so unexpected, so completely *foreign*, that for one confusing heartbeat she was speechless.

He surveyed the entryway with obvious wonder. "Beautiful room."

The spell shattered. Room? she thought with contempt. A butler thought the foyer was a room? "That's it." Emma grabbed his arm, spun him around, and pushed him out of her apartment.

He turned to look at her. His bright smile wobbled, fell. Confusion replaced the wonder in his green eyes. "Isn't the party inside?"

"Not for you, it isn't," Emma answered. "And you can tell your boss not to expect a dime from me."

"Isn't he here? I thought—"

"Nice try." She slammed the door shut in his face.

Emmaline spun on her heel and walked briskly back toward the parlor. Halfway there, she saw Michael Jameson heading her way with two glasses of champagne. She walked right past him. She didn't feel sociable right now, and besides, she needed something stronger than champagne.

Michael executed a quick pivot and fell into step beside her. "What happened? I saw—"

"I threw the idiot out."

He stopped. "You did what?"

It took Emma a few steps to realize that Michael was no longer walking with her. Slowing, she turned around and walked back to him. "Surely you're not going deaf, too. I threw him out. He's gone. And good riddance."

"But—"

"I know what you're going to say, and don't bother. I don't care a fig that a butler is the thing to have at a party. I am not about to pay top dollar for a late, deaf, incompetent server just so that Mrs. Astor—who wouldn't allow her dead body to be dragged into my home—won't be offended."

"He must have told you—"

She sighed. "Michael, I appreciate that you want this party to go well. It's your college that will benefit. But I had to decide quickly—another ten seconds and my Aubusson rug would have shrunk to the size of a postage stamp."

"Emmaline, will you let me speak?"

"Certainly."

A smile curved his lips. "That man was no butler."

"At least we agree on something." She grabbed one of his champagne glasses and took a sizable drink. "You should have seen what that old biddy at the employment house sent me. Even that fool you and Caroline engaged for your Christmas party was more competent."

"I *did* see him. I went to get a glass of champagne, and when I got back, he was gone."

"Like I said, good riddance."

"Emmaline," he said in a voice tinged with laughter, "that wasn't your hired butler." His smile graduated to a grin. "It was Dr. Digby."

She gasped in horror. There was a heartbeat's pause before he added, "I see you recognize the guest of honor's name when you hear it."

Dr. Larence Digby stared at the door. A frown worked itself across his face. Something was wrong. True, it was his first party, but he was pretty sure he was supposed to be *inside* the house. . . .

What had he done? Or not done? He'd read Duffey's *Ladies' and Gentlemen's Etiquette* from cover to cover. Of course, he'd thought the person answering the door would give him enough time to think. Problem was, he didn't think quickly. Never had.

He'd made his usual mess of things. He shouldn't have allowed himself to get so caught up in the beauty of the city at night. Ordinary people weren't mesmerized by the glitter of a fat raindrop as it slid down a streetlight's pane. Most people wouldn't even notice such a thing.

But Larence could no more overlook that singular

beauty than he could fly past it. The world was just too exceptional, too breathtaking, to ignore. After so many years of darkness, of *nothingness*, he simply couldn't ignore the many faces of light.

He'd forgotten that the people behind that door didn't notice a rainstorm, let alone the beauty of a single drop. They were the people who made the world go around, not the people who watched its pirouette. The businessmen. And tonight he'd meant to be one of them.

Ordinarily the thought would have brought a self-deprecating smile to his lips. The thought of him— *him*—fitting in with the hardheads behind that door was worth a good belly laugh.

Ordinarily.

He clenched his fists in familiar frustration. If only he could be like other people; if only he could care more about concrete, day-to-day things, and less about castles in the air and people who might have been.

After all the work, all the dreaming, all the planning, he'd botched it. The door stood between him and every dream he'd ever had.

What now? he wondered. Knock again or simply walk away? It wasn't in his nature to give up; neither was it easy for him to fight publicly for what he wanted. He'd lived too long alone, friendless, to be comfortable with strangers. Especially with the type of people behind that door.

But even as he asked himself the question, he knew the answer. They wouldn't have believed him anyway— wouldn't have believed *in* him. He'd simply have to find another way to get funding for his project. And find it he would, even if he had to wait a lifetime.

Turning, he started toward the elevator. On his second step, a familiar fire wrenched his left ankle. White-hot pain shot into his shin. He pivoted back toward the door, searching for support. His palm smacked against the carved mahogany of the front door and held him upright.

With one hand bolted to the door, he bent over. The top of his head brushed the wood. Shaking, he wiped the sheen of sweat from his forehead.

After so many years of living with the pain, he knew how to combat it. He focused his every thought on the next breath, and the next, until gradually his breathing normalized. The pain receded, cooled, slinking back into the damaged bone in which it lived.

Suddenly the door opened and he fell face-first through the opening and landed on the wet white carpet with a thud.

"Aah!" From somewhere above his head, he heard a woman's shriek. A bell-like burgundy velvet skirt rushed toward him. The soft fabric breezed across his cheeks, then stilled. He caught a glimpse of white lace and black shoes before the skirt settled primly into place.

Rolling onto his back, he found himself staring up into a woman's upside-down face. Silver-blond wisps of hair curled across the pale, perfect skin. Blue eyes peered questioningly into his own. Midnight blue, he thought dreamily, the color of advancing night.

She bent closer toward him. "Are you all right, Dr. Digby?" Her mellifluous voice flowed through him like warmed cognac. "I'm sorry I expelled you earlier; you see, I thought—oh, well, that's neither here nor there. The fact is, you're . . . welcome. I sent Mr. Jameson to announce your arrival to the men in the parlor."

Welcome . . . here! He grinned.

She immediately popped upright and backed away from him.

He rolled onto his stomach. Squishing his palm deeper into the rug, he pushed to his knees, then to his feet.

The first thing he noticed was the woman; she was staring at him in obvious distress. As if he'd already done something wrong. Her exquisitely beautiful face was screwed into the most austere pinch he'd ever seen. Her gaze plunged to the mud splotches on the rug and riveted there, narrowing.

He lurched sideways to get off the carpet. When he landed, pain jabbed into his bad ankle. He gritted his teeth and ignored it.

In less than a heartbeat he was able to dredge up a smile. Swiping the borrowed top hat off his head, he executed an awkward, but much practiced bow. "Larence Digby, at your service, ma'am."

Her intense blue eyes swept his attire from head to foot in a single glance. Disapproval tightened the corners of her mouth. "At *my* service, Dr. Digby? How comforting. I'll advise my housekeeper that you're here—finally. She can take your . . . cloak and direct you to the parlor. You may begin your presentation in one quarter hour. Will that be sufficient time?"

"Y-Yes."

Emma spun on her heel and headed for the kitchen. Her heels clicked in rapid-fire succession as she marched away from the disaster in her foyer. *Dr. Digby indeed.* One eyebrow cocked upward derisively. This fund-raiser was in serious trouble. No one would give hard-earned money to an idiot like Digby—especially not with the problems on Wall Street. People funded scientists who inspired confidence. Not laughter.

"Uh, ma'am?"

The sound of Digby's voice brought her to a reluctant halt. Without bothering to turn around, she answered him. "Yes, Dr. Digby?"

"I didn't catch your name."

"I'm Emmaline Hatter—your hostess."

"Oh . . . nice to meet you. I suppose I should have guessed," he said with a good-natured laugh.

"Yes. Now, if you'll excuse me, I'll go fetch Mrs. Sanducci."

"Uh, Miss Hatter . . . ?"

She pretended she hadn't heard and kept marching.

Precisely fifteen minutes later, Larence stood in the center of Miss Hatter's parlor, staring at the semicircle of important men who were staring back at him. Pungent swirls of tobacco smoke flitted around the room like ghostly apparitions, darting in and out of Larence's nostrils until his throat felt raw and dry. He swallowed hard, wishing he'd thought to ask for a glass of water. Sweat itched along his hairline. He rubbed his damp palms on the nubby wool of his trousers.

Placing his drawings on the wooden easel Michael had brought, Larence smoothed the long, white pieces of paper. Dampness seeped from his palms into the crisp sheets, making a yellowish smudge. Someone in the audience cleared his throat. The sound seemed to grab Larence by the neck and twist. Nervously he smoothed the paper again, although there wasn't a ripple to mar the artwork he'd slaved over.

Emmaline Hatter appeared at his side in a swirl of burgundy velvet. Rhinestones beaded her skirt and glittered in the pale glow of gaslight. She stood silently, her bare shoulders perfectly erect, her chin tilted slightly

upward. Her classically beautiful face was expression-
less, and yet Larence had the distinct impression that
she was worried about something.

She clapped loudly, and the conversation in the room
abruptly died. "Gentlemen, I thank you for attending
this fund-raising dinner party. You all know Michael
Jameson, president of Columbia College. . . ."

There it was again, Larence thought dreamily, that
wonderful voice. He closed his eyes, listening to its
soft, singsong sensuosity.

Suddenly she touched him. Larence's eyes flew open.
He stared disbelievingly at the hand resting on his forearm. Her fingers looked pale against the linty, damp
black wool of his sleeve. Pale and unfamiliar. Women
so rarely touched him. . . .

"And now I'd like you to meet Dr. Digby, Columbia's famous history professor, who's going to tell us
his startling new discovery. As we all know, everything
new takes money, and education is no exception. The
college needs our donations to fund an expedition to
prove Dr. Digby's theory, so please, be generous."

She was gone in a heartbeat. Taking a seat center
stage, she plaited her pale fingers in her lap, drew her
elegantly shod feet together, stiffened her spine, and
waited.

He could feel her gaze on him. Cold. Blue. Demanding.

Suddenly he knew why she'd touched him. For some
reason, it was important to *her* that he succeed tonight.
The touch had been her public blessing. But why?

She cleared her throat.

Larence jumped at the sound. It was time. Fifteen
years of research came down to this moment. This op-

portunity. He wet his paper-dry lips. *Please, God, don't let me fail. . . .*

He took a slim wooden pointer from his frayed canvas satchel, gripping it tightly enough to mask the trembling of his fingers. The audience shifted in their seats. A few hearty souls even leaned forward slightly. In the corner, Michael nodded imperceptibly. *You can do it,* he mouthed.

Larence took a deep breath, offered Michael a nervous smile, then turned for his notes. At the movement, another pain gripped his ankle. He stumbled sideways. His fist shot out for something to grab on to and connected hard with the easel. The tablet flew off the wooden stand, fluttered against itself, and fell to the floor. He clutched the thin metal frame with shaking fingers and steadied himself.

Larence's stomach knotted with shame. He squeezed his eyes shut, waiting for the agony to abate before turning back to the audience with a forced smile. "Sorry," he mumbled.

Clumsily he retrieved his work and rearranged it. Taking another deep breath, he said another silent prayer, smoothed his borrowed black suit coat, and launched into his presentation. "In Roman times—"

A single, deflated sigh swept the audience.

The words logjammed in Larence's throat. They didn't want to hear about ancient Rome.

Yet, he told himself resolutely. They didn't want to hear about it yet. Once he got into the wondrous tale of the seven lost cities founded by exiled Roman priests, they'd be enthralled. They had to be.

He wet his lips again. He'd planned this, practiced it a hundred times. He could do it. He could captivate and intrigue them with the legend that had fueled his dreams since boyhood.

He took a deep breath, focused his attention on the map of ancient Rome he'd drawn so carefully, and started over.

Chapter Two

By the time Dr. Dimwit reached the sixteenth century, Emmaline had lost all feeling in her lower body. She shifted uncomfortably on the hard, wood-slatted chair she'd rented for the evening, and immediately wished she hadn't. A thousand fire-hot tingles pinched her fanny and skittered in painful streaks down her shins. She took a deep breath, trying—futilely—to squash her irritation. It took all her self-control not to leap up and grab Digby's pointer from him.

Her groggy gaze shot to the mantel clock. Eleven o'clock.

The idiot had been talking for three solid hours. *Three*.

She refused to look at him, knowing that if she did, she wouldn't be able to keep the contempt from her eyes. And *that*, she knew, would be a big mistake. At all costs, the investors had to think she believed in Digby's stupid quest. To avoid looking at him, she pinned her glare on the clock. The slow, methodical march of the timepiece's metallic hands punctuated Digby's monotone ramblings. That and the quiet hush of heavy breathing were the only sounds in the parlor.

Rain no longer thumped across the apartment's pitched rooftop or slashed at the small windowpane in silver streaks. The howling wind had dwindled to a late night sigh. Even nature, it seemed, had fallen asleep.

Emma stifled a heartfelt groan. *Little wonder.*

She shot a surreptitious glance at Digby. The dimwit was wide-awake, and talking with a degree of animation normally reserved for children on Christmas morn. His attention, as usual, was fastened on his drawings. Not once in the past three hours had he actually *looked* at his audience. Oh, no. He was too busy staring at his multicolored chicken scratches to care about his listeners. Emma was half-blind from squinting at the ridiculous drawings.

Still, blind or not, she should at least *look* interested. It was the only hope she had of fulfilling her promise to Michael without having to dig into her own bank account. She had to find something—anything—in Digby's speech that would inspire the men in this room to fund the doctor's expedition, and unfortunately she could only do that by listening to him.

Straightening, she forced herself to concentrate on what he was saying.

"On the seventh day of March, in the year of our Lord 1539, Esteban, a Moorish slave, and Fray Marcos de Niza, a Franciscan friar, left Mexico City. Their quest: to find the legendary lost cities of Cibola . . ."

The sixteenth century . . .

With sudden, certain clarity, she knew it was useless. She'd never get the men to invest in the professor's harebrained scheme. The party was a disaster; Digby was a joke. Nothing, not even her considerable clout on Wall Street, would make the professor look like a good investment.

Strangely, the realization brought relief. Admitting defeat made it easier to accept. The starch slipped out

of her spine as she settled sleepily into the rented chair.
Her fingers unfurled. There was no point in pretending
to listen to him any longer. She might as well relax.

Digby's words droned on. And on. And on.

The monotonous cadence of his voice coaxed the tension from Emma's body. Her eyelids fell to half-mast.
Lazily she studied him through the spidery veil of her
lashes. He was spouting off about something. Probably
broken bits of pottery, or something equally vital to the
world order. She didn't bother listening. The last time
she'd paid attention, he'd spent half an hour on a bunch
of muddleheaded priests who founded a few secret cities. Men who'd taken vows of poverty definitely didn't
interest Emma.

Then, suddenly, he looked at her.

Emma lurched awake. Her heart skipped a beat.

A believer's passion shone from his bottle green eyes
like the full-blown rays of a midsummer sun, scorching
in its intensity. There was no mistaking it, even if one
hadn't seen that look before. And Emmaline had. She'd
seen it in her father's eyes a thousand times—every time
he'd talked about one of his schemes to get rich quick.

Digby immediately turned back to his drawings. Emmaline swallowed hard, shaken by the sudden remembrance. She'd spent years trying to forget her father's
farfetched dreams, and their cost to his family.

And now, unexpectedly, here they were again. Questions. What ifs. What if her father had been given the
chance Digby was botching so badly? What if the city's
richest men had spent a night listening to her father's
dreams? Would he be alive now?

Emma forced the questions from her mind, just as
she had done a thousand times before, by sheer force

of will. Her father, and his useless, empty dreams, were gone, buried in a pauper's grave in Potter's Field.

A dinner party wouldn't have helped her father any more than it would help this man. God knew Digby wouldn't be getting a dime from the men in her parlor. Businessmen didn't pay for dreams. They paid for results. It was a reality her father had never learned.

Money. Cold hard cash. That's what made dreams come true. Dreaming about anything but money, and the security it created, was just plain stupid. That was one lesson she'd learned the hard way.

It was so close, Larence thought excitedly. So close to coming true. The dream he'd cherished for almost half his life was inches away from being his.

He flipped the second-to-the-last sheet of paper over the easel's top. The final drawing filled his vision and sucked him into another world. He stared at it, transfixed. His monologue dwindled to a mumble and then trailed off altogether.

There it was, for all to see: the secret, rock-faced entrance to the legendary city of Cibola. A shiver of anticipation coursed through his body. His heart pounded with excitement. This was it. The moment he'd waited half his life for.

Like a sputtering engine, he found his voice again. The final, memorized sentence of his speech tumbled from his mouth. ". . . And with your generous support, I intend to use this remarkable diary to retrace Esteban's footsteps. Hopefully he will lead me to the legendary Lost City of Cibola.''

It took Larence's mind a moment to wend its way back to the present. As always, the past was so vivid in his thoughts that when he spoke of it, he lived it. Slowly he came back to earth, and realized that it was over. He'd finished.

His breath escaped in a long, trembling sigh of triumph. He'd done it. With nothing more than a few sheets of paper, and his own magical words, he'd recreated the wondrous, legendary Lost City of Cibola. A triumphant grin spread across his face as he turned to look at his audience.

What he saw made his heart stop. Not one of them was awake. Not even Michael. The parlor looked like one of those wild West saloons he'd read about, with men sprawled in chairs and slumped over tables. Snores rumbled through the room. Why hadn't he noticed the sound before?

Larence felt as if he'd been punched in the gut. His grin wobbled, flattened, vanished. He'd blown it. Suddenly his feet felt unsteady. He sank onto the settee and slumped forward, burying his face in his hands.

He'd spent fifteen years of his life gathering data and fueling his dream, and turning the impossible into reality. And now . . . now when he'd finally been given the opportunity to make it all come true, he'd *failed*.

Why? he thought desperately. Why was he so unable to communicate with people? God, he tried so hard. . . .

Emma wakened slowly. Something was different. Raising a hand to massage the aching crick in her neck, she coaxed her heavy eyelids open. Then she noticed it: silence. The professor had finished!

She snapped her head up and started clapping, slowly at first as her groggy mind cleared, and then louder. Out of the corner of her eye, she saw Michael stagger to his feet. He mouthed a single word: *disaster*.

She shook her head in disagreement, then hurried to

Digby's side. "Stand up," she hissed just loud enough for him to hear. Before he had time to answer, she clapped again for attention. "Ah, gentlemen . . ."

"They're asleep," Larence mumbled.

"Two hours ago they were asleep," Emma commented sharply. "Now they're in comas." She shot him an assessing, contemptuous glance. "I take it your specialty is research?"

He looked up at her through dull green eyes. "Yes. How did you know?"

"A wild guess. Now, stand up."

Larence eased himself to a stand as, one by one, the men around him roused themselves.

"Gentlemen," Emma said as the last guest wakened, "I know each of you would like to talk to Dr. Digby, but I'm afraid I must commandeer him for a moment." A sigh of relief swept the audience. Emma pretended not to notice. "So, please, have another drink, and make yourselves comfortable."

She plucked up her skirts an unfashionable but practical two inches. "Follow me," she said, already moving.

"But . . . but some of the men are asking for their coats."

Emma didn't turn around. "Rats have always known when to leave a sinking ship."

She marched briskly toward the door, her chin held high so that none of the guests would suspect her inner turmoil. Behind her, she could hear Digby's shuffling, awkward footsteps. Damn him, she thought again. He'd ruined everything. If he'd had half a brain, she could have convinced the men to invest. But Digby had given her nothing—*nothing*—to work with, and now *she* had to turn disaster into success.

Larence hurried to keep up with her grueling pace. Every time his left foot hit the hard wooden floor, hot shards of pain shot to his knee. He forced himself to ignore it. Instinctively he knew she was testing him. For some strange reason, she wanted him to fail, wanted him to give her a reason to slam the door in his face again. He gritted his teeth and plodded along behind her, one painful step at a time.

She pushed through a half-open door and disappeared. Larence picked up his awkward pace and followed her into a small, dimly lighted room. It took his eyes a moment to adjust.

She'd led him to a library of some sort. Row upon row of new-looking leather-bound volumes covered the wall beside him in muted shades of russet, brown, gold, and green. The smell of crisp new paper and good-quality leather perfumed the heavy, cloying air of a room whose windows were never opened.

Slowly the rest of the room came into focus. A forest green tapestried paper blanketed the upper portion of the remaining three walls, its primordially lush color disappearing at waist level into stark mahogany wainscoting. In the exact center of the room, facing no windows, was a huge mahogany desk, its mirror-bright surface dotted with carefully aligned piles of important-looking papers. A soft golden glow crept through the lamp's scrolled Japanese paper dome and cast pale fingers on the reddish wood.

Emmaline swept into the massive wooden chair behind the desk, and immediately turned her attention to the stack of papers nearest her hand.

Again Larence was struck by her beauty. In the lamp's light, she seemed to glow like a golden goddess. The claret-hued velvet of her gown made her skin seem almost ethereally pale. Flyaway strands of white-blonde hair curled across her brow and along her temple, softening the austere way she'd pulled it back from her face. If she'd smile, even once, she'd be the most beautiful woman he'd ever seen.

"Sit," she commanded in the distracted tone of one used to being obeyed without question.

Larence couldn't help himself. In the face of her imperious attitude, he was seized by an irrepressible urge to needle her. "Where?"

She looked up sharply. "I forgot you were a college professor. Perhaps you'd feel more comfortable if I offered a multiple-choice answer."

He laughed. "I take it you feel a certain . . . disdain for higher education."

If he thought she'd smile, he was wrong.

"Book-based education—I hesitate to use the term 'higher'—is something which I hold in supreme indifference."

"Indifference? But these glorious books—"

"Are decorations. I don't read, Dr. Digby." At his gasp, she smiled grimly. "Oh, I can, but I choose not to. You know the old saying, 'Those who can, do; those who can't, teach.' I do."

"But books invite us to other worlds, fuel our dreams, fill our senses. You miss so much by turning your back on them."

"The last thing I need is a bunch of useless dreams." She gave him a chillingly cold look and then eased the top desk drawer open. "Now, Dr. Digby, fascinating as this discussion is, I suggest we focus instead on the business at hand. As you may—or may not—have noticed, I have a houseful of guests to which I must attend. So shall we get on with it?"

He moved toward the chair facing her desk. On his second step, pain jolted into his ankle and shin. His leg buckled, and he stumbled forward, collapsing into the overstuffed velvet chair with a sigh.

He steeled himself for her show of concern, false though it would be. *Oh, dear, may I help you?* was a sentence he'd heard all his life from women—usually just before they left with another man.

She said nothing. Slowly he relaxed. One by one his fingers released their death grip on the chair's wooden arm, and his breathing normalized. When he finally allowed himself to look up, he found her looking directly at him. There was an intensity about her gaze that made him feel uncomfortable—as though she held his limp against him, or, more accurately, as though she saw it as a moral failing rather than a physical one. "Are you all right?" she asked in a clipped, matter-of-fact voice.

"Fine."

She looked about to say something. He leaned forward, eager to hear what a woman like her would say about someone else's pain.

"Good. Then let's get on with it."

He frowned, easing back into the chair. "With what?"

"What else?" she responded sharply. "What do people like you always want from people like me? Money."

Larence's heart stopped dead, then kicked into a gallop. "Money?" he whispered. It was something he hadn't considered, not even for an instant. That *she* would help him. "You mean you're considering funding my expedition?"

"Someone at this party has to, and after your . . . detailed presentation, no one else is willing."

"Or awake."

Her lips didn't so much as twitch upward. "Yes. So, as much as I abhor parting with money, I must. I owe a debt to Michael—and to Columbia, for that matter. He's counting on me."

Larence leaned forward. "As am I, Miss Hatter. Myself and all the world."

A quick rolling of her eyes relayed her opinion of that. "How much do you need?"

"Ten thousand dollars."

She flinched. "And for that amount, you'll get what?"

He was momentarily taken aback. "Get?"

"What is it you're looking for? Gold, silver, jewels, what?"

Cibola as he'd always imagined it filled his mind. He saw the buildings and streets and artwork of a civilization long gone. It was a sight he'd dreamed of seeing for half his life. Even as a boy, he'd known somehow that it was his destiny to find the lost city; his recompense from God for being a cripple. Finding Cibola would make him, for one bright and shining moment, whole.

But what kind of answer was that? He studied Emmaline's flawlessly beautiful, emotionless face, searched her exquisite, ice-cold eyes. She'd never understand an answer like that.

So he gave the second-best answer. The one he'd given to hundreds of his students, the one everyone in the world understood and accepted. "Knowledge."

She snorted. "You must be joking."

"Joking? Why would I—"

"Will there be gold in the city?"

He frowned. "I believe so, but that's unimportant compared to—"

"Silver?"

"Almost certainly, but again—"

"Treasures?"

"Undoubtably, but Miss Hatter—"

"Fine." She pulled a leather-bound ledger from the top drawer, and opened it slowly. "Eight thousand dollars, was it?"

"Ten."

She grimaced. "Oh, yes." Carefully extracting her scrolled silver black pen from its holder, she wrote out the check. Long, tense moments passed as the ink dried.

With a quickly suppressed shudder, she handed him the check. Larence's fingers shook as he took the piece of paper from her. She had just handed him the key to unlock his greatest dreams. Words of gratitude flooded his mind and clogged in his throat. All he could do was stare at her in awe.

She flipped open a small sterling silver box and took out a crisp, white card. "Here's my calling card. Send me a telegram when you find the city. I'll take half."

Confused, he looked down at the card in his hand, then across the desk at her. "Half?"

"Of what you find in Ciburra."

Larence's blood froze. "I don't understand. . . ."

She studied him with unconcealed disgust. It was obvious she considered him only slightly smarter than the stuffed owl perched in the library's corner. "And just what is it you don't understand?"

"About you wanting half of what I find. The treasures of Cibola belong to the world, not any one person. They need to be showcased in museums—"

"That's what you'll do with your half. My half, I'll sell to the highest bidder."

"*Sell!*" He could hear the horror in his voice, feel it

violating his soul. He felt the check slip out of his fingers, taking his dream with it.

"Yes, Dr. Digby, sell. Why would I make an investment of this size with no hope of turning a profit? I'm a businessperson, not a philanthropist."

"But surely you can't mean to profit on history?"

"Look, Dr. Digby, this discussion is becoming tiresome. Take my money, or don't take it, it's up to you. But if you take it, there's a price. I get half of whatever you find."

He squeezed his eyes shut. The image of treasures, thousands of years old, being hacked up and separated like so many parts of a chicken filled his mind. His stomach wrenched at the thought.

She clicked her jeweled gold pocket watch open. "*Now*, Dr. Digby."

"Without your money, I'll never find the city," he mumbled.

"Dreams have a price, Doctor. That's a lesson I have learned myself. Now, what's your decision?"

He tried to analyze the situation quickly. What other option did he have? What other choice? Without her money, he was back to the beginning—and it had taken him fifteen years to get this far. The thought of starting over made him feel queasy. Desperate.

She leaned forward. The muffled thump of her elbows hitting the hardwood caused him to jump slightly. Her gaze narrowed, scrutinized him. Amusement flickered through her eyes and then was gone, as if she was *pleased* by his dilemma. "Well, Digby?" Her words hung heavily in the silent, breath-laden air, and this time there was no mistaking her smile. "What will you do?"

It was another test, he realized suddenly. A test she

wanted him to fail. She wanted him *not* to take the money.

He smiled at his own deductive powers. It made perfect sense; she was a miser who'd unaccountably been put in the position of spending her money. The only way she could back out of her commitment was if *he* declined her offer.

A river of relief rushed through him. Her threat was only that—a threat; a smoke screen to keep him from thinking clearly. She wouldn't do it—not really. Not once she'd seen the treasures, touched them, seen their incredible value to the world. No one could sell the past to the highest bidder, could they?

The more he thought about it, the more sure he became. Perhaps she even *believed* she could sell the treasures, but once she'd seen them, touched them, she'd realize her mistake. Cibola and its treasures belonged to the world. Not to any one person.

"Very well," he said slowly. The moment the words slipped out of his mouth, he felt as if an anvil had been lifted off his shoulders. "I'll take your money."

"Oh," she answered, and the look on her face told him he'd been right. She'd wanted him to refuse the money. "When will you be leaving?"

"I don't know. It's all so unexpected. . . . A few months, maybe. It will take me a while to make all the arrangements."

"I'll expect to hear from you before you leave. Good luck, Dr. Digby."

He watched her sail out of the room with the controlled, regal bearing of a lioness. Not once did she look back at him. Larence looked down at the check in his hands. The stark white paper danced in his shaking fingers.

Ten thousand dollars.

There was nothing to stop him now. Nothing.

The adventure he'd waited a lifetime for had just begun.

Chapter Three

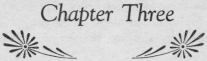

Emmaline walked briskly down the gray stone canyon of Broadway, her plain black satin umbrella set at
a no-nonsense angle above her severe, backswept coif-
fure. Rain thumped her umbrella and splattered in huge,
icy droplets on the flagstone sidewalk, splashing the
toes of her Pebble goat walking shoes. Wind snapped
at her thick woolen skirts. Chin up, eyes straight ahead,
she strode toward her usual Monday morning destination.

The morning's dark, rain-heavy air filled her lungs.
She inhaled deeply, savoring the familiar scent of New
York City's financial district during an early spring
shower. She loved this part of the city in the morning;
it was so vibrant, so alive.

Most people felt hemmed in by the towering buildings crammed against one another on either side of the
street. But not Emma. She loved the colorless blocks
of stone that encased the city's financial heart. It didn't
matter to her that their straining skyline blocked out all
but the hardiest rays of the ineffectual sun. When she
wanted sun, she went to her summer house in
Manchester-by-the-sea. When she wanted anything else,
she went to Wall Street.

Eagerness to begin the day quickened her pace. At

the corner of Broadway and Wall she looked up to check for traffic, and was surprised to find the street almost deserted.

Fools, she thought of her peers. *She* didn't let a little thing like foul weather stand in the way of getting to work. That's why she had succeeded where so many had failed.

Grasping her skirt and heavy gossamer overcoat in one gloved hand, she hurried across the street toward the Smitherton Guaranty and Trust Bank.

In front of the bank she stopped just long enough to adjust the tilt of her high-crowned Rainsford hat. Her fingers slid hesitantly toward her forehead, and she immediately frowned. A riot of blond curls had broken free of their moorings and were now wisping freely across her forehead.

Disgust thinned her lips. The curls always ruined her appearance. No matter how much water she slapped on her hair to straighten it, the tiny corkscrews broke free.

It was important that she look her best for bank president Eugene Cummin. She and Eugene had been engaged in a discreet, businesslike affair for nearly a year. Not an ordinary *affaire de coeur*, of course; Emma didn't believe in love, and she was fairly certain that he didn't either. More of an . . . economic and social liaison. A relationship that suited both of them to perfection—at least, it suited her well. She had never thought to ask Eugene whether it was equally satisfactory for him.

He would have found it odd if she had. They rarely talked about personal things. Even their bedtime talk was strictly business. Oh, occasionally they'd laugh, or tell a joke. But not often. Life on the streets of New York had given Emma an unconventional and practical opinion of sex. She'd learned long ago—too long—that everything she had was either an asset or a liability, and sex was no different.

Her relationship with Eugene gave their business dealings a spicier, more intriguing edge. And, most important these days, it pleased her. She actually rather enjoyed giving the priggish ladies of the Four Hundred something to gossip about.

He wasn't much to look at perhaps, but his financial skills more than compensated for any lack in his physical appearance. They were a solid money-making team. She had even considered the possibility of merging their fortunes when the time came for her to have children.

Heaving a sigh that strained the starched white pleats of her shirtwaist, she smoothed the intricately coiled Roman knot at her nape and plucked up her skirt. Climbing the massive pile of steps that led to the bank's entrance, she stared at the huge wooden doors that would any moment be flung open in greeting.

They stayed shut. Her smile faded. Surely the idiotic doorman didn't expect her—*her!*—to open the door for herself. Disgusted, she drew herself up to her full height of five six, threw her shoulders back, and barreled up to the closed door. She waited one-tenth of a second for it to open, then snapped her umbrella shut and rapped sharply on the portal's small window.

From behind the door came the sound of rushing feet, and then the door was whisked open. The doorman's watery eyes took one look at her and bulged in surprise. Color crawled up his accordion-wrinkled neck. "I-I'm sorry, Miss Hatter. It's just that . . ." His gaze plummeted to the brightly polished toes of his shoes. "I didn't expect you today."

Emma swept into the bank. "For ten years I've been

here every Monday morning at precisely eight-thirty A.M. And you," she added with a pointed look, "have opened the door for me every single one of those days."

"But today . . . well . . ."

She shoved her umbrella at him and began peeling off her damp five-button kid gloves. She didn't care a fig for the old geezer's excuses. It would serve him right if she reported his incompetence to Eugene.

She heard the door click shut behind her. The sound echoed in the unusually quiet lobby. Without another glance at the doorman, Emma jerked her chin to its proper tilt and started down the polished marble hallway.

"Good morning, Miss Hatter."

The unexpected greeting brought Emma to a halt. Turning, she noticed Miss Baxter waving at her from behind the polished brass bars of her teller's cage. A gloating smile wreathed the woman's pretty face.

Emmaline's frown intensified. Miss Baxter and she hadn't spoken since Emma had reported the teller's incompetence to Eugene.

"I didn't expect to see you here this morning," Miss Baxter cooed with a deepening smile. "I must say, I do admire your courage."

Emma snapped her gaze away from the teller and moved on, her rapid footsteps echoing loudly through the hushed, austere lobby of the building. She turned the last corner and strode up to Eugene's private office.

"Mr. Cummin, please," she said to the young man seated at the desk outside Eugene's office.

"And do you have an—" He looked up from his book and saw Emma. His smile wobbled and fell.

"Is there a problem?" she asked tightly. "I wish to see Eugene."

"O-Oh, of course. It's just that I didn't—"

"*Don't* say you didn't expect me today. Just tell Eugene I'm here."

The young man's expression melted into one of concern. "Go on in," he said in a soft, almost sad voice. "Mr. Cummin asked for your file not fifteen minutes ago."

With a brisk nod, Emma brushed past the reception desk and knocked sharply on Eugene's handsomely carved mahogany door. At his muffled answer, she swept into his office. "Good morning, Eugene."

Eugene looked up from the report he was studying. Emma offered him her brightest Monday morning smile, and began unbuttoning her caped gossamer. "I must say, it's been the oddest morning. Why, the doorman—" She caught the strange look in Eugene's eyes and frowned. "Is something the matter?"

He squeezed his eyes shut for a moment, then opened them slowly. Tired brown eyes stared deeply into her own. "Emmaline . . ." His normally strong voice was weak and washed-out. He gestured to the chair in front of his desk. "Sit down."

Emma felt the first stirring of fear. Something *was* wrong. Mechanically she moved toward the proffered chair and sat lightly on its tufted leather seat. "What's the matter, Eugene?"

"You haven't read the newspapers this morning."

"Of course not. You and I always read the Monday morning paper together."

Sighing heavily, Eugene plopped his bump of a chin into his laced fingers. Silent, suddenly nervous, Emma stared at him, her body angled imperceptibly forward. The slow, steady whirring of mingled breath was the only sound in the too quiet room.

"Eugene, you're frightening me—"

"The Pennsylvania and Reading Railroad declared bankruptcy today."

Emmaline gasped. Her fingers curled reflexively around the hard leather arms of the chair. "Oh, my God . . ."

He gave another tired sigh. "And that's not all. National Cordage should close by the end of the week— as will Drexana Mills. Stocks are crashing right and left. We expect a run on the banks by month's end."

Emma eased back in her chair, stunned. She'd invested everything she had, *everything*, in the railroad and textile mill stock. A crash would mean—

A full-blown, hammer-hard headache slammed into her temples. Pain throbbed at the base of her neck. She closed her eyes against the bright light from Eugene's desk lamp.

Think. She had to think.

"I'm sorry, Em," he said quietly.

She opened her eyes slowly. The pity in Eugene's eyes hit her like a fist in the throat. Her self-control slipped a notch. Fire-hot tears stung the corners of her eyes. She dashed them away with the back of her hand and shot to her feet.

Think! She lurched into action, pacing back and forth across Eugene's office while her mind tried to sort through the rubble. Her fingers coiled together, nervously twisting and retwisting with each step. "The railroads, the mills, the banks . . ."

"Insurance companies, trusts, farms," Eugene added. "They're all going under. There's simply been too much rash speculation in the last year. European banks are cutting off credit. They want their money back."

"I knew times were uncertain, but this . . ." Her words trailed off as she turned to look at him. "I . . . I always thought I'd start being conservative later . . . when I was old."

Eugene's pale lips worked, but no sound came out.

She mustered a small laugh. "So what exactly does it mean?"

He glanced down at the leather-bound folder on his desk, and as he did, the color seeped out of his cheeks. A knot of fear tightened Emmaline's stomach.

"It means you're broke."

The breath she'd been holding whooshed out of her lungs. She lurched into nervous pacing again, her fingers twisting painfully together with each step. "Broke is a relative term. . . . Do you mean I have to cut back my spending at Bloomingdale's, or that I can't afford the upkeep at my summer house anymore?"

"I mean," he said softly, "that after this month, you won't even *own* the summer house. You're severely overextended, and the bank has no choice but to call your loans."

She whirled on him. "Call my loans? Eugene—"

He cut her off with a wave of his colorless hand. "Let me finish while I have the nerve. You used all your cash, the summer house and its furniture, and the furniture in the Dakota apartment to collateralize your loan for the railroad and textile stock. Now that stock, and your other stocks, are worthless. If you can't make your payments next month, we'll have to repossess it all. We've already seized your cash." His voice shook. "I'm sorry."

Emma's hands balled into white-knuckled fists as she pivoted away from the pity in Eugene's eyes. It was all she could do to keep from screaming—but if she started, she was afraid she'd never stop.

"You can keep your jewels," he offered quietly.

Hysterical laughter bubbled in her throat. She clamped her teeth together to keep the sound from slipping out. "Jewels?" she repeated in a thick voice. "I don't have jewels. I put my money in what I believed in—this country. The United States *has* to grow; you said it yourself. We need railroads, and banks, and farms, and factories. *That's* where my money is, Eugene, and you damn well know it. Not in diamonds and pearls."

"Every decision you made was a good one, Emma; you're just ahead of your time. The rest of the world doesn't think as clearly as you do." He pushed back in his chair, and the sound of wood scraping on wood seemed thunderous.

Emma winced, her lips pressed into a white line to keep from screaming or crying or otherwise making an idiot of herself in front of the one man who mattered to her.

He was beside her in a heartbeat. "Em . . ." His reassuring voice coiled around her throat, making breathing difficult. She felt the whisper-soft flutter of his breath against her cheek. "Here," he said, "take the portfolio. Maybe you'll find some hidden asset. Something I missed."

She lurched sideways, afraid she'd succumb to the compassion in his voice and let herself cry. Tears never did anyone any good. She pinched her nose, hard, to keep the moisture at bay.

He reached toward her.

"Don't touch me," she hissed. She couldn't bear it; not now. One touch and she'd shatter into a million pieces. She grabbed the folder from him and hugged it to her chest like a shield. "I must go," she said shakily.

"Emma?"

"I'm fine, Eugene. Truly." She forced her chin up a notch and squared her shoulders. "But I have to go now. After all, I've a fortune to remake."

He smiled weakly. It was a lie, and they both knew it. "You're smart, you're young. You'll find a way."

Another lie. She tightened her grip on the leather portfolio to still the trembling of her fingers. "You're damn right I will."

Before Eugene could say a word, she turned and bolted out of his office. She hurried through the suddenly oppressive, overly quiet halls of the bank, her head held high as she sailed past Miss Baxter's cage. The teller's snicker nipped at Emma's heels, clawing at her confidence, but she set her lips in a grim line and ignored the laughter. At the door, she snatched her umbrella and gloves from the doorman and marched outside.

The doors slammed shut behind her.

At the sound, her composure crumpled. Her shoulders trembled and slumped, her chin sank.

Dear God . . .

It was over. After fifteen years of clawing and scraping and sacrificing, she'd lost it all.

Somehow she kept moving. Like a sleepwalker she glided forward, seeing nothing, feeling less. Moving, drifting, staring straight ahead through wide, painfully dry eyes. Sheer force of will kept her feet moving. The buildings on either side of her melded into one another, forming an indistinguishable blur of gray. Equally gray was the sky above; no sunlight penetrated the gloom or warmed Emma's cheeks.

She clutched the slick wooden handle of her umbrella with frozen fingers. Rain thumped the black pongee satin over her head, its staccato beat an echo of the headache behind her eyes.

Broke. The word repeated itself with every raindrop that hit the umbrella. Broke . . . broke . . . broke . . .

She squeezed her eyes shut to block the taunting word from her brain, and kept moving forward.

"Hey, lady!"

A hand curled around her forearm and yanked hard. She stumbled backward, slamming against a strong, barrel-sized chest.

She opened her mouth for a scathing retort, but before she uttered a single sound, an electric trolley rattled past her. Water spewed off the fast-moving car and splashed her face.

"You okay, lady?" It was the same voice, softer this time.

Okay? She felt as if her bones had turned to porridge. She'd almost walked into a moving trolley! Taking a deep breath, she turned to look at the man who'd saved her life. He was a big, burly, middle-aged man, a stevedore by the looks of him, and he was looking at her through the warmest brown eyes she'd ever seen. Gratitude filled her heart, but as usual, the words stuck in her throat.

He doffed his worn red cap and offered her a fatherly, concerned smile. "You okay, miss?"

She tried to dredge up an answering smile, but couldn't. The best she could summon was a small nod.

He led her back onto the flagstone walkway, and once there, she looked around. For the first time, she realized that she was no longer in the financial district. "Where are we?"

"I figgered you was lost. Don't get too many ladies like yourself on Mott Street."

Mott Street. Emma's heart lurched. Her throat seized up. It had taken fifteen years to scrape her way out of this cesspool of poverty. Now here she was again.

And dead broke—just the way she'd started. A chill crept across her flesh. Jesus, she thought with sudden, fierce desperation, had it all been a dream? Had she ever *really* gotten out?

"Why're you here, miss?"

The question lodged in her brain like a shard of glass. Why was she here?

The answer was obvious. Too obvious. It was one she'd run from all her life. *Because you belong here. You've always belonged here.*

Could it be true? she wondered with a rising sense of panic. Had a vengeful God given her the moneyed life on Eighth Avenue, only to snatch the goodness away at the last moment and plunge her back into the coldest darkness she'd ever known?

She shivered at the thought. It fit so well with her perception of the Almighty.

"You wanna come with me, miss? You don't look so good. The missus—"

Emma forced an answer past the lump of fear in her throat. "No, thank you. It appears I know where I am after all."

"You do?"

She felt his skeptical gaze on the expensive rubber- ized wool gossamer that protected her from the cold wind and driving rain, and the tiny, fashionable hat that perched just so on her perfectly coiffed hair. She licked her dry lips, then said softly, "I grew up in Rosare Court."

An odd silence stretched between them, as if he no longer knew what to make of the unfamiliar creature standing so primly before him. "Oh, well, then," he finally said. "Good-bye. Keep your eyes open this time."

"I will," Emma answered to his retreating back. She clutched the collar of her woolen cape and stared dully into the hissing, smoking gloom. The soft hum of the streets vibrated beneath her feet. She stood frozen, her gaze glued to the sidewalk stretched out before her. The slums seemed to be calling to her, beckoning in the same sly, taunting voice that had haunted her nights for as long as she could remember. They were ready, these pathetic, dirty streets, to welcome her back as one of their own.

The buildings melted into a gray, swirling layer of fog. Out of the colorless mist came the high, keening cry of a fishwife hawking her wares. *Whitefish, day-old whitefish* . . .

Emma shuddered. Above her head the elevated railway sputtered and rattled, sending a cascade of sparks to the wet pavement below. All around her, people scurried to and fro like ants, their pale, careworn faces turned in to the ragged collars of hand-me-down coats. The rain had stopped, but the air remained sour, thickened by the stench of long-forgotten garbage, darkened by the outpouring of smoke from too many chimneys.

She heard a high-pitched giggle and glanced toward the noise. Beside a rickety horse-drawn cab, a dozen or so dirty, half-clothed children chased an equally dirty mongrel down the streets. The noisy pack dashed between broken-down stalls and overfilled pushcarts, their bare feet splashing through the dirty puddles that pocked the cobblestone road. Everywhere they went, the sound of angry hollering and childish giggles followed.

Behind the children, a group of stoop-shouldered women was huddled around a broken hydrant. White water spewed over their feet and splashed across the cobblestone street. They hurried to fill anything they could find—shoes, hands, buckets—with the fresh water.

Emma bit down on her lower lip to keep it from trembling. Even now, after all these years, she remembered what it had felt like to stand at the hydrant, waiting, praying, to get even a cupful of water before the policemen arrived and shooed her away. Her hands had been dirty then, and cold. Always cold. And it had hurt like Hades to plunge her tiny fingers in the freezing cold water, but she had done it, and gladly. The poisoned, filthy water in the tenement's broken-down communal sinks had been undrinkable.

Emma wrenched her gaze away from the women clustered around the hydrant and slowly turned, knowing what she'd see: the alley's entrance.

She allowed herself only a moment of doubt, then squared her shoulders and forced her chin up. Clutching her umbrella in shaking fingers, she turned down the twisting, dirty walkway that was no more than three steps wide.

Gritting her teeth, she walked past one broken-down building after another until she came to the building that had haunted her dreams for years: Rosare Court.

The tenement's red-brown face was as blank as a dead man's eyes. No windows relieved the stark, straight pattern of the bricks, no flowers bloomed from boxes beside the closed door. The only ornamentation on the building was the crisscrossed ironwork of the fire escape.

Fire escape. What a cruel joke to call those useless ladders *escapes*. Emma still had nightmares about the night dozens of men, women, and babies had burned to death in a building exactly like this one. The escapes, they'd discovered too late, didn't reach the ground. The victims had burned to death staring down at the firemen and the water wagons clustered in the alley below. Even though she'd taken a job as a typist on Wall Street and moved to Catherine Street by then, Emma had been close enough to hear the screams. . . .

Something, some wisp of sound, floated to Emma's ears.

It was a lullaby.

Drawn almost against her will, she followed the sound to a tumbledown rear tenement less than fifty feet away. The top floors of the building disappeared into the low-slung layer of haze. Below the fog, clotheslines traversed the dirty backyard, and from their sagging expanses, wet, worn clothing snapped in the wind.

Sounds battered her ears, pulled her back in time: the barking of half-starved dogs looking for food; the bellow of an angry husband seeking his helpless wife; the soft shuffling of bare feet on rainy sidewalks. And above it all, the haunting strains of a mother's lullaby.

She walked to the sagging fence that lined the tenement's muddy backyard. Looking up to the second floor, she saw a woman huddled on the cold iron slats of the fire escape, and in her arms was a baby wrapped in a tattered blanket.

The child gave a violent shudder, then let out a loud, high-pitched hacking that was immediately followed by a wheezing wail. The mother sang louder, and reached a too-thin, blue-veined hand to the child's face.

"Shh, Jeannie. It'll be okay, love. . . ."

Emma turned quickly away. Tears stung her eyes and clogged her throat. The scene was so close. . . . She had sung the same lullaby to her dying mother, raised a similarly shaking hand to Mum's fire-hot bow. Whispered the same desperate, aching words . . .

Emma moved closer. She could barely make out the woman's face, for her too-pale, care-creased skin was almost indistinguishable from the cheap gray wool fascinator that wreathed her head and neck. The woman's drawn mouth worked softly, haltingly, and the lullaby left her lips in hesitant, painful spurts.

The child hacked again, harder this time. Emma had no doubt that the babe was dying; nor that the mother knew it as well. With half a chance, the baby might live, but here, in the hopeless pit of poverty, there was no chance at all.

Unless Emma herself made one. She stepped forward. Her knee brushed the rickety fence and a rotted slat fell onto the wet sidewalk.

The mother's head jerked up. Her tired, bloodshot eyes narrowed suspiciously when she saw Emma. Wordlessly the woman bundled up the baby and hurried back into her apartment. The door creaked, then slammed shut in her wake.

Emma stared at the closed door for a long time, the mother's glassy eyes etched into her memory. There had been no hope in those eyes; no hope in that quiet lullaby. No hope of escaping this hellhole. No hope of even surviving.

Once again Emma realized how lucky she'd been. Unlike most of the people in this neighborhood, who were beaten by poverty until they dropped, exhausted and depleted, into a waiting grave, Emma had never let herself accept life in the slums. Never.

Yes, she'd been lucky. And something else, something even more important. She'd been smart.

She was *still* smart, still lucky, still hungry for success. She'd made one fortune, and by God, she could make another. And once she'd made it, nothing on Heaven or Earth would pry it from her hands again.

Nothing.

Chapter Four

Emmaline looked up at the ornate chateau-styled town house and swallowed thickly. A flutter of butterflies nested in her stomach. She pressed a slim, gloved hand to her abdomen.

It was foolish to be nervous. She'd gone over this decision a thousand times in the last few days, and it seemed the perfect plan of action. She and Eugene should marry.

Marry. She suppressed a shiver of repulsion at the word. It was so . . . personal, conjuring up myriad disturbing images—joint checking account, shared power, female subservience.

"No," she said sharply, jerking her chin to a defiant tilt. It wouldn't be an ordinary marriage. Not one of those fluttering-eyelid sorts of affairs the socialites specialized in. Rather, she saw marriage to Eugene as a convenience. A merger. She got a place to live and enough money to start over, and he got an intelligent, sexually progressive, financially gifted wife. All in all, she thought, a good deal for both of them.

Plucking up the heavy folds of her pleated French sateen skirt, she climbed the marble steps and rapped smartly on the door.

The butler appeared almost immediately. "Miss Hatter," he said in a pinched, nasal voice, "is Mr. Cummin expecting you?"

She forced a smile. "No."

He nodded. "Very good, miss. Come in and sit down." He led her to a comfortable tapestried bench in the foyer. "I'll tell Mr. Cummin you're here."

Emma watched the uniformed man climb the stairs and disappear. Her breath escaped in a nervous sigh. Lord, she hoped she was doing the right thing. . . .

She sat stiffly erect and forced the anxiety from her mind. Glancing idly around, she studied the foyer. The decorations were expensive, but rather sparse. Elegant but poorly placed.

In need of a woman's touch, she decided. As soon as they were wed, she'd hire a woman to give it one.

"Emmaline," came Eugene's voice as he padded quickly down the carpeted stairs. "What a surprise."

She stood. "Good evening, Eugene."

"Come into the salon," he said, leading her into another sparsely furnished room. "Would you like a drink?"

Emma took a seat. Fanning her fashionably narrow skirt out around her legs, she shook her head. "No, thank you. I'm here on . . . business."

He poured a splash of bourbon into a cut-crystal glass, then turned to her. There was no mistaking the surprise in his eyes. "What business is that?"

She cleared her throat. "I thought it would be beneficial if we married."

He stared at her. "Married?"

"Yes. We've been . . . lovers for nearly a year now.

It makes sense that we formalize our partnership. I could make you a fortune, you know."

Eugene walked toward her. Emma noticed that his step seemed heavy and slow. The overstuffed velvet couch sagged beneath his weight as he sat down beside her.

Emma looked into his sad brown eyes and wanted to run. He opened his mouth to speak, and she wished suddenly that she'd taken the drink.

"Emma, I-I don't know how to say this without sounding like a cad. . . ."

"Just say it," she said, pasting a smile on her face.

He set his glass on the piecrust table at his left. "I remember when you first hired on at the brokerage. You were so young, so eager. I tried to talk to you a dozen times, but you never even gave me the time of day. I was just a kid, a nothing. But old man Lyndeman— him, you had time for. It didn't surprise me when you two became . . . friendly, or when he let you use your salary to buy stocks."

"Eugene, that's ancient—"

"Wait," he said, "let me finish. I watched you from afar for years, watched you develop into one of the greatest financial minds of our time. And all the while I was waiting to make my own mark with you. Waiting for you to look down from your lofty perch and notice *me*.

"It finally happened when I took over Mr. Olsen's job at the bank. Suddenly I was *somebody*, and for the first time, your beautiful blue eyes noticed me. I thought I was in Heaven. We went to the theater, out to dinner. . . . Everything was wonderful.

"Then we went to bed. That's when I first noticed it."

Emma frowned. "Noticed what?"

"The coldness. *Your* coldness. Oh, you went through the motions, made me feel great, but I never really reached you. I could tell you found our passion pleasant, but nothing more." A laugh that sounded forced escaped his lips. " 'Pleasant' is a bit rough on a man's ego. For a while I hoped you'd change, thaw. Then I sort of . . . accepted it."

He took her hand in his and looked at her. The expression in his dark eyes was infinitely sad and filled with regret. "We're not lovers, Em. We're business associates who occasionally sleep together. It's not enough for me, not for a lifetime. Marriage isn't a merger. It's something more. . . . It's laughter, hope, joy—emotions I've never known you to express. I'm sure you have them, don't get me wrong. But you're so . . . so withdrawn and self-centered. I admire your mind immensely—you're a brilliant, visionary businesswoman. But . . ." He shrugged, apparently at a loss for words, then he said quietly, "You're just not the woman I'd choose to share my life and raise my children. I'm sorry. . . ."

Humiliation stung Emma's cheeks like a slap. She'd always known she wasn't very . . . lovable. But to hear it in such cold, impersonal words—and from one of the few people whose opinion she respected—made her feel worthless and barren. Empty. She shot to her feet and spun away from the pity in Eugene's eyes. "I understand," she said stiffly. "I'm sorry for wasting your time."

"Emma, I—"

Without waiting to hear what he had to say, she yanked up her skirts and strode briskly from the room.

* * *

Two weeks later, Emma knew she'd hit rock bottom. It was over.

She rubbed her weary, overworked eyes, and sighed. Her head drooped forward, her elbows plopped onto the polished mahogany of her desk.

She stared at the papers strewn in front of her. The white sheets blurred; numbers melted together in a black stream of dancing dots. She'd spent every waking hour of the last two days going through the figures and documents in her financial portfolio, studying every piece of paper in every drawer. Time and again she'd wanted to give up, but she'd forced herself to keep looking, keep hoping that somewhere she'd find an asset she'd overlooked. Anything that would give her the money to start over. *Anything*.

At first she'd thought it would be easy, finding some scrap of redemption, but with each passing moment, each second, she'd believed in the possibility less and less.

Now she had no hope left at all. There was nothing. No asset, no hidden cache of money, no secret stock. Nothing. She was broke. And there was no more time to look. No more time to hope.

In less than ten minutes the movers Eugene had hired would arrive at her door. Everything of value would be carted off and sold to pay her staggering debts. The summer house had already been repossessed, and the small staff that had seen to her needs in both homes had been let go.

She had ten minutes left. Ten minutes in which to perform the most difficult, most painful task of all: clean out her desk.

She'd been putting off the task for weeks, but she couldn't put it off anymore. It was no longer her desk;

it belonged to the bank now. They wanted it, and they wanted it empty.

She grabbed the little brass handles on the top drawer, and gently eased it open. The first thing that caught her eye was the checkbook. She pulled it out and laid it on her desktop. Her fingers glided atop the high-grade, butter-soft leather almost reverently before she flipped it open.

More numbers leapt out at her, taunting her with the memory of her excesses. This was the one document she hadn't allowed herself to study. There had been no point. The bank had seized all the cash in the account.

She glanced down at the entries and felt the familiar tightness in her throat. Meissen vases, Sheffield silver, Aubusson rugs, Waterford goblets . . . She'd spent money like it was water.

Today the well had run dry. She glanced down the line of numbers, and noticed something odd. There was an empty entry line. A frown pulled at her mouth. When had she ever failed to record a payment made?

A knock at the front door interrupted her thoughts. She waited for one of her employees to open it, then remembered she had no employees. Heaving a sigh, she pushed tiredly to her feet and headed for the door.

She made her way slowly down the darkened hallway. Each leaden footstep took her closer to ruin. When she opened the door, it would truly be all over. By sunset tonight, there wouldn't be a stick of furniture in her apartment, and by tomorrow, there wouldn't even be an apartment. Not for her, anyway. Number 17, Dakota Apartment, now belonged to the bank.

At the door she took a deep breath and squared her shoulders. Wiping the emotion from her face with practiced ease, she opened the door.

"Miss Hatter?"

Emma studied the man with unconcealed surprise. He wasn't dressed in stained blue dungarees; nor was he big and burly. Instead, he was a small, bespectacled, stoop-shouldered man in a suit that was at least six years out-of-date. A *suit*, for God's sake. What kind of a furniture mover wore a suit? "You're going to need help with the piano," she commented dryly.

"Excuse me?"

"In fact, you may need help with the dining room chairs."

He pulled the lopsided brown bowler off his head and crushed it to his chest. "He told me you were . . . opinionated."

A bittersweet smile softened the hard lines of Emma's mouth. "That's what I like about Eugene. He's tactful. Anyone else would say I was rude."

"Eugene who?"

"Cummin."

"Oh, no, thank you. I can only stay for a moment."

Emma almost laughed aloud. "I didn't say 'Come in.' I said Cummin. You know, Eugene Cummin, the man who hired you."

"I was hired by Michael Jameson."

Emma frowned. "You work for Michael, at Columbia?"

The man's wrinkled face lit up. "I'm proud to answer yes to that one."

"And Michael told you I was opinionated?"

"Oh, no, ma'am. Mr. Jameson would never say such a thing. Not to me, anyway."

Emma felt a headache start. She pressed two fingers to her temples and closed her eyes. "Look, Mr. whatever your name is, I—"

"Doctor," he cut in. "Dr. O'Halloran."

That was when she knew. Emma's eyes flipped open. "You're a friend of *his*. That idiot doctor."

O'Halloran nodded eagerly. "Larence Digby."

"No confusion over *which* idiot, I see," she said crisply, crossing her arms. "Okay, O'Halloran, why are you here?"

"Larence sent me over here to give you this." He held out a tattered, dirty scrap of paper.

Taking the ruined calling card between her thumb and forefinger, Emma grimaced. What had Dr. Dimwit used it for? Dusting? "He sent you all this way to return my card? How . . . nice."

"No. He sent me here to tell you that he's leaving for New Mexico tonight."

"And he thinks I ca—" *New Mexico. Ciburra. Gold!* Emma's heart lurched into her throat. The missing entry in her checkbook! It was the ten-thousand-dollar check she'd written to Digby. She must have been too upset that night to record it.

Bits and pieces of Digby's speech came to the forefront of her memory. *Gold. Silver. Turquoise. Treasures.*

She grinned suddenly. "Well, Dr. O'Halloran, I appreciate you stopping by."

"My pleasure, ma'am." He put the bowler back on his balding head and turned to leave.

Before he'd reached the elevator, Emma called out to him. "Oh, Doctor, could you tell me where I might find Dig—Larence this afternoon?"

"I suppose he'd be in his office at the college. He's usually there until about suppertime."

"Thank you, Doctor. Thank you very much."

* * *

Less than two hours later, Emma stood at the closed door to Digby's office. Anxiety coursed like electricity through her blood. She was nervous, hopeful, and excited all at once. She'd found it. Her hidden asset. Ten thousand dollars was more than enough to start over; she could do with half that amount. Now all she had to do was get it back from Dr. Dimwit. And outsmarting *him* would be like taking candy from a baby.

At the thought, a smug smile settled on her face. Taking a deep breath to calm her racing nerves, she raised her gloved fist and rapped sharply on the hardwood.

"Come in," came a distracted voice from behind the door.

Emma squared her shoulders for battle, lifted her chin, and jerked the door open. She sailed into the room, her nose held so high that only a last-minute skidding of her heels kept her from hitting the wall.

A low, throaty chuckle reached her ears. "It's kind of a small room," said the well-modulated, masculine voice. "Lots of people hit the books at full steam. That's why the bookcase sags to the left."

Emma spun around. Digby was staring at her from behind a huge wooden desk. Behind him, a small leaded-glass window was open, and the last rays of a late afternoon sun bathed his face and glanced through his hair, making the messy brown strands appear gilded. Her first thought was, *Lord, he's not bad-looking*. Then she noticed his ridiculously happy smile, and the thought vanished.

"Miss Hatter," he said, "what a nice surprise."

"Hello Dr. Digby. Can I sit down?"

"I don't know. Can you?" At Emma's frown, Digby's grin expanded. "Sorry, professor humor. Please, do sit."

Emma glanced at the room's only chair and suppressed a shudder. Too bad she hadn't worn an older gown. She eased herself onto the chair's ripped seat. Horsehair stuffing fluttered to the floor. The smell of aged, dusty leather teased her nostrils. Perched precariously, she reminded herself why she was here. It was to ask a favor. At all costs, she had to be polite. Even to Dr. Dimwit.

Especially to Dr. Dimwit.

Slowly she raised her gaze, and found herself staring into his eager, bottle green eyes. He leaned forward, nodding in anticipation. She opened her mouth. Surprisingly, the words she'd practiced lodged in her throat. An unfamiliar pang of conscience struck her. Somehow, all of a sudden, outwitting him seemed like . . . well, like taking candy from a baby. Not a nice thing to do.

"I knew you'd come to wish me luck. I knew it! You couldn't stay away from what may be the most important quest of the century. You're a part of it, after all. A big part. Why, only yesterday I was saying to Dr. O'Hall—"

"Stop!" she said more harshly than she intended. At his surprised look, she swallowed hard. Her fingers twisted in her lap. *Go easy, Em. Don't upset him.* "I'm sorry, I didn't mean to interrupt you, it's just that . . . well . . ."

The eagerness in his bright eyes was replaced by concern. "Yes?"

She took a deep breath. "It's just that I need my money back."

He laughed. She shot him a sharp look, and his

laughter ground into an awkward silence. "You're kidding, right?"

"Dr. Digby, I'm sure you realize I'm not the kind of woman to joke about money."

His gaze hardened, turned assessing. For a split second Emma wondered if there wasn't actually a razor-sharp mind behind those guileless, friendly eyes. "Unfortunately for you, Miss Hatter, I doubt you're the kind of woman who jokes about anything."

She bit back the words *And I thought you were stupid* just in time. "Dr. Digby, I don't want to take up more of your valuable time than is necessary. There must be dozens of overprivileged minds just waiting to be shaped by your . . . eloquent teachings. So if we could discuss the matter of my ten thousand dollars . . ."

He leaned back to study her. The sharp, whining squeak of tired springs accompanied his every move as he settled deeper into his broken-down chair. Never taking his eyes off her face, he brought his hands up behind his head and rested his neck in the bower of his laced fingers.

Emma shifted uncomfortably, ill at ease with his scrutiny. She was the one who usually studied people, and it was disconcerting to have the shoe on the other foot. It was all she could do not to snap at him. By sheer force of will she kept her lips compressed into a firm line. She wouldn't say anything shrewish yet—not until she had the check in her hot little hands. But by God, then she'd—

"I don't have the money."

Her mouth gaped. "What?"

"I don't have the—"

"I heard what you said," she said through gritted teeth. "Explain it."

"I don't think there's any call to be rude—"

"Explain where my money is. Now!" Emma banged her fists on the desk and lurched to her feet. Her eyes narrowed to angry slits as she stared down at him.

He shrugged, clearly impressed by her anger. "My colleague, Dr. Henry Stanton at the University of New Mexico, kindly offered to outfit me for the journey to Cibola. I sent him the money more than thirty days ago. I only kept enough for train fare and traveling expenses."

"Let me understand this," she said slowly. "You gave all my money to a professor in New Mexico who *kindly* offered to spend it for you?"

"That's right."

"Digby, your ineptitude would be funny if it weren't so damned . . ." Her voice trembled, and she clamped her lips together.

So damned serious. Her mind finished the paralyzing sentence. God, what would she do now? She squeezed her eyes shut to block out the terrifying images jockeying for position in her mind. She didn't even have a place to sleep tonight.

Digby rose slowly and leaned forward. Emma felt the soft intake of his breath against her cheek. It was warm, and strangely reassuring.

She slowly opened her eyes and found herself staring into his compelling green gaze. Her throat went dry. There was something in his eyes she couldn't fathom, something that made her uncomfortable. It was as if he could see right through her angry, ice-hard facade to the scared woman within.

She opened her mouth to yell at him.

Before she could utter a word, his finger touched her parted lips. The sharp tang of homemade soap filled her nostrils. Her words backed into one another in her throat. She stared at him, stunned into silence.

"You have two choices," he said matter-of-factly. "Be civil or leave."

Emma's hands curled into fists. This was precisely why she hated to be poor. Poverty meant weakness, and weakness meant she had to take garbage like this from idiots.

It took a supreme effort to say her next words in a reasonable tone of voice. She'd rather throw herself in front of the el than apologize. But, unfortunately, she had no choice. "I'm s-s-sorry if I was rude. It's just that I need that money. I can't believe you simply gave it away."

A good-natured smile transformed his serious expression. "I never claimed to be J. P. Morgan, Miss Hatter. I never claimed—or pretended—to be anything other than a man who thinks he's found a key to a locked door. I'm sorry if you think I shouldn't have given *my* money to Dr. Stanton. Perhaps you're right. Perhaps not. Either way, the question is moot. I did. If you cared so much about the money, you should have come down here and supervised my spending. As it is . . ." He shrugged.

Supervised my spending. The sentence flared like wildfire in her brain. Had he just given her the solution to all her problems?

She proceeded cautiously, afraid to hope. "You gave the money to this Dr. Stanton, to spend as he sees fit, correct?"

Digby nodded, and Emma felt her excitement jerk up a notch. "So if you got to New Mexico and found that he'd spent it, say . . . unwisely, you'd simply ask for some of it back, correct?"

He frowned. "I doubt he'd spend it unwisely. He is, after all, an educated man."

God save me. Emma forced a false smile. "Nonetheless, if you *did* think he'd overspent, you could get some of it back, couldn't you?"

"I suppose so, but—"

"Good," Emma cut in. "When do we leave?"

"I have a sleeper train ticket for tonight at . . ." He stopped.

Emma's forced smile melted into the real thing at Dr. Dimwit's discomfort. She almost laughed out loud. Why, the good doctor looked decidedly ill. Maybe he'd just forget the whole thing right now and wire Dr. Stanton for the money. "Dr. Digby," she said in a sugary voice, "is something amiss?"

"Did you say 'we'?"

"Yes, I did. It's my investment. I think I'll just tag along to oversee your spending."

"Are you sure? It's a long, hard journey. An adventure." The last word was more breathed than spoken, as if it were too significant to be said aloud.

Emma stiffened. *Adventure.* How many times had she heard that ridiculous word from her father? "I'm sure," she answered tightly.

"That's great! We'll have a wonderful time. He jerked open a desk drawer and pulled out a big, leather-bound book. Flipping the book to a dog-eared page, he thumped his forefinger on a cruddy little line drawing of a plant.

Emma's eyes glazed over as he pointed again at the drawing and yapped some more. Thump, babble, thump, babble.

She shook her head in disbelief. The idiot was *happy* that she was coming along. She should have known.

"What time do we leave?" she demanded suddenly.

He looked up from the book. "The train leaves Grand Central Station at nine o'clock tonight. I hope you can get a ticket."

"I'll get one."

Nodding, he started flipping wildly through the book. "Here, before you go, look at this great picture. . . ."

"Sorry, I have to go home and pack."

"Oh." Reluctantly he closed the book.

With a curt nod, Emma pivoted on her heel and marched out of the cramped little office.

"See you at nine o'clock tonight. We'll have a grand adventure," he called out after her.

She exited the stuffy little office and slammed the door shut behind her. The sudden silence was heavenly.

Four days on a train with that? It was unbelievable. She'd be lucky if she didn't kill him by New Mexico.

She'd better not take a weapon. Just in case.

Larence let out his breath slowly, afraid that if he spoke, or moved, or even closed his eyes in relief, the spell would shatter. That Miss Hatter would barrel back into his office and say it had all been a lie.

He waited, his eyes trained on the crystal doorknob. It didn't move. The clock on his desk clicked forward.

Had she really meant it? Was she going with him?

He heard her walk past his open window, and a small smile teased the edges of his mouth at the sharp, no-nonsense *rat-a-ta-tat* of her heels on the walkway.

She wasn't coming back this way; she was leaving. She'd meant it! Relief spun so hard through Larence's mind that he felt dizzy from the force of it. He returned to the book on his desk, and opened it to page 287. A pen-and-ink rendition of a secret door leapt out at him. His fingers shook, his mouth went dry.

For the first time since taking the check from Miss Hatter, Larence felt completely at ease. Unafraid. Now she'd know it all, just as he knew it. The legend, the people, the countryside would become a part of her, worming its way into her soul as irrevocably as it had wormed into his. She'd never be able to sell her half of the treasures. Never.

No one, not even crabby Miss Hatter, could actually see the treasures and then dismantle them.

His expedition, his dream, was safe.

Chapter Five

He was almost there. Larence's heart pounded, his palms turned clammy, as he climbed the stairs to Grand Central Station. It was a moment he'd waited and planned and prayed for. The first steps of his very first adventure. If only his grandmother were alive to see him now . . .

You won't make it, Larry. You're not like other boys. You shouldn't try to be.

Larence stiffened at the unexpected memory. His step faltered; pain shot through his bad leg and he nearly stumbled.

You're wrong, he thought fiercely. Maybe you weren't wrong then, but you're wrong now. This time I *will* be like other men.

This time he wouldn't fail. He was tired of being alone and afraid. It sounded crazy, and he knew it, but somehow this quest was more than just an expedition to find a lost city. It was a quest to find himself.

"Don't let her make you afraid," he said aloud, taking comfort, as he always had, in the sound of his own voice. "You can make it. You can."

Banishing a lifetime of doubt, he hurried up the stairs,

and limped through the open doors into Cornelius Van-
derbilt's phenomenal station.

The place was chock-full of travelers. People scurried up and down the wide, cream-colored steps, their
muffled footsteps merging into a single, shuffling heartbeat of sound on the hard marble squares. They flowed
and ebbed together like dancers. Gas jets in huge, sparkling chandeliers cast glimmering rays of light on the
silvery tracks and shiny floor. Overhead, trapped in the
small, leaded-glass squares of a domed window, hundreds of stars sparkled like glitter-dust.

Awestruck, he limped down to the crowded concourse below, merging awkwardly into the throng and
letting it carry him forward. Several times along the
way, he tripped, and just barely kept himself from falling. He didn't care. He would have fallen flat on his
face a hundred times before he'd miss one second of
this glorious cavalcade of humanity.

A sound reached his ears. A hissing, then a loud,
jangled clanging.

Larence surged out of the crowd, dropped his valise
down on an empty bench, and hurried out to the platform's edge. The incoming train rattled past him. Cool
air whooshed through his hair. Hot steam pelted his
cheeks.

The train jerked to a hissing stop, and sat there,
steaming, clanging, rattling like a caged animal. The
floor shuddered beneath Larence's feet. He leaned
slightly forward, breathing in the smoky, humid air,
reveling in the flutter-soft feel of it against his face.

His fingers curled around the piece of paper in his
hands. The train was here, he had the ticket. Now all
he needed was his partner, and the adventure could begin.

What a time they'd have together. His heart raced as he thought of the wonderful things they'd share, the good times they'd have on the trail.

He scrounged through his bulging pockets until he found his nickel-plated pocket watch and glanced at the time: 8:54.

She should be here by now. Craning his neck to take full advantage of his six-foot frame, he scanned the crowded concourse. It took less than a second to find her.

She was walking—like she always walked, stiffly—down the stairs, her arms filled to overflowing with luggage.

He waved at her. "Over here, Miss Hatter."

Her lips thinned into the grimmest smile he'd ever seen. He limped toward her.

"Miss Hatter," he said, reaching her side, "it's great to see you again."

"Wonderful," she said through clenched teeth.

"May I help you with your bags?"

Emmaline groaned at the puppy-dog eagerness in his voice. God, she hoped she hadn't made a monumental mistake in coming here. Without bothering to slow down, she shoved three valises at him.

He grabbed them, wobbled precariously, but managed to keep moving. Emma grimaced and hurried ahead, trying to ignore the clomp, step, clomp, step of his gait as he limped along behind her. She stopped at the wooden bench. Digby rammed into her back, throwing her forward. She snapped over the bench's iron side like a rag doll. Her Piccadilly parasol and traveling satchel flew out of her hands.

"Sorry," came Digby's half-laughing voice behind her.

She righted herself slowly, forcing herself to swallow the scathing retort that sprang to her lips.

"Here you go, lady," said one of the station attendants as he came up beside her. Her trunk thumped to the floor. Wincing at the sound, Emma clicked open her handbag and burrowed through the wrinkled silk interior for pennies. *Pennies*. She scowled. The man deserved more. She knew it; he knew it. But it was all she had—and she was damn lucky to have that. She'd had to sell her gold watch to get enough money for traveling expenses, and the fifty dollars she'd gotten for that wouldn't last long. Until she reached New Mexico and retrieved some cash from Dr. Dimwit's buddy, she was pinching every penny.

The attendant's open palm appeared beneath her chin. She plucked a penny from her bag and dropped it in his hand.

"Gee, thanks, lady."

As the disgruntled attendant walked away, Emma's efficient gaze swept the bags piled on the bench. With some satisfaction she noticed how neatly Digby had stacked them. At least he was good for *something*.

"Where do I purchase my ticket?" she said without bothering to look at him.

Silence answered her. She turned to look at Digby, and shook her head in disgust. He was too busy ogling her trunk to notice she'd spoken. She sighed. This was going to be the longest trip of her life. "Digby? Digby?"

Larence was dimly aware that she was talking to—or rather, at—him, but he couldn't wrench his gaze away from her baggage. He shook his head in denial. All these bags and that huge trunk couldn't be hers. She had to know *how* they were getting to Cibola.

A sick feeling crept into his stomach. He had mentioned it, hadn't he?

He decided that with Miss Hatter, it was best to take the bull by the horns—and hope she didn't fling him through the air. "You can't bring all that. Dr. Stanton—"

"Is an idiot. I *need* all of these things. Surely you don't expect me to wear the same clothes every evening on the train? Now, where do I purchase a ticket?"

Larence let out a disappointed sigh. This wasn't going as well as he'd expected. He'd hoped the looming excitement of their adventure would soften her tongue. At least a little bit.

She snapped her fingers in front of his face. He jumped in surprise. "Where do I purchase my ticket?" she repeated in the slow, exaggerated tone of voice usually reserved for imbeciles.

He thrust a wadded-up scrap of paper at her. "Here."

She frowned. "What is it?"

"Your ticket. I felt it was the least I could do, since it was your money that financed the expedition."

Emma's mouth dropped open in surprise. Relief buckled her knees. She grabbed the bench's hard wooden back to steady herself. Suddenly the fifty dollars in her purse swelled like a fortune. "Why, Dr. Digby, that's very thoughtful of you," she managed.

"I figured we'd never get to sit together unless we purchased the tickets early. So I sent my assistant right over here after you left my office. He was able to get you a seat next to mine. And the very last one. How's that for luck?"

Emma's relieved smile froze. "Next . . . to you?"

"Yes, isn't it great? I'll be able to tell you all about

Cibola. Why, by the time we get there . . ." He frowned. "Are you all right, Miss Hatter. You're pale."

Emma's retort was cut in half by the loud whistle of a train and the booming words: "All aboard!"

"That's it!" Digby said excitedly. "That's the number Eighty-Two to Albuquerque."

Emma's fingers curled around the ticket in her gloved hand. Five days—and nights—on a train with Dr. Dimwit at her side. Her teeth ached at the thought of it.

She'd almost rather be poor. Almost.

"Let's go." Without waiting for Digby, she gathered her handbag, satchel, and parasol, and headed toward the train. Her expensive, scallop-edged twelve-button walking boots clattered like a Gatling gun as she marched toward the uniformed train attendant standing alongside the car nearest her. At her approach, the dark-skinned man offered her a warm, welcoming smile.

Emma cast a quick glance behind her. Larence was reaching for his ridiculously overstuffed, out-of-date valise. She breathed a sigh of relief. It would take him a while to flag down a porter and get their trunks and bags loaded on the train. She had a few precious moments without him.

She handed the attendant her ticket. "I'd like to trade this seat for another. Anywhere."

The man didn't even bother to look at her ticket. "Sorry, miss. Train's full up."

"I have money."

"I'm sure you do, miss," he said, taking her bag, "but that don't give this train mo' seats. Now, if you'll follow me . . ."

Emma's lips stretched into a tense smile. "Fine," she said between clenched teeth. "Lead on."

The uniformed attendant climbed the creaky metal

steps leading onto the car, then turned and offered his big, pinkish brown palm to her. Emma placed her white-gloved hand in his, hiked up her heavy wool traveling skirt, and followed him into the train.

The train. She thought of the two words as capitalized. *The Train.*

The Train in which she'd be sitting next to Dr. Dimwit from New York to New Mexico.

If only she were one of those people who suffered fools gladly.

If only he weren't so easily cast in the role.

Emmaline perched stiffly on the edge of the plush burgundy velvet seat, edging herself as close to the window as possible. Her hands were wadded in her lap, her back was ramrod-straight.

She waited for the telltale clomp, step, clomp, step of Digby's ponderous gait. At each passenger's entrance on the train, her vertebras tightened.

Calm down. It wouldn't do a scrap of good to go working herself into a snit. She was riding cross-country in this—her gaze shot to the small settee opposite her, and she groaned—this minuscule compartment with Digby, and that was that.

She breathed in and out slowly, forcing herself to calm down. Squeezing her eyes shut so that she wouldn't have to greet Digby when he finally worked his way to their seat, she leaned against the thick brocade shade that covered the window. The musty scent of aged fabric crept to her nostrils.

Then she heard it: Clomp, step, clomp, step . . .

"Here you are, Dr. Digby: 62-A."

Emma heard something land on the velvet settee opposite her. She could almost *see* that ragged old duck valise bouncing on the squabbed cushion.

"Thank you," Digby said in a voice that could only be described as breathless. "I hope that grandson of yours feels better soon."

Grandson? The idiot had asked the train attendant about his family? Emma groaned silently, waiting for the attendant to leave before she cracked one eye open.

Across from her, Larence scooted to the edge of his seat. Emma felt the soft brush of his wool-clad knees against hers. Before she knew what he was up to, he'd reached over and patted her clasped hands. One quick touch and then his hands were back in his own lap.

She stiffened in shock. People so rarely touched her. . . .

He smiled. White teeth flashed at her. "Isn't this great? I've been reading about . . ."

He launched into another monologue. Emma grimaced. It was time to set some ground rules. "Let's get something—"

The train lurched forward; she flew backward, cracking her head on the bench's mahogany back. As quickly as it had moved, the train stopped again. The car rattled, hummed, shook.

A headache burst to life at the base of her neck. Closing her eyes, she pressed two fingers to her temples and eased herself deeper into the settee. "Would you hand me my gladstone bag?"

Nothing. Not even a stupid answer.

She opened her eyes hesitantly. Digby had his nose buried in a scruffy, dog-eared copy of *Century Magazine* that was dated 1882. She stifled a groan. Only Digby would bring an eleven-year-old magazine to read.

She cleared her throat.

He looked up. Emma craned her neck for a look at the article's title: "An Aboriginal Pilgrimage."

She made a mental note not to accept any reading material he offered her. "Would you hand me my gladstone bag?"

"What gladstone bag?"

"The one I handed to you at the concourse." She glanced around the tiny compartment. "Where did you stow it?"

"I didn't."

Emma's headache intensified. "Didn't what?"

"Stow your bag."

"Then what did you do with it?"

"Nothing."

The train lurched forward. Emma's stomach dropped. "What do you mean, nothing?"

"I mean nothing. I didn't touch it."

With a cry, Emma snapped to her feet. The train bucked forward, and she staggered back, flopping onto the velvet seat. She yanked the gold silk tassel beside her. The shade jerked once, then bounced up the window and clapped around the metal rod that housed it.

Emma's gaze shot to the bench. There, piled neatly on the hard wooden surface, were her traveling bags. Leaning up against the bench was her expensive Crystal Maine iron-bottomed trunk. The leather trunk tag with her name and address swung forlornly against the wooden-slatted side.

Her hands flew to her mouth. For a heartbeat she was speechless. The she shouted at the top of her lungs: "Porter!"

The train pitched forward. She heard the long, drawn-out squeal of reluctant wheels, and then the slowly building *chug-a-chug-a-chug* of the mighty engine as the train started rolling forward.

She pressed her hands to the cold glass and peered out. Her breath clouded the pane until she couldn't see anything except the hazy outline of her bags on the bench, and then nothing at all.

The train wheezed out of the station. The inky black fist of night pressed itself against the window.

Emma stood frozen in shock. A desperate sob caught in her throat. Everything was in that trunk. Everything. Her toilet case, manicure set, hand mirror, Chlorate Dentrifice tooth powder, her favorite Hoyt's German perfume . . .

Clothes. The word crashed through her brain, bringing with it a tide of queasiness. Forget the tooth powder—she could purchase that in Albuquerque. What in God's name was she going to wear?

She spun away from the window and glared at Digby. What had he done? Just had his own trunks loaded and to hell with hers? "Who in the world would walk away from trunks without paying a porter to load them?"

"*You* did."

Emma's flimsy hold on her temper snapped. "I *handed* you my bags."

"And I piled them on the bench. I thought—"

"Ha!" Emma knew there was a hysterical edge to her voice, but she couldn't help herself. All she could think about were the gowns and garments and toiletries she'd packed so carefully. They represented everything she had left in the world. Now she had nothing. Nothing . . .

"You didn't ask me to carry them onto the train for

you,'' he said in a reasonable voice that made Emma want to smack his face.

''A lady doesn't have to ask a gentleman to carry her things. He just *does* it.''

''He does?''

She lowered herself slowly onto the seat, feeling suddenly old and alone. ''Of course he does. Where have you lived all your life—under a rock?''

Something—maybe pain, maybe embarrassment—flashed in his eyes and was gone. ''Do gentlemen really do that?'' he said earnestly. ''Always? Without being asked?''

She thought about saying nothing to him at all, or about yelling at the top of her lungs, or marching away. But what was the point? Nothing she did would get her trunk back.

Besides, it was her own fault. She was the one who'd walked off without her bags. She'd spent so much time with men like Michael Jameson and Eugene Cummin that she'd forgotten that gallantry wasn't universal.

And even worse, she'd relied on *Digby*. What kind of a fool would do that? By God, she deserved what she got.

''Who says?'' he asked unexpectedly.

She frowned, trying to remember what they'd been talking about. ''Who says what?''

''Who says men have to run along behind women and make sure their trunks get loaded on trains?''

''I don't know. Women, I suppose.''

''Oh.'' He paused. Then, ''I don't know many women.''

''No surprise there.''

Larence leaned forward, and for one horrifying moment she thought he was going to touch her again. "You had your name and address on everything, didn't you?"

"Yes."

"Then what's the problem?"

"You wouldn't understand."

"Try me."

She sighed heavily. What was the point? Only someone who'd lived in poverty could really understand the value of possessions. "Forget it, Digby. All I want right now is to go to sleep. Maybe when I wake up, I'll find that this was all a horrible nightmare."

"Yes, I'm sure it will all look better tomorrow."

"Oh, yes, I'm sure it will."

Her sarcasm bypassed him completely. "That's the spirit, Miss—"

"Call me Emmaline."

His eyes rounded. "Really?"

Hers rolled. "Really. What do I call you—Larry?"

"No," he said sharply. "Larence is good."

"Fine. Whatever. Call the porter, will you, and get him to let down our beds."

He looked quickly away.

Emma frowned. "Is something wrong?"

"That depends on your point of view, actually; I mean, we're both adults and . . ."

"What are you talking about?"

"My assistant, Ted—he's really a bright young man, good student—anyway, he tried to get you a sleeper ticket, but there weren't any. Except this one. He knew I wanted to sit with you. . . ." His sentence trailed off.

"And . . ." she prompted.

"And the upper berth is broken. We only have the one we're sitting on."

Emma stiffened. "Are you telling me we only have one bed for the two of us?"

"Yes."

Her gaze cut to the brass pull-ring embedded in the mahogany overhead. It was almost impossible to believe that there was a bed lurking behind that elegant wooden facade; it was even more unthinkable that there wasn't.

She saw the hairline crack that slithered from one end of the wood to the other. With a sinking feeling, she examined the remaining berth. Two seats—Larence's and her own—faced each other, forming a four-foot-by-six-foot enclosure. Tonight, when the porter came by, he'd fill in the space between the seats, slap a sheet on the mattress, and *viola!* a bed would appear.

A bed.

She grimaced. One bed. Two bodies.

And not just any body—but Dr. Dimwit himself.

"You propose to share this bed with me, then?" she said thinly.

"Well, actually, it's my bed."

She gasped. "You mean you'd actually—"

Larence's mouth tilted in a quickly suppressed smile. "I suppose a gentleman would give up his bed without a fight?"

She nodded stiffly. "He would."

A smile tugged at one corner of his mouth. "Duffey's etiquette book didn't say a word about relinquishing one's bed."

It took Emma a moment to realize he was teasing her. She had no idea how to respond; it had been years since someone had joked with her. She stiffened, trying to maintain a cool, emotionless facade. "I believe this is the sort of thing the author would take for granted."

"I guess you silver-spooners know a thing or two about unwritten rules."

She blanched. "I wasn't born with a silver spoon in my mouth," she said quietly. "Quite the opposite."

Larence focused on her with the same single-minded concentration he'd shown his magazine. An unexpected intelligence, deep and penetrating, shone from the bottle green depths of his eyes.

Emma shifted on her seat. She didn't like the way he was looking at her, as if he were searching her soul for secrets. God knew she had enough of them.

They stared silently at each other. Across the aisle an elderly gentleman coughed. The phlegmy sound vibrated in the thick, pipe-smoke-filled air.

"I think maybe I knew that," he said finally.

Emmaline's throat closed up at his quiet observation. She didn't like the turn this conversation was taking. Not one bit. It was getting entirely too . . . personal. "So," she said, restiffening her spine and hardening her stare, "do I get the bed or not?"

"Of course."

It was strange, really, the way the victory made her feel. Almost disappointed. Not at all as she usually felt when besting someone. "Where will you sleep?"

He shrugged, and she could tell that it was a heartfelt response. He really didn't care where he slept. She shook her head in amazement. It was astounding how happy he was just to *be*.

Fool. The word came automatically to her mind, but for some unfathomable reason, the familiar venom was absent.

He turned back to his reading, and Emma found herself studying his downcast face.

He wasn't a bad-looking man, if one was attracted to the smiling, boyish type. He had . . . something. A joie de vivre that made her feel vaguely old. Almost elderly, in fact.

It would be difficult for him to find a place to sleep on this crowded train. He was—

(crippled)

—a tall man, taller than she'd first thought, and he'd have to curl up like a cinnamon roll to sleep in one of the parlor car's chairs. Assuming, of course, there was a vacant one.

She tried to think about something else. The treasure, the weather, anything. But her mind kept returning to the word it wanted: *crippled*.

He was crippled. She was stealing a crippled man's bed. That was low—even for her.

Reluctantly her gaze slid down his long legs to the scuffed toe of his walking boots. His left foot was tucked protectively behind his right.

Emma rarely thought about other people; not their pleasure or their pain. Yet now she found herself thinking about his crippled ankle. About him. He was just dumb enough to sleep curled up in some little chair and never once complain.

Damn him anyway. His silence would make her feel guilty and selfish—and she hated feeling anything but pleased with herself. No doubt she was going as soft in the head as he was, but she knew there was only one thing to do. "You may share the bed with me."

"But—"

"Don't say anything," she cut in sharply. "I might change my mind, and I don't want to."

A smile shone like the first rays of an August sun in his eyes. She felt its warmth in every fiber of her body.

Places that had been cold and dark for years felt a glimmer of heat. "There might just be a chance for you yet, Emmaline Hatter."

His observation was like a slap in the face. She looked him square in the eyes. "Don't count on it."

Chapter Six

Emmaline stared at the bed. White sheets stretched across the mahogany-sided berth, their starched rims turned precisely down across equally white blankets. It looked like a thick layer of new-fallen snow in a smooth, red-gold box.

It was so *small*. Somehow, when she'd been sitting across from Larence—fully clothed—the area between them had seemed big enough for a good-sized bed. Not nearly so . . . confining. Now she saw the space for what it was: a dining-table-sized mattress made for one.

She cast a sideways glance at Larence and almost smiled in spite of herself. If possible, he looked more uncomfortable than she felt. His lanky, broad-shouldered body was ramrod-stiff, and he was staring at the bed as if he expected a cobra to slither out from the crisp sheets at any moment. A striking cobra, at that.

"Will that be all, Doctor? Mrs. Digby?"

The porter was finished.

"Yes, yes." Larence handed the man a coin. "That will be all, thank you."

"Sleep well." Then the porter left. And they were alone. *Bedtime.*

Emma turned to Larence; he turned to her. Silence

thudded between them. He cleared his throat. She nibbled on her lower lip. Both of them did their best to avoid looking at the bed. Neither had much success. Emma knew it was ridiculous to be so uncomfortable, but she couldn't help herself. The last thing in the world she wanted to do was sleep with Digby. Just the *thought* made her edgy.

"Nice bed—"

"Looks comfort—"

They spoke at once, and the sudden cacophony of sound punctured the sleeper car's quiet. Their sentences ground into an awkward silence. Emma racked her mind for something witty to say, but nothing came to her.

"Why don't you go in first, and change your clothes?" Larence ventured. "I'll wait out here."

Emma almost laughed in relief. Her awkwardness vanished. His stupid words had returned them to the status quo. Life was back on track. She felt better, more in control. She gave him a look that would shrivel grapes. "I don't have any clothes."

His eyes bulged and he looked quickly away. Right at the bed. His gaze bounced once, then ricocheted to the ceiling. Color crept slowly along his Burnaby-style shirt collar and fanned up his throat. "Sorry."

"Oh, this is ridiculous," Emma said sharply. "We're acting like children. I refuse to allow this absurd situation to be exacerbated by unnecessary awkwardness. You said it yourself: We're adults. Let's act like it."

He nodded, obviously relieved. The idiot smile came back.

It calmed her to talk. So she added, "I mean, it's not like we're a couple of virgins on our honeymoon. We've both slept with members of the opposite sex before."

He swallowed so hard, his Adam's apple bobbed against his collar. ''Well, actually—''

''Don't!'' Emma flung her hands up to ward off his next words.

His mouth clamped shut.

Emma stared at him in shock. He'd been about to confess he was a virgin. She was sure of it.

No. It wasn't possible, she told herself firmly. Who would disclose such a thing, and to a perfect stranger? No man she'd ever met. She stared hard into his guileless, intelligent green eyes, and slowly shook her head. *No . . .*

There *had* to be women who were attracted to dreamy dimwits. Louis Pasteur had found Marie Curie, hadn't he?''

''I'll sleep next to the window,'' she said at last.

''Okay.''

But what if you were right? nagged a little voice in the back of her mind. Wouldn't an inexperienced man be dangerous in this sort of situation? What if his suppressed urges kicked into high gear while she was sleeping? She plucked a hatpin from her hat—*just in case*—and held it out in front of her like a miniature sword. ''I'll expect you to keep a respectable distance.''

''What's that?''

Emma looked down at her hand. ''A hatpin.''

''No, what's a respectable distance?''

Pain thumped her in the back of her head. It occurred to her that when he opened his mouth, she almost invariably got a headache. Without a word, she swept up her skirts and clambered onto the bed. On her knees, facing Larence, she grabbed hold of the heavy velvet curtain that partitioned the bed from the aisle.

''Just don't touch me,'' she said. Then she whipped the curtain shut, and she was alone.

Blessedly, wonderfully alone. She breathed a heartfelt sigh of relief and began to undress.

An hour later, Emma lay stiff and unmoving beneath the sheets, her head cradled deep in the pillow's cushy softness. She could feel the raised pattern of the railroad's monogram beneath her head.

She couldn't see a thing. Thick, forest green velvet curtains were drawn tight along Larence's side of the bed. No hint of light sneaked through the infinitesimal crack between the two sheaths of material, and the tapestried window blind kept any slivers of moonlight at bay.

Relax, she told herself for what had to be the thousandth time. But she couldn't accomplish it.

For all her bluff and bluster, she'd never actually slept with a man before. Had sex, yes; slept, no. Long ago, when she'd lived on the cold, dark streets, and slept huddled beneath sagging eaves, she'd dreamed of sleeping with a man, of waking up with one. Of cuddling and warmth and caring. But that had been a lifetime ago. Longer. Before she'd stopped dreaming of princes.

Now she believed in protecting herself. She had sex when she wanted to, and she always chose the partner. She orchestrated everything, down to the smallest detail. It was the only way she knew to keep absolute control of the situation.

Somehow, spending the night with a lover had always implied an intimacy she'd never wanted, a level of trust she'd never let herself feel. Sex was easy—fast, furious, impersonal. And, generally speaking, she enjoyed it. But intimacy was different.

Intimacy required vulnerability. The relinquishment of the one thing she could never give up. Control.

She thought of all the men, including Eugene, who had asked her to spend the night, and of the way she'd turned them down. Flat. Cold.

Yet here she was, sharing her first slumber with a grinning, dreamy-eyed professor whom she didn't even like. In a very, very small bed.

Her body started to tingle from the effort of remaining so motionless. She took a deep breath, and slowly, inch by inch, began to relax.

Gradually she became aware of the sensations swirling within the penetrating layer of darkness. It felt as if she were floating in a sea of ebony-hued velvet. Larence's soapy, masculine scent filled the air, becoming an almost tangible presence between them. The movement of the train rocked the bed in a muted lullaby of sound and motion.

She felt the warmth of his body alongside hers. Even with him pressed as far as possible against the far edge, there wasn't more than an inch separating their bodies. Heat radiated between them, firing the sheets, prickling her flesh. Perspiration crawled in the valley between her breasts.

This was ridiculous.

She forced herself to think about something else. *The treasure*. For the first time, she wondered whether it could be true. Whether Dr. Dimwit could really lead her to gold and save her life.

"Larence?" she said softly.

He fell out of bed with a thud and a groan, then scrambled back in beside her. "Y-Yes?"

"Will we find the treasure?"

"Yes."

"How can you be so sure?"

He shrugged. The movement pulled the blanket snug

against her chin. "It doesn't sound very scientific, but in my heart I know it's there."

Emma closed her eyes. She was traveling cross-country with a man who knew *in his heart* that the treasure existed. The thought depressed her greatly. For, of all the organs in the human body, the heart was the least reliable.

She let out her breath in a long, defeated sigh. She was as much a fool as he.

"Good night, Emmaline."

"Good night, Larence."

She heard him roll over, and within moments the soft, even cadence of his breath told her that he was asleep. Envy stabbed her. He went to sleep with the ease of a child. Her fingers, still curled in a death grip around the hatpin, loosened. She stabbed it in the mattress's far corner.

Maybe he slept easily because he believed in something.

Idly she wondered what it would be like to believe in something, and thought that, perhaps, it would be the sort of thing that helped a person sleep at night. Lord knew it had worked for Digby.

He had such big, big dreams.

She didn't have a single one. She'd stopped letting herself believe in anything except the security of cold, hard cash on the day her father killed himself.

And she hadn't gone to sleep easily since long before that.

Larence spread his papers and pens and pocket tapes out on the table he'd had the porter set up between him and Emmaline. Carefully extracting his brand-new Woodsman's Reliable compass from its leather pouch, he laid it alongside the pens. Then, very gently, he pulled the diary out of its special place in his valise, opened it to page one, and began rechecking his distance calculations.

"What are you doing?" she asked, sipping her morning tea.

He smoothed the map of New Mexico, his gaze riveted to the forested patch of terrain between Cibola and the *Malpais*. "Checking the map Stanton gave me against the landmarks in the diary."

She set down her cup and reached for the compass.

"Don't touch that."

She drew her hand back. "I wasn't going to steal it."

He got out his straightedge and drew a line between two points, then looked up. "Sorry," he said with an easy smile. "Sometimes I get sort of . . . caught up in things. Of course, you're welcome to look at the compass."

She glanced over at it and nodded. "Nice."

"Michael gave it to me for the trip. It's the very best one on the market. Oxidized case, hinged cover, automatic stop, jeweled needle." His words ground to a chuckling stop. "I guess you don't care much about the compass."

She stifled an unexpected smile. "I guess not."

"Maybe we could talk about something else."

She pondered that for a moment, clearly hesitant. "Maybe . . ."

He pulled out his cherished copy of *Century Magazine*. The one with Frank Cushing's article about his travels in Zuñi country. "Would you like to see—"

"No, thanks."

"How about my map? I could show you—"

"I don't think so."

He frowned. "Well, then *you* think of something we could talk about."

"Stocks?" she said hopefully.

He shook his head. "Sorry. How about plants?"

"No. Economy?"

"Nope. History?"

Silence stretched between them, thick and awkward. Larence heard the quiet ticking of his watch as they stared at each other.

"Well." They both said the word at precisely the same moment.

Larence chuckled at their mutual discomfort. "I think I'll go back to work," he said.

She nodded. "That's an excellent idea."

"Good."

"Good."

Emmaline plucked up the old financial newspaper she'd found in the parlor car, and began to read. Larence turned his attention back to the map and began to mark off watering holes and rivers along the journey.

Larence sighed in his sleep, burrowing closer to the warm body spooned tightly against his own. Something tickled his nostrils. He wiggled his nose and pushed the offending strands of hair off his face. The delicate scent of roses reached him.

His arms tightened around her body, his leg slid atop hers. He felt the heat of her skin through his long underwear. She rolled over. Warm, firm breasts and hardened nipples pressed against his chest.

The contact jolted him awake. His eyes blinked twice in rapid succession, then widened at the sight that greeted him.

Emmaline was curled like a contented kitten in his

arms. Her face was turned up to his, and their lips were no more than a strand of hair apart. Her even, peaceful breath teased his face and lips.

He stared at the long, spiky lashes that fanned her pale cheeks and had a sudden, almost overwhelming urge to move his face the barest fraction forward, to touch his lips to hers. To take his first kiss.

It took all his willpower to remain stock-still. His heart skidded against his rib cage and thumped hard. His skin itched with the need to touch hers. He'd never in his life known a moment so fraught with emotion: exhilaration, fear of discovery, desire. And laced through it all, this pervasive, compelling feeling of well-being.

They'd slept together for four nights, but somehow last night they had crossed a boundary. In their sleep, at least, they had found a common ground, a zone of comfort. He prayed they could find such a place in their waking moments, although he knew it wouldn't be easy. Emmaline was not an easy person to like, even for him. And *she* didn't like anyone.

He studied her porcelain-perfect face. So soft, so lovely, and yet so hard. During the past few days he'd seen things in her eyes that disturbed him. Every now and then he'd say something innocuous—something like *do you have any family*? And quick as a flash he'd glimpse a pain so pure, so elemental, he'd feel its impact like a fist in the gut. It only took her a second to drop the impersonal curtain over her eyes, but pain was something Larence recognized.

She wasn't what she appeared; of that he was sure. She was running from something in her life, something painful and ugly and raw. Running fast.

He felt a rush of compassion for her. He knew what it felt like to be afraid.

Without thinking, he pushed a cornsilk-soft lock of hair out of her face. She sighed. Her eyelashes fluttered.

Larence's hand froze in place. The last thing he wanted was to get caught staring at her; she'd probably slap his face. He slammed his eyes shut and pretended to be asleep.

Emmaline wakened slowly, reluctantly. For the first time in years, she felt at peace. Almost happy. No nightmares had terrorized her slumber. She'd slept long and well, and she felt like a million dollars.

She stretched. That's when she noticed it: the leg draped so casually atop hers. Heavy. Warm. Masculine.

Her eyes popped open. Larence's nose was practically touching hers. His hand, entangled in her hair, was resting on the side of her face. She froze, afraid even to breathe for fear of waking him.

Good Lord, how had this happened? The last few nights together had been restless, pinned-against-the-wall kind of nights. Never, not once, had she so much as *thought* about easing toward his side of the bed, and now, here she was curled up against him like a lover. And on his side of the bed, too.

She groaned inwardly. *Please don't let him wake up and find me like this. . . .*

Moving slowly, deliberately, she plucked up his hand and eased it off her face. When his fingers were about a half inch above her skin, she allowed herself a small sigh of relief. So far, so good.

She eased her leg out from underneath his.

Footsteps thundered in the aisle.

Emma froze. Her heart thudded against her chest. *Please don't let him—*

"Albuquerque, next stop!" The conductor's voice boomed through the car.

Larence's eyes opened. They stared at each other for a single heartbeat before the scramble began. She clutched her lacy, scoop-necked chemise to her throat and clambered backward. Her muslin underskirt bunched like a mushroom in the middle of her bare thighs. She stared in horror at her naked legs, then, with a gasp, she shoved the Hamburg lace hem back to her ankles and scuttled backward at full speed.

She hit the window hard. Behind her, the blind thumped once and bounced up the window. Harsh sunlight streamed into the cubicle.

Larence scooted backward. His back thudded into the solid mahogany wall; the compartment vibrated, the curtain shimmied.

They stared at each other, both breathing rapidly. The sound seemed thunderous in the confined, velvet-curtained space.

"Sleep well?" he asked nervously.

She cleared her throat and tried to look casual. "Fine, and you?"

"Fine. If you'll just hand me my trousers and shirt, I'll be out of your way in a second."

"Good."

"Good."

Emma grabbed his clothes from the foot of the bed and shoved them at him. He pulled them under the sheets and dressed quickly, then rolled out of the bed with a plop. She saw the shadow of his body move protectively across the space between the two curtains to ensure her privacy.

She reached for her wool traveling suit. Wrinkling her nose at the clothes she'd been wearing since she left

New York, she burrowed through the pile for her corset. Drawing a deep breath, she squeezed into her Dr. Strong's celebrated corset, which, as advertised, gave her the perfect hourglass shape.

She laced it up. Her breathing shattered into a series of sharp, pained pants as she wiggled into her now wrinkled shirtwaist, wool skirt, and hip-length coat. She sat stiffly erect and perfectly still, taking short, shallow breaths. When the familiar dizziness passed, she adroitly twisted her hair into a Roman knot and pinned her hat in place.

Dressed, she felt better. More in control.

What in the world had come over her? she wondered with some irritation. She hadn't had a moment's modesty in years—and yet in Dr. Dimwits' arms, she'd blushed like a schoolgirl.

It defied all logic. She shook her head. There was something about him that crept past her guard. Confused and irritated her.

Whatever it was, she'd simply have to be more careful in the future. She'd worked hard to become cold and detached. The last thing she needed was some muddle-headed idealist with a bright smile turning her carefully ordered world upside down.

Fortunately they were in New Mexico now and they wouldn't be sleeping together anymore. It would be easy to keep him at arm's length.

Preferably farther.

Chapter Seven

Larence bounced nervously on the balls of his feet. His hands clenched, stretched, clenched. Craning his neck, he tried for the thousandth time to see the station.

No luck. All he could see was a smoke-clogged blur of yellowish brown beneath a layer of bright blue sky. The iron couplings beneath his feet bucked and clanged. The cars on either side of him rattled. Wind pelted his face, stung his eyes. Tears streamed across his temples and burrowed into his rustling hair. His hold on the cold brass handrail tightened.

Any minute now, he thought. Any minute . . .

Executing a wobbly half turn toward the sleeper car's narrow, shaking door, he looked through the cloudy, rectangular window and saw Emmaline standing in the line of passengers. She offered him a stiff, cheerless wave, and an even stiffer smile.

The pure, unadulterated *joy* of having someone with whom to share this spectacular moment welled up in Larence. Grinning, he crooked his index finger in a motion of invitation.

She shook her head violently, pointing to the ridiculous little scrap of a hat perched on her head.

A long, high-pitched whistle rent the air. Larence

spun back around. The couplings banged together; the puckered metal floor clattered and shook. He clutched the handrail harder, remaining erect by sheer force of will.

Black smoke billowed past the opening in a noxious cloud. The train's huge metal wheels locked with a clang. Wheels screeching, the train eased up to the station's long, wooden platform.

He was in Albuquerque.

Emotion clogged in his throat. After all the years of waiting and praying and believing, he was here. Nothing could stop him from finding Cibola now.

He took a deep breath. The hot, arid air seared his lungs, reminding him with painful clarity that he was here, in Albuquerque, where his dream began.

Emma tasted grit before the train door even opened. Trapped in the center of a centipede of humanity, she inched her way forward. The floor beneath her feet rattled and hummed with the vibrations of the train; the velvet drapes of the sleeping compartments shimmied. Smells assailed her—the sharp tang of bodies who'd traveled too long on a packed train, the gunpowdery scent of old dust, the pervasive aroma of perfume and cigar smoke. The odors closed in on her, coiling around her throat like a noose. She squeezed through the narrow doorway and emerged onto the rattling metal platform between cars, her parasol and bag tucked tightly beneath her arm.

"Over here, Emmaline!"

She slanted a gloved hand over her eyes and squinted into the bright noontime sun. Larence was standing on the empty platform, waving like a windmill. He was wearing his trademark "the world's a great place" smile.

"Here! Over here!" More waving.

Did he really think she could miss him? She took a deep breath—and immediately felt as if she'd just inhaled a bolt of lightning. Her ability to breathe sputtered and died. She coughed, gasped.

Air. God, she needed air.

She bolted down the swaying steps and staggered onto the platform with a thud. Hot air smacked her in the face again, stung her eyes. She gasped, doubled over, trying desperately to draw a normal breath. All she could manage were short, painful pants.

She started to straighten, and a wave of dizziness hit her. It was so strong, she didn't know whether to vomit or faint. Her knees buckled.

Larence was beside her in an instant. "Are you okay?"

"I . . . can't . . . breathe."

"Relax. Take little breaths. Here, like this: *ha, ha, ha.*"

She had an almost overwhelming urge to coldcock him. "H-How come . . . you can . . . breathe? The . . . air's so dry . . . and dusty and . . ." *And what?* What made the air so unbreathable?

Larence's hand moved soothingly up and down her back. She thought about wrenching away, but didn't have the energy, and strangely enough, the contact was comforting. After a few moments, breathing came easier.

"It's the altitude. Remember, I told you Albuquerque was almost fifty-four hundred feet above sea level?"

Her bleary sideways glance told him she'd forgotten to memorize that scintillating bit of information.

"I told you not to wear your corset."

An *I told you so* from Larence? She groaned. "I . . . thought . . . it was . . . fashion advice."

His arm curled around her waist and steadied her. She swallowed, tasting the acrid memory of nausea on her tongue.

With a herculean effort, she straightened. Slowly.

"Are you—"

"Fine," she wheezed. "Where's . . . Stanton?"

"We're meeting him at San Felipe de Neri." Larence eased his arm away from her waist and checked his pocket watch. "He'll be there in thirty minutes."

"Let's go." She took a small, mincing step forward. Her stomach roiled at the motion; her breathing quickened, became painful.

Larence appeared beside her. "May I just hold on to you for a moment? My . . . my ankle hurts and I'm a bit dizzy."

She breathed a silent—painful—sigh of relief. She didn't want his charity, but she wouldn't mind—just this once—accepting his help. She wouldn't have asked for it, but by God, she needed it.

"Sure." She held out her arm for him.

His answering smile was awfully bright for a man in pain, but that was one thing Emma had learned about Larence. He suffered his pains in silence. Not like her.

His forearm slid underneath hers, palm up. Warm, surprisingly strong fingers slipped between hers and curled tight. She leaned against the steadying perch of his forearm, and allowed herself a rare smile of relief.

"Ready?" he asked.

She nodded, feeling better already. "Ready." Plucking up her heavy woolen skirt in her other hand, she allowed him to lead her through the station. They crossed the dark, relatively cool room and reached the

double doors on the other side. Larence limped ahead
and yanked the door open.

Harsh, bright sunlight streamed through the opening.
By the time she could finally focus, she and Larence
were standing on a landing, several steps above the
street.

Emma glanced at the buildings with contempt, noticing the false storefronts that created the impression of
two-story structures. They'd actually painted windows
on the fronts to make poor passersby think they were
in a city instead of a shabby little cow town.

Larence squeezed her hand again. ''Isn't it beautiful?''.

Her mouth dropped open. Were they looking at the
same town?

A horse-drawn wagon rumbled past them. The big
wheels crunched forward, sending a plume of gray-
brown dust hurdling into the air. More grit insinuated
itself into Emma's mouth and eyes. Infinitesimal gran-
ules stung her eyes. Tears ran in zigzagging brownish
streaks down her face.

Soon, she told herself. Soon she'd have her money
back and be on her way east.

She had no doubt about the outcome of her meeting
with Stanton: She'd get her money back. There was no
way Stanton or Larence could justify spending ten thousand dollars on this backwater expedition. A few well-
chosen observations about where the budget could be
pared down, a steely-eyed order coupled with a full-
blown feminine smile, and voilà, she'd have her money
back. And then she'd be gone. Good-bye, dirty down-
town Albuquerque; hello, Wall Street.

She didn't want all of her money back. All she needed
was a couple of thousand dollars. A few measly thou-

sand. Larence would still have plenty of money to find his precious city—and she'd have enough cash to start over.

Start over. The words were a balm that soothed her, gave her a goal to fight for. She already had some good, solid ideas. *Those zipper fasteners W. L. Hudson had recently patented looked interesting enough to finance. And Villard and Morgan's new endeavor, General Electric Company, showed some real promise. . . .*

She couldn't help smiling. It felt good to think about money and how to make it again.

Her plan was perfect. Flawless. There was a train leaving for New York tomorrow morning—the only one until next week—and she intended to be on it. With her money.

"Shall we walk?" Larence's question interrupted her musings.

She took a shallow, close-mouthed breath. "How far?"

Bad question. With an eager grin, Larence plopped his duck valise on the ground, squatted beside it, and started burrowing through the cluttered bag.

"Here it is," he said, extracting a carefully folded piece of paper. Before Emma could utter a word, he'd opened the Rand McNally map of New Mexico to its full three-foot-by-three-foot size, and was poring over the spider-leg scrawls.

She peered over his shoulder. "How far?"

Pushing slowly to his feet, he began to refold the map.

"Larence?"

"The church isn't listed by name."

A terrifying question flitted through her mind. "It is in Albuquerque, though. . . ."

He nodded. "Yes, I'm sure of that. In the early seventeen hundreds, there was a priest named—"

"I believe you," she said quickly to forestall another scintillating historical monologue.

The loud, pealing jangle of a brass bell announced the arrival of a draft-horse-drawn streetcar. Emma almost buckled with relief when it came to a creaking halt in front of them.

She jabbed Larence in the side. "Ask him where the place is." *And it damn well better be in Albuquerque and not Atlanta.*

"Sir?" Larence inquired of the man perched on a three-legged stool in the thrusting lip of the streetcar. "Do you go to San Felipe de Neri?"

The man squinted up at them. "You in a hurry?"

"No—" "Yes—" They answered at once.

The driver laughed. "Well, if you ain't in a hurry, hop on. If you are, you'd best walk. Me an' Bullet here, we take our sweet time."

Larence grinned at the driver. "A man after my own heart," he said, offering Emma his arm.

Ignoring him, she grabbed her skirt and descended the wide, pale-colored stairs to the dusty, dirty strip of land that Albuquerqueans ambitiously called Railroad Avenue.

Naturally, with ten empty seats on the streetcar, Larence squeezed in beside her. She jabbed her parasol between them and rammed her satchel on her lap. Her gloved fingers curled around the smooth leather handle and didn't let go.

Emma stared forlornly at the town as it unfolded before her. The street was nothing more than a long, wide stretch of loose sand and dust. Buildings were crammed on either side of the street like a child's building blocks.

All wood, all the same height, all false fronts, and all boring.

She pressed a hand over her mouth as a filter against the dust churned up by Bullet's huge, plodding hooves. Thank God she wouldn't be here long.

Larence edged forward on the streetcar's hard wooden seat and peered around Emmaline's stiff shoulders.

Albuquerque unfurled in front of his eyes like something out of one of Mayne Reid's dime novels.

His gaze darted up and down the street, greedily storing images to take out later and savor like fine pieces of chocolate. Horse-drawn wagons and ox-drawn *carretas* churned down the street, creating a cloud of rolling dust.

They passed the White Elephant saloon, and Larence craned his neck for a better look. The saloon's front door was flung open in greeting, giving him an unobstructed view of the dark, smoke-filled interior. Body-shaped shadows shifted and moved in the hazy half-light. The warbling strains of a poorly played accordion and the tinny clang of an old piano drifted into the dusty street.

It was exactly what he expected. *Exactly.* A dime novel hero's perfect haven. He closed his eyes for a moment, imagining the scene inside the saloon. Dozens of hard-bitten, hard-riding men sidling up to a massive wooden bar, swilling rotgut and laughing about the day's work. Pretty, scantily clad women sidling up to the men, laughing softly, propositioning.

Slowly the streetcar clanked on by. The warbling, hard-edged sounds of the saloon drifted on the air for a long, exquisite moment, and then drifted away.

Gradually the new part of town gave way to the old. The western frontier town became an age-old, much-loved Spanish village. Pale adobe buildings squatted one after another along the wide street, their doors connected by a long, covered boardwalk. Across from the small plaza, a beautiful, white-picket-fenced park appeared like an oasis in the middle of the dusty street.

People drifted through the marketplace. Horses and mules and burros clomped up and down the hard-packed street, their heavy footfalls accompanied by the occasional snap of leather reins on a dusty hindquarter or the grinding squeak of tired wagon wheels.

"Whoa, Bullet."

The streetcar came to a stop. The driver twisted around on his perch to look at them. "Here yah are, folks. Old Town."

"And the other part was 'new'?" Emmaline said under her breath. She shot a disgusted glance at the flesh-tone adobe buildings, and wrinkled her nose.

Larence started to frown, then stopped himself. No, he thought ferociously. I won't let her dourness affect me. It was too bad she couldn't see the beauty around her, but if she couldn't, it was her problem. Not his.

Emma lurched to her feet. Jamming her parasol and bag under one arm, she pushed past him into the aisle. "Let's go."

Her boot heels clicked rapid-fire along the floor, then thudded onto the dirt street.

Larence sighed wearily. Forcing a smile he should have felt but didn't, he grabbed his valise and followed her out.

"Hurry up!" she hollered.

He stared after her in awe. She was about ten feet in front of him, and she was moving. Fast. Her back ramrod-straight, her nose in the air, her feet and skirt hem obliterated by a cloud of dust, she looked like a general headed onto the battlefield. There was no hint that she was uncomfortable—and she had to be downright *sweaty* under all those layers of wool.

Suddenly she stumbled, clutched her side. The parasol wedged beneath her arm wobbled precariously, tilted.

"Emma!" He surged forward as fast as his bad leg allowed. He wasn't fast enough. Before he could reach her, she was off again, striding hell-bent toward the walkway's meager shade.

He hurried along behind her, listening to the rasping, broken tenor of her breathing. At the covered sidewalk, she bent in half like a broken doll, clutching her sides. Her satchel thunked to the ground.

Gritting his teeth against the pain of running, Larence finally reached her. "Are you all right?"

She took another gasping, wheezing breath, then slowly grabbed her bag and drew herself erect. She looked up at him, and there was spiritless blue fire in her eyes that chilled him to the bone. "Let's go."

She rejammed her parasol under her arm and forced a path through the other shoppers. He watched her barrel through the makeshift marketplace and felt a sharp stab of sadness for her. Nothing caught her attention. In fact, he doubted if she even noticed the people she was plowing through to get to her destination.

Oh, well, he thought with a shrug. He couldn't change her.

But she wouldn't change him, either. This was his adventure, and he was going to enjoy it.

On that cheerful thought, he shoved his free hand in his pocket. Whistling softly, happily, he ambled lazily down the wide, shady pathway.

"Larence . . ." His name, buried in an impatient

huff, was followed by the unmistakable tapping of her foot. Larence listened to the *ra-ta-ta-tat* and smiled, casting a surreptitious glance to where she was standing. Her foot tapped ceaselessly, creating a cloud of dust around her high-buttoned walking boots and black skirt.

Whistling a bit louder, he squatted down beside an old Indian woman and admired her handiwork.

Emma stopped tapping and started stomping. "I'd like to find Stanton sometime this century," she grumbled.

Larence handed the woman a coin and pushed to a stand. When he reached Emma, he flashed her an innocent smile and offered her his arm. She took it with obvious reluctance, and together, they started across the street.

His smile turned into an eager grin as he gazed at the adobe church that had presided over this square for nearly two hundred years. White crosses glinted in the warm April sun. Ignoring the pain in his ankle, he stepped up his pace. Beside him, he was dimly aware of Emmaline wheezing and hacking at the dust his feet churned up. He knew he should slow down, make it easier on her, but he didn't want to. Not this time. Just this once, he wanted—needed—to be selfish.

With each step, his excitement grew. Any minute, Stanton would come around that corner, and the adventure would really and truly begin. Any minute—

I'll get my money back. It was that thought—and that thought alone—which kept Emmaline from complaining about Larence's world-record pace. Head down, fingers curled tightly around his forearm, she struggled to match him step for dust-billowing step.

Her feet caught in her skirt and she stumbled. Only

her ironclad grip on Larence's forearm saved her from falling. He slowed for a millisecond, then reaccelerated. Her hold tightened. She leaned almost imperceptibly toward him. For once, she didn't care if she looked weak. She was. Weak as a kitten.

Refund. Refund. Refund. The word was her mantra, her salvation. It slammed through her brain with every crunch of her heel, reminded her time and again of why she was here. Any minute now, she'd meet Dr. Stanton, prove to the doddering coot how poorly he'd spent her money, and demand enough of a refund to start over.

Refund. Just thinking about it made her feel stronger, better.

"Stanton!"

Larence's voice reached her dust-clogged ears. She dragged her chin up and squinted into the vicious sun, trying to make out the dark shadow waving at them from across the street.

God help me, another windmill. She blinked.

The stoop-shouldered old man shuffled toward them, his right hand already outstretched in greeting. "Larence, my boy, it's good to see you."

"Good to see you, too, Henry," he said, shaking his mentor's hand. "I'd like you to meet Emmaline Hatter."

Henry cocked his head at her. "The financier?"

"Of course," she answered.

He looked back at Larence. One bushy white eyebrow lifted questioningly. "Interesting development."

"Isn't it great? She's fascinated by Cibola."

"Fascinated," she murmured sarcastically. "Look, Henry, I'd like to speak with you about—"

"First things first," he said, and promptly turned his back on her.

Emma's teeth came together with a snap. What sort of man turned his back on a woman while she was speaking? The answer came to her immediately: the sort of man who left a woman's bags piled on a station bench.

Professors, she thought with disgust.

Shaking her head, she plucked up her skirts and followed Tweedledee and Tweedledum across the street.

Halfway to the supply wagon, she felt the hairs on the back of her neck stand up. *Someone was watching her.*

She looked around. Not more than ten feet away from the wagon was a group of Indians. The serape-ed men were standing together in a half circle, laughing softly and talking among themselves.

Nothing unusual about men talking, Emma told herself firmly. Then she saw him.

A tall Indian man stood out from the crowd of short, squat men like a hundred-year oak in a grove of alder. He wore no hat and no shirt, and his bronzed, barrel-chested torso glinted copper in the bright sunlight. The only adornment on his body was a thick green band that encircled the largest part of his bicep. He was staring right at her.

Emma felt a flicker of unreasonable fear. Her fingers tightened nervously around her gripsack's leather handle. He inclined his head at her almost imperceptibly. Slowly, as if he were *trying* to frighten her, he crossed his arms and leaned back on his heels to study her. Narrowed eyes stared at her, followed her every move. She felt a thick, almost tangible sense of malice emanating from him.

Nothing wrong with a man looking at you, Em. Calm down. She was letting her imagination run riot. With a snap of her chin, Emma broke eye contact, and the moment she did, she felt better. There was no sense in worrying about something that didn't concern her. That man was nothing to her. Nothing.

"Here's your horse, Larence," Henry said as Emma reached the men. "His name's Diablo. He wasn't cheap, but he's worth every cent."

Cheap. The word was like a gift from God. Emma stepped forward. "Now, that's just what I wanted to talk to you about, I—"

"He's a beautiful animal, Henry. Thanks."

Emma tapped Henry's shoulder. "About what you spent—"

"My pleasure."

Emma gritted her teeth. They were acting as if she weren't even here. As if she weren't important.

She squeezed her eyes shut and counted silently to ten. She didn't want to alienate Henry. Without his help, she wouldn't retrieve a dime of her money. When she'd calmed down, she tried again, "Dr. Stanton, I'm anxious to—"

Larence curled an arm around her shoulders and drew her close to him. Emmaline stiffened instinctively. "She's as anxious as I am to get going, Henry. How long till we get started?"

"You'll leave at dawn tomorrow. I've made reservations for you at the Armijo House. We'll unload the supplies now, and then go have dinner."

Emma almost sighed with relief as Henry began unloading the wagon. Finally they were getting somewhere. All she had to do now was figure out where to save money.

Henry yanked three slatted crates from the back of the wagon and dropped them to the ground.

"There it is, Larence. Your supplies."

Emma snorted. "Three little crates of food cost ten thousand dollars?"

Henry frowned. "Is there a problem, Miss Hatter?"

Larence chuckled. "With her, there's *always* a problem, Henry."

She shot him a quelling stare. "Not at all, Dr. Stanton. As long as your expenditures are . . . reasonable, there shouldn't be a problem in the world."

"Good. For a moment there, I thought you were questioning me."

"I was."

"Emmaline," Larence said in a low, warning voice.

Emma didn't even spare him a sideways glance. "Let's see what you've used my money for, Dr. Stanton. Shall we?" She stepped around him and peered into the nearest crate. A rifle stuck butt-first out of the closest box, and she stifled a quick shudder at the thought of Dr. Dimwit with a weapon. One by one, she studied the boxes, cataloging in her mind the contents. Tent, sleeping bags, canteens, ropes . . .

At the last crate, relief swamped her. Henry couldn't possibly justify the expenditure of ten thousand dollars. She turned around, her smile held firmly in check by years of practice. "How can that be ten thousand dollars worth?"

"It's not."

Her heart soared. She slapped her palm out in front of Henry. "Then give me what's left."

"There's nothing left."

"Nothing? Three crates full of—" she bent over and yanked out a five-pound bag of sugar "—foodstuffs, and there's nothing left?"

"Actually, I had to spend fifteen of my own dollars.

Larence and I figured the expenses on the tightest budget possible.''

Emma dropped her bag of sugar. It landed with a dusty plop. "What 'expenses'?''

Henry pulled an envelope out of his breast pocket, opened it, and extracted a piece of paper. Unfolding it, he began to read: "Sugar, flour, corn meal, rolled oats, evaporated potatoes, evaporated onions, beef extract—''

"Try and find something that costs more than five dollars,'' she cut in impatiently. *I have a train to catch tomorrow morning.*

"Diablo cost two hundred fifty.''

"Aha!'' It was all she could do not to clap her hands in glee. "That's more than Eugene paid for his blooded carriage horse.''

"True,'' he said, "but it takes a special horse for this job, and 'special' translates to expensive.''

Emma cast a speculative glance at the big red horse. "He doesn't look too 'special' to me.''

"He is. Anyone can ride him. Even someone who's never ridden before, like Larence. Around here, a calm desert horse is worth more than some scatterbrained thoroughbred.''

Emma's smile fell flat. How could she argue with the law of supply and demand? "Fine,'' she said, running a sweaty, gloved finger inside her damp collar. "The horse was a legitimate purchase. Let's move on.''

Henry consulted his list. "The pack mule—''

"How much?''

"Twenty dollars.''

"Look, Henry, let's not make a production out of this. I have a simple question; I expect a simple answer. You spent a few thousand dollars on supplies—I understand that. All I want to know is, where is the rest of my ten thousand dollars?''

Her question hung in the hot, dry air. She felt the ticking of each second as an almost tangible tightening around her neck. *Please God, all I need is—*

"The church," Henry said at last.

Emma stared at him blankly. "Excuse me?"

"To get control of Esteban's diary, I had to 'donate' eight thousand dollars to the Mexican priests who found it."

She gasped. Metal stays stabbed her skin at the sudden intake of breath. "Eight—" The word lodged like tar in her throat. "Eight thousand dollars for a book?"

"*The* book."

"Eight . . . nonrefundable thousand?"

Henry frowned. "Of course. Why would Larence want the money back?"

Hope hit the dust at Emma's feet. Desperation twisted her stomach into a hard knot.

It had all been for nothing. The terrible train trip across the country, selling her last possession, putting up with Larence's bumbling good humor, wearing the same clothes for almost a week . . .

All for nothing. She'd return to New York City as poor as she'd left it.

No. She refused to even contemplate a defeated return to New York. She'd been poor once, and she refused to fall into that soul-less hole again. She'd do anything—*anything*—to remake her fortune. And once she had it, by God, nothing on earth would pry it from her fingers.

Think, damn it, that's what you're good at.

She couldn't get her money back; that much was painfully obvious. So, what now?

The treasure. The thought plunged into her mind with blinding force, and she grabbed at it desperately. *The treasure*. Of course. Without the money, it was her only hope.

And it all depended on Larence.

Her heart sank into her stomach. God only knew how long it would take Dr. Dimwit to find the treasure. And time was the one thing she didn't have. The fifty dollars she'd gotten for the watch wouldn't last long. If she didn't do something, and fast, she'd soon be selling wilted flowers in the Bowery and living in Rosare Court.

She had to make sure Larence hurried, and there was only one way to do that. She swallowed hard, forcing down her disgust at what she had to do. There was no choice. She was going to Cibola with Larence.

"Let's get started," Henry said. What do you want to do first? Meet the men I hired to accompany you on the expedition?"

Emma frowned. Men? *Men?* They had hired people to go with them? On a *treasure* hunt?

She shook her head in disbelief. How could anyone—even these two muddleheads—be so stupid? Hadn't they ever heard of *robbery*, for God's sake?

Well, one thing was certain: No one was going with her and Larence to the secret city. She'd make damn sure of that. It was her treasure hunt as much as it was his, and she couldn't afford to lose a single gold doubloon to some backstabbing hired hand. Larence might see the world as a fairy-tale place where dreams came true and people were kind, but she didn't. She knew better; the world was a dog-eat-dog arena where people killed for a dollar, much less a fortune.

Her lips thinned into a grim, determined line. She was just about to lay down the law when she heard a soft rumble of laughter coming from her right. The sound had a low, masculine sound to it. Quiet and mocking. Threatening.

Realization struck. And struck hard.

The men I've hired to accompany you . . .

Chapter Eight

Emma turned. The tall, bare-chested Indian was still staring at her. At her glance, his laughter dwindled. The air thickened in sudden silence.

Dark, deep-set eyes held her captive, stealing the breath from her lungs and making her heart thump like a rabbit's. Thick lips which hinted at an intense, silent pride were drawn into a taut, disapproving line.

A chill mingled with the perspiration itching along her spine, but she forced herself to stare right back at the man. She wouldn't let him see her fear. Not him or anyone.

I won't be afraid. I won't be afraid. . . . With each repetition of the words, she felt stronger. More in control. She wouldn't allow this man to frighten her. Frightened women were weak women, and Emma was far from weak.

She strode over to Henry and Larence, who were burrowing through the crate of foodstuffs. "No," she said firmly.

Both men turned to look at her. "What?" they said in unison.

"I won't travel with those men."

Henry offered her a smile that made her stomach turn. Emma could almost *feel* him patting her head. "I un-

108

derstand," he said in one of those disgusting I-know-what's-best-for-you male voices. "Most gentlewomen are afraid of Indians, but you needn't be. Really. I know almost every man in that group, and I'd trust my life—or my wife's—with any one of them."

"It has nothing to do with their race. Nothing at all. I just think—Wait a minute, what do you mean you know *almost* all of the men?"

"Ka-Neek over there—you see the big man without a shirt?—he's the only one I don't know."

"I'm sure all the men will be great, Henry," Larence said quickly, smiling.

Emma would have laughed if it hadn't been so damned serious. Didn't they know anything about the real world, for God's sake? Half those men looked like thieves, and the other half looked like rapists. And the man called Ka-Neek looked like both.

She squared her shoulders for battle. "They aren't going."

"What?"

"I refuse to spend the next two weeks worrying about being killed or robbed or—" she lowered her voice "—worse."

"Every man over there is honorable," Henry said with a deepening frown.

"They also look poor. You can trust them all you want, Henry; I don't have to. And I don't have to travel with them."

"Larence, talk some sense into her. You two can't go into the desert alone."

"Why not?" she demanded.

Henry stuttered for a moment, as if at a loss as to where to begin. "You'll get lost."

Emma turned to Larence. "Can you or can you not read a compass?"

"I can."

"Can you follow the map and find us water?"

He nodded.

She shot Henry a triumphant look. "The issue is settled. We're going alone."

She was just congratulating herself on how well she'd handled the unpleasant situation when Larence took her by the arm and led her to a private spot a few feet away from the wagon.

"Henry has worked very hard on this expedition, Emmaline."

"I'm not going with them."

His penetrating gaze focused on her face. She dropped her chin and stared at her toes. She didn't want him to see her irrational, humiliating fear of Ka-Neek.

"What is it, Emmaline?" His voice was quiet. Compelling.

He laid his hands on her shoulders. Warmth seeped through the hot, damp fabric of her jacket and tingled along her skin.

"Em?" The sound of his voice was soft, gentle, and it sparked a sudden, unexpected wave of longing within her breast. She'd waited a lifetime to hear someone say her name like that.

She pulled away, struggling to maintain at least a facade of control. "Are you deaf? I'm not going with those men, and that's that."

He swallowed the distance between them in a single step. Emma felt the cool of his shadow fall across her face. She quickly looked at the ground.

His forefinger slid beneath her chin. She felt its hard

warmth like a brand against her skin. Slowly he tilted her face up.

The concern in his eyes almost did her in. She squeezed her eyes shut in a feeble attempt to maintain her composure. *Don't let him see your weakness. Don't give him that power over you. . . .*

"Open your eyes, Em." When she didn't budge, he added, "I'll wait all day."

He probably would. Reluctantly she did as he asked—and found that he had leaned toward her. His nose was nearly touching her own. She felt the feather-soft caress of his breath against her cheek. His knowing eyes imprisoned her, made the breath stumble in her throat.

"That's better. Now, tell me the truth. What are you so afraid of?"

Resentment surged to the forefront of her mind. She hadn't revealed her fear, and yet somehow he'd seen it. Those damn eyes of his had done it again.

Now there was no choice left but to tell Larence the truth and hope he didn't use it against her.

"Please . . . I . . ." The confession stuck in her throat. She looked at Larence helplessly, shaking her head. She couldn't tell him; too many years of training and self-imposed solitude made it impossible for her to admit to fear. She'd spent a lifetime building an emotional barrier to the world, and the walls just wouldn't come down so easily.

Her nervous gaze cut to Ka-Neek to see if the man was still staring at her. He was.

Larence's gaze followed hers. Turning, he stared long and hard at Ka-Neek, and then, slowly, he brought his gaze back to her face.

She held her breath. *Please . . .*

"Okay. We'll go alone. It'll be more of an adventure that way, anyway."

Emma's breath came out in a rush. *Thank you, God . . . and Larence.*

With a concerted effort, she stilled the trembling in her fingers and limbs. She was being a fool, she knew it, but somehow the knowledge didn't help much. She'd been afraid there for a moment, really afraid, and it left her feeling shaken and weak.

"Let's tell Henry," she said, forcing strength back into her voice.

"Emmaline?"

She didn't look at him. She couldn't. Not yet; not while relief and fear still lurked in her eyes. It was bad enough that he'd seen her weakness and acted upon it; she didn't want him to know just how relieved she was. If he knew that, he'd know how truly afraid she'd been, and she'd learned a long time ago that it was never smart to give out information about yourself. It gave people a power over you, a way to hurt you.

She'd given Larence enough of a weapon. She'd be damned if she'd give him any more. As it was, she'd have to spend the rest of the trip wondering when he'd use it against her.

Without sparing Larence a glance, she grabbed his arm and propelled him toward the wagon. Henry looked at them expectantly.

"We won't be needing the Indians," Larence said.

"But the two of you can't go alone. It wouldn't be safe."

"Safer than going with *them*," Emma responded.

"And it wouldn't be proper," Henry added with a pointed, fatherly look.

"Now, *that's* something I care about," Emma said.

"But the curse—"

"What curse?" she demanded.

Henry shot an uneasy glance at the Indians, then lowered his voice. "There's supposed to be a curse on seekers of the lost city. Over the years, many have tried to find Cibola; all have failed, most have died—"

"Rubbish. Larence and I don't believe in any silly local superstitions, do we?"

"Nope."

Henry sighed dramatically and threw his hands up in the air. "All right, I'll send them home. They won't mind getting paid for doing nothing, but I can't recommend—"

"Paid? *Paid?*" Emma parroted. "They won't be getting paid, Doctor."

"Now, see here, Miss Hatter—"

"No, Doctor. You see *here*. They're not going; they're not getting paid."

"Yes, they are." The voice was soft, so soft, and yet it was rock-hard. Emma blinked in surprise. Larence—*Larence* had disagreed with her. It was like having Santa slap your hand.

She frowned. "But—"

Larence shook his head. "It wouldn't be right. They're ready, willing, and able to come. The money is theirs to keep."

A headache started, slow and thudding, in the back of Emma's skull. She could tell by the implacable set to Larence's square jaw that his mind was made up. "Fine," she spat. "Just throw the supplies in the wagon and we'll get started."

"Wagon?" Henry and Larence said together.

A sick feeling crept into Emma's stomach and twisted.

"I thought I told you," Larence said. "The only way to Cibola is by—"

No. No. No.

"—horseback."

She squeezed her eyes shut. God, she didn't even like *paintings* of horses. "How long?"

"About a week. One way," Henry answered. "Of course, that's assuming you're not walking."

Emma's eyes popped open. *"Walking?"*

"I didn't plan for you when I outfitted Larence's expedition. So there's only the one horse—and I had to go all the way to Santa Fe to find a beginner's mount. Everyone out here rides." He studied her. "I don't suppose you're much of a horsewoman?"

Emma thought about the one time she'd tried to pet a cab horse. The ungrateful beast had bitten her fingers. She flashed Henry a sarcastic smile. "I don't suppose so."

"There's the pack mule. . . ."

She stared at him in disbelief.

"No, I guess not." He frowned in thought for a moment, then shrugged. "I guess you'll just have to walk."

She didn't even dignify that with an answer.

"You could take my horse."

The offer was made so quietly, she almost missed it. Hope flared, then fizzled. Guilt curled in her stomach for even *considering* his offer. She wouldn't give two cents to a dying man, and he—a cripple—would give up his horse so that she wouldn't have to walk. She licked her overly dry lips and shook her head. "You couldn't walk that far. . . ."

"Wait a minute," Henry said, "I just thought of something. *Javi!*"

A squat, dark-skinned man emerged from the crowd of Indians and shuffled over to where they stood. "Yes, Professor Stanton?"

"Would you be willing to sell Is-ta-shi to this lady?"

Javi pulled the battered straw hat off his head. His dark, dirty fingers twisted the pale brim as he stared at Henry. "I don't know . . . my Tashee's a smart one, and the children love her. . . ."

Emma sighed impatiently. "How much?"

Javi shot her a startled look. "Pardon?"

"How much do you want for the nag?" Emma glanced around. "Where is it, anyway?"

"Wait a minute, miss, my Tashee is—"

Henry laid a pale hand on Javi's serape-ed shoulder. "She's from the city."

Javi looked at her warily. "Ah . . ."

"The thing is, Javi," Henry said smoothly, "my friends need Tashee. Just for a few weeks—maybe they could rent her?"

Javi thought about that for a moment, then nodded slowly. "Okay. I will rent her for thirty dollars."

"Thirty dollars!"

Henry grabbed Emma's arm tightly. "That would be good, Javi. Tack included?"

"Sure, but you don't need no tack with my Tashee. She follow like a baby lamb."

"Good," Henry said with a smile.

"Thank you," Larence said softly. "We appreciate your generosity."

Javi grinned and hurried off.

Emma snorted. "Generosity. Ha! I could buy a thoroughbred stallion for that."

"You know, Miss Hatter," Henry said, "this is New Mexico, not New York. You might try—"

"Don't bother, Henry," Emma said with a wave of her sweaty, gloved hand. "Better men than you have tried to change me. I *like* the way I am." That said, she slammed her arms across her chest and closed her eyes against the sun's bright glare, waiting impatiently for her mount.

"Here she is," Javi said, his voice thick with pride.

Grimacing, Emma opened her eyes. And froze. "No way," she mumbled, shaking her head and taking a step backward.

Larence grinned at her. "No way what?"

A loud bray split the silence. Sour breath slammed into Emma's nostrils. Big, square, yellow teeth laughed at her.

"I am not riding an ass to Cibola."

Chapter Nine

She was riding an ass through the desert. *Unbelievable.*

Thank God it would be a short trip. All she wanted to do was get to the city, get the gold, and get out.

Already impatient to be making better time, she glanced at the deserted landscape stretched out before her. The desolation of it made Emma feel a twinge of anxiety. She'd never been out of the city in her life. . . .

"Don't be a fool," she soothed herself. "If you could survive in Rosare Court, you can survive anywhere."

The realization brought the expected calm. She settled deeper onto the strange combined pack and riding saddle Javi had provided as "tack." The animal's backbone made even modest comfort impossible.

With an irritated sigh she flicked open her utilitarian steel pocket watch and checked the time again. It was 5:45. Soon it would start getting hot. Henry had told her that yesterday's weather had been unseasonably warm, but not at all unusual. At her frown, he'd laughed, telling her that nothing from snow to eighty-degree weather was "unusual" for New Mexico in April.

She hoped she hadn't made a mistake by refusing to accept the clothes he'd offered her.

No, she told herself, she'd made the right decision. The black wool traveling suit she'd been wearing for nearly a week would do just fine. Even if it *did* bunch up around her thighs. After all, there was no one out here to notice the way her pantaletted legs swung like cotton-clad pendulums on either side of Tashee's squat body. No one but Larence; and God knew, he didn't matter.

She might be down on her luck, but she wasn't a Mexican peasant, and she refused to dress like one.

Emma's lips pursed in disapproval. Clinging, off-the-shoulder cotton blouses, free-flowing skirts, thin leather slippers . . . Ha! She wouldn't be caught dead dressed like that.

Larence twisted around in his saddle to talk to her. "I think—*oof*!" He hit the dirt, hard.

A cloud of dust puffed up around him. Coarse, hacking laughter echoed from within the dirty brown haze. Sputtering, hacking, he waited for the dust to clear, then pushed to his feet. The first thing Emma saw was the bright white of his smile.

"Quite a fall, huh?" Suppressed laughter and inhaled dust thickened his voice.

Emma bit back a sharp retort. God help them, they weren't one hundred feet from Albuquerque and he'd already fallen. She pulled out her pocket watch and studied the stark, undecorated face.

"Six o'clock." She snapped it shut. "Let's get going. Henry said it would probably start getting hot around eleven."

Larence dusted himself off and wandered back to Diablo, who'd stopped dead when his rider fell. "Hi, boy. It'll take a little getting used to, I guess. Hope you'll help me out."

He was talking to his horse.

Diablo whickered softly and rubbed his broad face up and down Larence's denim-clad leg.

Emma rolled her eyes. "Are you going to ride him or marry him, for God's sake? Let's go."

Larence cast her an amused glance, then awkwardly remounted. When he hit the seat, Diablo lurched into a trot.

Tashee surged forward. Emma flopped backward, landing hard on the burro's bony spine. Her left toe slammed into a big rock, and a pain sliced through her foot.

She stifled a curse and clung to the wooden X that made up the saddle's makeshift horn, bouncing atop the burro's bone-jarring trot. She squeezed her eyes shut. *Please let me stay on. . . .*

The trot turned into a manageable walk. Emma let out a sigh of relief. She'd made it. Her fingers released their white-knuckled grip on the wood and regathered the reins she'd dropped.

It took her a moment to open her eyes, and after that, a moment to realize what she was seeing.

Diablo's huge butt.

Emma's lips thinned with disgust. She tugged on the reins and tried to turn Tashee. The burro shook her head and kept plodding forward, her wet, snotty black muzzle pressed to Diablo's tail.

She yanked on the reins again, harder this time. Tashee gave a snort, threw her head back, and bucked.

Emma hit the dirt before she even knew she was falling.

"Larence," she cried, choking on the dust clouding around her.

Diablo stopped, swung his head around, and stared

at her. She could almost read the animal's thoughts—and she didn't like what he was thinking.

Larence twisted in his seat. When he saw her sprawled in the dirt, his mouth twitched. "Need help?"

She scowled. Mr. Horseman was fighting laughter.

"Don't you dare," she said thickly, tasting grit on her tongue.

"Me? Never."

Just then a warm, wet muzzle pushed against Emma's cheek. A moist tongue streaked up her throat. With a cry of disgust, she slapped the nose away and glared at the pack mule who was nuzzling her. "Get away from me."

The mule got back in line behind Tashee. Emma got to her feet slowly, testing her backside for bruises. Shaking the dust from her clothes, she grabbed her hem, pulled it between her legs to make a makeshift riding skirt, and climbed back in place.

Grabbing the reins, she nodded curtly to Larence. But he wasn't looking at her face. His eyes were riveted to her drawer-clad legs. His openly interested gaze traveled down the length of her leg and back up again. Slowly. Almost appreciatively.

With a snort, she shoved her skirts down as far as they would go.

Laughing, he turned back around. "Let's go, Diablo."

They were off again, plodding toward the bridge.

Bored, Emma glanced around. New Mexico stretched out before her like a length of flat, camel-hued wool. Here and there, dots of squat, lonely, gray-green shrubs defied the sun, and along the twisting, greenbelted bosque of the Rio Grande, a few cottonwoods held the desert at bay.

But mostly there was nothing here. No birds spiraling through the hazy predawn light; no snakes slithering across the cool morning ground; no buildings or homes or offices; no swirling current of a clear mountain stream.

There was only the thunking sound of hooves hitting the planks of the bridge. And then, when they'd crossed the river, even that was gone.

Every time Emma looked at Diablo's butt—and she could hardly miss it—she felt a growing surge of resentment. It stuck in her craw to ride *behind* Larence. Her place was in front of him, leading. At the very least, she belonged beside him, an equal. But thanks to the traitor of a female beneath her, she was riding along behind like a dutiful wife.

For the next week she'd see nothing but rocks, dust, dirt, and a horse's ass. "Perfect," she muttered to herself, "just bloody perfect."

"Isn't it?" Larence's enthusiastic answer floated on the resin-scented air. "I'm so glad you decided to come. I knew that once you were out here, you'd see how wonderful everything is." He twisted in the saddle to talk to her. "I'll bet you never—*oof*!"

He was down.

Diablo stopped dead. Tashee rammed into his backside and bounced backward. The pack mule hit Tashee's butt, and the little burro crow-hopped in response. Emma wobbled and slid sideways, landing with a soft plop on the ground beside Tashee.

She clenched her fists and slugged the hard-packed earth, fighting the urge to scream at the top of her lungs.

Walking would have been faster.

Hell, crawling would have been faster.

* * *

The sun continued its slow, inexorable trek into the sky. Quickly warming rays slid across the ground, casting the harsh, inhospitable landscape in late morning light. The spikes and thorns of a thousand low scrub bushes glinted green, and the dirt beneath the horse's hooves shone like gold dust.

A red-tailed hawk glided effortlessly in a giant, spiraling arc through the cloudless blue sky. Larence leaned back and looked up.

The movement upset his precarious balance, and he fell, hitting the ground with a thud. His first reaction was to laugh. The pure, clear sound of his joy rose into the bright spring air, and made him feel even better.

God, it felt good to be alive. He turned his face toward the morning sun, reveling in the warm feel of it against his cheeks. A sigh-soft breeze ruffled his hair, caressed his flesh.

A thick curse shattered his peace. He glanced at Tashee and saw a blur of black and then a cloud of dust.

Emma hit the ground beside him. Waves of gray-brown dust wafted over to him, insinuating its gritty, peppery fingers into his nose and eyes.

He waited for her laughter to join his. He didn't know why he expected it—she hadn't laughed yet, and she'd fallen almost as many times as he had. But still he expected it. Wanted it. Missed it.

He was always doing that—expecting people to take the same joy from life that he did. And with Emma, he was always wrong, always disappointed.

He shifted slightly to ease the ache in his ankle and noticed the treasure beside him. A flowering hedgehog cactus. Its beauty nearly stole his breath.

Swiveling to face it, he pulled the small, leather-bound notebook from his shirt pocket and began sketching the cactus.

He heard Emma get to her feet beside him, heard the no-nonsense crunching of her heels in the loose dirt as she dusted herself off and remounted. But he didn't bother looking up. His fingers were flying now, capturing the haphazardly placed gray-green spikes on the blank page.

"Hey, Emmaline," he called out, excited as the first bloom materialized perfectly beneath his pen, "come look at this."

She didn't, of course, come anywhere near him, and he hadn't expected her to. Still, he couldn't help asking—hoping.

"Oh, for God's sake, Larence, it looks just like all the other scrubby little dirt-weeds you've been jumping—or falling—down to draw since we left Albuquerque."

Larence shook his head in amazement. How could anyone *choose* not to see the beauty in life?

He looked at her, long and hard. She was, as usual, sitting board-straight, her no-nonsense blue and white striped parasol cocked against the sun. Her black skirt billowed like twin balloons over her hips and down to her knees, and below the dusty brown hem, her cotton-clad legs dangled to the ground. Dust-caked black walking boots wiggled just above the dirt.

He consulted his pocket thermometer. It was seventy-five degrees out here. And there she sat, ramrod-straight in a wool traveling suit that had to be killing her. She looked ridiculous.

But Larence didn't laugh. He wanted to; oh, how he wanted to. But every time he realized how ridiculous she looked and started to smile, he'd look in her eyes. And the laughter would shrivel in his throat.

She was not a woman who liked to be laughed at. Normally that wouldn't have stopped him, but anger wasn't the only emotion that flashed in her eyes when he made fun of her. There was something else, something fleeting and quickly suppressed that made him feel uncomfortable. Made him feel he'd actually *hurt* her.

He studied her profile, drawn as he always was to her pale, classic beauty. She stared straight ahead, apparently fascinated with Diablo's hindquarters. Only the taut, clenched line of her jaw and the white-knuckled curl of her fingers around the reins betrayed the impatience she felt.

He found himself wishing she'd look at him. On rare occasions, like when he'd told her that they'd leave the Indians behind, he'd seen her eyes without the protective barrier that so often hardened them. In those moments, he'd seen something that made his heart thud against his rib cage, made his breath quicken. Something he longed to see again.

But those moments were so rare, so transient, that after they'd passed, he was left wondering whether he'd dreamt them.

He sighed. If only she'd relax. Let that glorious hair tumble down, loosen her nail-straight spine, and let herself *enjoy* this wonderful adventure. She could be having as much fun as he was. They could be sharing the joy.

"*Larence . . .*"

Through the swirl of his thoughts, he heard her voice, knew it was *her* voice, and yet, in his mind it was his grandmother who spoke his name so harshly.

"Larence, come away from that window. There's no use watching the other boys play. You'll never be able to join them." And if he didn't move at once, it came again. That voice, that word. Harsher. More impatient. *"Larence . . ."*

"Damn it, Larence—"

At the sound of Emmaline's voice, he snapped out of the past. Instinctively his hands balled up, his cheeks turned hot.

He'd spent the ten years since his grandmother's death reinventing self-confidence and teaching himself to love life. And he'd be damned if he'd let Emmaline plow through his dream and turn it into rubble. She could live in a shriveled-up soul if she wanted to, but by God, she wouldn't suck the life out of his. He wouldn't let her.

Ramming his fists into his pockets, he strode over to her. Astride the little burro, she was almost eye level with him.

She turned to look at him, and there was no mistaking the impatient anger in her eyes.

He stepped closer.

She frowned, leaned back, trying to maintain her precious distance.

He took another step toward her. His heel crunched on a loose stone. She winced. He heard her breath stumble.

Good, he thought with a surge of self-confidence, *let her wonder what I'm going to do.* "Emmaline," he said without preamble, "do you want to take the compass and the map and lead us to Cibola?"

Her frown intensified. Wariness replaced the uncertainty in her eyes. "No."

"Then it's time to set a few ground rules. Rule number one: This is my expedition. I'm in charge. When I say go, we go. When I say stop, we stop. If you don't like that, or can't live with it, turn around. Because I won't be hurried—not by you or anyone.'' He leaned closer, close enough to see the tiny navy blue flecks in her sapphire eyes. ''Understand?''

She licked her lips. ''But—''

''Understand?''

She nibbled on her lower lip. He could almost *see* the wheels turning in her head. She'd give anything to seize control of the expedition right now, to take the compass and map and lead them to Cibola. But she couldn't. He knew it. She knew it. Nothing in her life had prepared her to lead this expedition. It was his and his alone.

After a long, silent moment, she swallowed hard. ''I understand.''

Triumph surged through Larence. He had to turn around quickly to hide his burgeoning grin. He started toward Diablo on feet that felt like they were inches off the ground.

Point one. Larence makes the scoreboard.

God, he felt good. Suddenly he hoped this expedition lasted forever. He was having the time of his life.

Chapter Ten

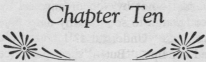

They were in hell.

Emma lifted a damp hand to her even damper brow and let out a long, quivering sigh of pure defeat.

She was being punished for all the years of missed church services. In her religious naïveté, she'd thought only dead people landed in hell, but she'd made a fatal mistake in her thinking: She'd underestimated a deity. And she was paying for it now.

The sun's hot fist slammed through the ineffectual barrier of her two-dollar fashion parasol and hit her face. Perspiration trickled down her cheeks and collected inside her tired stand-up collar. Hot, wet cotton clung to her parched throat. The salty, humid scent of her own sweat clogged her nostrils.

With a bare, shaking hand, she swiped at the stringy blond curls plastered against her brow. The effort was almost too much for her. Panting like a puppy in July, she reached into her breast pocket for the saturated scrap of lace that once had been a hand-woven Irish linen handkerchief. Balling the wrinkled white square in her wet palm, she dabbed at her sweat-slicked forehead.

The linen soaked up a feeble amount of moisture, and left the rest streaking in hot rivulets down her cheeks. With another sigh, she let her limp wrist drop onto her lap. The monogrammed white handkerchief fluttered like a surrender flag against the black wool of her skirt. Emma eyed it with open hostility. The tiny bit of fabric had obviously been designed by men for women who "glowed."

Well, she'd "glowed" until about nine o'clock this morning. From nine to eleven, she'd perspired. And in each of the lifetime-long seconds since lunch, she'd sweated. Buckets. Bathtubs. Troughs. There wasn't an inch of her skin that wasn't soggy-wet and itchy beneath her clothes.

Larence's carefree whistle floated on the infinitesimal stirring of air that constituted a breeze. Emma gritted her teeth—not a difficult thing to do since they were coated with dirt—and tried to ignore him.

Out of the corner of her eye, she caught a glimpse of something green. Hope surged through her blood, giving her the energy to actually lift her chin.

She used her sleeve to wipe the sweat from her eyes. The moist, harsh wool scraped across her sunburnt skin, setting off a thousand pinpricks of pain, but she didn't care.

A *tree*. Could it be the one? She held what little breath she had. Please, God, she prayed, let Larence pick this one.

All she wanted now was to slide off this damn burro, fall face-first on the welcoming ground, and sleep for ten hours. It wasn't so much to ask. . . .

He rode right past it.

Her shoulders sagged, her chin bobbed back down to her chest. She swallowed thickly, wishing, inanely, that a fraction of the moisture crawling along her flesh would puddle in her throat. Only the thought of having to later relieve herself kept her from reaching for her canteen.

She'd already squatted behind one bush today—while Larence had sat on that stupid horse not more than fifteen feet away from her makeshift necessarium, *whistling*—and once was bloody well enough.

God, she felt awful. The inside of her mouth felt like a sunbaked riverbed. She was hot and tired and cranky and—worst of all—she was unable to control Larence.

That she—*she*—Emmaline Amanda Hatter, the great and feared "Mad Hatter" of Wall Street, should have to sit in silence *behind* him was . . . was—

Think about something else.

Yes. She had to learn to make the best of this horrid situation; she had to learn to—she gulped at the thought—follow.

Larence stopped whistling for a second and said something to her. She couldn't make out the words and didn't try. Why should she? All of his comments were the same: garbled, laughter-tinged babble about how beautiful something was, or how grand it was just to be alive.

She scowled at the bright yellow and white stripes on his serape. Any second now he'd probably slide off Diablo's broad back, grab his sacred notebook, and start doodling.

He babbled something that sounded suspiciously like "Look! A desert shrew!"

Before she even had time to roll her eyes, he was off Diablo and limping toward the furry little rodent.

Emma saw her chance and seized it. She slid off Tashee's back and plopped onto the hard, bone-dry dirt. The bunched-up muscles in her thighs screamed in protest. She grabbed hold of Tashee's wiry mane and kept herself upright until the painful tingling in her legs subsided. After a few seconds, she let go of Tashee's mane and stepped away from the little burro.

She was standing. *Standing*. Relief spread through her body, rejuvenated her spirits. *Thank God.* A sudden breeze came up and ruffled the curly tendrils of hair that had escaped the thick coil at her nape. She tottered toward the pack mule.

"What are you doing?"

Emma winced. *Damn.* She'd hoped it would take longer to draw a rat than that. Oh, well. There was nothing to do but answer. "Getting my things. I thought we'd stop here for the night."

Deep, rumbling laughter floated to her ears, raked down her back.

"Turn around, Emma."

Reluctantly she did.

"*You* thought we'd camp here for the night?" A quick, cocky smile punctuated his sentence.

She licked her paper-dry lips and nodded. "I did."

He limped toward her. The pointedly teasing look in his eyes made her stomach clench in angry frustration. She'd seen that look in his eyes before, when he'd offered her the compass: it was his "lesson" look.

The thought of a second lesson from Larence was almost more than she could bear. She backed away from him and found herself pinned against the mule's sweaty flank.

He came close and stopped. She forced herself to return his steady gaze. As they stared at each other, the hint of a breeze evaporated, leaving in its stead an oppressively hot silence. Emma felt each breath like an anvil in the chest. The only sound for miles was the soft threading of their breath in the hot, motionless air.

Her overtaut nerves snapped. "Spit it out."

"Only the leader of an expedition can decide where to camp for the night."

Emma's fingers itched to slap his face. She balled her hands into tight white fists. "Fine." Without another word, she pushed him aside and staggered back to Tashee. Remounting, she stared dead ahead.

Still smiling that same irritating, obnoxious smile, Larence ambled lazily over to Diablo. Within seconds, the melodic warble of his whistle floated across the desolate landscape.

Emma glowered at him, a thousand silent curses jockeying for position in her mind. A dozen dark, angry emotions pulled at her, but the strongest of them was regret.

She should have taken the damn compass when she'd had the chance.

"We'll camp there by the river."

The words wrenched Emma out of her heat-induced stupor. She lifted her head. The world spun crazily. Diablo's hindquarters went in and out of focus.

She blinked to clear her vision, and immediately wished she hadn't. It felt as if sandpaper were scraping against her aching, too-dry eyeballs. She squeezed her eyes shut.

Gripping the reins in slick, white-knuckled hands, she ran her tongue along the cracked, dry surface of her lower lip and recocked her parasol against the lowering sun. Then, hesitantly, she opened her eyes.

They were in a narrow valley, alongside a thin, twisting ribbon of water. The brownish stream chattered with swirling ripples, lapped against the low, sandy bank. Dozens of old cottonwood trees lined the river's edge, their arching branches raised like defiant fists against the hostile sun. Golden-white beams of light streaked through the cathedral-like dome of rustling leaves and mottled the sandy earth.

Surprise rendered Emma momentarily speechless. It was . . . pretty. Not beautiful perhaps, but *pretty*, in a harsh, raw sort of way. For the first time all day she noticed how blue the sky was, how white the clouds. . . .

"Here we are, home sweet home."

She was afraid to believe the words. No doubt the heat was playing tricks on her, and what Larence had actually said was, *We're halfway there. Just another sixteen hours and we'll make camp.*

"We're here?" she breathed.

He twisted around and gave her a bright white smile. "Yep. We're here."

"Yep?" she said to herself. *"Yep?"* Where was he getting his dialogue? Bad dime novels?

He eased out of his saddle and dropped to the sandy ground. A low, masculine groan of pure pleasure accompanied his every movement as he bent and stretched.

Emma clicked her parasol shut and tossed it to the ground, then eased off Tashee's sweaty back. The second her boots hit the soft-packed earth, her legs turned to jelly and she crumpled to her knees in the dirt.

"Yep. The beauty makes you want to get down on your knees and pray."

Emma was too stunned by the stupidity of his remark to reply.

He didn't seem to notice that she was glaring at him. Quite the contrary, in fact. His smile got bigger. And whiter. "Did I ever tell you that I once wanted to be a priest?"

She shook her head in disbelief. He took it as an answer and nodded. "I did. Only problem was, I couldn't settle on one religion. Each one is unique and has so much to offer. Why, the Buddhists . . ."

She stopped listening—all he ever did was give her a headache, anyway. With one quick, indrawn breath, she grabbed hold of Tashee's mane and hauled herself to her feet. After what felt like hours, the strength returned to her legs. Cautiously she let go of Tashee's mane and took one experimental step backward.

Pain shot up her shins. Her teeth came together with a click. An ache twisted her inner thighs and flared in her lower back. She clenched her jaw and took another hesitant step.

A dry twig snapped beneath her heel. The noise startled Tashee, and the little burro jerked her head up and crow-hopped to the right. Her hoof came down hard on Emma's toe.

"Ouch!" Emma jerked away and grabbed her foot, but she was too unsteady to stand. She tottered, flailing for balance for a heartbeat, and then crashed to the ground.

Larence was beside her in an instant. "You okay?"

She sputtered, waving a hand through the dust cloud to keep it from settling in her nose and mouth. "Great. Just great."

A hand punctured the dust. "Here, take hold."

The urge to smack it was strong—but not as strong as the need for help. Swallowing her pride—and apparently half of New Mexico—she clutched his hand and let him drag her to her feet.

"Better?" he said.

She stumbled out of his grasp and hobbled to a big

rock beneath a tree, plopping onto its hot, flat surface with a groan of pure relief.

"What are you doing?" he asked.

She leaned against the tree's scratchy trunk and closed her eyes. "Dying. Show some respect."

Larence laughed—that same soft, joyful sound she'd heard all day. Her teeth ground together, and the urge to smack him came again. She lifted her lids just far enough to glare at him, but it was a wasted act. He wasn't even looking at her. He was standing alongside Diablo, petting the tired old beast's sweaty neck and flipping through those stupid drawings in his notebook. And he was smiling.

She groaned. He was *always* smiling.

The longer she looked at him, the angrier she got. How could he look so . . . so cool and collected and happy? There wasn't a drop of sweat on his face or threaded through his hair. And he was *clean*. How could he be so damn clean? He'd fallen at least fifteen times today, and yet he looked . . . perfect.

Even his teeth made her angry. How could they be so white? Hers, she knew by running her tongue across them, were mottled with dirt and as gray-brown as everything else in this godforsaken desert.

She hooked one sweaty finger inside her collar and pulled the sticky cotton away from her skin. Maybe it was the clothes.

She studied his bizarre attire. Brand-new navy blue jeans hugged his long legs and disappeared into ornately stitched brown cowboy boots. A big yellow and white striped serape spread over his broad shoulders and hung to the top of his thighs, completely covering the pale blue shirt he wore underneath. Around his neck he wore a bright red bandanna. And that hat! Lord help her. He had a high-crowned black Stetson pulled low over his eyes.

Obviously he'd never gotten to play cowboys and Indians as a child.

She realized suddenly that he was watching her watch him. Beneath the brim of his black Stetson, his eyes glowed like those of an exotic cat, green and glittering. She stiffened in shock, preparing for one of his idiotic and yet strangely perceptive comments. Something definitely masculine, like *Seen enough*?

"We should make camp before you sit down."

"In case you haven't noticed, I'm already sitting down."

"I mean, before you sit down for good. Come on, get up and we'll get started."

She sighed heavily, feeling an ache in every joint and muscle and bone of her body. They'd only been traveling since dawn, and yet it felt like months since she'd mounted up this morning. She reclined against the tree and let her eyes slide shut. "Pretend we've made it. You're good at that—just tell me what it looks like."

"Shall we pretend to eat, too?"

Eat. Food. Emma's stomach growled on cue. She hadn't eaten anything since that hideous scrap of seasoned leather he'd given her at noon. She cracked one eye open. "More jerky?"

"Nope. Real food."

That did it. Emma staggered to her feet. "Okay, where is it?"

"Where's what?"

She had a brief but strong urge to slug him. Instead, she pasted a thin-lipped smile on her face. "The food."

"Oh, we can't eat yet," he answered, pulling another book from his saddlebag and flipping through the worn, yellowed pages. She limped toward him on her mashed-up toe, ready to grab the little book and throw it in the river, when the title caught her eye. *The Everyman's Guide To Survival in the American Desertlands.*

She came to a halt. Lord knew she didn't want to get in the way of *survival*.

After a second, Larence thumped his forefinger on one of the pages. "Here it is. How to make camp." His gaze flicked down the page. "The first thing to do is dismount."

She cocked a brow at him. "Another eight-thousand-dollar book?"

He didn't bother to look up. "Next, we need to un-pack the mule, unsaddle the mounts, and water the animals."

"You can do all that later. For now, just unpack the food and fix me something to eat. I'm starving."

He glanced at her sharply. "*I* can do it later?"

"Good. Now that that's settled, why don't you start a fire? A cup of coffee sounds good."

She crossed back to the shady grove of cottonwood and sat on a big, flat rock, carefully fanning her dirt-smudged skirts out around her. Lord, she was hungry. Closing her eyes, she conjured up an image of the last meal she'd had on the train: thin-sliced roast beef, mashed potatoes smothered in rich, creamy gravy, suc-cotash, flaky rolls . . .

She heard the uneven shuffle of his walk, and groaned. God, she didn't want to listen to him, or, worse yet, see some stupid chicken scratch of a draw-ing. All she wanted to do was get something to eat and then crawl into her sleeping bag and sleep for a month.

The crunching stopped. "Emmaline?"

His quiet voice held a hint of suppressed laughter,

and something else, something new: a core of steel that made Emma open her eyes in spite of herself. "What?"

He hunkered down beside her. "Who did you think was going to cook on this trip?"

"You, of course."

His lips twitched. "Do I look like a cook?"

"No, but you don't look like much of an adventurer, either, and here we are."

The twitch became a full-blown grin. "Looks are deceiving, I guess. I *am* an adventurer. What I'm not is a cook."

"Good thing you brought all those books to help you out. That's the one good thing about professors. They learn quickly."

"I didn't bring a cookbook."

A small frown puckered her eyebrows. "How will you make dinner, then?"

"I won't."

Emma felt the first stirring of uneasiness. "When you planned this expedition, you didn't know I was coming. You couldn't have expected *me* to cook."

"Nope. I sure didn't."

Her breath rushed out in a relieved sigh. "Who, then?"

He leaned back on his heels and studied her. Barely contained laughter glittered in his eyes. "The Indians were supposed to cook. But seeing as how they're not here . . ."

The Indians. Emma's mouth dropped open in shock. The Indians she'd fired had been their *cooks*? She shook her head in denial.

"Yep," he said with another dazzling grin. "Henry hired them to help us find the city and to take care of us along the way. Now . . ." He shrugged, and there was a wealth of silent meaning in the action. "Now we're on our own. So do you want to cook or take care of the stock?"

"Don't tease me," she snapped. "I'm good with *stock*. But I wouldn't touch that mangy pack mule with a ten-foot pole."

"So you'll cook."

Emma shuddered. The thought of her cooking was enough to bring on another headache. She was too hungry to eat her own cooking. But *someone* had to feed them.

"Emmaline?"

"You win. I'll cook."

He touched her shoulder. "It's not a win-or-lose proposition, Emmaline. Life isn't—"

She wrenched away from him. "Don't you tell me what life's about, *Doctor*. While you've been hiding from it in your ivory tower, I've been living it. And believe me, it's always about winning and losing—and about winning a lot more than you lose. Now, where's the damn stove?"

Emma winced as the box came flying her way. It landed with a thud and a rattle at her feet. She eyed the wooden rectangle disbelievingly. It *couldn't* be the stove, she told herself. She had hat boxes that were bigger.

The longer she looked at the box, the sicker she felt. She pressed a trembling hand to her roiling midriff. Anxiety unfurled like a river of ice inside her.

If only she could be angry—maybe even furious. Anger was an emotion that had always suited her well, had always spurred her to accept greater and greater challenges. It had gotten her out of the slums and kept her out.

But what good did it do to be mad at yourself? As much as she'd like to yell and scream and beat her fists into the dirt, it would be a waste of time and energy. This predicament was her fault and hers alone. She'd fired the Indians, and now she had to learn to do their jobs.

She glanced at her sunburnt, scratched hands and groaned aloud. Larence expected these hands to cook dinner—these hands, which only knew how to make money, were supposed to *cook*.

"Emmaline, are you going to start dinner?"

She jumped at the unexpected sound of his voice. "Uh . . . yes . . ."

"Good. My stomach's rumblin' something fierce."

She rolled her eyes. More cowboy talk. Scooting forward on the flat rock, she flicked the box open. The first thing she saw was the silver-hued dome of a coffee pot lying on its side.

Coffee. Hunger surged through her, made her mouth water in anticipation. As she reached for the pot, she heard the quiet grinding of Larence's boot heels on the hard-packed dirt. He stopped beside the stove and dropped a load of flat, brown chunks at her feet.

She looked up suddenly, surprised. "What—"

"Cow chips," he said, squatting down beside her to start a fire. "Henry packed enough to get us to the forested part of the trip, and I found a few over by the river."

Emma eyed the compact circles with disgust, but didn't ask the obvious question. If they were cooking their food over cow . . . dung, she didn't want to know.

Food. Cook. Her panic lurched up a wrung. What

could she make for dinner? As if to punctuate her silent question, her stomach rumbled loudly.

"Guess you're as hungry as I am," Larence said as he dropped a burning match onto the pile of cow chips and grama grass. Flames zipped along the fuel's hard surface.

Emma's nerves flared as brightly as the flame.

Calm down. You're an intelligent woman. You can do this. She simply needed to set her razor-sharp mind to the problem.

She frowned in thought. First things first: What foods were prepared over an open fire?

Oysters on the half shell.

She brightened. *Yes.* Jean-Claude, the chef at Delmonico's, had once told her that oysters tasted best when cooked right over an open flame.

Her spirits deflated a second later. *Right, Em. Henry packed fresh oysters for a trail ride across the desert.*

She shot a quick look at the small pile of boxes and bags and tins that were their foodstuffs. There probably wasn't a single thing in those supplies she liked to eat. No bluefish in cream sauce, no cold boiled tongue, no thinly sliced lemon-flavored veal loaf, no fresh strawberries or—

Stop it.

She had to concentrate, to think of something she could make that would be edible. She tried to remember the things her mother had cooked in the old days. The good days. But the memories were either gone or locked away too tightly to grasp. All she could remember were the dark days after her mother had died and her father had committed suicide. In those days she'd been forced to feed herself, but even then, she hadn't cooked. There'd been nothing *to* cook. An old crust of bread, a bruised apple, a discarded tin of sardines . . .

Warm, comforting fingers curled around her shoulders and squeezed. "How about canned beans?" came Larence's steady, even voice from somewhere above her. "I think you just heat them up."

A river of relief gushed through Emma. For once, she was thankful for his perceptiveness. "If that's what you want . . ." She winced at the tremulousness in her voice.

"Sounds good. You go ahead and get started while I take care of the stock."

"Okay." Emma scooted closer to the box and started unpacking it. In a few moments she was sitting amid six sets of silverware, six white enamel cups and plates, a coffeepot, four lengths of pipe, a baking pan, a frying pan, a washbowl, and three camp kettles. Finally she pulled out the heavy Russia sheet-iron stove and carefully placed the iron grate over the cheerful fire.

Within moments the beans were in the pot and sending a plume of mouth-watering steam into the evening air. She shot a quick glance at Larence, to see if he'd noticed how efficiently she'd unpacked the utensils and set up the stove. He hadn't, and for some odd reason, she was disappointed.

He was standing by Diablo, trying to figure out how to halter the beast—and without much success. Just as he was about to toss the contraption away, Diablo shoved his nose through the opening.

"Hey, Emmaline! Did you see that?"

Emma found herself smiling. "It's just a suggestion, Larence, but I wouldn't call attention to the fact that you're dumber than a horse."

His answer was a good-natured laugh.

Emma almost laughed with him. She felt surprisingly good. She was doing something important. It wasn't much, perhaps. Not something difficult, like trading stocks or financing companies, but it was something she'd thought she couldn't do.

She glanced over at Larence, who was now fiddling with something that looked like a leather figure eight. "How long until you want to eat?"

"I don't know. I've got to figure out how to hobble Diablo."

"Just put it on the ground. Diablo the wonder horse'll probably step into the thing and snap it with his teeth."

Larence's bright, clear laughter floated into the air. "A joke, Emmaline? How bold."

She bit back a chuckle just in time. "Heavens, no. Merely an observation."

Chapter Eleven

A surprising sense of satisfaction filled Emma as she repacked the pots and pans in the stove's wooden box. The beans hadn't been good—sort of lukewarm and chewy on the surface, and crispy and burnt-tasting from the bottom of the pan—but even so, she felt pleased that she'd actually cooked.

True, warming canned beans didn't take a philosopher's intellect. But at least she'd done *something* on this trip that mattered.

Thunk. Behind her, something heavy hit the ground. Laughter followed the sound.

Clicking the locker shut, she pressed slowly to her feet and glanced across the campsite. Her good humor vanished. About six feet away from the fire, Larence was struggling to erect their tent.

No, she amended, struggling was too kind a description. It looked more like active warfare—and the tent was winning. Emma snatched up her skirt and headed his way. "What are you doing?"

Larence and the tent collapsed in a heap. He grinned up at her. Bright white teeth flashed through the shadow-cloaked planes of his face. "I have no idea. But I know what I'm *not* doing, and that's putting up a tent."

143

Emma thrust her hand at him, palm up. "Instructions."

He handed her a scrap of paper. She grabbed it out of his hand and squatted down by the fire to read.

The Montgomery & Ward Company's Protean tent is undeniably the best all around tent for camping purposes. Frowning, she skimmed down the page. *Compact, roomy, easy to put up . . . only one pole required . . . fits easily in mule-pack panier . . .*

She looked up. "These aren't instructions."

"Exactly."

A headache banged to life behind Emma's eyes. She pressed two fingers to her temples and sighed. It struck her suddenly how achingly, bone-searingly tired she was.

"I always wanted to sleep under the stars."

"What?" Her head snapped up. "Oh, no, you don't. Pick up that pole and try again."

"Nope, I'm too tired to concentrate. Tomorrow night I'll start putting it up earlier. We'll be okay for tonight; the snakes won't—"

"Snakes?" She flung her pointed finger toward the heap of white canvas. *"Get the damn tent up!"*

"Nope. If you want it up so badly, you do it. I'm happy to sleep outside." He started to brush past her on his way to the fire. "It's just another bit of adventure."

"Adventure?" She grabbed his cotton sleeve and spun him around to face her. "It's an engraved invitation to bugs and snakes."

He frowned at that for a moment, then shrugged, as if the matter were of no import. "Too bad we don't have a hair rope."

She eyed him suspiciously. "What's that?"

"Snakes won't cross a strand of hair."

She gave a disbelieving snort. "Oh, that sounds reasonable."

He nodded. "It's true—I read it in *Diamond Dick's Deadly Deeds*."

Balling her fists in frustration, she stomped to the sleeping bags Larence had laid side by side next to the fire, and started removing the hairpins from the sagging Roman knot at the base of her neck. She cast a longing glance at the pile of canvas.

If only she could erect it herself. Unfortunately, building things was substantially below cooking on her list of skills.

"You'll like sleeping outside, Emmaline. Honestly It'll be fun—just like the time Diamond Dick—"

"Shut up."

She had yanked a half dozen pins from her hair before she realized Larence was staring at her. Turning, she glared at him.

Larence immediately dropped to his sleeping bag and pulled off his boots. Beneath her watchful eyes, he burrowed into the bag, twisted onto his side, and stared at the little gray rocks that rimmed the fire.

Emma quickly unbuttoned her wool jacket and laid it on the rock at her feet. One by one the despised garments were stripped away. When the corset plopped into the dirt, she took her first comfortable breath of the day. It felt absolutely heavenly to be clad in nothing but drawers and chemise.

She closed her eyes, reveling in the feeling of freedom. The night breeze slid across her bare arms. Goose bumps tiptoed across her flesh.

She felt his gaze on her body like a tangible presence. Almost a touch. Slowly she turned her head. He was propped up on his elbows, his long legs buried in the sleeping bag. He looked . . . hypnotized by the sight of her in her underclothes.

Their eyes met, held. The warmth in his look sent a shiver skittering along her exposed skin. The cotton of her underclothes seemed somehow thinner, the night colder. "Turn around."

When he did, she gritted her teeth and yanked a strand of hair out of her head. "Ouch." The word slipped out involuntarily. She cast a quick glance down at Larence to see if he'd heard.

He had. The amused look on his face made her feel like an idiot. "Turn around," she ordered again.

"Why are you pulling your hair out?"

"If you must know, I'm making a hair rope."

He had the nerve to laugh.

She yanked again. "Laugh all you want, Larence. But if a rattlesnake bites you, you'd better hope Diamond Dick is rounding up dogies in the area. Because I'm not sucking one drop of poison out of you."

"I'd do it for—"

"Turn around!"

Ignoring Larence's quiet chuckle as he settled into his sleeping bag, she carefully laid her strands of hair in a big circle around both bags. When she was finished, a weary sigh escaped her lips.

Lord, she was tired. Her whole body ached.

She sank to her knees on the bag's harsh, waterproofed duck exterior, and with a herculean effort, crawled inside its sheepskin-lined warmth.

As she stretched out, every bone in her body seemed to dissolve. Her eyelids became as heavy as boulders and slid shut. Oh, God, sleep . . .

"Hey, Em," came Larence's quiet voice from beside her, "look at the stars."

"No way. Night, Larence."

She heard the unmistakable rustling of his sleeping bag as he sat up. "But it's our first night out; I thought—"

"Don't think. Sleep."

"But the legend of Cibola is so perfectly suited to—"

"Good *night*, Larence."

He thumped back to the ground, his breath expelling in a disappointed sigh. "Night, Emmaline."

Emma sighed with relief. *Thank you, God.* The last thing she wanted to hear was pointless babble about the city. It was either there or it wasn't—who cared about some boring old legend?

Within seconds, she was sound asleep, and dreaming of gold.

Larence burrowed into the woolly warmth of his sleeping bag and stared up at the wondrous display of stars. It was so immense, this desert sky. He felt as if he'd fallen upward, and instead of staring into the exquisite sky, he was now a part of it.

He wished he had someone with whom to share this moment. If only Emmaline were the kind of woman who would lie beside him in the darkening margin of the day and gaze up at the stars and feel what he felt. The aching, almost religious sense of awe. There was nothing he would love more than to be able to reach out right now, and take her hand.

Another dream, he realized with a self-deprecating smile. Emmaline wasn't that kind of woman.

He told himself it didn't matter. He'd spent a lifetime dreaming alone. He was used to it.

Wind crept into the campsite, brushing across his exposed cheeks in soft, cool waves. In its wake, the fire snapped and crackled, the leaves overhead rustled one against the other. And threaded through it all like a heartbeat was the lap, lap, lap of the river against its sandy bank.

The sound was hypnotizing. Larence felt its rhythm pulling on his senses, lulling him into a state of pure relaxation. Still smiling, already dreaming, he fell asleep.

He came awake with a start. Nothingness curled around him, coal black and suffocatingly thick. Tension vibrated in the night air. He lay stiff as a nail in the warmth of his sleeping bag, listening.

There was no wind. Above his head, the leaves were motionless and silent. Even the steady licking of the river against its bank was muffled, almost undetectable.

He felt surrounded, watched. Fear pressed like an iron fist against his chest. His heart sped up, thudded loudly in his ears. He glanced wildly around, searching for some pinprick of light—anything—to banish the darkness. But there was nothing. The fire had long since died away. A dense, charcoal-colored cloud had obliterated the pearl-bright moon and killed the starlight.

It was so dark. So terrifyingly—

Stop it. He tried to banish his rising fear beneath an avalanche of calm, rational thoughts. He seized on the soft, regular cadence of Emmaline's breathing. The sound was like a lifeline in the darkness, and he clung to it with the strength of a drowning man.

If only he could touch her. As a child, when the nightmares had come, he'd always believed that if he could touch someone, could feel the warmth of human contact, the terrors would scurry back into the lightless holes from which they'd sprung. All he needed to fight them was the security that came from not being alone.

But he'd never had that touch, never been able to test his theory. Until now.

He sent his hand scouting across the sleeping bags for the woman who lay so quietly beside him. "Emmaline?"

His voice floated in the darkness, a disembodied echo of sound that went unanswered. Memories clawed their way to the surface of his mind. They were old memories; old but not forgotten.

Would they ever be? he wondered with a building sense of panic.

Images battered at the closed door of his mind, slipping through the cracks and keyholes, drawing strength from his fear. He weakened, and in that split second a memory flashed through his thoughts with blinding force.

A small, brown-haired boy lay curled on his hard, solitary bed. His small fingers were fisted tightly enough to leave half-moon-shaped indentations in his sweaty palms. He was trying desperately not to cry—not for the parents he'd lost, not for the gnawing pain in his leg, not for the aching void in his soul where laughter used to live.

Granny, it's so dark. . . . But she hadn't listened to the words or the whimpers that slipped beneath the crack of his locked door.

Granny . . .

Quit sniveling, Larry, and go to sleep.

It was then, in those endless, pain-ridden nights, that he'd begun to dream of a great adventure. He'd created the dream and clung to it with shaking fingers until its seductive promise had eased the ache in his soul. Then and only then, with the dream insulating him from the reality, had he learned to sleep alone.

But he'd never really gotten over his fear of the dark. It was always there, ready to rip him from a peaceful slumber or keep him from closing his eyes. Always there, always waiting.

You've done it. You're in New Mexico. Nothing can hurt you. . . . Slowly he felt himself calming down. One by one his fingers unfurled, his breathing slowed.

The cloud in front of the moon let loose its anchor and moved on. Pale blue moonlight spilled across the flat desert landscape, backlit the jet black stand of cottonwoods.

He let out his breath in a long, tired sigh. The battle had been waged and won again. This time.

His eyes slid shut, and he concentrated on the steady in-and-out of his breathing until the fear receded. He hadn't been able to touch Emmaline this time, but perhaps next time he would be luckier. Perhaps next time he would take her hand in his and find the courage to keep the darkness at bay.

The thought brought a sense of peace, and within moments, he was asleep again, dreaming of the countless Indian children who would one day learn of their ancestors' greatness.

Not far away, a campfire burned low. Shadows and light leapt like spirits from the flames, twisting and dancing across the somber faces of the three Indian men who huddled around its warmth.

The eldest, a stoop-shouldered, gray-haired old man with a hawklike nose and narrowed eyes, jabbed a pointy stick into the fire. Sparks spiraled up into the pitch-dark sky and floated away. "Falls with a Laugh will not find what he seeks."

Ka-Neek lurched to his feet. "You cannot be sure of that," he said in the clicking language of the Zuñi. His moccasined feet wore an angry groove on the loose-packed soil as he paced back and forth in front of the fire.

"Sit," commanded the eldest in a time-graveled voice. "You make us dizzy."

Ka-Neek stopped pacing instantly. Striding back to the group, he bent on one knee before the old man, his father's father. "It is our job to protect. If there is even a chance . . ." He let his words hang, thick with warning, in the dark, spark-gilded air.

The old man didn't answer. His stick fell to the ground. He watched it land in a puff of dust, then picked up his pipe. Drawing deeply on the ancient buffalo-bone pipe that had been his father's, and his father's before that, he stared into the fire. After a moment, his drawn, age-creased lips parted almost imperceptibly. Smoke climbed up the shadowy planes of his face and drifted toward the fire. The gray haze formed myriad magical, mystical shapes as it rose into the night sky.

He watched the images for a moment, a small, sad smile lurking in the wrinkled corners of his mouth, and then, slowly, he turned to look at the two men sitting with him. Their dark eyes were on him; he felt the silent burden of their stares. Effortlessly he read the sum of each man's thoughts.

Long, silent seconds passed before he spoke. "Falls with a Laugh and Pinched Face are like the other crazy white men who have come before and who will come again. They will fail. What seeks to stay hidden will not be found."

Ka-Neek leaned toward the old man. "But—"

He held up a gnarled hand for silence. "My mind is strong. We will not stop them yet. We will wait. And we will watch."

Ka-Neek grimaced, but said nothing. He knew better than to argue with his leader. Any words of disagreement would be wasted, and they would be disrespectful.

They would wait.

But when the order came to stop the intruders—and the order *would* come—he'd be ready.

A mourning dove cooed. The sound vibrated through the still, cold predawn air.

Sunlight caressed Larence's closed eyelids, urging him gently to waken. He yawned lazily, taking a deep, satisfying breath of the cleanest, purest air he'd ever known.

He blinked away the last sandy vestiges of sleep and opened his eyes. An immediate stab of disappointment made him frown. He'd missed the sunrise. Mentally vowing not to make the same mistake again, he lifted his arms for a nice early morning stretch.

Every muscle in his body shrieked in protest at the movement. He grinned and kept stretching, reveling in the burning ache that accompanied his every move.

For once in his life, he'd *earned* his pain. He didn't hurt because of a carriage accident that had happened too long ago to remember; he hurt because he'd pushed his body too far.

God, it felt good.

Levering himself onto his elbows, he took another deep breath and looked around. In the crisp morning air, the desert glittered around him; everything seemed sharper, clearer, closer. Hoarfrost turned the bosque's new spring grass into a bed of diamond-bright silver-gray spikes. A soft gurgle of sound drew his gaze to the river, and he watched, mesmerized, as a fallen leaf spiraled through the current and disappeared from view.

His gaze climbed, and what he saw made his breath catch in his throat. Above and all around him was the biggest, brightest sky he'd ever seen. Cloudless, vibrant, it didn't start at the mountaintops, nor even at the treetops. This endless New Mexico sky began at his feet and washed across the world in an infinite sea of pale blue.

Awe filled him. Nothing stood between him and his God except the rising sun.

The realization brought with it the most profound sense of peace Larence had ever known. Here, on the trail to Cibola, he'd found the church he'd sought all his life.

He crawled out of his sleeping bag. With every movement, the sheen of white hoarfrost that layered his bag crinkled and crackled.

Shivering, he rubbed his hands together. Breath shot from his mouth in a steady stream of white as he grabbed his boots. He was just about to put them on when he remembered Diamond Dick finding a rattler in his boot on the trail to Taos. Gingerly Larence tilted both boots and checked. Nope, no snakes. Grinning at his own ingenuity, he shoved his stockinged feet into his cowboy boots and crawled toward the ashes of yesterday's campfire. Kneeling, he started the fire.

Moments later, the hardy snap and crackle of the cook-fire echoed through the otherwise silent air, and the dusky scent of smoke wafted across his nostrils.

Emma fought consciousness with every breath. She

tried valiantly to ignore the crackle of the fire and the soft melody of Larence's whistling. All she wanted to do was burrow deeper into her woolly bag and sleep for another twenty-four hours.

"What time is it?" she mumbled.

A watch clicked open. Larence stopped whistling long enough to say, "Five forty-five."

She groaned. "Wake me at eight."

"Yesterday it was seventy-five degrees by eight."

And ninety degrees by ten. She groaned again. God help her. She was living a nightmare.

Something clanged. After a few moments, she heard a pop, hiss, pop. And then she smelled it: the aroma of cooking bacon. Her stomach rumbled loudly as she unsnapped a section of her sleeping bag and sat up. At the movement, a cry of pain shot past her lips.

At the sound, Larence looked up suddenly and smiled at her. "Morning. Sleep well?"

She squeezed her eyes shut. It was too early in the morning to look at Larence. His kid-in-a-candy-store good humor irritated during the day; at this hour of the morning, it was enough to make her contemplate cold-blooded murder.

No jury in the world would convict her. . . .

"I did," he said, and immediately the whistling started up again. "My Darling Clementine."

"If you have to make that racket," she grumbled, "whistle something appropriate."

"Like what?"

"How about the death march?"

His rich, rumbling laugh floated her way.

Emma scowled. Suppressing another groan of pain, she rolled gingerly onto her left side and eased to a sit.

"How does a cup of coffee sound?" he asked.

She licked her lips in anticipation. "Wonderful."

"Good. I thought so, too."

The coffeepot hit the ground beside her with a *thwack* and a clang. Her eyes popped open.

He answered her unasked question. "I'm making bacon. Fair is fair."

God, she hated it when he was right. She watched him through narrowed, resentful eyes as he pushed to his feet and headed toward the animals. He was limping along just as he always did. And he was whistling. *Whistling.*

Why wasn't he in pain? The man should be crawling, for God's sake, not ambling along as if he didn't have a care in the world.

She frowned. He had to hurt as badly as she did. He *had* to.

He hunkered down and started unbuckling the hobbles on Diablo's forefeet. "The coffee's there by the stove," he said without looking at her.

Coffee. The word made her mouth water.

It was time to get up. Grimacing, she curled into the fetal position and rolled onto all fours. Pain radiated through muscles she hadn't even known she had. Her breath came in short, hacking gasps.

After a few agonizing seconds, the fiery pain in her legs melted into a dull, thudding ache. She waited a few minutes—just to be sure it had abated—then dressed.

Coffeepot in hand, she staggered to her feet. At her first step, a white-hot shaft of pain shot from her heels to her groin. Her teeth clamped together and bit off a strangled cry.

"Hurts like a son of a gun, doesn't it?"

She grimaced. Leave it to Larence to come right out and admit his pain.

Ignore him. Gritting her teeth, she inched to the river and filled the coffeepot, then turned around and tottered unsteadily back to the fire. Inch by painful inch.

Larence took the pot from her and set it on the stove's grilled surface. With a sigh of relief, she collapsed on her sleeping bag. Moisture droplets from the melted hoarfrost seeped through the thick wool of her skirt and brought goose bumps to her flesh.

She drew her legs up and hugged herself, dropping her chin onto her knees. In some distant part of her mind, it dawned on her that she looked awful. Her hair, unbound and unbraided, hung down her back in undulating, leaf-and-twig-infested waves. Dust darkened her bare feet and discolored the hem of her skirt. No doubt there were circles the size of bowling balls under her eyes.

Not that she cared, of course. Who was there to impress out here in the middle of nowhere? Certainly not Larence. All she cared about was getting a drink of coffee, eating a few strips of bacon, and sitting absolutely, positively still.

Larence handed her a blue can and calmly walked away.

She took it in her scratched, sunburnt hands. The label read *Maxwell House Coffee*. She turned it round and round, searching for directions, but there wasn't so much as a tip for the unschooled chef. Apparently if you didn't know how to make coffee on your own, you shouldn't be drinking it.

Oh, why hadn't she ever watched Mrs. Sanducci in the kitchen? Emma cast a surreptitious glance at Larence, who was busy rolling up their sleeping bags. He was still whistling, and he looked suspiciously happy—like he might break into song at any moment.

No way would she ask him for help. If Dr. Dimwit had been able to make coffee last night, then she could make it this morning.

She grabbed a handful of the coarse mixture and tossed it in the boiling water. Cloudy white bubbles foamed to the surface. She eyed it questioningly, then added another handful for good measure.

She liked her coffee strong.

A half an hour later, Emma felt almost human. She'd brushed most of the tangles and leaves from her hair, rewound the mass into a nice, professional-looking Roman knot at the base of her neck, and washed her face and brushed her teeth.

Behind her, the coffeepot's lid clanged and clattered. Puffs of steam spiraled up from the bouncing lid and melted into the warming air.

"Bacon's ready." Larence slapped crisp strips of bacon on two tin plates and smiled at her.

She crawled over to the fire and reached eagerly for the coffeepot.

Larence's hand snaked out with lightning speed and grabbed her wrist in an iron grip.

"Ouch! Damn it, Lare—"

He let go. "The pot's hot. Here, use this rag to pick it up."

Color climbed up her cheeks in hot waves. *Saved by Larence. A new low.* "I knew that."

He grinned. "Of course you did."

She wrenched the blue and white checked dishrag out of his hands and wrapped it around the pot's metal handle. Careful not to spill a precious drop, she poured two cups of the steaming, pit-dark brew and gave one to Larence.

"Thanks," he said, handing her a plate with four strips of crisp, done-to-a-turn bacon.

Emma closed her eyes and breathed deeply of the rich, mouth-watering aroma of the bacon. Beside her, she heard Larence reach for his cup and take a sip of coffee.

He set it down fast. She opened her eyes and looked at him questioningly. "Everything okay?"

"Sure."

"Good." She reached for a piece of bacon.

"You want a spoon?"

Her hand halted midway. "No, thanks. I don't eat bacon with a spoon."

"How about soup? You eat that with a spoon?"

"Of course. But what in the world does that—"

He shot a meaningful glance at the coffee. "Take the spoon."

Chapter Twelve

The next morning it was ninety degrees by eleven o'clock, and the dust churned up by Diablo's huge hooves was even worse than usual. *The dust Larence never saw . . .*

Emma sat as stiff as a knife blade on Tashee's back. The once gay and now grayed parasol lay limply against her shoulder, its dirty blue and white dome a dismal barrier to the blinding sun.

The burro picked a careful path in the rock-strewn, steadily rising plain. Swallowing thickly, Emma tried to dislodge the layer of dust and grime that clung to her tongue and teeth.

A cloud moved across the sun, giving Emma a brief moment of respite. She took a greedy drink from her canteen. The hot, metallic-tasting water seared her lips and burned a trail to the empty pit of her stomach. Wincing, she backhanded the moisture from her cracked lips and retied the canteen in place.

Idly she stared at the scratches and scrapes on her hands. A small frown tugged at her mouth. Her hands hurt. Everything hurt. She felt like a dog that had been kicked six ways to Sunday and left to die on the side of the road.

Except the dog was luckier—he got to lie down. She

swallowed thickly, disgusted by her own train of thoughts. Things were bad when being left for dead on the side of the road actually looked *good*.

She was falling apart. And not just physically—a few cuts and bruises, she could handle. What scared her, terrified her, in fact, was what this expedition was doing to her mind. Never in her life had she experienced this kind of eyeball-searing, lung-sapping heat, and it was beating her down, weakening her.

"Look, Emmaline—a pancake prickly pear in full bloom."

She squeezed her eyes shut and ignored his steady stream of gibberish. Through a distant, detached part of her mind, she heard the quiet *thud* of his boots hitting the dirt.

"Over there—look!" he cried a moment later.

The perfect campsite . . .

"It's a kangaroo rat."

Emma tightened her hold on the reins and battled the tide of disappointment rising within her. Her eyes opened slowly, reluctantly, and veered away from Larence, who was squatted down by some dirt-weed, drawing. She tried to think of something—anything—that would take her mind off her partner's irritating cheerfulness and her own aches and pains.

"Gold," she whispered aloud, letting the word work through her like a balm.

Gold.

Every horrible, too-hot second of this trip was taking her closer to the gold. *That's* what she had to hold on to and take strength from. She had to remember that Larence was nothing, her own discomfort even less. Gold was the important thing. And for enough of it, she could endure any hardship New Mexico could fling at her. Even two weeks with Larence.

Soon they'd be at the city and she could shower herself in gold doubloons, curl her fingers around the cool, metallic—

A rousing, whistling rendition of ''Jeannie with the Light Brown Hair'' sent the kangaroo rat bounding toward the nearest rock.

Gold. She'd get her gold and get the hell out of this godforsaken heat. Away from Larence.

After a few interminable moments, Larence closed up the notebook and remounted.

They were off again, moving at their snail's pace across the desert. Gradually the heat wore Emma down, liquified her bones. She closed her eyes, giving in to the gentle sway of Tashee's step. Sleep beckoned her, promising the cool of darkness. The slow, painful panting of her breath melted into an even rhythm.

Her chin bobbed onto the wrinkled cotton of her collar and she fell asleep.

She came awake slowly. Blinking groggily, she glanced around. A red-cliff-bordered valley stared back at her. Silent, lonely, somehow watchful. The hairs on the back of her neck prickled. She had the unmistakable sense that they were being followed. Watched . . .

Something whirred in the air above her head. She looked up sharply.

A hawk banked left and swirled in a huge, effortless circle against the dark, cloud-thickened sky. Its keening screech split the silent air and echoed off the black-coned line of volcanoes in the distance. The bird did a last, spiraling dive toward them.

Instinctively Emma ducked and closed her eyes. The impact never came. A shadow crossed her face, and she looked up. Beady black eyes blinked at her; whooshing air from the hawk's mighty wings brushed her face.

The bird cut through the air and sped away. Emma watched him become a little brown dot against the cloud-layered sky.

She shook her head, forcing a smile she didn't feel. She'd obviously been in the sun too long. Hawks didn't kill people, and no one was out here. She was a fool to think they were being watched or followed.

They couldn't be more alone. Since morning, they'd been steadily climbing; not a steep, breath-stealing rise, but rather a slow, even escalation. The windswept plain of Albuquerque had gradually given way to a rocky, cliff-rimmed plateau dotted with dormant volcanoes and low-lying mesas.

Overhead, clouds sped across the sky, creating a shifting kaleidoscope of shadowy patterns on the harsh, stone-covered ground.

The shadow play fascinated her. In the three days since they'd left Albuquerque, Emma hadn't seen more than four clouds in any given afternoon. But today the sky was darkening, boiling with countless gray-white clouds that gave welcome respite from the too-hot sun.

Diablo sped up unexpectedly. Emma grabbed hold of her saddle's makeshift horn just in time. Tashee followed her leader into a bone-jarring trot.

A sound, far away and strained, threaded the wind's sigh. Like the soft whimper of a woman giving birth, the sound began slowly, throatily, and gradually deepened into a mournful dirge. Wind danced low across the plain in a dozen swirling eddies, then gave a loud, wolflike howl and trebled its speed. Dust flew upward, darkened the air.

She clung to the wooden X above Tashee's withers, bouncing like a sack of potatoes on the burro's bony back. Her parasol thumped hard against her shoulder.

Diablo came to a sudden stop. Tashee rammed into the horse's tail and immediately backed up.

Emma reached blindly for the wooden X, but it was too late. She fell like a ton of bricks.

Larence swiveled around to look at her. His gaze landed on the empty pack saddle and slid to the ground. "What are you doing down there?"

She glared at him, thankful—for once—for the mouthful of dust that made speech impossible.

"Something's up," he shouted. "We're going to make a run for that indentation in the cliff over there."

The word hit Emma like a blow. *Run.* They were going to run? As in gallop? She shook her head in denial.

"Get on Tashee."

She shook her head again. A creosote bush tumbled past her, its fingers splayed out like earthen tentacles.

"Don't make me come and get you, Emmaline."

She staggered to her feet and remounted. She had time for one quick, dust-infested breath before Larence yelled, "Whoopee!" and kicked Diablo into a trot.

They were five minutes too late. A fast-moving gust hit them like a steam-driven locomotive. Larence crammed his hat to his head and bent into the onslaught.

Emma curled her body into the wind and tucked her chin against her chest. For once, she was glad to be behind Larence. Hair snapped across her face, stung her eyes. Gritty wind whipped her face and wrenched the parasol out of her tired grip.

Instinctively she reached for it. Fists of wind-driven dust rammed like hot pokers into her eyes. A flood of warm, wet tears streaked across her temples and disappeared in the hair flapping against her face. The umbrella bounced end over end and lodged in a flattened cactus.

Thousands of glass-sharp particles stung her cheeks and forehead, stabbed her exposed throat. Dust clogged her eyes and nose. Blinded, she squinted into the darkened, fast-moving air, trying to see Larence. He was a huge, shadowy blur in front of her.

She hunched forward, bowed her head, and clung to the wooden X on the front of her saddle. Her fingers curled, shaking and white, around the piece of wood.

Over and over again her mind taunted her with images of what it would mean to fall off right now. Larence wouldn't know, wouldn't stop. She'd lie in some forgotten heap on the hard desert floor, tired, thirsty, in pain. And that wasn't the worst of it: This wind would reduce her to a pile of sun-bleached bones before Larence could find her. If, in fact, he ever could.

She forced her mind away from the gruesome images. Curling into as small a ball as she could on Tashee's back, she stared at the dirty, bloodless ridge of her knuckles until everything seeped out of her mind except for a comforting blankness. Time lost all meaning. Nothing mattered except hanging on.

She wasn't even aware that they'd stopped when Larence's arm curled around her waist and squeezed gently. At the warm, reassuring contact, a shudder sped through her limbs. She lifted her heavy head and stared up at him through dull, dispirited eyes.

Wind howled around them, pulled at their hair and clothes and whipped across their faces.

"It's okay," he said, easing her off Tashee's back.

She let herself slide into his comforting embrace and didn't protest when he picked her up. She wrapped her arms around his neck and buried her face in the dust-caked flannel of his shoulder.

He bent into the storm. Tightening his hold on her, he clamped his hat hard against her back and limped past a huge hump of sandstone that jutted out from the mesa's dun-colored wall. In the narrow, U-shaped indentation behind the sandstone barrier, he set her down gently. Then he threw his hat into a protected corner of the sanctuary, flung his arm across his eyes, and went back for the animals.

Emma almost grabbed him. *Don't go*, she wanted to say. *Stay with me.*

But of course, she said nothing. Just watched him limp past her and disappear.

Shaking, she leaned back against the rough sandstone wall and pulled her knees into her chest. The trembling in her arms and legs intensified, clattered through her aching bones. Tears scalded her eyes. She slammed them shut and buried her face in her hands.

"You okay?"

She eased her hands from her face. Larence was sitting beside her. White teeth flashed in a dirt-dark face as he reached out and touched her. His hand, warm and solid, pressed against the hollow between her shoulder blades and began moving in a slow, comforting circle. "Some windstorm, huh?"

At his touch, she remembered how good it had felt to be in his arms.

Humiliation writhed in her stomach. God, she'd let

him *carry* her as if she were a helpless child. Self-disgust swelled, made her feel sick.

And yet, even now the compassion and the caring in his eyes made her want to forget about silent strength and curl up beside him. . . .

Damn him, she thought. Damn the heat and the dust and the wind and the pain. But most of all, damn him. What was it about him that turned her into a weak-willed, simpering schoolgirl? Her emotional armor hadn't cracked more than three times in the fifteen years she'd worn it; and now, around Dr. Dimwit, it seemed to splinter at every turn.

She wrenched away from him and staggered to her feet.

"Emmaline?"

Don't look at him. She stumbled to the sandstone lip that protected them from the driving wind. Hugging herself tightly, she stared at the storm's fury. Wind screamed past their hidden sanctuary. A howl like that of the hounds of hell echoed through the valley and bounced off the mesa's walls.

God, what a miserable place. Excruciating heat, never-ending dust, sweat, snakes, bugs, and now this—wind that moved faster than a train and ripped up everything in its path.

But the real danger, she knew, wasn't the weather. It was Larence, always Larence, just waiting for her to break so he could pick up the pieces and put them back together.

If only she could be sure it wouldn't happen, then she could relax. Maybe even let down her guard enough to talk to him. But she couldn't. In this godforsaken hell of a land, she couldn't be sure of anything. Especially her own strength.

At least she'd made it through today, she thought dully, staring at a creosote bush as it hurtled past the opening. And what could possibly be worse than a windstorm?

That was when the first raindrop hit.

Chapter Thirteen

Emma huddled against the cold rock. Her cheek was pressed to the damp, gritty sandstone. Rain hammered her head, thumped a hollow beat on the supplies piled alongside the animals. The hard-packed dirt floor had turned into a shallow pool of paste-thick mud. The odor of wet animal hair, horse droppings, and moist earth hung thick and heavy in the stone-rimmed enclosure.

A particularly large droplet landed in Emma's left eye. She winced and swiped at it with her saturated sleeve. She should have taken Larence's hat when he'd offered it. *Stupid pride.*

She moved slightly, eased her cheek away from the wet sandstone. A sharp *thunk* of released suction accompanied the movement. Lifting her face just a fraction, she saw Larence, who sat about five feet away from her against the other wall.

He was a blur of yellow and white stripes. She blinked to dispel the water streaming into her eyes. When that didn't work, she wiped the rain with the back of her hand and tented her eyes with her sleeve.

Like her, he was curled up against the wall. Unlike her, he looked relatively comfortable and considerably drier. His knees were drawn against his chest, and that ridiculous-looking serape covered his entire body, from throat to toes. Water skidded down the thick, oil-treated cotton and puddled on the ground around him. His hat, pulled low on his brow, protected his face and eyes from the onslaught. Rainwater streamed in a thick, silver line from the brim, plunking in a splashing pool between his boots.

She should have taken the serape when he'd offered it. Now it didn't look so ridiculous; it looked . . . practical. Sighing at her own stupidity, she rested her head against the wall again.

God, she was tired. Bone-melting, blood-draining tired.

So why couldn't she sleep? She cast an envious glance at Larence. It wasn't right that he should be snoozing away while she was wide-awake, wet, and miserable.

In the distance, an animal howled.

Fear brought Emma's head up again. Adrenaline coursed through her body, made her breathing speed up. She sat as stiff as a new pin, her whole body poised and shaking, her blurred gaze pinned to the opening.

The animal howled again. Emma imagined she saw a pair of feral eyes gleaming gold against the darkness beyond the pack animals.

"Calm down, Em," she said through chattering teeth. "There's nothing there." She forced her eyes shut and tried to blank everything out of her mind. Concentrating on each harsh, rasping breath, she felt some control return.

She was so focused on herself that it took her a moment to realize the change. It was quiet.

Cautiously she opened one eye, then the other. It was true! The rain had stopped. Relaxation slid through her blood like a warm, magical elixir. Her cheek plopped back against the harsh stone wall, but this time she didn't notice the minuscule grains of sand that scraped her skin. She closed her eyes and was asleep within moments.

Half an hour later, she came awake with a start. At first she thought she'd been dreaming about ants crawling all over her body, then she realized the truth.

Damp wool clung to her flesh. As it dried, tiny strands poked through her thin undergarments and stabbed her skin in a thousand itchy sparks.

A low, miserable moan escaped her lips. The need to scratch was almost overwhelming. Her fingers tingled with the temptation, but she knew that if she scratched, even once, she'd be scratching until the sun came up.

She curled her fingers into shaking, white-knuckled fists.

One thing was certain: She wouldn't sleep tonight.

"Look at that—over to the east—it's a red-tailed hawk. . . ."

As usual, Emma didn't listen. She couldn't; it was all she could do to stay awake and erect on Tashee's back. She leaned forward slightly, clinging to her makeshift saddlehorn as her mount lurched up the rocky embankment. Scrubby bushes decorated with razor-sharp thorns clawed at her skirt, poked the raw, cotton-clad columns of her legs.

She closed her eyes and hung on tight. When they'd cleared the arroyo and were back on the plain, Emma let herself relax again.

The two days since the storm had been the longest, most uncomfortable forty-eight hours of her life. Whether on Tashee's back or sitting cross-legged beside the campfire, she'd alternately sweated and scratched and tried to keep from screaming. The days were interminable; hotter than hell and drier than dust. And the nights were worse. In the lonely hours between dinner's end and bedtime, silence curled around her like a musty velvet cloak, smothering her until sometimes the need to speak, to make contact with another living soul—even Larence—was so strong, she actually opened her mouth.

Fortunately, nothing ever came out. She hadn't uttered a single word to Larence in days. Not one.

Two days ago it had been stubborn pride that had compelled her to keep her mouth shut. Now it was self-preservation. She was afraid that if she opened her mouth—even once—she'd scream like a coward facing the gallows, and she wouldn't be able to stop.

It was all because of that damn storm, she thought dully. That night, sitting huddled next to the rock face, itchy and exhausted and alone, she'd felt the beginning strains of fear.

Now she felt it all the time. It sat on her shoulder like a vulture, waiting patiently for the moment to swoop down and devour her. With every second of this trip, each mile traveled, her hold on her emotions unraveled. Building inside her was a loss of control so complete, so terrifying, she couldn't even contemplate its magnitude. It took all her concentration to keep her anger and frustration under control.

So she kept her mouth sealed. As long as she was silent, she maintained the illusion of dignity. And right now, illusion was all she had.

If only she could sleep, she thought for the thousandth time. If she could sleep, even for a few precious hours, she would have the strength to fight. But that blissful state eluded her, floated just out of her grasp;

no matter how hard she reached for it, she came up empty-handed. A catnap here or there kept her functional, but at night, when it counted, her eyes remained achingly wide and painfully dry.

She pulled the flimsy, unfashionable hat lower on her sweaty brow, and immediately felt a tiny bit of relief from the hot sun. Thank God Larence had brought an extra hat. If he hadn't, her face would be lobster-red and cracked by now.

She glanced tiredly around. It was like another planet, this sloping, rising plain that twisted in and out of blue-topped mesas and eons-extinct volcanoes. The easy days of simply sitting on Tashee were gone; now they were constantly going up and down, weaving their way through rocky, cactus-thick arroyos that scared Emma to death.

The land was barren, burnt and empty. Somehow menacing.

Mountains, steel-hued humps against the eye-splitting blue of the sky, sat along the horizon, watchful and unfriendly. Huge, red sandstone walls rose up from the shrub-studded earth, and grayed, pointy spires thrust up beside them like ancient, accusatory fingers.

Nothing was normal or even remotely familiar about this land. You couldn't even trust what you saw. They had been moving steadily toward the largest of these mesas for two days. And they were no closer now than when they started. The damn thing seemed to be re-treating at the same pace they were advancing.

Rarified atmosphere. Larence had used those words to describe why the mountains actually *moved*.

"Look, Emmaline, a dwarf *piñon* . . ."

Emma rolled her eyes. Could he possibly believe she cared? He'd been rambling on since dawn, pointing out each and every bit of flora and fauna that dared to survive under this scorching sun, as if she really wanted to know the name of every dusty little leaf between here and Arizona.

When she had first stopped talking to him, he'd repeatedly turned in his saddle to speak to her, apparently thinking she didn't answer because she didn't hear. But after a while even Dr. Dimwit had gotten the hint. Now he understood that she was ignoring him on purpose. He hadn't turned to speak to her in hours.

Fortunately he no longer dropped down to draw at every change in the wind's direction. The steep, rock-strewn arroyos and thorny bushes had encouraged da Vinci to remain mounted. It was the only good thing about this part of New Mexico.

Emma sighed, feeling a sharp jab of metal against her bottom rib at the exhalation, and tried to find a comfortable position on Tashee's bony back.

Larence's detailed travelogue rolled around her, swirling into a vaguely comforting rhythm of monotonous sound. Exhaustion rounded her shoulders. Her eyelids felt like weighted curtains; no matter how often or how diligently she lifted them, they persisted in falling back to the closed position.

God, she was so tired. . . .

Within moments, she was asleep.

Ten minutes later, Tashee followed Diablo up a steep, rock-strewn embankment. Emma's sleeping body bobbed with each of the burro's lurching steps.

A long, thorn-studded branch grabbed Emma's heavy woolen skirt and yanked hard. She hit the earth with a thud. Her head smashed into a hot, flat rock. Stars shot across her eyes, and nausea bubbled in her stomach.

Tashee walked past Emma, her snotty black nose still buried in Diablo's tail.

She opened her mouth to scream at Larence, and sucked in a fistful of dirt. Her yell died in a fit of coughing.

The pack mule ambled along beside her prone body, climbing the embankment with ease. His tail whipped across her face. At each hoof-fall, gritty, gray-brown dust slammed into her nose and mouth, mixing with her saliva to form a thick, muddy paste on her tongue. Hacking coughs racked her lungs, made her throat go dry.

"Look, Emmaline," Larence's cheerful voice floated back to her. "Another jackrabbit."

Stop! Oh, God, please stop . . . She tried to scream, but couldn't force a single sound up her bone-dry throat. Panic sluiced through her blood, made her heart hammer in her chest. She surged up the rock-strewn embankment. Her fingers clawed wildly at the loose earth, but the faster she climbed, the faster the ground gave way beneath her. She slid downward in a cloud of rolling, puffing dirt.

Coughing, eyes watering, she started up again. Sand embedded itself in her fingernails, clogged her nose and eyes. Thorns grabbed hold of her clothing, biting into tender skin beneath.

After what seemed like hours, she reached the top of the bank. Panting hard, she stared in helpless horror at the pack mule's hindquarters. It was getting smaller— all three animals were getting smaller. The little caravan marched single file across the desert in a moving mushroom of dust. Their steady clip-clopping steps echoed across the dry land, the sound threaded with the lilting cadence of Larence's whistling.

Larence . . . stop! The words blared through her mind, loud and commanding; they squeaked out of her parched lips in a breathless, rasping whimper.

She tried desperately to get to her elbows. At the effort, her head swam; the queasiness in her stomach trebled. She collapsed like a broken doll.

How long she lay there, lost and alone, in the gray-black hinterlands of semiconsciousness, was a mystery to her. All she knew was that suddenly she was awake. She strained to hear the steady beat of the horse's hooves, or even Larence's idiotic whistling, but there was nothing; no sound save the hushed whisper of the wind through the grama grass. Hot, cloying air pressed in on her.

She blinked, and the sight that greeted her brought another stab of panic. They were gone. With all the strength in her body and soul, she crawled through the hot, dusty dirt. But the desert was stronger. The heat and the dust and the pain conspired against her, robbing her of willpower.

Finally she collapsed, panting for breath. She lay there, beaten and afraid, and closed her eyes. Tears burned her eyes and wrenched her throat. She didn't even try to stem the tide; there was no one to see her weakness. They streaked down her cheeks and disappeared in the hot earth.

No one—not even that traitor, Tashee—noticed her absence. Oh God, why hadn't she talked to Larence? If she had, even once, he might turn around in his saddle to speak to her, might notice her absence. But as it was . . .

She shivered at the thought and forced it out of her mind. But it came right back, louder and stronger and unable to deny.

How long would it be before he realized she'd fallen off? Dinnertime? And how far away would he be by then? Too far to do her any good . . .

Despair and defeat consumed her. She'd fought all her life. And what had it ever gotten her except a lonely mansion and a broken heart? God, she was tired of it all. Maybe it was time to say *enough*. Time to let go . . .

"Larence." The word came out in a cracked, broken whisper of pure defeat. Would it really have cost her so dearly to talk to him? A harsh, self-deprecating laugh grated in her throat at the obvious answer: Certainly her silence had cost her more.

She rested her face against the hard ground. The sun-hot earth pressed against her cheek, the arid scent of the high desert filled her nostrils.

She swallowed, trying to dredge up some hidden bit of saliva to slide down her parched throat. The swallow died, stillborn, on her swollen tongue. Without a hint of moisture, it was impossible. Too bad the canteen hadn't fallen off with her. Then she might have had a chance. As it was . . .

A shadow slithered across her body. She tilted her face and looked skyward. A huge, brown-winged bird circled a few feet above her head. Beady, unblinking eyes stared down at her. A sharp yellow beak glinted in the sunlight.

A vulture, already? She felt a racking shiver of fear. *Oh, God . . .*

Larence heard something and stopped whistling. He cocked his head toward the noise, listening.

It was the far-off keening wail of a hawk. The high-pitched screech echoed off the distant mesas, reverberated through the still, heavy air.

He smiled, remembering the majestic red-tailed hawk that had swooped alongside them this morning. He wished he had the talent to capture the effortless, gliding circles of its flight on paper.

Something on the ground caught his eye. A blur of grayish-green.

He glanced down at it. His breath caught. It was a perfect specimen of *Agave parryi*. Perfect.

He reined Diablo to a stop and dropped to the ground, hurrying toward the compact cluster of rigid, spadelike leaves. The tip of each leaf, a vicious thorn, glinted like a drop of sterling silver in the hot afternoon sun.

Whistling, Larence squatted by the cactus and began to sketch.

It was a full five minutes before he realized that something was wrong. He frowned. What was it?

Emmaline. He couldn't hear her exasperated, impatient breathing. She hadn't spoken to him in days, so he didn't expect to hear her voice, but whenever he stopped to draw, she had always made her frustration known by breathing in short, angry pants.

He shot a distracted glance her way. And gasped.

Tashee was riderless.

''Oh, my God!'' He crammed the notebook and pen back in his shirt pocket and ran awkwardly to Diablo. Vaulting into the saddle, he turned the horse around, waited for the mule and burro to follow, and then kicked Diablo hard in the sides.

The horse moved into a pounding trot. Larence clung to the saddle horn, bouncing hard on the leather seat. Only his toes, rammed deep into the stirrups, and his white-knuckled grip on the saddle horn, kept him from falling off. Every time his butt hit the seat, pain vibrated into his rib cage. His innards rattled and shook, and an involuntary groan shot out of his mouth. He gritted his clattering teeth and hung on, thankful, for once, for having learned to live with pain.

When had she fallen off? And why the hell hadn't she said anything?

Maybe she hadn't been able to. . . . The idea sliced through his thoughts like a lance.

It was his fault. In the past two days he'd given her too much freedom. He never should have let her get away with her childish silence. He should have insisted she take an active part in this expedition, should have forced her to change instead of letting her retreat deeper and deeper inside herself.

When he found her, things were going to be different. She was going to talk, do her share of the chores. By God, he'd even make sure she learned to laugh—and at herself first.

If he found her . . .

He kicked Diablo again. The horse responded by moving into a more manageable lope. Larence sat deeper in the saddle, riding his mount's rocking gait with relative ease.

A piercing, high-pitched screech rent the quiet air. Larence snapped his chin up and looked around.

The hawk was off in the distance, gliding in a small, perfect circle. How far off, Larence had no idea—the atmosphere at this altitude made it impossible to judge how far away things really were.

His heart sped up. The bird was flying low to the ground in tight, controlled circles. It was irrational, he knew, and yet somehow Larence was certain that the hawk was leading him. . . .

He jerked the reins to the left. Diablo turned toward the bird with lightning speed, and ate up the ground with his thundering gait.

An hour later, Larence finally saw the first faint outline of the body lying prone on the ground beneath the hawk's gliding circles. She was a heap of black wool and white cotton and blond hair.

Heart pounding, palms sweating, he pressed up onto the balls of his feet and peered over Diablo's head.

Please God, let her be okay. . . .

At their approach, the hawk gave one long, screeching shriek and flew away.

Larence grabbed his canteen, wrapped his leather reins around the saddle horn, and leapt out of the saddle. When his boots hit the dirt, his knees buckled. Pain radiated up his bad leg. Wincing, he raced to Emma's body and dropped to his knees beside her.

She was lying spread out on the hot ground, one arm pinned to her side, and the other curled protectively beneath her cheek. Strands of dirty blond hair fanned out across her sunburnt cheeks and disappeared against the pale gold earth. Her lips were cracked and colorless.

Larence swallowed thickly. Fear lodged in his throat like a lump of burning ash. Hesitantly he reached for her. His fingers slid along the flesh of her exposed throat, feeling, testing. God, she was so hot. . . .

Then he felt it: the gentle, thudding beat of life. His whole body buckled with relief.

"Emma?"

Nothing. He gently rolled her onto her back and slid one arm behind her neck, lifting her toward him. She lay in his arms like a wet dish towel.

He pried his canteen open and tipped it, letting a few

precious drops of water slide down his fingers and pool in his palm. Then, careful not to move her too harshly, he dipped two fingers in the water and rubbed it along her parched mouth. It took a couple of times before her lips parted, but when they did, Larence felt like whooping for joy.

"Come on, Em, that's it. Lick my fingers."

Her tongue darted out and tasted the cool wetness on his forefinger. A strange shiver sped through his body at the whisper-soft gliding of her moist tongue against the rough flesh of his finger.

When all the water was gone, a low, pained groan issued from her cracked lips. He pulled her into his arms and held her folded body, crooning to her as if she were a child. He talked softly of little, inconsequential things, anything that came to mind. The sun, the weather, Cibola.

After a few minutes, her tongue slid along the bumpy, chapped surface of her lips. Her throat bulged in a thick swallow.

Her eyes cracked open.

She immediately blinked at the harsh sunlight. Larence yanked his Stetson off and used it to shield her eyes from the bright light. "Hi, Em."

Her mouth opened slightly, but nothing came out. Still, he could see the makings of his name. He nodded in understanding. "Of course it's me," he answered, stroking the side of her face.

She closed her eyes and sank deeper into his arms.

"Here," he said after a moment, "drink this."

He held the canteen to her mouth. Her eyes flipped open. She grabbed it in both hands and wrenched it out of his grasp. Tilting the canteen, she gulped the hot water greedily. Rivulets ran down her throat and along the sides of her face, seeping into the coarse denim of his pants.

"Whoa, there, slow down," he urged, tugging the canteen away from her and setting it on the ground beside him.

She looked at him then. He saw in her eyes an aching, deep-seated despair. And more than a hint of defeat. It was a look he knew well. Too well. But seeing it in *her* eyes, in invincible Emmaline's eyes, was somehow worse than seeing it in his own. He had a strong, sudden urge to fill her eyes with laughter. To teach her to smile.

You came, she mouthed.

Invisible hands clutched his heart and squeezed. Had she really thought he'd just leave her out here to die?

"Of course I came." He wondered if she heard the thickness in his words.

She tried to smile and failed miserably. "Thanks."

He forced himself not to answer. Tonight, when she was more relaxed, he'd begin his attack on the emotional barriers she'd obviously spent years erecting. But not now, not when she was so close to breaking.

"De nada," he answered lightly. "That's what Diamond Dick always says to his partner, One-Eyed John. It means, 'Think nothing of it.' "

Emmaline groaned and rolled her eyes.

He grinned. Tightening his hold on her, he stood up. The small effort it took to hold her surprised him. His grandmother had been wrong: he could carry a woman up the stairs or across the threshold. Maybe even farther.

"Larence?"

Her face was so close, he could see the grains of sand still clinging to her pale brown eyelashes. Her blue eyes seemed huge against the sunburnt darkness of her skin. She stared at him without blinking, and for once, the shuttered look was gone. He felt as if he could see straight into her soul—and it was a frightened, vulnerable place like his own.

"I mean it," she said in a dry, brittle voice. "Thanks."

Some emotion he'd never felt before and couldn't name made his heart slam against his rib cage. The slow, warm patter of her breath brushed his cheek, the even beating of her heart thudded against his chest.

He searched for something light to say. "Well, if you're through here, how 'bout we make camp someplace a bit prettier?"

Amazingly, she smiled.

At the soft curving of her lips, Larence felt something inside him break free and float.

She licked her lips and said in a thick, cracked voice, "We'd better get going."

His smile turned into a grin. Leave it to Emmaline to come back from the brink of death issuing orders. Setting her down, he limped over to Diablo. A feeling of camaraderie clung between them, something new and fragile, and Larence was loathe to let it go. So as he rearranged the supplies to make room for two riders, he said over his shoulder, "Next time you decide to rest a minute, Em, why don't you ask for the notebook. I sure would've appreciated a sketch of that greasewood over there."

A clot of dirt hit him in the back. There was a moment of stunned surprise, and then they both laughed.

Emma couldn't believe she'd laughed. Somehow the sound had tumbled out of her, unbidden and unwanted, and yet strangely *necessary*. As if it had been a substitute for screaming.

Now laughter was the furthest thing from her mind. Seated on Diablo behind Larence, with her cheek pressed to the warm cotton of his serape, and her arms curled around his midsection, she wanted desperately to cry. It took every ounce of strength, every ounce of willpower she possessed, to keep the hated, humiliating tears from creeping down her cheeks.

She tried to force her mind away from what had happened, but couldn't. The image of herself lying alone and forgotten in the desert pounded through her mind, demanded a reaction.

Her teeth started a low, quiet chattering. She clamped her mouth shut, whether to stop the chattering or keep the scream bottled up, she no longer knew. No longer cared. All that mattered was hanging on to her last shred of dignity. All that mattered was not crying.

Tears burned. The need to shed them ached behind her eyes, gave her a pounding headache. She'd been so scared, so alone. And she hadn't thought he'd come. Not really.

But he had, she reminded herself firmly. So why did she want to cry? Why now, when it was all over and she was safe?

She didn't have an answer. All she had was a need, building with every heartbeat, to open the floodgate on her emotions and let herself fall apart. It swelled within her like a rising tide, slipping past every nook and cranny in her armor.

Larence would feel the wetness against his back. The thought was like being hit with a bucket of cold water.

She couldn't take the humiliation. And what good would it do, anyway? Crying was a useless waste of energy. Hadn't her father cried for days before he'd shot himself?

Fat lot of good the tears had done him . . .

She squeezed her eyes shut, letting anger at her father's death consume her fear. Almost instantly, the trembling in her body subsided, the rapid pumping of her heart slowed. Her tears dried into a hard, aching lump in her chest. Control returned.

Emma sighed and almost smiled.

She'd beaten it again.

Not too far away, on a mesa to the east, a hawk screeched loudly, then flapped its huge brown wings and settled onto the uppermost branch of the tree. The limb shook; green needles shuddered and dropped to the sandy soil.

Ka-Neek gave the bird a respectful nod, then turned his attention back to the two gray-haired men sitting cross-legged by the smokeless fire. "How much longer shall we wait? They are close. Too close. The secret—"

"Enough." The word was spoken quietly, with no emphasis but for the slow raising of a gnarled, sundarkened hand. In the silence that followed, the leader took a long, whistling drag of his pipe.

Ka-Neek jerked away from the tree and started pacing. Dust spiraled up from the worn leather soles of his moccasins. The haliotis-shell necklace he wore clacked with each of his angry steps. "I cannot stand by and watch the cursed white men destroy what this family has protected for five hundred years. I say—"

"We know well what you say, son," Me-lik broke in harshly. "But it is not you that matters, is it?" He turned to look at the old man beside him. "What say you, Father? It cannot be denied that they draw near to the Forbidden Place. Perhaps too near.''

The ancient one let out a last, lingering curl of gray-white smoke, then set down his pipe. Picking up a stick, he poked its sharpened end into the fire. Sparks hissed loudly and fluttered upward like a thousand freed fireflies.

The bright orange flames reflected in his eyes. Shadows twisted across the chiseled, wrinkled hollows of his cheeks. With great care, he eased a limp lock of ash-hued hair out of his face, curled it behind his ear. ''Ka-Neek is right,'' he said at last, reluctantly. ''It is time.''

Chapter Fourteen

Larence stood at the riverbank, breathing deeply of the resin-scented air.

The stream, a braid of silvery water cutting through the dun-colored dirt, reflected the now-darkening sky. Shadows curled along its bank and clung to the whispering leaves of the cottonwoods overhead. Water lapped lazily against the bank and rustled the rushes.

Fingers of wind trailed Larence's cheek. Cool air ruffled his hair. He glanced up at the early evening sky, mesmerized by the beauty of it. The sun had changed from a burning, eye-searing star to a pale yellow layer of lingering light. Billowing gold and blue clouds crowned the steel rim of mountains in the distance.

It was so incredibly lovely. Emmaline should be seeing this. . . .

He turned around, and what he saw stole the smile from his face. Emmaline sat perfectly still, her gaze riveted to the fire, her fingers curled tightly around a long-cold cup of coffee. Her back was knife-blade-stiff, as if she was afraid to let herself uncoil even a fraction. In the black dress, with her skirts puddled around her, she reminded him of a bereaved widow sitting at her husband's freshly dug grave. The only thing missing from the picture was tears.

186

He limped over to the fire and dropped to his knees across from her. She didn't even bat an eye at his arrival. She just sat there, as stiff and silent as a marble statue.

He didn't know what to do, how to reach her. With each mile traveled today, he'd seen her fortify the wall of icy indifference she'd erected around herself, seen her retreat further and further inside herself.

She snapped her head up suddenly. "Quit staring at me."

"Why?"

She gave an irritated sigh. "Don't you have some unpacking to do so I can start dinner?"

"Worried about the animals' welfare, Emmaline?" he teased.

"Leave me alone."

His half smile faded, and his voice dropped to a near whisper. "I can't do that, Em. Not this time."

Their gazes locked. The color seeped out of her face. She opened her mouth to say something, then clamped it shut again and yanked her gaze back to the fire. The cup in her hand began to shake.

Larence studied her downcast face. She was hanging on to her self-control by a fingernail; trying pathetically hard to be invincible. But he could see past her facade even if she couldn't. And the scared, lonely woman inside tore at his heart, reminded him of a little boy curled on a hard, cold bed, trying not to cry. Fear and the painful loneliness of battling it alone was something he understood.

He knew the signs. Throughout his youth he'd hidden his pain and anger, tried to pretend they didn't exist; that he was stronger than any emotion. But it had never worked for long. Sooner or later the emotions always broke through the barriers he'd constructed to contain them.

She was afraid of the emotions, just as he'd been. Unfortunately, the only way she'd realize her own strength would be to hit rock bottom and realize she could survive it.

An almost aching tenderness unfolded within him. The need to reach out, to thread his fingers through hers, rose like a wave in him. He wanted to take her in his arms, without words, without even a whisper. To let her know it was okay to break down, okay to be human, and that, for once, she wasn't alone.

"Em . . ." Her name, spoken so gently, hung between them.

Slowly she lifted her gaze to his. In her eyes he saw a faint, hesitant stirring of hope.

Her beauty nearly took his breath away. His heart thudded against his chest and crept into his throat. "You're so . . ." The words congealed in his throat. Why would someone like Emmaline care that he thought her lovely? Better men than he had undoubtably told her that a thousand times. If she had an answer at all, it would be a laugh.

He said the next thing that came to mind: "—tired. Would you like to go to bed?"

A wan smile touched the edges of her mouth. One eyebrow arched mockingly upward. "Propositioning me, Larence?"

Yes. Maybe I am. The realization stunned him into momentary speechlessness. He stared at her, trying to think of something—anything—to say. Something clever, worldly, something that would sweep her off her feet. But nothing came to him except the same amazing, unexpected words, over and over again: *Yes, maybe I am.* . . .

"Don't bother answering." She gave a harsh, bitter laugh. "I know how you feel about me."

"It's not—"

She cut him off with a wave of her hand. "Don't bother. You go feed and unpack the animals. I'll start dinner."

"You don't have to cook tonight."

"I *want* to help. It's time. And besides, I owe you for coming back for me."

Larence felt like he'd been punched. "It wasn't a business transaction, Em," he said quietly.

She paled. "It's . . . easier for me to think otherwise. Business I understand; debts and payoffs make sense to me." Their gazes locked. "Anything else . . ." She shrugged, forcing another lackluster smile, and let her sentence dangle.

Larence felt a surge of hope. It was the most—hell, it was the *only*—personal thing she'd ever told him. He leaned forward, knowing his eagerness was obvious, but unable and unwilling to mask it. "Emmaline, I—"

Something cracked into the back of his head with a sickening thud. Pain exploded behind his eyes. He wobbled. Emma's sharply indrawn breath echoed in his ears.

Everything slowed to a crawl. He felt as if he were being sucked down a long, lightless tunnel. Through a distant, fuzzy part of his brain, he heard a woman scream, heard the high-pitched screech of a large bird and the whisper-soft shuffle of feet.

He had one cogent thought: *Emmaline.* He grasped desperately for consciousness. It crumbled at his touch, and blackness consumed him. With an agonized groan he pitched face-first into the dirt.

Emma heard footsteps coming toward her. She screamed, strained desperately to see through the velvet darkness that wreathed the campsite.

Nothing.

Panic seized her. She started to scramble backward, seeking the anonymous blackness beyond the fire's feeble glow. Halfway there, she stopped.

Larence had helped her when she was in trouble. *Damn.* She almost wished he hadn't. Now she had to think about someone besides herself. It had never been one of her strengths. . . .

She crawled shakily to her knees and worked her way around to where Larence lay facedown. Beside him was a thick chunk of wood smeared with blood. She shuddered at the sight. Someone was out there, in the darkness. Watching them. Waiting. Someone who wanted to hurt them—and knew how.

"Larence?" She winced at the loudness of her whisper and nervously glanced around.

He didn't move. Every instinct she possessed screamed at her to run for her life, but for once, she stayed.

Hesitantly, she tested the dark smear on the back of his head. Slick, warm blood oozed over her fingers. Nausea gurgled in her stomach and throat.

She squeezed her eyes shut, fighting the urge to vomit. The sharp, metallic taste of bile flooded her mouth and made her gag. Clamping a shaking hand against her roiling midsection, she waited for the nausea to pass, then forced herself to do what needed to be done.

She untied the kerchief from around his throat and pressed it to his wound.

A low, moaning sound came from his throat.

"Thank God," she breathed. "Larence?"

She heard something then. A butterfly-soft movement; more a gentle whirring of air than a human noise. Suddenly a pair of moccasined feet appeared in front of her. She gasped. Her hand flew instinctively to her throat.

"*Larence,*" she hissed.

A rifle appeared. Emma swallowed hard, staring at the gun's sleek metal barrel. A big, brown hand curled around the wooden handle and lifted. Cold steel pressed against her throat.

"Get up, woman."

Her mouth went so dry, she couldn't speak. If she could have, she'd have pleaded, or cried, or done *something*. Anything except what she was doing—which was sitting like a frozen lump. But it felt as if her legs had turned to cold marble, and her throat to dust. Her blood was pumping so fast, it thundered in her ears.

A hand reached out of the darkness and grabbed her. Cold, merciless fingers coiled around the fleshy part of her arm and yanked her to her feet. She bit back a yelp of pain and stumbled into a man's naked chest. A big, round shell sliced into her cheek. Warm streaks of blood slid down her throat.

"Look up."

Emma thought about refusing, but didn't dare. Hesitantly, trying to swallow her fear, she did as she was told. And looked into the slitted, pit-dark eyes of the Indian from Albuquerque. Ka-Neek.

"*Larence!*"

Ka-Neek dragged her away from the fire. She stumbled along beside him, tripping and being wrenched to her feet like a reluctant child.

"Lare—"

He jerked her against his side. She rammed into his stone-hard body and gasped at the pain.

At Tashee, he stopped. She fell against the burro's familiar side with a momentary sense of relief. His painful hold on her arm eased. Then, in a blur of motion, she found herself sitting on Tashee's back, with her wrists bound and tied to the wooden saddle horn.

Emma tried to wiggle free. Her feeble attempts brought a low, dangerous chuckle. "Get off and I'll shoot you."

She didn't doubt him. In fact, she got the distinct impression that he *wanted* her to run. . . .

"Go ahead and yell," he said in a too-quiet voice that sent icy rivulets of fear down her stiffened spine. His eyes added: *Give me a reason to shoot you.* A hawk screeched overhead, and the sound grated down Emma's stiffened spine.

Screwing up her courage, she said in a single breath, "My partner . . . please, he needs . . ."

Ka-Neek grabbed Tashee's reins and pulled. After a short, reluctant bracing of her feet, the little burro gave in, and plodded toward the magnificent paint standing alongside Diablo. The Indian vaulted onto the animal's back and they were off.

Walking. Somehow that was the most frightening thing of all. They were *walking*. Not galloping, not cantering, not even trotting. It was as if Ka-Neek wanted to be followed. Or knew they wouldn't be.

The thought brought the sting of tears to Emma's eyes. She squeezed her fingers around the wooden X, feeling the warm slickness of Larence's blood in her palm.

Please, God, she prayed, take care of him. . . .

She had no prayer for herself. God had never once listened to her prayers, and she didn't expect Him to hear her now.

She was, as always, on her own.

A dull thudding ricocheted through Larence's head. Each hammer-stroke brought a stab of pain cracking through his skull. He frowned, tasting something metallic. Groggily, with a shaking hand, he raked the hair off his face. Something slid off the back of his head and plopped in a cloud of dust in front of his nose. He tried to focus on the thing and couldn't. It was a bloodred blur.

The thudding intensified; the pain trebled.

Damn neighbors, he thought distractedly. Who was hammering at this hour of the morning?

Memory jerked him upright. At the sudden movement, his head spun. Nausea boiled in the pit of his empty, roiling stomach. He clutched his midsection and scanned the campsite. He was alone.

Emmaline. Someone had taken Emmaline.

Terror, colder and more debilitating than any he'd ever known, suffocated him. His mind went chillingly blank. He stared at the little scrap of red that had fallen off his head, transfixed, unable to move. Harsh spurts of breath shot past his lips.

"Calm down, Larence. *Think.*"

He forced his breathing to slow down, and gradually his nausea subsided. The scrap of red turned into his bandanna, haphazardly folded. His fingers reached out, grazing the sticky, still warm smear of blood.

She had tended his wound.

He went weak with relief. *She was alive.* But where?

He crammed the bandanna into his jeans pocket and lurched unsteadily to his feet. Nausea hit again, harder, thicker. He battled it, clutching his stomach and concentrating on each breath as he made his shambling, hunched-over way to Diablo and the mule.

"It's up to you, boy," he whispered to Diablo, thankful now that he'd never gotten around to unpacking for the night.

Diablo whickered in understanding as Larence grabbed the pack mule's lead line, wrapped it around the saddle horn, and climbed awkwardly into Diablo's saddle.

"Okay, boy," he said, wheezing from the exertion, "find her."

Diablo took off at a ground-gobbling extended trot. Larence's fingers tightened around the horn, turning white with the effort it took to hold on. Strands of hemp from the twisted lead rope poked his flesh. He swallowed thickly, trying to block the pain hammering behind his eyes.

It was useless. With each pounding hoofbeat, Larence landed hard on the seat. Pain burned through his body and stabbed behind his eyes. Vomit inched up his throat.

Diablo stumbled, throwing Larence forward. His midsection rammed into the horn, and the battle was lost. He just had time to lean sideways as his sickness splatted on the dark desert floor.

When the nausea passed, he felt better. Stronger. The pain behind his eyes melted into a manageable headache.

Not that it mattered. He'd endure whatever pain he

had to. Nothing would stop him from saving Emmaline. Nothing.

He tightened his hold on the horn and hung on.

Two bone-shattering hours later, Larence finally caught up with them. He'd heard the unmistakable sounds of two moving animals for more than an hour, but now, finally, he could *see* them. Two slow-moving black specks in the eerie, occasional half-light of a setting sliver of moon.

The duo ahead of him stopped at the base of a huge, shadowy mesa.

Larence reined Diablo to a stop about fifty yards away from them. Hidden from view by the night and a grove of dwarf piñon trees, he dismounted as soundlessly as possible and hobbled the two animals. Retrieving his specially fitted Acromatic Spy Glass from his saddlebag, he limped silently toward the grove's last tree.

Something snapped under his heel and he froze. Every muscle in his body spasmed taut. The harsh, ragged tenor of his breathing scored the silence.

After a few moments, he forced himself to relax. His fingers unfurled. No one had heard. He dropped noiselessly to his knees on the cool dirt and lay down. Bringing his elbows up in front of him, he lifted the cold rim of the spyglass to his eyes and turned it toward the campsite up ahead. The kidnapper was hunkered down, doing something with his hands. In seconds, a bright fire flickered to life, bathing the man in pale golden light.

Thick ropes of silky black hair concealed the enemy's face, swung gently against the huge, squared muscles of his bare chest. Shadows cavorted on his downcast face, giving the man a sinister, evil countenance.

Larence felt a flash of fear at seeing his adversary, but conquered it quickly. He wouldn't do Emmaline any good if he was afraid. . . .

You won't do her any good anyway, came his grandmother's taunting voice. *This situation requires a real man, not a half-broken excuse for a hero.*

No, he mouthed determinedly. He *could* save her. *Would* save her. But how?

Formulate a plan. Yes, that was it. He needed a plan of action, a way to save her. But what? This wasn't exactly the sort of situation Harvard had trained him for. Nothing in his ivory-towered life had prepared him to assume the role of romantic hero. . . .

Suddenly he remembered Diamond Dick. There was a kidnapping scene in the hero's latest dime novel. Certainly *that* would give some inspiration. Larence scrambled to his feet and limped quietly to Diablo, searching through the saddlebags for *Diamond Dick's Deadly Deeds.* Finding it at last, he squatted behind a dwarf piñon and lit a match, flipping through the warped, yellowed pages for the kidnapping scene.

He found it quickly and started reading.

Black Bart listened to the soft, muffled sounds of the woman's whimperings. His mouth twisted into a cruel smile. Tonight was going to be fun, he thought. Just like the old days.

He lurched drunkenly to his feet and tottered across the shadowy campsite toward the woman he'd taken a few hours back.

"Git up," he said hoarsely.

She huddled into an even tighter ball and shook her head. "Please, don't . . ."

He yanked her to her feet and pressed his hunting knife to her throat. Her quickly indrawn breath made the ache between his legs grow stronger. He slid the blade under the top button and cut the threads. The button slid down her chest and plopped to the dirt.

"What you doin', Bart?"

Bart heard Diamond Dick's voice and froze. He shoved the woman away from him and spun around. "You got no bizness here, Dick."

Dick didn't move. "You got my woman. I want her back."

"Dick!" she screamed, running toward him.

Just as she reached Dick, Bart cocked his gun and pointed it at her. "Shut her up, Dick, else I will. That caterwaulin'll bring the law fer sure."

"Kill him!" she screamed, clinging to Dick's arm. "Kill him!"

Dick shut her up with a kiss. When it was over, he pulled back slowly, whispering, "Count to three and drop to the ground."

The second she hit the ground, Dick fired. His bullet drilled Black Bart between the eyes, and the desperado thudded to the ground in a lifeless heap.

Larence closed the book. It would work, he thought. He could act like Emmaline was his woman and demand her return. He could even offer money if he had to. They had a little left.

All he had to do was act dangerous. And hope the Indian didn't drop him with a single bullet.

* * *

Emma saw the lone man before Ka-Neek did. At first her heart lurched upward in hope, then it spiraled into her feet.

It was Larence. Larence come to save her.

God help them both.

Chapter Fifteen

Larence set his face in a killer's remorseless expression. At least, it *felt* remorseless; he couldn't be sure.

His eyes were narrowed, almost slitted. His mouth was drawn into a thin line. He tried to dredge up a frown, but couldn't do it without feeling like an idiot.

Not an idiot. A dangerous killer. A man you didn't want to tangle with.

He hooked his thumbs through his belt loops, letting his fingers splay loosely across the blue denim of his jeans, and started toward the small circle of firelight up ahead. The shotgun felt foreign and useless wedged beneath his armpit. He wished fleetingly that he had a pair of pearl-handled Colts instead. Just for looks.

He stepped into an indentation in the ground. His ankle twisted hard, and pain ricocheted up his shin. He bit his lower lip to stifle a gasp. The metallic taste of blood filled his mouth.

Wiping the moisture from his lower lip with the back of his hand, he forced himself to keep going. But he couldn't help thinking that he didn't need a damn pistol. He needed a healthy leg.

Every step reminded him of the limp that marred his image and made him look frail and weak. Diamond Dick hadn't limped a day in his life—not even when that Comanchero had knifed him in the thigh. Dick had walked all the way to Ogalala that day, and not a single step had been off balance.

Larence fought the tide of self-pity he'd always despised. As a child, he'd prayed every night to wake up healthy and whole, without the damaged leg that kept him cooped up in the darkness of his grandmother's house. Even as an adult, he'd occasionally wished for a respite from the pain and embarrassment of his disability. But never, not in all the long, lonely nights when he'd writhed in agony, had he wished to be whole and healthy as fervently, as desperately, as he wished it now.

Heroes were supposed to be perfect physical specimans, not broken-down, deformed shells that—

No. He refused to think about it. If he gave self-doubt a hint of purchase, it would devour him whole, turn him into a useless shell of a man. He knew; he'd been down that road a thousand times in his life. Before he'd started searching for the positive in life, he'd been mired in the negative. Strangled by it.

Not this time, he vowed. This time he had to be strong and in control for Emmaline.

Emmaline. The word gave him strength. Forcing his face into a hard expression, he kept moving toward the light.

As if sensing Larence's presence, the Indian looked up. Emotionless black eyes scanned the shadowy veil of night, searching.

It was Ka-Neek.

Larence froze. The hairs on the back of his neck stood up. Sweat seeped out of his skin and itched across his forehead. Fear strangled him, made it impossible to move. Emmaline had been right; Ka-Neek *had* meant them harm.

He stared at the gun lying across the Indian's crossed legs. Firelight and shadows slithered along its steel barrel, giving the weapon a twisting, snakelike life. No doubt the Indian was a crack shot. God knew he threw wood like an expert.

Larence swallowed hard, forcing away fear. *You're Diamond Dick. You can do it.* When he almost believed it, he schooled his features into a hard mask and emerged from the darkness.

"Larence!" Emma burst out of the shadows and barreled toward him.

"Don't!" he hissed.

Their eyes met, and even in the half-light, he could see the fear in hers. He prayed she could see the silent warning in his. Her run melted into a shuddering walk and then disappeared altogether. She stood as stiff as a statue, her wide-eyed gaze darting from Larence to Ka-Neek and back to Larence. Only her bound hands, twisting together against her midsection, hinted at the emotions roiling inside her.

Please keep quiet, he thought. *I need to concentrate.* . . .

She did.

He took a deep breath and looked down at Ka-Neek, who was looking up, measuring him.

Larence steeled himself. A bead of sweat slid down the side of his face. "You took my woman." Incredibly, his voice sounded calm, strong. Maybe even dangerous. The small success gave him courage. "I want her back."

A slow, mocking smile tilted one side of Ka-Neek's mouth. It was the only indication that he'd heard.

"If it's money you want—"

"No!" Emma cried out unexpectedly. "It's not your—"

Larence shot her an uncompromising glare. "Be quiet, Em. *Now*."

Her tirade ended in a sharply indrawn breath. Seconds later, he heard the rapid-fire tapping of her booted foot.

To Ka-Neek he said, "We don't have much gold, but perhaps—"

"No!"

"Goddamn it, Emmaline, *shut up*."

She marched up to him, her face set in that pinched, don't-mess-with-me expression he'd seen a thousand times.

"*You* don't have money, Larence, *I* have money. And I refuse to give it to this obnoxious, overbearing sav—"

He yanked her against him. She slammed into his chest with a surprised gasp.

Her eyes bulged. "What in the hell—"

He kissed her. She gasped again, tried to wrench away, but he was too quick for her. His hand glided up the stiff column of her neck and fastened in her thick, silver-gold hair.

He meant to do it quickly, like Diamond Dick had. Just long enough to shut her up. But once he felt the softness of her lips against his, he couldn't pull back, couldn't ease away.

He expected to feel a stinging slap against his cheek, and then remembered that her hands were bound. She couldn't stop him.

He was being a cad; taking advantage of her when she couldn't fight back. He knew it, and couldn't stop himself. This kiss, the feel of her, it felt so good, so incredibly *right*.

Just one more second . . .

The world slowed to an aching, exquisite crawl. Larence's hold loosened, became more an embrace than a possession. The feminine taste of her filled his senses. Warmth seeped through the tired cotton of her shirt-waist and dampened his flesh. Blood tingled in Larence's veins, thrummed through his body. All thoughts of Diamond Dick vanished; now he was just Larence. And he was holding the woman who'd haunted his days and filled his nights since the moment he saw her.

Something banged against his chest. It was a moment before he realized that she was hitting him with her knotted fists. Hitting him hard. He pulled away. Cold air immediately rushed in, breezing across his lips and reminding him that the kiss was over.

She glared up at him, breathing hard. Her eyes were icy-cold and filled with disgust.

The fire in Larence's blood chilled. His broad shoulders sagged. For a second there, he'd thought they had come close to something special.

No, he reminded himself sharply. *They* hadn't been close to something special. *He* had, and as usual, he'd been there alone.

"How dare you," she hissed. "No kiss is going to shut *me* up. And we aren't going to give that sav—"

Larence clamped a hand over her mouth.

Angry-sounding words muffled against his palm. Her eyes narrowed, shot blue fire.

"I'm going to take away my hand now. But I want you to be quiet, okay?" He eased his hand from her mouth.

"Why, you—"

"Bad move." He yanked the bandanna from his pants pocket. Before she could stutter a word, he gagged her.

Her eyes bulged.

"What do you expect?" he whispered. "You can't go around calling people 'savage.' Especially not people with big guns. You left me no—" Her fist slammed into his chest, and his breath expelled in a rush.

He straightened. "Now, that wasn't—"

She kicked him in the shin.

He groaned and backed out of the field of fire. He'd deal with her anger later, when they were both calmer. Right now he had more important things to do. Taking a deep breath, he wiped the expression from his face and turned to speak to Ka-Neek.

The Indian was gone. So was his horse.

Frowning, Larence walked over to the fire and squatted down beside its bright warmth. His fingertips grazed the sandy soil, searching for some sign of Ka-Neek's presence. But there wasn't so much as a crease in the dirt. Nothing. No hint of the man who'd been sitting there only moments before . . .

What in the hell was going on? Certainly they hadn't imagined Ka-Neek? He laid a hand to his thigh and started to push to his feet.

Then something caught his attention. He plucked it up and moved closer to the fire's light. It was a perfectly formed circle of tanned leather. Curious, he flipped it over and saw a blackish red symbol.

He gasped. With half an ear he heard Emmaline come up behind him, but he didn't turn around. He couldn't. He was frozen to the spot.

Now he knew why Ka-Neek had taken Emmaline. It wasn't to rob or kill them; it was to give them this message.

She squatted beside him. A few muffled words reached his subconscious, but Larence ignored them.

She rammed her shoulder into his. The suddenness of the movement wrecked Larence's always precarious balance. He grabbed Emmaline for support, but it was too late.

He hit the dirt with a thud. Emma landed hard beside him, her bound wrists making it impossible for her to break her fall. She started to roll backward, into the fire. Larence scooped her into his arms and rolled away. When he came to a stop, she was lying flush atop him, her face a hair's breadth from his own.

He stared at a spot just to the right of her ear, too deep in thought to notice Emma at all. What did it mean? Was the Indian threatening to kill them? Or was he trying to save them with a warning?

She grunted angrily and brought her bound wrists up to his chest. Absentmindedly he untied the leather restraints. She untied the gag and yanked it out of her mouth.

"You gagged me," she screamed.

He frowned up at her, baffled. Had she said something? He couldn't remember—his mind was too filled with the image of the bloody marking that meant danger.

"*Gagged* me! How dare you! I've never been so humiliated in my entire life; why, I ought to . . ."

Larence winced at the loudness of her voice. "Now, Emmaline, I—"

"Don't you 'now, Emmaline' me, you . . . you . . ."

A headache started. He couldn't think with her caterwauling like this, and right now he had to think.

He stopped her screeching the Diamond Dick way.

* * *

Emma smacked his cheek with all the force she could muster. The loud *crack* echoed through the night's darkness. Before he could utter a word, she threw herself backward.

"Em—" He reached for her. She wrenched out of his grasp and clambered to her feet.

Standing above him, she had a hysterical urge to laugh. The sound welled up inside her, threatening to spill out. She clamped a hand over her mouth and twisted away from him, stumbling mindlessly away from the fire.

He advanced.

Emma felt him coming toward her, and she retreated. She didn't want to talk to him, didn't want to get near enough to touch him. The memory of his lips, so soft and undemanding and *caring*, against her own sent a flood of ice-cold water down her back. She didn't want to think about that. Not now. Not ever.

Turning to face him, she intended to yell at him to stay away, but something in his eyes made the words clog in her throat. She took a hesitant step backward. Her hands twisted the nubby wool of her skirt. "Don't you come near me," she said, angered by the breathy sound of her voice.

She sounded like a woman who'd just been kissed—a woman who wanted to be kissed again, and that made her even madder.

Anger brought her chin up. How dare he make her feel this way? How dare he take her out in the middle of nowhere and put her on a burro and *lead* her as if she were a worthless child toward some city she didn't even believe in? Suddenly it all came crashing in on her: the windstorm, the rainstorm, being abandoned in the hot desert, half-dead, and now this. She'd been kidnapped by a half-naked savage and dragged across the desert—only to be rescued and *kissed* by Larence. It was too much.

"Stay away from me." She backed up. He came closer. Her fingers balled into a fist—just in case.

He didn't hesitate, kept moving toward her with that same quiet, limping gait. Every footfall echoed in her ears like the fall of a hammer against hard-packed earth. She winced, trying to block out the sound.

His hand came out, stretched toward her.

She stared at the flat, pale circle of his palm. Unbidden came a wave of longing. God, how good it would feel to place her hand in his, to let his fingers thread through hers and squeeze. . . .

Run. Now! Before you shatter into a million pieces.

Biting hard on her lower lip, she lunged away from him. Skirting the fire, she ran to the firelight's quivering edge. There she stopped. Uncertainty tugged at the edges of her mouth, trembled in her fingertips. Beyond, the darkness beckoned, promised anonymity and a place to be alone. But she couldn't take the step. Her feet stayed close together, ankle to ankle, rooted in the gray-brown dirt.

She felt, rather than heard, Larence come up behind her.

"Emmaline?"

His voice, so rich and welcoming, curled around her. She shivered, clutching her arms across her breasts like a protective shield. She felt as if she were standing on a great precipice, her toes jutted foolishly over the edge. Below was a great chasm of darkness; a fall that would break her neck and shatter her soul.

The trembling in her fingertips moved up her arms, rattled through her body, and chattered in her teeth. Her tearful gaze darted left to right and up and down. Surely there had to be someplace to run, somewhere to go? If she didn't move soon, and fast, she was terrified the angry panic building inside her breast would explode. And what would be left of her after the explosion? *What?*

The touch was so soft that at first she didn't notice it. Then it tightened. Fingers curled into the tensed flesh of her shoulders, squeezing gently.

"Emmaline?"

She relaxed for a single beat of her heart, then she jerked taut. In one quick, self-defensive move, she spun around and raised her hand to smack his face again.

His hand stopped her in midswing. His fingers curled around her wrist and held fast. She felt the heat of each digit like a brand.

Larence's eyes impaled her, pinned her in place. She had a sudden, terrifying feeling that he could see *inside* her, see her fear and hysteria and weakness.

Panic clawed through her determination. Wild-eyed, she searched for an escape route. A place to be away from Larence, from this damn desert, from herself . . .

"Emmaline," he said softly, "it's okay to be afraid."

Okay to be afraid. The words slid through the chinks in her armor, swam like melted butter through her nervous system. One by one her trembling fingers stilled, the irritating chattering of her teeth subsided.

Okay to be afraid.

A single tenuous spark of hope flickered in the darkness of her fear. Was it? she wondered tentatively. Was it okay to admit she'd been afraid? That she was still afraid . . .

She ran her tongue along her lower lip and swallowed hard, then slowly tilted her face up. Shining, uncondemning green eyes stared down at her. Tendrils of curling warmth seemed to reach out to her, offering her a hand to cling to. A place to belong.

She stood riveted to the spot, afraid to move or even to breathe. All her life she'd waited for this moment. Waited for someone to say *I care*. And yet now that it was here—*might be here*, her mind qualified—she was afraid to believe. God help her, if she reached for the light he offered and found that it was an illusion, she didn't think she could survive it. The only thing that had kept her going since her parents' deaths was her stubborn independence. Nothing and no one had ever been important to her since. She wasn't weak and needful like her father. . . .

Until now. Until Larence. In his silent strength and understanding, he was offering her something she'd never even dreamed of: a safe harbor. A place to be weak and afraid.

Okay to be afraid.

Tears burned behind her eyes. A single drop slid down her face and burrowed into the corner of her mouth. The salty moisture slid along her tongue, and the taste of her own tears brought an image so strong, so unexpected, she almost buckled.

She was standing by her father's dead body. It was Christmas morning; just two days after her eleventh birthday. He was slumped facedown on the splintery, lopsided kitchen table. Even now she could hear the plop, plop, plop of his still warm blood splattering the hardwood floor. Terrified, she'd reached out, her fingers pale and shaking in the room's insufficient light. *Daddy—*

"Emma?"

Larence's voice ripped her out of the past. She yanked

her hand out of his grasp and wiped the humiliating tears off her face. But another tear fell, and another. Faster than she could wipe, tears squeezed past her lashes and coursed down her face. She was crying, for God's sake. *Crying*.

Cold, dark panic swirled at the edges of her mind. She wrenched the crumpled, dirty handkerchief out of her pocket and raised it to her face.

He grabbed her hand. "Let them fall, Em. I'll take care of you."

The simple sentence made Emma's breath catch. It was one she'd never heard before, and long since despaired of ever hearing. She thought about Larence for the first time, really *thought* about him. About the way he'd let her use his arm at the train station and let her keep her pride by pretending *he* needed the support; about the way he smiled at her, as if he *liked* her; about the thousand tiny things he'd done to make the trip easier on her.

Okay to be afraid. Slowly the words took on a new meaning; gave her new hope. Maybe, she thought for the first time in her life. Just maybe, with Larence beside her, they were true. . . .

Chapter Sixteen

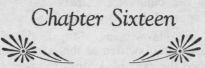

Larence gathered her into his arms.

She closed her eyes and leaned forward, letting her forehead rest on his chin. His day's growth of beard prickled her flesh, reminding her of times long gone. A father long gone.

At the memory, her last remnant of control shattered. She gave a great, heaving sigh and let the tears come.

One after another they fell. She began crying for herself, for the fear and uncertainty and pain of this expedition, for her new poverty.

Then, inexplicably, she was crying for all of it: for the mother who'd died too young, for the dream-laden father who'd been too weak to live without his much-loved wife, for the child who'd wandered the dark slums in search of food when she should have been curled in her mother's arms.

Emma shivered. Larence's arms wrapped more tightly around her trembling body, held her close. Warmth seeped from his body to hers, taking the edge off the chill in her soul and reminding her forcibly that she was in New Mexico. Far, far away from the apple vendor and his fat, greasy hands.

"It's okay . . ." He whispered the words above her head. Over and over. She knew they should make her feel stupid and childish, but they didn't. Coming from Larence, they made her feel safe and cared for. For the first time in years she felt . . . protected.

She burrowed closer to his chest. The scent of damp cotton and salty tears clung to the fabric of his shirt, filled her nostrils.

Gradually the terrible trembling in her limbs melted away. The torrent turned into a halting, sniffling drizzle, then trailed off altogether. She felt warm and cozy and . . . and what? Something elusive, something she'd never felt before.

At peace, she realized. She felt at peace.

She tried to remember a time she hadn't been afraid, hadn't felt alone and lonely and one step ahead of something dark and terrible. She thought perhaps that once, long ago, before poverty killed her mother and weakness her father, she'd felt this way all the time.

She couldn't be sure, of course. It had all been so long ago. . . .

"Em?"

She stiffened, afraid suddenly to look at him. Uncertainty filled her. No one had ever seen her like this, weak and afraid and needy. How should she act? What should she say?

His forefinger slid beneath her chin and forced her gaze up. At the sight of his green eyes, so clear and uncondemning, something wonderful unfurled in her soul.

She tried to smile. The effort resulted in a trembling, hesitant tightening of her lips. "Thanks." The knot in her throat made it impossible to say more—even if she had been able to think of something else worth saying.

"My pleasure," he said with a grin that sent warmth

sliding through her body. "God knows my shirt needed the washing."

Unexpected laughter crept up Emma's throat. She almost clamped a hand over her mouth to stifle the sound, then thought: *What the hell.*

She was as surprised as he by the bright, musical sound of her own laughter. It had been so long since she'd heard it. Larence joined her, and their mingled laughter bounced off the mesa's tall stone walls and echoed through the night.

Emma stared up at him. A breeze wandered through the campsite, ruffling his hair. Moonlight cast him in a cameo of pale blue light. Her breath caught. The laughter died in her throat and was replaced by a quiet sigh of wonder. In that instant she realized how truly handsome he was, how his eyes weren't simply green, but rather the color of magnolia leaves after a rain.

The moment spun out, seemed to lengthen. Larence's laughter dwindled and died, and a thick, charged silence followed. A cloud drifted past the near-full moon. Velvet blackness wrapped around them, closed out the world beyond.

Before she even knew she was going to move, Emma had touched his face. She brushed a lock of hair from his eyes. Her hand strayed to the strong, straight line of his cheekbone and followed it in a single, brushing stroke.

Words, dozens and dozens of them, turned through her mind, but not a single one made it as far as her mouth. What could she say to this man who'd rescued her, not once, but twice? Who'd given her back her smile and made her *laugh*?

Silence stretched around them, broken only by the gentle duet of their breathing. Overhead, the wispy black cloud covering the moon moved on, and an undulating blue-white pall stole across the shadowy desert. A breeze picked up in the east and blew gently through the campsite, jiggling the dancing flames as it passed. Light throbbed in the darkness.

And still they stood there. Quiet. Content.

Finally Larence broke the spell. His hands slid down her arms and dropped to his sides. "I better go get Diablo and the mule. They'll be needing some water and grain."

He started to walk away, and Emma grabbed his hand. "Stop!" The minute the word was out of her mouth, Emma wished it back. What was wrong with her? Surely she could be alone a few minutes. She'd been alone all her life.

But it wasn't that she was afraid to be alone. She just didn't want to be. Something had happened between them tonight, something special, and she didn't want to let it go, not even for a moment. It might never come back.

He turned back to her, his left eyebrow lifted upward in a silent question. She wanted to answer him with a flip, sarcastic retort that showed how strong she was, how in control. But nothing came to mind. Not a single syllable.

"I'll be right back," he said, giving her hand a squeeze that said *I understand*.

She forced a shaky smile. Of course he'd be back, she told herself. What had happened between them wasn't a tangible thread that would drift away like a spider's web if tested. It was a thick rope, a lifeline. Something strong and lasting.

Right then she made up her mind to change. No more

Miss Selfish on this expedition. From now on they were partners. Share and share alike.

The decision lifted a huge load off her shoulders. For the first time since her parents had died, she felt hopeful. From now on, she was a new person. A better one.

"No," she said firmly. "I'll go. I know it's painful for you to walk."

He offered her his hand. "How 'bout we go together?"

Together. It was as if she were hearing the word for the first time. "Sure," she said, slipping her fingers between his. Strangely, it felt *right* to be holding his hand. "We'll go together."

She'd helped him feed and water the animals, and set up the tent. And she'd done it with a smile. A *smile*.

Larence shook his head, still amazed.

Now, replete from a satisfying dinner of canned beans and gooey rice, he stared across the fire at Emma, watching her stack the last clean pan in the box. The sight of her brought another smile to his face.

Orange-yellow flames snapped and hissed and filled the quiet darkness with staccato bursts of sound. Sparks gilded the night air. Behind them, the animals stood quietly, their heads bowed low to the ground. Moonlight filtered through the trees overhead and cast a thousand glasslike shards of blue-white light upon the shadowy earth.

Larence reached forward. Wrapping a dish towel around the pot's blackened handle, he eased the pot off the stove and carefully poured two cupfuls of steaming evaporated milk. After adding a dash of cinnamon and sugar in each, he handed one to Emma.

She took the cup silently, curling her fingers around

the hot metal and lifting it to her face. A thin stream of steam caressed her mouth. She closed her eyes, as if savoring the feel of the wet warmth against her lips.

He took advantage of her closed eyes, and settled back to study her.

Tonight had changed her. It was as if, before the tears, she'd been as much a cripple as he, trapped in a cage wrought of fear instead of pain. Somehow, sometime, she'd gotten it in her head that it was weak to cry, and that it was bad to be weak. And so she'd been strong. Viciously, self-destructively strong.

Until tonight. Tonight she'd finally let go of that iron will and let herself be frail.

She opened her eyes suddenly and caught him looking at her. His breath hesitated. He waited for her to turn away, but she didn't. She just sat there, inches away and perfectly still, returning his gaze. He felt his heart slow to a snail's pace then speed up.

Her beauty struck him like a blow. He'd always thought she was flawlessly, coldly beautiful, like a marble statue. But now, with the pain gone from her eyes and a soft smile shaping her lips, she was a Madonna— a flesh-and-blood woman of incredible loveliness. And it was he—Larence Alexander Digby—who'd erased the pain from her eyes and made her smile.

The realization brought a quiet sense of wonder. For the first time in his life, he felt . . . important. Special.

A sigh of breeze swept through the camp, ruffled through her hair. Strands clung to her nose and mouth. She eased the hair from her face and tucked it behind her ear. Her tongue glided along her lower lip, leaving a glistening trail.

Something deep inside Larence clenched. Sweat dampened his palms.

Love. The word came out of nowhere, driving through his thoughts like a locomotive. He could fall in love with Emmaline.

Never had he believed that he would be given the gift of love. He'd told himself a thousand times that love didn't happen to men like him; men who were inexperienced and tongue-tied and . . . crippled.

And yet, here it was, fluttering around him like a butterfly. He could feel the petal-soft whirring of its wings even now, brushing against his heart.

It was dangerous, he knew, this business of falling in love. More dangerous even than their quest, because Emma would never return his love. Affection, yes. Respect, hopefully. But love? Never.

Women like her didn't fall in love with men like him.

No, if he fell in love, it would be alone. Unreturned. Unrequited.

So what?

Hadn't he waited all his life for the chance to feel what other men felt? Wasn't that the reason he'd embarked on this journey in the first place? To be like other men?

He wouldn't run from the opportunity to fall in love; not even if it meant he'd be in love alone. Even if it meant getting hurt. After all, he'd been alone all his life, and he'd learned long ago to deal with pain, both physical and emotional. He could certainly handle the pain of eventually losing her.

Better to have loved and lost . . .

He smiled. Yes, he could handle it.

And yet, even as he thought it, he knew there was another answer. . . .

"Larence? Do you know where we are?"

The sound of her voice was so unexpected, he almost

jumped. Running a hand through his tangled hair, he shook his head. "Nope. But don't worry, I'll figure it out. I know you're in a hurry and I want to—"

"Not anymore."

She spoke so quietly, it took Larence a second to realize he'd been interrupted. He turned to her, and the look in her eyes made his throat go dry. He felt as if he'd just been given an extraordinary Christmas gift. The desire, almost a need, to touch her swelled through his body, made his fingers tingle.

Dangerous, he thought again. Very dangerous . . .

That night Larence woke up with a start and sat bolt-upright in bed.

At first he thought a nightmare had wakened him. Groggily he rubbed his eyes.

Then he remembered: *the marking*. How had he forgotten it?

Fear made his heart hammer in his chest. His breathing accelerated, sounding loud and serrated in the tent's darkness.

Calm down. Calm down.

Slowly he lay back down. His head settled into the warm pillow of his folded jeans. Beside him, Emma slept peacefully on.

He squeezed his eyes shut, wishing he could just go back to sleep and forget all about Ka-Neek and his dangerous message.

But of course, he couldn't. He lay wide-awake, thinking, his eyes staring blankly into the darkness. He didn't believe there was any real danger—if Ka-Neek had wanted them dead, they'd be dead.

The real danger lay in Emmaline's reaction. If she

got scared, or didn't trust in Larence's instincts, she'd want to turn around. For her the quest would end.

His stomach twisted into a hard, cold knot. The thought of losing her now, when they'd come so far and been through so much, made him feel sick to his stomach. Something had happened between them last night; they'd begun forming a bond. But their new feelings for each other were tangible threads, too easily broken, and once the strands snapped, they would never be forged again.

There's one thing you could do to keep her. . . .

Larence was disappointed in himself for even thinking it. Yet he couldn't stop himself. There was a surefire way to keep her—if he were willing to lie. A single untruth would keep his quest safe. And not even an active lie; just a simple failure to speak. *What she didn't know about couldn't frighten her.*

He had to admit it sounded good.

But he couldn't do that to her. She was an intelligent woman who deserved to have all the facts. If she chose—and he prayed she didn't—to leave him and the expedition, it was her choice.

The morning dawned crisp and clear. Sunlight glowed through the tent's white canvas, and still Larence lay wide-awake. Waiting. With each minute that passed, each second, he felt the noose tightening around his neck. *She'll leave you.*

"Morning, Larence," she said quietly beside him.

He flinched, stared straight ahead. "M-Morning."

"Is something the matter? You look . . . tense."

With a ragged, tired breath, he rolled onto his side and found himself looking directly into Emma's eyes. Close enough to see the tiny network of sleep lines that crisscrossed her cheeks, he felt an almost overwhelming urge to take her in his arms and hold her tight. To lie to her and pretend nothing had changed.

He wrenched his gaze away from her face and dug into his jeans pocket. Pulling out the scrap of leather, he tossed it onto her bag. It landed with a muffled plop.

Emmaline picked it up, studied it. Then she looked over at him, a frown etched in the valley between her eyebrows.

"It's a Cibollan marking," he answered her unspoken query.

"Where did you get it?"

"Ka-Neek left it by the fire."

"What does it mean?"

He felt as if a great weight were pressing down on his lungs. When at last he spoke, he barely recognized his own voice in the haggard words. "It's the ancient symbol for danger."

She went perfectly still; so still, he couldn't even see the steady rise and fall of her chest. The color seeped slowly out of her cheeks. "Is it a warning or a threat?"

"I don't know."

She lifted her gaze to his. It seemed to take forever before she spoke. "If Ka-Neek wanted us dead, we'd be dead. But it doesn't matter, anyway, does it? We're going forward."

He hadn't known he was holding his breath until that moment. "It could be dangerous."

She laughed. "Hell, Larence, I've lost a fortune, almost died alone in the desert, and been kidnapped. And that's just since Monday."

He smiled, as proud of her in that moment as he'd ever been of anyone in his life. She had the courage of a lioness. "Not alone, Em," he said quietly, "never alone."

After breakfast, Larence got out the diary, his map of the area, and his compass. As he settled in to do a few computations, Emmaline came up beside him.

"You know, Larence," she said tentatively, "I was thinking . . ."

"About what? General Electric?"

She flashed him a smile. "About that mesa behind us. I know I'm no explorer, but the damn thing seems big enough to be on *somebody's* map."

Larence cocked his head and looked over his shoulder.

The blood drained from his face. "Oh, my God!" He lurched unsteadily to his feet, spilling coffee down his pant leg as he turned around to study the mesa. He took a few cautious steps backward, then a few more and a few more until he was practically running backward.

"Larence!"

Through a distant, detached part of his mind, he heard Emmaline calling to him, but the words sounded far away and unimportant. Turning, he ran as fast and as far as his bad leg would allow, until, wheezing for breath, he finally stopped and turned around. Now he could see the whole thing.

The mesa rose out of the grass-strewn plain like a huge, flat-topped table of red rock. Behind it the sky was an intense, cloudless blue. He dropped to his knees in awe.

The Sky City. It had to be, though it was bigger than he'd ever imagined. He knew from his research that the mesa was 365 feet tall, but he'd never realized how *high* 365 feet was.

He lurched to his feet again, ignoring the pain caused by the sudden movement. The early morning scents of pine resin, blue lupine, and nameless wild things wafted to his nostrils, but he didn't notice. Not this time. All he could see now was the city he'd read about since childhood. *Acoma.* The Sky City. Quite possibly the oldest continually inhabited pueblo in the country.

On the mesas's top, something glinted in the harsh sunlight. Excitement surged through Larence's blood. He tented his hand over his eyes and squinted, trying to see. Maybe it was the light glancing off a knife blade, or a woman's silver earring, or—

He heard the quiet, steady crunching of Emmaline's heels in the dirt and felt an almost blinding joy that she was here with him. To have someone with whom to share this moment was the answer to his every boyhood dream.

He grabbed her hand and pulled her close, pointing at the mesa. "That's Acoma."

"A what?"

"Acoma. The Sky City."

Emma squinted into the rising sun. "City?" she repeated doubtfully.

He nodded eagerly. "There's a whole city full of people on top of it. Some claim the pueblo was founded as early as 600 A.D."

"Wait a minute, you mean that's *the* city?"

"No," he answered with a laugh. "Ka-Neek wasn't *that* nice. He probably thought he was taking us miles out of the way, but what he actually did was take us to the diary's starting point. Esteban's recorded journey began here, at the base of the Sky City."

"Acoma." She said the word a couple of times, as if trying to remember where she'd heard it. Then, finally, she shook her head and muttered, "Worthless book."

"What book?"

"I learned history from a book called *The History of the United States Told in One-Syllable Words*. I knew it was sort of . . . abbreviated, but I didn't think the damn thing was wrong."

Larence chuckled. "It's not wrong, not according to most other books. The men who wrote the books—all the books—care only about white man's history.

"But look around you, Em. This is the birthplace of this country. The real core. The Anasazi, the Ancient Ones, were here, living and building, while the Europeans were living on a flat continent surrounded by make-believe sea monsters."

His words tugged at her, tapping into some deep, fundamental emotion. Emma found herself getting caught up in his excitement. For the first time she had an inkling about what this trip was about. About what it meant.

"We could prove it to the world," he said quietly. "We could show everyone that Jamestown wasn't the first important settlement in this country."

"How?"

He took her hands in his and stared down at her. "Cibola. Think about it, Em. You and I can change history, right an ancient wrong. If we find Cibola, the world will be forced to acknowledge the Pueblo Indians. Everyone will know that the first Americans were great artisans and great builders—like the Egyptians and the Romans." His voice dropped, caught. "And even more important, the Indian children will see proof of their forefathers' greatness, and they will hold their heads up with pride.''

Tears stung Emma's eyes, blurred her vision. When had she ever cared about anything except the almighty dollar? And what had she ever given the world, except a few more gold coins?

Then sanity returned. Ruthlessly she quelled the traitorous emotions that threatened everything she believed in. Everything she'd spent a lifetime working for.

He'd tricked her, damn him, tricked her with his puppy-dog eyes and wistful voice. And she'd been such easy prey. *She*, who should know better, had been tricked by pretty words and grandiose dreams. . . .

Fairy tales were something she knew a great deal about; her father had spun a thousand of them for her, each grander and more farfetched than the last. For years she'd even *believed*.

She'd been about seven years old when reality had hit—and hit hard. She'd awakened early that morning, freezing cold and hungry. Tugging the worn, holey blanket tighter around her shivering body, she'd glanced at their room. And in that gloomy predawn morning she'd finally seen the place for what it was. Not Cinderella's temporary home, but a dark, dank, cheerless hovel.

From then on she'd seen the world through her own eyes, not her father's. She stopped waiting for the prince to rescue her from the coldness of her home and stopped believing in her father's schemes to bring them wealth. Never again had useless imaginary dreams reached her.

Until now. She glared up at Larence. She felt— absurdly—betrayed. He *wanted* her to feel this way, wanted her to care about a bunch of long-dead people and their way of life. That's why he'd told her his story.

Well, his teary-eyed dramatics and rambling on about a few Indian children wouldn't work. She wouldn't let it.

Oh, she might let herself change. Might make the occasional dinner or roll up the sleeping bags, might even let herself be Larence's friend. But change only went so far. Being a better person didn't include being a poverty-stricken person. No way.

She'd never change when it came to how she viewed money. She couldn't afford to.

Neither could she afford to get tangled up with Larence's vision. Dreams were a useless waste of time.

Larence could change the world if he wanted to. His kind always did. People who'd never been poor could give money to charity and sleep with a clear conscience. But those who'd eaten off the street and slept in the dark on a cold floor didn't care much about the pride of a few small children. They couldn't afford to.

She couldn't afford to.

Changing history wasn't her dream, and she wouldn't let herself be swayed by its seductive pull. She was in this for the gold. Beautiful, shining gold.

She might let herself cry in front of Larence, might even let herself like him, but the one thing she'd never, ever do was let him steal her future. It was all she had; all she ever hoped to have.

Half the gold was hers, by God. Indian children or no Indian children, half that gold was hers.

And she intended to get it.

Chapter Seventeen

That day Emma finally rode beside Larence like an equal. A short equal, she admitted with a smile, but an equal nonetheless. She tented a hand over the brim of her straw hat, extending the shade a small bit, and glanced up at him. He was a foot or so above her, sitting tall and proud in the saddle.

She shook her head in amazement, still unable to believe the change he'd wrought with a simple whisper. Emma had tried to get Tashee to give up her favored spot at Diablo's tail for days; she'd kicked, screamed, hit, and pleaded with the little burro, and all to no avail.

Not so Larence. He'd whispered once and patted Tashee's neck. A whisper and a pat—that's it, and voilà! Tashee trotted eagerly to Diablo's side as if that was where she'd wanted to be from the beginning.

Maybe there's a lesson in that. . . .

A quiet, companionable silence filled the air. Now and again Larence pointed out and named some bush or animal, and surprisingly, Emma found herself *listening* to him, and if she allowed herself to admit it (and she wasn't entirely sure that was a good idea), even enjoying his soft-spoken monologue.

But now he was silent. The hot sun pressed down on

them, made Emma slump lazily on Tashee's back. She swayed side to side, her thoughts far away and pleasant.

She was so relaxed, it took her a moment to realize that something was different. There was a noise. And out in the great, waterless alone, that was something worth taking note of.

She straightened, listened.

The sound increased, drew close. *Pitter-pat-pitter-pat.*

She looked down and couldn't believe her eyes. A bird—quite possibly the ugliest one she'd ever seen— was running along beside them. Running!

As if aware of her scrutiny, the funny-looking little bird cocked his head at her. Beady eyes stared up at her, and she thought for one amazing moment that he actually *smiled* at her.

"Larence, look!"

The second she spoke, the bird lowered his head again and dashed forward, zipping in and out of the animals' path like a drunken sailor and then disappearing in the distance.

Larence didn't even glance at the bird. He was looking at her with a cocky grin. "Noticing wildlife, are we?" he drawled. "I've got this notebook . . ."

Emma couldn't help laughing. Lord, she felt . . . good. It had been years—forever—since she'd been so relaxed and ready to smile.

And it was all because of Larence.

She felt . . . comfortable with him. She shook her head in disbelief. Who would have thought it possible? In all the years she'd known Eugene, she'd never once felt comfortable or relaxed around him.

Comfortable. The word conjured all sorts of ordinary images—images she'd spent a lifetime banishing to the darkest corner of her mind. *Holding hands. Whispering. Laughing. Walking in the park on Sunday. Cuddling . . .*

Images that no longer seemed frightening or the least bit threatening. In fact, now she wondered how she'd lived so long in fear of such simple emotions.

Maybe if she hadn't worried so much about ending up like her father . . .

But she *had* worried about it. Every day and every night of her life she'd worried about needing someone so desperately that she couldn't survive without that person. The fear had kept her bound up so tightly, she'd never unfurled, never let herself even consider what she was missing.

Until Larence. With his simple declaration, *It's okay to be afraid*, he'd offered her a light. A way out of the darkness.

She thanked God she had taken it.

"Let's stop for lunch."

Emma groaned in relief. They'd been riding for hours. She pulled back on Tashee's reins and slid from the animal's back before the little burro had even stopped moving.

"I'll make something to eat in a second, Larence," she said, staggering over to a piñon tree and collapsing in the shade beneath its lowest branch. "Just give me a second to die."

She closed her eyes and leaned back, resting her head against the thin trunk. A shower of greenish gray needles sprinkled her face and throat. The sharp, refreshing scent of pine surrounded her. Absentmindedly she wiped the needles away. She'd just rest for a few short minutes, then she'd get up and pull her weight.

"Lunch is ready."

She sat bolt-upright. Guilt made her wince. "I fell asleep?"

Larence studied her over the rim of his coffee cup. "It's okay," he said quietly, "I like watching you sleep."

Something hot and dry curled in Emma's throat. His eyes were like pools of promise, beckoning and calling to her. Holding her. *Trust me,* those eyes said. *Smile with me.*

She did. "What are we having?"

"Canned stew."

She groaned. "Again?"

He grinned. "Come on, it's not that bad. Besides, I was hoping that if I kept serving you canned beans, maybe one day I'd get lucky."

She eyed him suspiciously. "What do you mean?"

"Maybe you'll make real stew. I've got plenty of dried beef and beef extract—all you need is a few herbs and plants."

She ambled over to the fire and sat down beside him. "What do I look like, Molly the pioneer wife? I wouldn't know an edible herb from a lump of coal."

"There's a book in my saddlebag that'll tell you everything you need to know."

A picture of herself "herb-hunting" flashed through Emma's mind and made her smile. "I'd probably serve up a tasty batch of poisonous mushrooms and kill us both over coffee."

Twilight had turned the night sky a brilliant fusion of bright pink and canary yellow when Emma noticed the small cabin in the distance. "Look, Larence. Over there."

Larence reined Diablo to a stop and started digging through his saddlebags for his map. Carefully unfolding the yellowed paper, he studied the landmark indications Dr. Stanton had made.

After a long moment, he shook his head. "I don't know. There isn't supposed to be anything here. I wonder if we're off course."

Emma groaned. They'd been riding for hours and hours. If they were riding the wrong way—

"No," he said more to himself than to her, "I know this is right."

"I hope so," she said.

He grinned down at her, and Emma couldn't help smiling back. "Let's go find out if anyone's home."

Half an hour later, they reached the cabin's front gate. By then the shadows had thickened to ankle-deep curls along the ground; the dwelling lay shrouded in shifting patterns of charcoal gray and midnight black.

The crude wooden structure, butted up close to a low, bloodred rimrock bench, looked lonely and deserted. No smoke spiraled up from the brick chimney; no welcoming light escaped the closed windows.

"Looks like no one's home," Larence said, and Emma could hear the disappointment in his voice.

Then she smelled the pungent scent of burning tobacco.

She sat up taller, sniffing, listening, looking.

Beside the west wall a shadow stirred; then came the barely heard crunching of tiny rocks.

Emma straightened. "Who's there?"

An old Indian man, leaning heavily on a gnarled walking stick, emerged from the darkness. Larence dismounted and limped eagerly to the man, his hand outstretched in greeting. "Hi there. I'm Dr. Larence Digby, and this is my associate, Emmaline Hatter."

The old man stared at Larence's hand for a long time, and then very slowly—and, Emma thought, reluctantly—slipped his own skeletal hand into Larence's palm. "*Hai*. I am Pa-lo-wah-ti," he said in a voice that sounded like the rusty turning of long-unused wheels. "There is not much food inside, but you may share what I have."

"Thanks, but—" Emma spoke quickly.

"We'd love to," Larence finished for her.

Pa-lo-wah-ti picked up a lantern. Striking a match, he lit the wick, and was immediately bathed in light.

The first thing Emma noticed was his eyes. She swallowed hard, fighting the shiver of fear that trailed down her back at the sight of them. They were blue and yet not blue. The color of pale seawater muddied by foam. Pale, pale.

Blind, she realized suddenly. He was blind.

Emma finally tore her gaze away from his eerie, sightless eyes and noticed his strange attire. He was bareheaded, his stringy gray hair cut in a no-nonsense shelf across his eyebrows and drawn in a tight knot at the base of his neck. Two thick locks swung freely on either side of his hollowed face, just brushing his shoulders. He wore a black shirt and red cotton pantalets, slitted from the knee down to expose pencil-thin legs and moccasined feet. A dozen or so strands of beads coiled around his neck, seeming to drag his head down with their weight.

Without a word, he turned and disappeared into the cabin.

It wasn't until much, much later that Emma thought

to wonder how the blind man had known to shake Larence's hand.

Larence couldn't believe their luck.

He turned the animals loose in the small corral out back, then followed Pa-lo-wah-ti into the cabin. Lantern light brightened the room, casting fingers of warmth across the scarred, lopsided table and the rusted iron stove. Burlap sacks of corn hung from the thick rafters, giving off a sweet, homey scent. Pale moonlight turned the window into a perfect square of tarnished silver.

Pa-lo-wah-ti pointed to one of the rawhide-covered chairs. "Sit."

Larence did. Emmaline didn't. She stood at the doorway, her hands clasped nervously together. She looked hesitant to enter the dwelling.

Larence turned in his chair, pinning an implacable, uncompromising stare on her. "Sit down. Pa-lo-wah-ti has offered to share a meal with us." He waited for her to move. When she didn't, he added, "It's an *honor*. Now, *sit down*."

Reluctantly she crossed the room, her skirts swirling atop the planked floor and sending up spirals of pale gray dust. At the table, she lowered herself to the rickety chair. The rusted wires screeched in agony at her weight. She sat stiffly, her hands folded tightly in her lap.

Pa-lo-wah-ti served thick strips of a colorless meat wrapped in wafer-thin cornmeal tortillas. Larence couldn't help grinning. Here he was, on the road to Cibola, having dinner with a man who could well be a direct descendant of the first true Americans, and eating his first real Indian meal.

He felt something jab him in the side. Distractedly Larence glanced up from the steaming food on his plate.

Emma was staring at him. The first thing he noticed was the lack of color in her cheeks. The second thing was the way her lips were drawn into that tense Wall Street grimace.

He frowned. "Are you all right?"

Pa-lo-wah-ti looked up from his plate. "Yes."

Emma threw the old man an exasperated look. Then she turned her full attention on Larence. Her gaze shot down to the food, then cut back to his face. Her eyes bulged in silent question.

"What?" he asked.

She leaned closer. "What is it?" she hissed under her breath.

Larence shrugged. "Who cares? It's great."

Emma sighed impatiently. "*I* care. I'm not about to—"

"Snake," came Pa-lo-wah-ti's time- and tobacco-graveled voice from across the table.

"Snake?" Emma's fork hit the table with a clang.

"Really?" Larence took another bite, marveling at the chickenlike taste. "You ought to try it, Em. It's really good."

"I'm sure it is," she said, pushing her plate toward the center of the table. "Reptile meat has always been a favorite of mine."

After that, no one said a word. A few times Larence tried to start a conversation, but the Indian seemed more inclined to stare at him and Emmaline than he did to speak. Finally Larence accepted that the man was a loner, and simply shut up.

After the meal was eaten and the few tin dishes

washed, Pa-lo-wah-ti said, "There is but one sleeping room. You will sleep outside."

"Certainly," Larence said. "Is there somewhere we can wash up? We've been on the road a long time and we're pretty dirty."

"There is a shower outside by the snubbing post. You may use that."

With quick thanks, Larence grabbed his saddlebags and headed outside.

Emma was left alone with the old man. Repeatedly she told herself it was foolish to be afraid of an old blind man. There was nothing *wrong* with him; certainly he wasn't evil or mean or dangerous.

But she couldn't quite believe it. Whenever those muddy, sightless blue eyes landed on her, a chill splashed down her stiffened spine. Silence stretched between them, thick and uncomfortable. She cleared her throat, forcibly unwinding the bloodless ball of her fingers. "Is there something I can do to help . . ."

"Leave." The word came unexpectedly, jarring Emma to sit up straighter.

"Leave? You want us—"

He turned suddenly. His narrowed eyes hit on her face with an accuracy that made Emma's stomach lurch.

A slow smile spread through the brown wrinkles. But it was a smile that didn't reach his eyes. "I am making a joke, of course. You will forgive a senile old man for speaking out of turn. I am happy to have you and your man here."

Before Emma could say *he's not my man*, Pa-lo-wah-ti shuffled across the room and entered his bedroom. The door clicked shut behind him.

Emma stared at the closed door. Senile? she thought with a grim tightening of her mouth. Hardly. The old man might be many things, but senile wasn't one of them.

He wanted them to leave. He hadn't meant to say it, perhaps, but he meant it.

The question was, did he want them to leave his home—or New Mexico?

Emma stepped outside, closing the door quietly behind her. The balmy night wrapped her in velvety warmth. She crossed her arms tightly across her chest and let her head loll back against the splintery door, reveling in the wind's soft caress against her cheeks. The thin fabric of her underskirt fluttered in the breeze, lapped against her legs.

"Hi, Em."

Larence's voice mingled with the sounds of the night and made her smile. Forgetting her ridiculous fear of the old man, she glanced up and started to wave. Her hand froze in midair. The reciprocal greeting jammed in her throat and fractured.

He was standing near a structure that looked like a small women's dressing room with a wooden barrel suspended above it. Behind him, the corral was a collection of slow-moving shadows. The slivered moon hung high in the night-dark sky, a scythe of the purest gold.

Pale lantern light haloed his half-naked body. He stood tall, proud, his long legs sheathed in tight, dripping-wet jeans.

Emma's gaze snagged at the top button of his pants. It was open. Invitingly open. She swallowed hard and forced her eyes up. Her gaze skidded up the wet, hair-darkened muscles of his chest and landed on his face.

Grinning, he ran a hand through his wet hair and shook his head. Water dripped down the side of his face and plopped onto his shoulder. Light reflected off the drops of water, turning them into diamond chips. Mesmerized, she watched a single droplet zigzag down his chest, through the soft matting of hair that veed his collarbone. Like a streak of sterling, it glided down his flat stomach and disappeared into the slack, open waistband of his Levi's.

Something irritatingly akin to desire made her breathing speed up. She brought a shaking hand to her throat.

"Come on over. The water's great."

Her feet turned to stone. She stood there for what seemed like hours, her hand plastered protectively to her throat, her gaze pinned on his eyes. Only his eyes.

He flashed her a challenging smile. "You want me to come and get you?"

"No!" Setting her chin at a defiant tilt, she plucked up her skirt and headed across the backyard. With each step, it seemed he grew taller. More naked. Her confident step faltered.

When she reached him, Larence slung a still damp towel around his neck and hung on to both ends. "It's a shower—can you believe it? No Motts' Needle Shower, maybe, but a shower."

Another droplet plopped onto his chest—right next to his nipple. It bumped over the puckered brown circle and glided downward. Emma swallowed hard and bolted into the shower, banging the door shut behind her. Safe now, she gave a shaky sigh and leaned her forehead against the door's cool, damp wood.

She was having a physical reaction to Larence. Unbelievable.

She closed her eyes and tried to slow the rabbit-fast patter of her heart. They were friends, for God's sake. Not lovers.

It was celibacy, she realized. She'd been too long
without a man in her bed. Eyeing the rain barrel suspended overhead, she smiled. Yes, a cold shower was
precisely what she needed.

She stripped off her shirtwaist and skirt and slung
them over the side. At the removal of the dreaded corset, she let her breath out in a long, appreciative sigh
of freedom. The torture device fell to a heap at her feet.

As she unbuttoned the top button of her chemise, she
noticed the small brown package sitting on the bench
beside her. She picked it up, turning it over in her
hands. "Larence, you left something in here," she
yelled.

"It's for you."

Frowning, she untied the strings and peeled back the
brown paper wrapping.

Her breath caught. It was the skirt and blouse Dr.
Stanton had given her.

Gratitude at Larence's thoughtfulness filled her. It was
so like him to think of her comfort—even back in Albuquerque when she'd been so spiteful toward him. She
could just imagine how it had happened: After Emma
had stuck her nose in the air and informed Dr. Stanton
that "Emmaline Amanda Hatter didn't dress like a
Mexican peasant," Larence had no doubt whispered to
his friend. *Give them to me, Henry; she might change
her mind. . . .*

Emma smiled. Carefully setting the blouse—what had
Dr. Stanton called it, a *camisa*?—and skirt out of the
way, she pulled the cap off the rain barrel's exposed
pipe. Cool water splashed her face and plastered her
dirty cotton chemise and petticoat to her body.

She scrubbed every trace of dirt from her body and
clothes, then peeled off the clinging wet undergarments

and slapped them over her woolen skirt. Standing directly beneath the pipe's mouth, she lolled her head back. The water splashed her exposed throat and pelted her breasts and arms. Beneath her feet the planked floor rattled from the onslaught.

She stood there until her skin felt tingly and alive and *clean*. God, she'd forgotten how good it felt to simply be clean.

Finally, reluctantly, she replugged the pipe and dried off. Plaiting her waist-length hair, she flung the thick skein over one shoulder and picked up the *camisa*. It was cotton, the hue of faded denim, with long, full sleeves and a drawstring neckline. Small gold buttons marched single file from neckline to hem. A pale gold string peeked in a dotted line along the shoulders and throat, coming together in a little bow in the center.

She shoved her arms through the sleeves. The blouse fluttered around her head for a second, then slid into place. She plucked the drawstring taut, and found to her dismay that the top of the sleeves came no higher than the crests of her shoulder. Her entire neck and collarbone area was exposed, as was a good swell of breast. And with no underwear on underneath, the outline of her nipple was unmistakable.

She shivered. The moist fabric clung to her naked breasts. Without a chemise, the feel of the damp cotton against her nipples was strangely erotic.

It was entirely too revealing, of course, but there was nothing she could do about that—other than putting her dirty clothes back on. And there was no way she'd do that.

Slipping into the skirt, she exited the showering area. When she was halfway to the campfire, Larence looked up.

Their eyes met and held. There was something in his gaze she hadn't seen before. It sent an icy-hot shiver through her body. She ground to a halt, suddenly acutely aware of her nakedness beneath the skirt and blouse. A sigh of breeze slid through the campsite, jostling the fire and teasing the flyaway hairs around her face. At the sudden chill, her nipples hardened, poked against the thin cotton. She felt surprisingly . . . desirable.

Larence cleared his throat and looked away.

Emma wrapped her arms around herself, tilted her chin, and walked resolutely to the fire.

They sat there for a long time, side by side, both lost in their own thoughts; Larence staring up at the twinkling scattering of stars in the sky, Emma staring at the flames licking on the twisted mesquite root of their fire.

She wondered what he was thinking about.

He wondered what she was thinking about.

But neither of them said a word. Instead they listened to the quiet strains of their mingled breathing and the snapping crackle of the fire.

The cabin door cracked open and banged shut. Slow, shuffling footsteps came toward them.

Emma stiffened instinctively, shrinking toward Larence as the old man moved unerringly toward them.

"I join you," he said without question.

"Of course." Larence pointed to the rock across from them as if the man could see.

Pa-lo-wah-ti sat. Folding his wiry legs beneath him, the old man pulled a buckskin bag of tobacco and a cigarette paper out of his breast pocket. Rolling a smoke with quick, sure fingers, he stuck the pointed end in his seamed lips and lit up. Smoke curled across his face. His eyes narrowed, boring through the gray cloud to fix on Larence. "What brings you here?"

The words were spoken casually, but they sent a tendril of ice sliding down Emma's back. Perhaps it was the tone of his voice—deceptively low, with a razor edge—perhaps it was the complete lack of question in the question. She didn't know. But something bothered her. . . .

Larence scooted forward. "Cibola."

A sharp, mirthless laugh shot past the dangling cigarette. "Legend. Myth."

"No—it's more."

Pa-lo-wah-ti pulled the cigarette out of his mouth and tapped it. Flecks of grayed ash fluttered to the shadowed earth. Then he, too, leaned forward, until his face and Larence's were almost touching. "Many have tried to find this place. All have failed. Some have died."

"I'm different."

Another harsh laugh. He leaned back. "How?"

"I have proof."

The old man took a long, wheezing drag and expelled a cloud of charcoal gray smoke. "There is no proof."

Emma looked into Larence's eyes at that moment and was reminded of the first time she'd met him. Once again the believer's passion shone from his eyes, turned them from comforting, bottle green eyes into something else. Something mystical and compelling.

Larence began slowly to speak.

"Three hundred years ago a priest named Fray Marcos de Niza set off with a few other priests and a Moorish slave named Esteban to find the famed Seven Cities of Cibola. As they walked northward from Mexico, through pueblo after pueblo, the Indians spoke of the Seven Cities; they told of riches beyond belief, of gold and silver and turquoise."

At the word "gold," Emma perked up.

"Fray Marcos sent Esteban ahead to scout for the Seven Cities, instructing him to send word back if Esteban found something of value. He was to send a 'white cross the size of Marcos's palm' if it was a good find; a larger cross if it was a great find; and an even larger cross if the find rivaled the Aztec riches. A few weeks later, Esteban sent the first cross."

"How big?" she breathed.

"It took two men and a mule to carry it."

"Tuh," Pa-lo-wah-ti repeated with a wave of his skeletal hand. "Children's stories."

"With respect, I disagree."

Anger flashed in the old man's muddy blue eyes. "Fray Marcos was a liar. He claimed to see the city with his own eyes, but when the Mexican government sent Coronado to rape the gold from Cibola, there was no city. None at all."

"True," Larence answered simply.

"Fray Marcos claimed to see the city?" Emma said with a frown. "What about Esteban?"

Larence grinned. "That's just it. Esteban sent two crosses—*two*—and then disappeared. The textbooks say he was killed during a battle at a pueblo east of here, but no one saw him fall. He just . . . *disappeared*. No one ever saw him again."

Pa-lo-wah-ti spat into the fire. The goo hissed on the log and turned into a spiral of gray steam. "You think Esteban, a heathen, matters?"

"He matters," Larence answered simply. "He and another man, a young Spaniard named Diego Parroquin de Escobar, found the city. And I found their diary."

Pa-lo-wah-ti puffed thoughtfully on his cigarette, his sightless eyes trained on Larence's downcast face. Wind swirled between them, jostling the yellow-gold flames until they quivered. The sharp scent of wildness, mingled with the pungent tang of cigarette smoke, gave the night a hard edge. "A dead man's words will not lead you to the city. That which seeks to remain hidden will not be found."

Larence looked up suddenly. His gaze captured the old man's, held it. They stared at each other for a long, breathless moment. The fire hissed, sending a spray of red-gold sparks in the night-dark air, and Emma felt a quiver of energy leap between the two men.

"I don't need the diary to find the city," Larence said in a soft, compelling voice. "That's just the proof I needed to get money. The real map is in here." He patted his heart. "I've seen the city a thousand times in my dreams."

For the first time, Pa-lo-wah-ti looked nonplussed. A frown pleated the tired skin between his bushy gray eyebrows. He looked at Larence sharply, and it seemed to Emma that the muddiness in his eyes evaporated, leaving twin ice blue pools. "A vision?" He took a deep, thoughtful drag. Smoke curled across his face. "Describe it."

"Streets paved with gold, hammered silver doors and doorways, turquoise windowsills . . . a great kiva hewn in a moon-shape against the red-gold sandstone, a pool the color of the finest jade . . ."

"Cibola." The word slipped out of the old man's mouth. Slowly he shook his head, spraying ash across his crossed legs. "This vision came disguised in sleep?"

"Dreams, yes."

Pa-lo-wah-ti eased the cigarette from his wrinkled lips and tapped the cone of gray ashes into the flames. His eyes never left Larence's face. "You are not like the other white men who have sought this place. You *believe*.''

''Yes.''

Emma couldn't contain her excitement another minute. ''Streets paved with gold—really? Silver doors—would that be *sterling* silver? And turq—''

''Emma.'' Her name was buried in a sigh of disappointment. ''Can't you see the *historic* value?''

Pa-lo-wah-ti shook his head, and a peculiar sadness flitted through his eyes. ''You are not like the other white men who have come, Larence; destroyers of the land and intruders on the past. But she is.''

''All I did was ask a sim—''

''Leave.'' At the hard, cold word, Emma's sentence stopped midstream. The old man stabbed her with his eerie, sightless and yet all-seeing eyes. ''Now. While you still can.''

The next day Emma woke slowly. Half the night she'd lain awake, wishing they could simply steal away from this deserted-looking homestead like thieves in the darkness. It was only the knowledge that Larence would laugh at her fears and suspicions that kept her from speaking out. And so she'd waited, patiently, all through the long, sleepless night. It had been nearly dawn when she'd finally fallen into a fitful, troubled sleep.

But now it was dawn, and it was time to go.

She pushed up to her elbows and brushed the thick curtain of hair from her eyes. Larence's sleeping bag was gone. She got tiredly to her knees and crawled toward the tent flap fluttering in the early morning breeze. She poked her head out and immediately squinted. The dawn was like all the late spring morn-ings before it: crisp and clear, with a sky so big and blue, it stung the eyes.

She turned around and crawled back into the tent. The pale, white canvas curled protectively around her. She plucked up her carefully folded clothing and felt a sharp surge of joy. New clothes!

Her corset slid out from its hiding place between the skirt and blouse. It plopped like a surrender flag onto the drab green fabric of her sleeping bag.

She groaned. The thought of worming her way into that torture device made her stomach drop.

Why bother? she thought suddenly. What good did it do out here in the middle of nowhere? An hourglass figure didn't mean anything if you couldn't breathe, and she hadn't taken a decent breath since arriving in this godforsaken state. She shoved the corset deep in her sleeping bag.

Feeling better than she had in weeks, she donned her clean underclothes and slipped into the new clothes. Crawling out of the tent, she quickly rolled up her bag, disassembled the tent, and stuffed it back in its canvas sack.

Then she stood, stretching as she inhaled the fresh morning air. Her skirt swung gently against her legs, and the blouse allowed soft fingers of breeze to graze her flesh. For the first time since boarding the train in New York, she was actually comfortable. She could *breathe*.

She felt so good, in fact, she could almost forget about the horrid old man and the way he'd looked at her.

Leave. Now. While you still can.

After uttering the blood-draining words, he'd stared at her. No, that wasn't quite accurate. He'd stared *into* her. She'd felt those impossibly sharp eyes bore into her, and a bone-rattling shiver had shaken her. She'd felt alternately cold and hot and—craziest of all—afraid. Not of the old man, either; that's what made it so crazy. She was afraid of herself. Afraid *for* herself.

The expression on his seamed, sun-darkened face had been unmistakable. He'd seen deep into her soul and found nothing of value.

She shot a worried glance at the closed cabin door. No smoke was rising from the chimney. The place looked as deserted as it had when they'd first arrived.

She breathed a quick sigh of relief that he wasn't awake yet. Plucking up her skirt, she crossed the small backyard and headed toward the corral, where Larence was just finishing packing and saddling the animals.

"Hi," she said, scooping the saddlebags off the ground and holding them out to him.

Turning, he started to reach for the bags. "Thanks, I—" He looked at her, and his sentence ground to a halt. He stared down; she stared up. Neither of them said a word.

The silence seemed charged with invisible sparks of electricity.

Larence's slid down her exposed throat, stopped fleetingly at the swell of her breasts, then kept going. All the way to her toes. A breeze kicked up, molded the thin cotton to her body. The sun seemed suddenly hotter, brighter. Emma's skin tingled; she was acutely aware of the missing corset.

Touch me. The two words charged like a bolt of lightning through her mind. Instinctively she leaned a hairbreadth closer, tilted her face up.

Larence turned to ice. His fingers tingled with the need to touch her skin, to feel the beat of her pulse. He curled them into white-knuckled fists and bolted them to his thighs.

Don't touch me, he thought desperately, inching away from her tempting lips. *If you do, so help me God, I'll make a fool of myself. . . .*

Behind them, a door creaked open. The long, whining screech of long-forgotten hinges sawed through the morning's quiet like a rusty blade through metal. Slow, deliberate footsteps shuffled through the rock-strewn dirt toward them. Tension made Emma's jaw clench, her spine stiffen. The electricity in the air vanished.

Larence called out, "Over here, Pa-lo-wah-ti—at the snubbing post."

Emma spun around. The old man ambled toward them in an unerring line. Dirt puffed up around his tan moccasins, clouded the thin, blue-veined shins that peeked through the slitted red cotton of his pants. Overhead, a hawk spiraled in controlled, gliding circles.

He stopped beside Larence. *"Hai."*

Larence frowned. "Are you okay, Pa-lo-wah-ti? You sound tired."

"Old men are often tired. It is the great Ka-ke's way."

"Perhaps we could stay another day and help you?"

"No." Tilting his chin, he looked up at Larence. A sadness that reminded Emma of defeat flitted through his sightless blue eyes. "Turn back, Larence. You cannot find what you seek. You are missing something—"

"A clue?" Emma asked sharply. "How do you know?"

An irritated frown puckered the old man's forehead, and Emma had the distinct impression that he was loathe to be reminded of her presence. Without bothering to look at her, he answered, "*You* might think it a 'clue.' "

Emma scowled. *Because I obviously have the intelligence of an earthworm.*

Larence laid a hand on the old man's shoulder, and Pa-lo-wah-ti smiled up at him. *Smiled.*

Emma couldn't help rolling her eyes. Beneath the softly rustling folds of her skirt, her toe picked up an impatient beat.

"Turn back, Larence," the old man said again, even more softly this time. "I feel . . . danger for you on this quest of your vision."

It seemed to Emma that Larence waited six weeks to answer. Her foot tapped faster. Dust spiraled up from her feet and obscured her hem.

"I can't," Larence said finally.

Pa-lo-wah-ti's eyes slid shut. "This, too, I know. It is meant that you search—but not that you find. Or keep. I am sorry."

"Oh, for God's sake, Larence, let's just go. He doesn't know any more about the damn city than you do. And his mumbo jumbo is irritating me."

Pa-lo-wah-ti spun on her with an amazing speed. "You are meaningless on this journey of his. You cannot even hear the whispering of the dead and the murmuring of the gods, let alone *listen* to them. Go then, seek your golden treasure. And pay the price for your greed."

Before she could utter a word, the old man turned his back on her and clasped Larence's hands. "Stay together in the city," he whispered in an urgent voice. "Always."

Emma snorted in response and yanked Tashee's reins

free of the fence post. Mounting up, she said, "Let's go, Larence. *Now.*"

Pa-lo-wah-ti stepped back, releasing his hold on Larence's hands. "Yes. Go."

When Larence had mounted Diablo, he looked down at the old man. "I'll see you again, won't I?"

The barest of smiles touched the man's mouth. He nodded solemnly. "In thirty days."

"Thanks, but no thanks," Emma said sharply. "In thirty days we'll be in the city."

His muddy blue gaze impaled her. "Will *you*? Perhaps. But there is much danger, much danger."

"But how will we fi—"

"Do not worry, Larence, *I* will find *you*."

When they'd been riding about fifteen minutes, Emma turned to look back at Pa-lo-wah-ti's cabin.

She studied the small cabin intently. Something wasn't right, but she couldn't put her finger on what it was.

The place looked deserted, almost . . . hazy. She tented a hand against the brim of her hat and squinted into the rising sun.

What was it?

Finally she gave up. Whatever was wrong, or different, she couldn't discern it. And it didn't matter, anyway. Shrugging, she turned her attention back to the desert stretched out before them.

Later—and she was never quite sure how much later—she turned around again.

The cabin was gone.

She squinted, certain the sun was playing tricks on her.

But it wasn't; no matter how long or how hard she

looked, there was no mistaking the truth: The cabin was gone.

Maybe she'd fallen asleep, she told herself.

Or maybe it was behind the mesa. . . .

But no matter how hard she tried to convince herself, or how doggedly she tried to ignore it, a thought returned.

Or maybe it never existed at all.

Chapter Eighteen

※※　　　　　※※

Emma slumped in the saddle, letting her chin droop forward. Warm sweat slid through the damp hair plastered to her cheeks and drizzled down the valley between her breasts. She sopped the moisture from her shoulders and throat with the crumpled white shirtwaist she'd ripped in half at lunch.

Her tired gaze lifted to the immense, twisting river of rock-hard black lava laid out before her. Here and there, clumps of hardy green grass grew in the cracks and crevices, but otherwise, the land between these sand-hued mesas was desolate and dead.

Only Esteban and Diego remembered this place. They had forged a path through the wasteland and found water along the way. And from the grave, they'd pointed the way.

"Look!" Larence said suddenly.

Emma squinted into the brilliant yellow sunlight. The cracked, lifeless landscape shimmied before her eyes, waved like a length of black silk in a light breeze. On her right the huge mesa called *Cebollita* weaved side to side.

Damn mirages. She rubbed her sweat-clogged eyes and tried again to focus.

The *Cebollita* mesa anchored, became once again an

immobile, timeless wall of stone. The shimmering curtain of heat in the distance stilled. One by one, other colors crept along the horizon; yellow, nutmeg red, green. No more black!

Relief rushed through her, bringing a trembling thankful smile to her lips. "Oh God . . ." was all she could think of to say.

She realized then that she'd thought they'd die out here, all alone in the land called the *Malpais*, the badlands.

Larence smiled down at her, but it wasn't his usual boyish grin. For once, she could see the tiny network of lines that fanned out from his eyes and the furrow that creased his brow. He'd been uneasy about their chances, too.

"We made it," she breathed.

He reached down. The hard, callused tip of his forefinger grazed the sweat-slicked hollow of her cheek, and the unexpected touch sent a hot shiver through her body.

"Of course we did. Together we can do anything."

Together.

Emma was still thinking about that simple word as she crouched by the small pool, washing the dinner dishes.

Together.

She dunked a pan in the pool, reveling in the soothing coolness of the water as it wrapped around her aching fingers. Overhead, clouds scuttled out of the moon's path, and tenuous strands of blue-white light crept across the puddle's mirrored surface. The metal pot in her hand glimmered like sterling silver in the moonlight. Scattered clumps of cholla jutted fistlike from the ankle-deep shadows.

Together. She closed her eyes, thinking about that single word and his unexpected use of it. *Together. You and I.*

She didn't hear Larence approach, but suddenly he was there, beside her, hunkering down. "Hand me the kettle. I'll dry."

A few days ago she would have denied him on principle, but tonight the thought didn't even cross her mind. Wordlessly she passed him the pot.

Their fingers brushed, and at the contact the full import of what they were doing hit Emma. Washing the dishes together was somehow so personal. It was one of those day-to-day things she'd never done with another person. Before she'd made her fortune and been able to afford a housekeeper, she'd done her dishes by herself, silently and alone. Always alone.

Her parents had always done chores together. Every night after dinner, they'd stood at the rusted, dented washbasin on the tenement's sagging porch and washed dishes. Mum washed; Da dried. Their quiet, mingled laughter had often floated to Emma's corner of the room, keeping her awake. Curled up on her narrow cot, beneath the tattered remnants of a hand-me-down blanket, she'd watched them. The love, the joy of their union, had wrapped her in comfort and been her lullaby. She'd gone to sleep a thousand nights dreaming about the man who would one day love her as much as her da loved her mum.

Her throat constricted. Tears scorched her eyes. When had she stopped believing that such a man, such a love, existed for her?

But of course, she knew; she knew the minute, the

second, the hour her dreams had ended. Eight-thirty Christmas morning. A Tuesday . . .

From that day on, she'd been as hard and cold and uncaring as she knew how to be. No one had ever filled the void left by her parents' deaths; she'd never let anyone get close enough to even realize there *was* a void.

But Larence had snuck up on her. Somehow, when she wasn't looking, he'd wormed his way past her defenses and made her realize she'd missed something in life. Something important and special and worth fighting for. Because he believed in her, she began to believe in herself.

A smile touched her lips. Eugene had been right; she *had* spent a lifetime being cold. Uncaring. And it had cost her more than she'd thought possible. The self-imposed solitude had chilled her soul, bit by bit, until there was nothing left but ice.

She'd always wanted to reach out. God, how she'd wanted to. But she'd been so desperately, desperately afraid that she was like her father. That deep inside, too deep to see or touch and just barely deep enough to *feel*, she was weak enough to someday kill herself. Ever since the day she'd found him, slumped and bleeding and dead at the kitchen table, she'd seen the seeds in herself. Seen the possibility.

And so she'd run. From herself and everyone else.

Then she'd hit Albuquerque, and there'd been nowhere to run. And then, finally, with Larence beside her, there'd been no reason to run. *Okay to be afraid* . . .

"The plate can't get any cleaner, Em," Larence said with a chuckle.

Smiling, she leaned against him and handed him the

plate. Together they held each other upright. Both supporting; both seeking support. It felt so good being near him. So right.

She stared at the plate in her hand but didn't really see it. Her mind was filled with images of her and Larence as they'd been in the last few days. Laughing, joking, caring.

Together.

Afterward, Emma sat by the cheerful, crackling fire, sipping a cup of cinnamon-laced tea. And watching Larence.

She couldn't help herself. Time and again her gaze was drawn to him, almost against her will. She was half-afraid that if she turned her back—for even a heartbeat—she'd find that it had all been a lie. That Larence and the friendship he gave her was nothing but an illusion created by a lonely heart.

The friendship he gave her.

She sat up straighter. Certainly he'd given her his friendship, there was no doubt about that. In a thousand tiny ways. But had she been reciprocal? Had she given the same immeasurable gift in return? Or had she merely been her old self—taking and taking and never giving?

"Aah!" Larence groaned again and staggered sideways. The canvas tent bag he was carrying slipped. He cried out, reached for it, but the bag hit the dirt with a thud.

"Larence!" She was on her feet in an instant, running fast. She reached him just as he collapsed.

She dropped to her knees beside him and instinctively reached out. Then stopped. Her hand hovered for a heartbeat; uncertainty made her gnaw at her lower lip.

Don't be a coward, not this time. Let him know how much you care. . . .

She touched him.

He jerked at her touch, then stilled. In the night's silence, his rapid breathing sounded like the fall of a hammer against hardwood. She felt the trembling in his body beneath her palm.

He kept his head down. "Go away."

It might have been a total stranger speaking. His voice was thick, tortured. The ragged sound of it tore at her heart.

A feeling of uselessness welled up in her. What could she do—or say—to help him?

She had no idea. She hadn't given comfort since her father died—and obviously she'd done a damn poor job of it then or he wouldn't have killed himself.

She pushed away the familiar doubt and focused instead on her instincts. Her *feelings*.

Swallowing thickly, she began to rub his back in soothing circles. Words, she thought desperately, *talk* to him. Let him know he's not alone. Only one sentence came to mind: "It's okay to be . . ." She stopped. Heat crawled up her throat.

Fool. Idiot. You couldn't comfort someone in canned, copied language.

He looked up unexpectedly. Their eyes met. Pain clouded his, drew little lines in his forehead and tightened his mouth. And yet, even in the midst of his own pain, there was an empathy in his eyes, an understanding of her frustration. He mumbled something.

She leaned closer. The soft, soapy scent of his hair mingled with the coffee and woodsmoke smell of his clothing and surrounded her, wrapped her in familiar warmth. She threaded her fingers through the brown hair that fell over his eye and pushed the curly lock out of the way. "What did you say?"

Tension etched in lines around his mouth; shame darkened his eyes. A soft night breeze slid through his hair, making it flutter against the sides of his face and rustle against her fingers. "It . . . embarrasses me to be seen like this . . . by you."

Emma felt as if a huge hand were squeezing her heart. Tears stung her eyes, blurred her vision. "Oh, Larence . . ." Her voice thickened, cracked. "You saw me at my worst—and helped me. Let me do the same for you. *Please*."

"No one can help me, Em. It's a—" his voice fell to a shamed whisper "—defect."

Emma swallowed the lump in her throat and forced a thin smile. "You should know better than to challenge the infamous 'Mad Hatter' of Wall Street."

Using her smaller body as a crutch, Emma levered Larence to his feet. Together, one step at a time, they headed for the fire. By the time they reached the small circle of light, Larence's face was a taut, gray mask of pain. His breathing was fast and shallow, and sweat beaded his forehead. He said nothing, though, and his silent strength moved Emma as words never could have.

He half stooped, half collapsed beside the fire. His breath expelled in a groaning sigh. "Thanks," he said without meeting her gaze.

Kneeling beside him, Emma stared at his profile, willing him to look up at her, to use those perceptive eyes of his to read what was in her heart.

His gaze remained transfixed on the fire.

She turned her attention to the dusty pointed tip of his boot. *Do it . . . For once in your life, give some-*

thing back. . . . She scooted backward until she was even with his feet. Hesitantly, she reached out.

He yanked his foot out of her grasp. "What are you doing?"

She met his gaze head-on. Fear curled cold fingers around her heart. "Don't stop me, Larence," she said in a voice so quiet, she knew he had to lean toward her to hear it. "Please . . ."

They stared at each other for a long moment. Neither one of them moved or spoke.

"Please," she whispered again.

Slowly, so slowly, Larence's booted foot slid through the dirt toward her.

Relief brought a shaking smile to her lips as she gently removed his boot. Easing his foot into her lap, she carefully peeled away his red woolen sock and dropped it in the dirt beside her.

She looked down at his bare foot, so colorless and swollen against the pale blue of her skirt, and felt a tremor of pity at the pain it must cause him.

He jerked his foot out of her lap. "I don't want your pity." Anger flashed in his eyes, anger and something else. Something that made her feel about two inches tall.

Humiliation.

"Don't do that," she said quietly. Give me your foot." She took hold of his twisted ankle and gently but firmly drew it back into her lap. She stared at it for a long moment, seeing the tiny, uncontrollable tremble that shook his toes.

Please God don't let me hurt him.

Her fingertips began to glide in small, barely felt circles against his cool flesh. Down along the pale skin of his foot to his toes, then slowly back up to the crisp brown hair that stopped just above his ankle. She carefully avoided the swollen, discolored ball of his ankle. Her fingers kept moving, massaging, until the tremble in his toes disappeared.

As she felt him relax, she glanced up at him. His head was thrown back, his eyes were closed. The tiny network of pain lines around his mouth had disappeared, and the color had returned to his cheeks.

It was working, she realized. She let her gaze fall back to his foot. Swallowing thickly, she decided to take a chance: She touched his ankle. Her palm formed to the damaged bone, warmed it.

He stiffened. The trembling began anew. She knew instinctively what he was thinking. He thought she'd be repulsed by touching his deformity. He was embarrassed by it, ashamed. Any second now he was going to pull away.

Her hold on that most damaged part of his flesh tightened. His pulse throbbed beneath her fingertips, matched the rapid beating of her heart. With a caring and a gentleness she'd never before possessed, she began to massage his foot. By touch she told him that he was perfect and whole in her eyes.

In massaging the aches and pains from his foot, Emma found a peace she'd never expected, a sense of freedom she'd never known existed. Amazingly, it made *her* feel good to give him comfort, made her happy to be needed. How long had it been since someone needed Emmaline Amanda Hatter for anything except a signature on a bank draft?

"You stopped it," he said in a voice filled with quiet wonder.

Emma felt a surge of pride. Impulsively she gave his toes a squeeze, then looked up. In his eyes she saw the same quiet wonder she'd heard in his voice, and it filled her anew with pride. Her fingers dangled familiarly on either side of his foot.

"No one's ever done that before. I didn't even know it was possible. Thanks."

She swallowed. "Sure."

"Come here," he said quietly, reaching his hand toward her. "Sit by me and look at the stars. I'll show you the constellations."

She was powerless to resist. She scooted over to him and huddled close. Together they lay back, staring up at the stars.

Long into the night they lay there, side by side, staring up at the sky and talking like the best of friends. They talked about the little things in life and the big; about the desert at night, about Cibola, about the world economy and the stock market crash, and about everything in between.

"Michael told me you'd made your money yourself," Larence said finally. "When I first met you, I thought you'd inherited money and then been smart enough to turn it into a fortune. But you started with nothing. How did you do it?"

Emma squinted in the darkness, remembering. "It was an inauspicious beginning. I stole a typewriter. I practiced on it day and night, until I could type without even looking at the keys. Then one day I bundled it up under my arm and went to Wall Street.

"I went to the biggest brokerage house and tried to get an appointment with the president. No one took me seriously, of course—and why should they? A sixteen-year-old kid in a dirty, ragged dress. But I sat down in the middle of the hallway and refused to move. I sat there for six hours until finally Mr. Lyndeman came out. He took one look at me and said, 'Girl, if you're half as good with the typewriter as you are at getting on people's nerves, you have a job here.' "

She smiled at the memory. "I worked there for ten years. Mr. Lyndeman taught me everything he knew and let me trade stocks. Fortunately for me, I was good at it."

"Could you live without the money?"

She didn't even hesitate. "No. But I've learned a few things on this trip. I wouldn't do it quite the same way again. This time I'd slow down a bit. Maybe make a few friends."

"You didn't have any before?"

"No. I was so busy getting what I wanted—and keeping it—that I never bothered socializing with anyone who couldn't help me in some way. I never had the time or the inclination to make friends."

His arm curled around her shoulder and drew her close. "Until now," he said.

"Yes," she whispered with a smile. "Until now."

Darkness closed in on Larence, wrapped around his face like a shroud of black velvet. Thick. Airless. Deceptively soft. It covered his nose and mouth, pressed hard against his lungs, suffocating him. Invisible hands pushed him down. His breath came in sharp, gasping pants.

He flailed, moaning quietly in his sleep, fighting, always fighting. Once again he was a little boy curled on a hard, cold cot. Pain throbbed in his leg, radiated in razor-sharp shards into his thigh. Tears burned behind his eyes, ached.

Granny . . .

He came awake with a start and sat bolt-upright.

Heaving for breath, he shoved the sweat-dampened hair out of his eyes and glanced wildly around, trying to see something—anything.

Cold, black nothingness surrounded him, battered his mind and fed the childhood fears. Disorientation clouded his thinking. Where was he? Where?

No answer came to his frazzled mind. He might have been in a tomb, buried alive. The world was a black pit in the middle of nowhere, without moon or fire or lantern to give it light.

Fear coiled around his throat, squeezed his lungs. Panic flooded into his brain. His heart thudded in his chest, pounded against the cage of his ribs. Each breath became a fire-hot gulp of air.

Out of the pitch blackness came a sound; quiet at first, then building. It began in his mind as the gentle lapping of water against warm sand, and then became air—whooshing softly in and out.

Breathing. It was breathing.

Emmaline!

Memory burst through his fear-clogged brain. He was in a tent on the trail to Cibola, and Emma was sleeping beside him. *He wasn't alone.* All he had to do was reach out and touch her.

This time he could do it. He could beat the nightmare, maybe beat it once and for all.

His hand moved across the harsh, bumpy fabric of her sleeping bag, scouting for her body.

"Emma?" The word hung expectantly in the jet black night air. His breath jammed in his throat. Hope cut like a hot knife through his thoughts. *Please wake up . . .*

"Larence?" Her voice sounded groggy, disoriented,

but it was the sweetest sound he'd ever heard. "What is it?"

"Touch me." He winced as the weak, unmanly words slipped from his lips. He wished he could call them back, laugh about them, but he couldn't. Not this time and perhaps never. The need was too strong, too all-consuming, the terror too real. . . .

She rustled around for a few moments, and then, miraculously, he felt her fingertips graze his upper arm.

At her touch, fear faded, sneaked back into that black pit from which it had come. The darkness eased, became manageable. It was as he'd always thought: It was loneliness that fueled the fear and gave it life. Simple loneliness.

And he wasn't alone anymore.

Her hand plopped onto his chest. He covered it with his own. And finally the last vestige of his childhood fear dissipated.

But as the fear subsided, embarrassment rushed in to take its place. He felt awkward and vulnerable in the aftermath of his outburst. He gave a shaky, self-conscious laugh. "I guess you think—"

"I don't think in the middle of the night, Larence," she said quietly, threading her fingers through his and squeezing. "Now, go to sleep."

Amazingly, he did.

Chapter Nineteen

The next morning dawned bright and clear. Larence woke to the crackling hiss of a well-made fire and the mouth-watering aroma of simmering coffee. He snapped upright in his sleeping bag.

Emmaline had wakened first—and made breakfast!

He clambered out of his bag and crawled to the front of the tent, peeking his head out. She sat hunkered down by the fire, poking a fork at the bacon popping in the frying pan. Oatmeal simmered in a pot alongside the bacon.

"Morning," he called out.

She tottered sideways and glanced back over her shoulder. "Good morning. Breakfast is almost ready."

His stomach grumbled at her words. Larence quickly rolled up his arctic bag and crawled out of the tent, buttoning his Levi's as he went.

Outside, he pushed slowly to his feet. A taut grimace of pain tightened his mouth as the familiar morning pain shot from ankle to thigh.

As always, it passed quickly. Grabbing his shirt from the tent pole's apex, he started to put it on, then decided against it. It was such a glorious, beautiful day—warm, and not yet hot—and it felt good to be unclothed. The morning breeze trailed cool, shiver-inducing fingers along the flat plane of his stomach.

He wrapped the shirt around the low-slung waistband of his jeans and tied the sleeves in a knot. The faded, wrinkled shirt hung to his knees, flapping soundlessly as he moved toward the fire.

Emmaline looked up at him as he reached the fire. Her gaze skidded to a halt at his chest, and a blush crept up her cheeks. But she didn't look away.

Stunned, Larence watched the pinkness inch up her throat. He was suddenly painfully, exhilaratingly, aware of his nakedness.

And so was she. A slow, cocky smile spread across his face and shone in his eyes. He jammed his hands in his pockets and rocked back on his heels.

"Breakfast's almost ready," she said crisply, and turned her attention to the bacon. "And put your shirt on."

That night sparks fluttered like dancing orange fireflies above the fire. The castanet crackling of the burning mesquite roots peppered the darkness with noise. Still pungent, the scent of coffee hovered in the cool air, mingling with the jumbled aromas of resin, pine, and arid dirt to create the desert's own particular perfume.

Emma laid the coffeepot on its side and closed the stove's wooden box. She had never felt so absolutely relaxed. Leaning back on her elbows, she stretched out along the fire with almost feline pleasure. Her gaze turned to the heavens. Millions of stars twinkled against the midnight blue night sky. "Look, Larence, there's the big scooper."

His soft laughter knocked at the door of her heart, bade her welcome. Coziness curled around her, warmed her toes and made her smile with him.

"Big Dipper," he said.

"Whatever," she responded with an airy wave of the hand. What mattered was not that she was wrong, but that she'd finally noticed the stars at all. Since last night she'd been consumed by an almost boundless energy. As if the realization that life was good, that *she* was good, had in some way rejuvenated her soul. She moved like a woman walking on air, and smiled almost all the time.

She rolled onto her side and stared at Larence. He sat cross-legged and hunched over with a Hogarth drawing pad in his lap. The faint scratching noise of his pen gliding atop the paper floated to her ears. Strangely, she found herself wishing he'd look up at her, wishing he'd come sit by her. "Do you want to play poker?"

"Nope."

Then he did something odd. He frowned. The expression was so alien on his face that it piqued Emma's curiosity. Standing, she peered over at him. "What are you drawing?"

"Come see for yourself."

Clasping her hands behind her back, she sashayed around the fire. "I don't know why I'm bothering," she said, coming up behind him. "I've already seen enough cactus and bi—" She gasped.

It was a drawing of her, perfect in every detail.

Unsteadily she sank to her knees beside him, and with a silent *oh*, turned toward him. He was staring down at the paper, still frowning as his pen expertly re-created the stunning burgundy velvet Worth dress she'd worn the night they met.

"Oh, Larence . . ." The word slipped out alone,

with nothing to follow it. The drawing, and the memory it represented, sent heat rippling through her body.

The pen stopped, raised a hairbreadth from the paper.

Their gazes met. Emma felt his every breath like a whisper of promise against her lips.

It occurred to her that if she leaned forward, no more than half an inch, she'd be kissing him. Cool fingers flicked along her spine, made her shiver. She had a strange feeling that she was close to something magical, something she'd waited for all her life. . . .

"Do you like it?" he asked quietly.

Transfixed by the slow, sensual movement of his lips, it was a moment before she realized he was talking to her.

He'd said her name twice—twice—while she stared like an idiot at his mouth. Self-consciousness consumed her, left her feeling foolish and awkward. "Y-You have quite a memory," she said, despising the breathy, hesitant sound of her voice.

He flipped to the next blank page. "For some things." His pen started moving again. "Like this . . ."

A couple of quick, sure strokes of his pen, and a door began to appear on the page. It was the door to her Eighth Avenue apartment—right down to the cracked center window.

She couldn't believe it. "That was a hairline crack. *I* could hardly see it, and I was the one who broke it. How in God's name can you remember that?"

He grinned. "You see a lot when something's slammed in your face."

Emma felt the blood rush out of her cheeks. She squeezed her eyes shut in shame. "I . . ." A thickness coiled around her throat, made it difficult to push the words out. "I shouldn't have done that."

With gentle fingers he cupped her chin and forced her to look at him. "Open your eyes."

She shook her head.

"Open your eyes. Now."

Reluctantly she did, and found him looking at her. The easy forgiveness in his eyes made her shoulders sag with relief.

"You're so serious about everything, Em. Relax. Have fun with life. Remember the good things; forget the bad. Like, remember when I stepped on your rug? You should have seen the look on your face. . . ."

His smile was so infectious, Emma couldn't help herself. Her lips twitched. "It was only a hundred-year-old Aubusson."

"And they were just muddy, wet, out-of-date creed-more walking boots."

"A *white* hundred-year-old Aubusson." She burst out laughing.

Larence laughed with her, and the happy, rolling sound echoed off the nearby mesas and smoothed the day's rough edges.

Gradually it dwindled away, melted into a comfortable, friendly silence. Long into the night they sat around the campfire, laughing and talking and smiling.

Sometime around midnight, just as the moon sneaked behind a thick gray cloud, Larence slipped his arm around Emma's shoulder and drew her close. She leaned against the strong, hard curl of his shoulder and slid her arm around his waist. Her cheek rested comfortably against the cottony fabric of his shirt.

It seemed like the most natural thing in the world.

* * *

The next morning they hadn't been riding half an hour when Larence noticed the first earth-shattering flora specimen. Emma knew she should groan when she heard the trademark *Look a perfect blah-blah-blah*, but for some reason, she didn't. In fact, she found herself actually smiling as Larence limped eagerly toward a flower.

Squatting down beside it, he waved her over. "Come on, Em. Look at this. It's beautiful."

It *did* look sort of pretty. *Maybe just this once.* Glancing left to right, as if she were afraid of being seen, she hopped off Tashee's back and sauntered over to Larence. "What is it?" she asked in as disinterested a voice as she could muster.

It wasn't disinterested enough. He looked up as if he'd been shot. And she knew why. He'd asked her to join him at some stupid plant or another a hundred times since leaving Albuquerque; not once had she deigned to even answer, let alone actually *follow* him.

Beneath his pointed perusal, Emma shifted from one foot to the other. "You can't draw much looking at me."

A slow, decidedly sensual smile spread across his face. Emma felt its impact all the way to her toes.

"You're right," he said, pulling out his notebook and turning his attention to the flower. "Here, sit."

Emma kneeled beside him. His pen moved atop the paper like a young girl at her first dance, in breezing, effortless circles. Transfixed, she stared at the strong, tanned fingers curled around the silver cylinder.

She felt hot. Then cold. Unbidden came a fantasy of those same fingers, gliding with the same scientific precision and attention to detail across her bare skin. A shiver rippled through her. Gooseflesh bubbled along her arms.

She swallowed dryly and forced her attention on the drawing. A beautiful, daisylike flower began to emerge.

"Wait, that's not right." The words popped out of her mouth before she knew she was going to speak.

The pen lifted. Larence turned to look at her. Their faces were close, so close Emma could see the tiny gold flecks that lightened his green eyes. His breath, a soft mixture of tooth powder and coffee-scent, brushed her cheeks. Bright morning sunlight gilded his hair, turned it the color of molasses. Once again she thought that if she just leaned the tiniest bit forward . . .

"What's wrong with it?"

She swallowed hard and forced her face and eyes to go blank, but she had a horrible feeling it didn't work, because a quick smile tilted the left corner of his mouth.

"The center should be darker." The words came out in a breathy rush. Wincing at the sensual sound of it, she snapped to her feet and strode away from him. Her walking boots crushed dozens of early spring flowers, but she didn't notice.

Once she was safely beside Tashee, Emma's breath expelled in a rush. She reached for her canteen and froze, staring at her fingers in horror.

She was shaking. *Shaking*.

The reason hit her like a lightning bolt and rocked her to the core of her being.

She was sexually attracted to Larence. *Larence*.

She shook her head in denial. *No* . . .

Unbelievable. Unthinkable.

Undeniable.

It wasn't that she'd been too long without a man in her bed, either. That answer was too simple. In New

York she might have been able to make herself believe
it, but out here, in the middle of nowhere, she couldn't
lie to herself.

"You're right, Em. I had it looking too much like a
daisy."

His words floated to her, and all of a sudden the irony
of the situation struck her. She burst out laughing.

She was in the middle of nowhere with no chaperon
and a man whom she found sexually appealing. Ordinarily, it would be considered ideal.

Except that the man was—quite possibly—the only
male virgin in existence.

As jokes went, she had to admit it was a good one.

That night Emma lay awake a long time. Stretched
out beside Larence, she stared at the tent's sagging canvas sides, turned a pale, glowing shade of amber by the
light of a full moon.

His regular, quiet breathing filled the tiny space with
calming, comforting sound. At least, it *should* have
been comforting. But it wasn't. Not tonight. With every
breath he took, every tiny, fluttering sound he made,
she was reminded of her attraction to him.

She'd come a long way from her first horrible initiation
to sex. She no longer despised and feared it; long ago it
had become a fear to conquer. And conquer it she had.
Now sex was merely part of life, something she did because she felt like it. It was a pleasant, enjoyable way to
spend an evening, and if she was often left feeling frus-
trated and aching for something—she didn't know what—
then that was simply part of life as well.

She wanted Larence. The fact still amazed her, but
Emma was not one to lie to herself. Facts were facts.
She wanted Larence in her bed.

Why? He had nothing to offer her, not really. He couldn't give her stock tips, or help her find that perfect investment, or introduce her to the "right" people.

And yet there was something about him that made all her previous criteria about men seem small and petty. In a thousand little ways he'd made her wonder if maybe—just maybe—sex couldn't be something more than practical and pleasant. She doubted it, of course. Everyone knew that sex wasn't supposed to be good for women, and yet ever since she'd touched Larence's foot, she'd felt . . . strange. Restless. As if she were searching for something, some door, and he was the key. And that small, niggling question, that quickly suppressed hope that sex could be . . . exciting . . . was too compelling to deny.

Ordinarily, of course, getting a man in bed was no problem. But nothing about Larence was ordinary.

One thing she knew for certain: He wouldn't make the first move.

Somehow that made it even more compelling. More challenging.

Because if he wouldn't make the first move, then she had to.

It wasn't working.

Emma sat up straighter on the rock, trying to get his attention.

Nothing. No reaction at all.

Larence was sitting cross-legged, close to the fire, reading each and every page of that damned diary as if it held the secret to eternal life. Every now and then he muttered "Ah-ha!" as if it meant something, but other than that, he hadn't spoken to her since dinner. She bit back an irritated sigh. It took all her concentration to keep an alluring expression in her eyes—especially since he hadn't looked at her in fifteen minutes.

She refused to let his scientific idiosyncracies beat her. No one bested Emmaline Amanda Hatter when she had her sights set on something—or someone—and she definitely had her sights set on Larence. Tonight.

She fanned the pale blue skirt out around her legs and cocked one shoulder up. The *camisa* slid enticingly down her shoulder. She waited for him to notice. He didn't. Next she tried uttering a low, sensual-sounding sigh.

Nothing.

Irrilaled, she tried the routine again. Except this time her right shoulder jerked up so hard, she almost lost her balance on the rock. Her arms flailed sideways. She grabbed hold of a little pine tree for support.

Larence looked up. "Be careful, Em. That's the second time you've almost fallen."

She offered him a thin-lipped, humorless smile. He flashed her a blinding grin and went back to his reading.

Emma slammed her arms across her chest and fumed silently. He hadn't even *noticed* the inviting way her blouse slid off her shoulder. . . .

Then suddenly he looked up again, and Emma was so surprised, she almost fell off the rock. He leaned forward and grabbed her just in time. "You better get down."

This was her best shot all right. Her cleavage—what there was of it without a corset—was right in front of his nose. "With you?" She purred.

He looked genuinely confused. "Of course."

Fighting the urge to roll her eyes, she tried again. "You look . . . excited."

"I am."

Her heart sped up. She leaned closer. "Really?"

He nodded eagerly. "Tomorrow's Cibola. I feel it in my bones."

"Cibola," she repeated woodenly, shaking her head in disbelief. There was no doubt about it; she was wasting her time trying to seduce Larence. Temporarily defeated, she slid off the rock and landed beside him in a puff of dust. Resting her elbows on her bent knees, she plopped her chin in her hands and gave a disgusted, tired sigh.

"Let's do something," he said unexpectedly. "I'm too hot to sleep."

Hot? Emma immediately straightened. Maybe her decision wasn't wrong; maybe she'd just taken the wrong tack. Perhaps honesty would work better than subtle innuendo. God knew subtlety had never been her strong suit anyway. Or his, apparently.

"Actually, Larence, I've been thinking about—"

"Let's play that game of poker you're always bugging me about."

"Poker?"

He whipped a deck of cards out of his saddlebags and started shuffling. His fingers moved awkwardly, flipping cards right and left.

Irritation surged through Emma. She couldn't be *that* unappealing. Men had been lusting after her all her life. What was wrong?

The answer came as quickly as the question: Larence. Larence was what was wrong. Nothing about him was easy or normal or as expected. She'd have to think smarter, *be* smarter. Somehow she'd just have to figure out a way to get him into her bed. Maybe she should try *touching* him. . . .

A card hit her right between the eyes.

"Oops, sorry," he said with a chuckle.

She glared at him. "I do *not* want to play poker."

"I'll let you win."

Let me win? Why, of all the—"

Another card flipped in her lap. Emma heaved a disgusted sigh and rolled her eyes. No one, but no one, *let* Emmaline Hatter do anything.

She snatched the cards from him and shuffled them expertly. Then she yanked her blouse's sagging shoulder up and started dealing. "Okay, Doc, let's play poker."

By the time they finished, Emma had "won" Diablo, Tashee, the pack mule, the tent, and practically everything else of value. She was so pleased with herself, she'd forgotten all about sex with Larence.

Winning was something she understood. Had always understood. It was the only thing she'd ever found that made her feel good about herself.

She tossed the cards down and leaned back lazily against the trunk of a medium-sized tree. Lord, she felt good. Content. "Well, that's that. There's nothing else to play for."

Larence took a slow, thoughtful sip of the freshly made coffee. "How about adventure?"

Emma eyed him suspiciously. "What do you mean?"

"The tent," he answered casually, taking another sip. "You win, we sleep in the tent. I win, we sleep under the stars."

"That's a sucker bet, Larence. You haven't won a hand all night."

One eyebrow cocked upward. "Afraid?"

"Don't be absurd." She grabbed the cards and started shuffling. "Five-card draw?"

"Stud."

Emma's fingers spasmed. The soft, seductive tone of his voice flustered her for a moment, and sent a quick tremor of apprehension skittering through her body. She looked up sharply.

He was smiling like a choirboy.

No, she thought, shaking her head. He couldn't be *hustling* her. Not Larence.

She dealt the cards expertly, then peeked at her hand. A pair of kings.

She immediately relaxed. Larence hadn't had a hand this good all night.

"I open with a night under the stars," he drawled.

Emma flashed him a cocky grin. "I see your bet and raise it. Loser cooks breakfast *and* cleans up."

"I'll see that bet and raise it. No hair rope."

"No beef jerky for breakfast," she countered.

"Call."

"Call yourself." She laid down her cards. "Two kings."

Larence's smile dimmed; Emma's brightened. The sounds of the night died away, leaving the world strangely silent. She leaned forward, peering intently at the boldface Tally-Ho trademark on the back of his cards.

One at a time he laid them face-up in the dirt. *Three. Queen. Jack.* Emma smiled in anticipation. *Two. Nine.*

It took Emma a moment to realize they were all hearts.

Her smile flattened. A flush.

"Good game, Em." He pushed slowly to his feet and

stretched. ''Damn, but the fresh air will feel good tonight.'' Then he winked down at her. *Winked!*

Emma felt as if she'd been turned to stone. She sat
frozen, staring after him as he made his ambling, limping way to the pile of supplies. The soft, warbling
strains of his whistle floated back to her.

A grudging respect made her smile. He *had* hustled
her; played her along like a trophy fish and then reeled
her in.

Who would have thought him capable of it?

Absentmindedly picking up the fallen cards, she made
a mental note not to underestimate him again.

Chapter Twenty

Larence stretched out in his sleeping bag. The warm, woolly fleece cocooned him, wreathed him in warmth. A deep, contented sigh escaped his lips as he cradled his head in his laced fingers and stared at the exquisite night sky.

It was an inky cloak speckled with thousands upon thousands of twinkling white stars. Again he was struck by the immensity of the New Mexican sky, the sheer magnitude of it. Nearby trees whispered quietly among themselves, rustling in the late night breeze. The sweet, almost vanillalike scent of ponderosa pines floated to his nostrils, mixed with the arid, harsh aroma of hard-baked earth and grama grass. He sucked in a big breath of pine-scented air and shut his mouth. The trapped air burned his lungs, but he wouldn't let it out. For one split second, with the air hot in his lungs, it felt as if New Mexico itself were inside his soul.

Reluctantly he exhaled, and the feeling of oneness with the universe seeped away.

Slowly he became aware of Emma. She was standing beside the fire, stiff as a ruler, her body haloed in the tenuous, dancing light of the dying flames. Her back was to him, and he could see tension in the board-straightness of her spine.

"Emma?"

She jumped. "Y-Yes?"

"Are you coming to bed?"

She didn't answer; she just stood there for a moment longer. Then her head tilted upward and her shoulders squared. He had the distinct impression that she'd just made an important decision. Then, slowly—unusually slowly—she turned around to face him.

Even in the meager light he could see the paleness of her skin, the slight worry lines that parenthesized the flesh between her eyebrows. She walked stiffly toward him, her fingers twined together in a telltale sign of anxiety, her eyes trained on the shadowy earth.

At each crunching of her heel in the dirt, Larence felt his confusion mount. What was wrong with her? She was acting . . . nervous. Maybe even shy.

Emma? Shy? He dismissed the thought.

That left nervous. But what would *she* have to be nervous about, for God's sake? He was the one who had to hide his every thought and feeling. He was the one in love alone.

He stretched a hand out toward her. "What is it?"

She didn't respond.

He wiggled his fingers to get her attention. "Em?"

Reluctantly she moved toward him. Still staring at the darkened earth, she reached out. Their fingers brushed. He thought for a moment she was going to pull away, but then her fingers laced through his.

He felt her tremble at his touch. Instinctively he thought she was repulsed. *No woman would want to touch you, Larry. Not with your . . . defect.*

He winced at the viciousness of his grandmother's words, but for once, they didn't sadden him, didn't coil around his heart and burn. Granny was wrong. Emmaline had massaged his crippled ankle—and had done it with a smile that even now had the power to warm his soul.

She mumbled something that sounded like "It's now or never, Em." Then she let go of his hand.

"Emma, what—"

"I'm going to undress."

Larence's stomach flip-flopped. "O-Okay."

She didn't move or turn. Standing perfectly erect, her shadow-darkened body outlined by the throbbing firelight, she reached for the bow on her bodice. She plucked one end of the golden thread, and the limp bow evaporated. Her neckline sagged immediately, exposing a pale, milky swell of breast.

Larence swallowed dryly. He knew he should look away, but he couldn't. His gaze was riveted on the shadowy valley between her breasts. On the smooth-as-silk curve of creamy flesh that disappeared beneath the loosened blouse.

She cocked one shoulder, and the *camisa* slid down to her elbow. Her fingers moved nimbly from one button to the next, and with each motion, more and more skin was exposed. Then, all of a sudden, the blouse fell downward, landing in a heap of sky blue cotton on the sleeping bag's green exterior.

She stood stock-still, staring at her feet. Her naked breasts rose and fell in shallow, rapid waves. Bolted to her sides, her fingers flexed and curled, as if she were fighting the urge to cover her nakedness.

Larence couldn't tear his gaze away. His throat went bone-dry. He had a fleeting urge to pinch himself to see if this was real, but decided not to. It if *wasn't* real, he didn't want to know.

God, she was beautiful. . . .

Next came the skirt. She unbuttoned the waistband, and the blue muslin puddled around her feet. Now she was wearing nothing but a clinging white eyelet underskirt.

She kicked the fallen skirt out of her way and took a step toward him.

Larence's breathing accelerated, came in quick, burning spurts. Surely she didn't know he was watching her, didn't know the firelight illuminated her body so clearly.

His heart pounded, thudded in his ears until he couldn't hear anything except the workings of his own body. He had to look away, *now*. Had to change the course of things. If he didn't, if he kept looking at her and wanting her so much he ached, he'd make a fool of himself.

He couldn't, couldn't actually make a move toward her. No matter how badly, how desperately, he wanted to touch her, he couldn't. The risk was too great, and he'd never been a gambling man. Alongside his tensed thighs, beneath the cover of the sleeping bag, his hands curled into fists. Yet even fisted tight, his fingers trembled with the need to touch her.

But he wouldn't—couldn't—let himself.

When she left him—and she *would* leave him, of that he had no doubt—he'd have only memories. Remembered images of a glorious, laughter-filled month in the New Mexican desert with the woman he loved. Good memories to balance a lifetime's worth of bad ones. He couldn't risk losing those images by getting slapped in the face, or, worse, laughed at. One laugh, no matter how quickly suppressed or unintentional, would mar his picture of her forever. And then he'd lose both her and the perfect memory of her. The risk was simply too great.

He rolled onto his side. The earth felt cool and dry beneath his cheek, and the overpowering smell of dirt filled his nostrils. The night seemed to grow preternaturally silent; no breeze threaded the trees, no faraway animals cried. He tried to steady his breathing.

His heart was pounding so loudly in his ears, it took him a moment to realize she was saying his name.

"Larence?"

He winced. *Damn.*

"Larence?"

Cautiously he rolled onto his back and pushed up to his elbows. He tried to plaster a casual expression on his face, but one look at her sent his heart racing again.

She was standing not more than six feet away, wearing nothing but the clinging white cotton petticoat. Firelight outlined the shapely columns of her legs beneath the sheer fabric. Her hair was a waterfall of golden-white and silver threads waving gently around her face and against her arms. Her breasts looked soft and pale and touchable.

He gulped, trying to think of something that would keep his mind off the terrible, aching need building in his body. "Y-You want to hear about Cibola again?"

She shook her head. A smile lifted one corner of her mouth. "No, Larence. I want you."

His heart came to a searing halt. Uncertainty and confusion consumed him. What did she mean? Certainly not that she wanted to—

"Come here, Larence."

Her soft, seductive voice washed over him in waves, drew the will from his body like a poultice. He shivered in response. Without conscious thought he pushed back the heavy sleeping bag and moved awkwardly to his feet.

On the first step, his bad ankle twisted. Pain wrenched through his body and pounded in hammer-blows along his shin. He stumbled, then caught himself. Grimacing, he steadied himself. But he couldn't look up, couldn't see the disgust in her eyes. . . .

"It's okay, Lare. Don't *you* be afraid."

He lifted his chin and met her gaze. What he saw in her eyes melted the years of hardness on his soul, left him feeling stripped and bare and able to believe.

He saw desire. Honest-to-God desire. For *him*.

Afraid to believe it, afraid not to believe it, he limped toward her and took her outstretched hands in his. He stood there for a moment, touching and yet not touching her, wanting to be closer and yet afraid. The quiet whispering of the pines intensified. Cool night air swirled in eddies around their feet, rustled the flyaway strands of spun gold around her face.

Her hands slid upward and locked behind his neck. Larence felt her drawing his head toward hers, felt the infinitesimal lifting of her body as she pressed onto her toes to meet him.

Tentatively he let his hands inch down her bare back. Her flesh felt warm and silky-soft. She shivered and drew closer; he heard the quickened pace of her breathing, felt each exhalation like a butterfly wing brushing his face.

Her lips touched his. Feather-soft at first, then more firmly.

He closed his eyes, becoming familiar with the feel of her lips against his. The sweet, vanilla-scented air wrapped around them, removed them to another, distant place. A place where there was nothing and no one except the two of them. His hands settled in the hollow at the base of her spine, pulled her close. It felt so good, so *right* holding her like this. . . .

Her tongue slipped through his parted lips and touched his. At the contact, a jolt of pure electricity shot straight through Larence's body and landed hot and hard in his groin. A thick, garbled moan inched up his throat and disappeared in the moist darkness of her mouth.

Was *that* what he was supposed to do? The thought terrified him, reminded him with razor-sharp clarity that he was inexperienced and she was not.

Clumsy dolt. Fool. Do it right. The words sliced through his head, taunted him. He wanted to do it right. *Ached* to do it right. To make her feel all the wonderful, glorious things she was making him feel. But how? he wondered desperately. How could he compete with the experienced, worldly men she'd undoubtedly known in her life?

Doubt assailed him, made him feel useless and weak and *crippled*. Slowly he lifted his lips from hers.

She didn't look away. Blue eyes, wide with wonder, stared up at him. The soft night wind teased the hair around her face, whipping golden strands along the moist, still-parted pinkness of her lips. Her scent, a mingled bouquet of long-dried dust, sun-warmed cotton, and something else, something uniquely *her*, floated to his nostrils.

He expected her to yell at him, to berate him for his clumsiness and ineptitude. But she didn't say a word; she just stood there, rooted to the ground, her eyes riveted on his.

A dizzying sense of hope unfurled within him.

Maybe—just maybe—she'd felt it, too. That incredible sense of *rightness*, of coming home at last.

He brushed his knuckles along the warm, bare column of her throat, grazed the soft pinkness of her lower lip. She shivered beneath his touch and closed her eyes, leaning toward him.

"Em . . ." The breeze whipped the word away, and Larence was left with nothing to say.

She opened her eyes and pressed one thin, trembling finger to his lips. "Don't talk." Without another word, she pressed onto her tiptoes and kissed him.

It was a real kiss, this one. Not a halting, inexperienced expression of hope and affection like the first one, but a real, honest-to-God, rise-in-your-body-temperature kind of kiss. Blood tingled in Larence's veins, thrummed through his body.

Her body formed to his like warm tallow. An intense vibration sped through his flesh. His knees buckled, started to give way, and he stiffened, ignoring the shooting stab of pain in his bad leg. Her arms tightened around his neck, steadied him, and the strength of her touch banished the pain. It receded, slunk back to the cold, dark corners of his body where it lived. And when it was gone, he felt strangely at peace.

Her willingness gave him confidence, and confidence made him bold. His hands roamed freely up and down her naked flesh, exploring every ridge and hollow from her shoulder blades to her small waist. A tiny sigh slipped from her mouth, and the trembling sound of it coiled around Larence's heart.

His tongue teased her lips, urged them to part. She responded quickly, eagerly, and touched her tongue to his. She tasted like melted honey and wildflowers, like all the things he'd reached for in his life and never quite attained. Never until this moment even hoped to attain.

Sensations hammered his body. Every nerve ending in his body quivered and came alive. He thought for a moment that his heart would burst out of his chest.

Suddenly holding her wasn't enough. He needed to feel every inch of her body. His hands slid down the wrinkled, bumpy fabric of her underskirt and cupped her bottom, dragging her closer. The vee between her legs settled intimately against him. Where they touched, his flesh grew hot, damp, and a need more intense than any he'd ever felt flared like a lit match in his soul.

Instinct took over. He began to move in a slow, rocking motion. His hips pushed and rubbed against hers. She matched him move for move until they were both panting and aching for more.

Then suddenly she pushed away from him.

Larence felt an ice-cold splash of fear. He squeezed his eyes shut, trying to control the ragged tenor of his breathing. It was over. Now she was going to slap him. Or laugh at him, or—

"Let's lie down."

His eyes opened. She grinned at him like an over-eager schoolgirl and stripped out of the petticoat.

"Come on," she said, taking his hand and pulling him toward the sleeping bags. He moved woodenly alongside her, his gaze glued to the pale round moons of her fanny.

She dragged the sleepings bag together and laid them side by side, then spun around and dropped to her knees onto their cushiony middle.

"Sit down," she said, patting the space beside her.

Larence couldn't move. He needed a moment—just a moment—to savor the look of her right now. To store every detail so that later, when he was alone and lonely, he could pull the memory out like a favorite photograph and stare at it. And remember . . .

God, she was beautiful. Sitting there atop the dark green ducked fabric, with her streaming white-gold hair and cream-hued flesh, she looked like an angel plunked down on earth.

For now—for tonight at least—she was his. He didn't know why; didn't care why. All he knew was that God had given him this gift, and he was going to take it. The Devil take tomorrow. He limped over and sat down beside her.

He brought his hand up, and in a tentative, hope-filled gesture, touched her cheek. "Come closer," he whispered.

She did.

He curled his hand around the nape of her neck and anchored her to him. His eyes fastened on hers. Now was the time to tell her the truth. The awful, humiliating truth. He swallowed hard, feeling heat creep up his cheeks. Although he wanted to, he didn't turn away, didn't take the coward's route. "You know I've never—"

She kissed him, a quick, short kiss that told him what he needed to know. She knew he was a virgin and didn't care. "You know I have?"

He took her face in his hands and gently tipped her chin. Gazing down into those luminous blue eyes, he felt . . . larger than life. Something deep in his soul expanded. An aching, loving tenderness filled his heart.

Emmaline Amanda Hatter, whether she loved him or not, was the woman he'd love until his dying day. He knew it more certainly than he'd ever known anything in his life.

This time Larence kissed Emma. As if he'd kissed a thousand women, he took charge. His lips molded to hers and moved slowly, sensually.

The kiss lasted forever and beyond. With each second, each lick of her tongue against his, Larence felt his need for her swell, until he thought he would burst from wanting her.

His free hand cupped her shoulder, kneaded the warm, silken flesh, then slid down the length of her arm. A groan slipped from her mouth and she leaned closer, fumbling urgently with the buttons on his shirt.

His shirt slid off before he knew it, bunched around his waist. She tossed it aside and went to work on his pants.

Larence felt her fingers moving nimbly from one button to the next, and his breath caught. Tentatively he let one finger glide up the sensitive skin of her inner arm. She shivered. Her fingers worked faster.

His forefinger continued up her arm, then followed the hollow indentation of her armpit and eased down toward her breast. The roughened pad of his finger brushed her nipple, and the peak hardened instantly. He brought his thumb up, and the two fingers began a slow, gentle laving.

She eased her lips away from his and let her head loll back. Her back arched, her breasts strained toward him. He did the only thing that made sense: He took a breast in each hand and touched the hardened peaks with his tongue.

"Oh, Larence . . . take your pants off."

"Already? I thought—"

She grabbed him by the waistband and pulled him close. He felt the rapid, heaving strains of her breath against his face, saw the passion-darkened pools of her eyes. "Take your pants off. *Now*."

He got to his feet and wrenched off his pants. Throwing them God-knew-where, he dropped back onto the sleeping bags and took her in his arms.

She rolled on top of him and kissed him again. He felt her naked breasts pressing hotly against his chest. Her hair streamed around his face, curtaining the moon's soft glow and plunging him in utter darkness. With his sense of sight impeded, his other senses burst to life. He heard the quiet sighing of the leaves above, felt the flicker-soft touch of her hair against his naked shoulders, smelled the wildflower-fresh scent of her skin, and tasted . . . Oh, God, what he could taste . . .

His hands moved to the base of her spine and roved upward, gliding up and down the soft curve of her back, pinning her to him. Naked flesh fused to naked flesh as her hips began a slow, sensual movement against his.

Desire exploded in Larence's body. Pure, white-hot passion. He'd never felt anything like it in his life. It was an aching, burning *need*. . . .

In one motion, he rolled her beneath him. She stared up at him through wide, night-darkened eyes. He could see the swelling of her lips, the faint scratch marks on her chin from his day's growth of beard.

I love you. He imagined himself saying the words, ached to say them. "Em, I—"

Her hands clutched his buttocks, and his sentence shattered, his ability to speak evaporated. That need, stronger and more intense, throbbed between his legs. Her hands squeezed, urged him to move. He ground his hips against hers, rubbed himself against the crisp, damp hairs between her legs. Her knees came up around his waist.

"Now," she whispered thickly. *"Now."*

Larence groaned aloud and buried his head in her shoulder. Cupping her tightly, he pulled her close and entered her.

She moaned; the breath felt warm against his cheek. He rocked against her, glided in and out of her in harder and harder drives. She clung to him, matching him thrust for thrust until sweat slicked his back and dotted the valley between her breasts.

Her bent legs slid in sweaty streaks up and down the sides of his body. Where they touched him, his flesh burned. Together they moved faster and faster. Their breath came in burning, panting gasps, and Larence heard himself saying her name over and over again, but the word seemed drawn-out and filtered through a long, dark tunnel.

His body spasmed, went taut. She grabbed his shoulders, and he thought he heard her whisper, "Not yet," but it was too late.

Release burst through him like an explosion of dynamite. He was spiraling through a lightless void where nothing mattered but the sensations pulsing through his body. . . .

Slowly he drifted back to earth.

Emmaline was staring up at him with a half-bemused, half-frustrated look in her eyes. A tiny, reluctant smile tugged one side of her mouth.

He kissed her lips and the smile grew. Rolling onto his back, he slid one arm behind her neck and drew her close. She snuggled up beside him, threw her left leg casually across his thigh. The easy intimacy brought a smile to his lips.

"That was great," he said, giving her shoulder a squeeze. "Really great."

He waited for her response. When none came, he pushed up onto one elbow and looked down at her. "Em? Aren't you going to say anything?"

Her mouth twitched. "It was . . . energetic."

He frowned at that. "Isn't it supposed to be?"

"Yes . . ." she said, but the word was so elongated, he wondered whether she meant it.

He chewed thoughtfully on his lower lip, then said, "Do you have any . . . suggestions for improvement?"

"Well . . ." Her gaze twinkled up at him. "Next time you might try making it last a little longer."

Next Time! Larence pulled her close against his side and flopped onto his back. In the darkness he grinned like the Cheshire cat. There was going to be a next time.

Long after Emma had fallen asleep, Larence lay wide awake, staring at the blanket of stars above.

Last longer. The words rolled around in his head, reminding him of the *Kama Sutra* and other Eastern books he'd read on the subject of sex and erotica.

Yes, he thought with a confidence he'd only just discovered. He could make it last longer if that's what she wanted.

A lot longer.

Chapter Twenty-one

From somewhere far away came the high, screeching cry of a hawk. Emma woke up slowly, lazily. Stretching like a contented cat, she yawned. She couldn't remember the last time she'd woken up feeling so good.

Every muscle in her body felt hammered and pounded . . . and joyfully alive. Curling onto her side, she snuggled against Larence's naked body. She eased her leg across his thighs and slipped her hand around his waist, laying her cheek on his chest.

She marveled at how relaxed she felt. She'd always wondered what it would be like to waken with a lover, but whenever she'd considered letting Eugene spend the night—and even considering it had been rare—her stomach had twisted into such a small, nervous knot, she'd practically pushed the poor man out the door. And yet here she was, curled up like a wife against her husband, and loving it.

She felt an intimacy with Larence she'd never known before. It liberated her, made her feel hopeful and free, and there was something else, something even more fragile slipping gently into her consciousness: trust.

She realized with a sense of awe that she trusted him with her emotions. He was the first person, including her parents, with whom she could just be herself. Aggressive, angry and bitter, or quiet, afraid, and laughing, she could simply be herself.

With that admission came the most encompassing, most compelling sense of well-being she'd ever known. Wordlessly she curled closer to him.

Sunlight kissed her skin. All around her the desert glittered and came to life. The morning air smelled of freshness and sunlight and . . . passion. Thick, sweet, new passion.

Emma smiled sleepily. Sex had been different last night. Never had she been so . . . abandoned.

Maybe it was her role as teacher that had excited her so much. Absentmindedly she twirled a finger through the dark brown hairs on his chest. She'd never had sex with a virgin before. It was a surprise to find, after all her experience, that inexperience was such an aphrodisiac.

For the first time, sex had been something more than simply pleasant. It had been . . . fun.

Her smile broadened. Yes, definitely fun.

That fact was especially amazing considering how . . . unsatisfied the entire play had left her. He'd brought her close—closer than she could ever remember being, in fact—to that elusive *something* that had always been missing from sex for her. For one brief, heart-stopping minute last night, she'd even thought it was going to happen. But, of course, it hadn't. He'd pulled out of her—like they all did—while her body was quivering with need and *waiting* for release.

Even so, she knew she wanted him again—and again.

"Morning, Em." He pushed up on one elbow and peered down at her. She plopped back into the sleeping bag's wool. In the morning's pale light, his eyes were the exact color of the leaves overhead. An unruly brown lock fell over one eye, and in a couple of places, spikes of hair stood at attention. He offered her a lazy, loving smile and pushed the hair out of his eyes. It fell right back.

Emma's heart squeezed.

He leaned down and kissed her, a long, slow, wet kiss that spoke of time and love and caring.

"How did you sleep?" she asked quietly, brushing the wayward lock from his eyes.

He grinned. "Never better. You?"

"Never better."

He slid his arm around her shoulders and drew her close. Together they stared up at the pink-and-blue-streaked sky. Dawn crept across the grass-strewn basin and gilded the mesa beside them. As usual, the red-tipped hawk was spiraling high above their heads.

"Today's the day," Larence said, and Emma knew exactly what he was talking about.

"Tell me about it again," she whispered, unwilling yet to let this moment together end.

Pulling her close, he began to spin out the legend of Esteban and Fray Marcos and the magical lost city. Again Emma found herself awed by the magnitude of his vision. His ability to dream astounded and humbled her.

For as long as she could remember, she'd discarded dreaming as a frivolous waste of time. But never once had she considered the price to her soul of such prac- ticality.

Now, in Larence's arms, she saw the cost clearly. Warmth, laughter, hope—these were the "trivialities" she'd discarded like so much trash. God, she'd missed so much in life by wanting so little—and needing that little so desperately. She'd let everything hinge on money—such a little thing, but she'd needed it so fervently. And God help her, she needed it still. . . .

Once again Larence's dreams spurred thoughts of her father's feeble, grasping prayers. She tensed, waiting for the familiar surge of resentment to hit her. Amazingly, it didn't. All she felt was an aching, almost overpowering sense of loss.

Something tantalized the edges of her mind, something elusive and yet important. She reached for it, tried to take hold of the insight that had eluded her for years. Somehow she knew Larence was the key. She tried to come up with the connection, but had no luck. Whatever the revelation was, she'd have to have it another time. Snuggling closer to Larence, she asked, "What made you first start looking for the city?"

"It started as nothing more than a dream. I was young then, and in a lot of pain. The dream . . . made me want to live."

"Oh," she said quietly as he went back to his description of the city and legend surrounding its disappearance. But she was no longer listening to him; she was thinking. The revelation slipped silently into her mind and changed her point of view.

Was it possible that she'd had it backward all these years? Had it been the dreams that had kept her father alive during the long, cold years of their poverty? He'd always lived in a dream world, always told her that tomorrow would be different. Better.

What if he hadn't been able to believe his own dreams, or if he hadn't been able to dream them at all? Would life have been so terrible, so dark and unbearable, that he'd have killed himself years before?

Emma chewed on her lower lip. Could it be true?

If it was, then the dreams hadn't made him take his

life; the death of those dreams had been the culprit. Perhaps when Mum died, she took the last of his dreams with her—and he simply didn't have the strength to live without their light.

She felt as if a ten-pound rock had been lifted from her shoulders. Maybe it was dreaming, and believing in dreams. That made life wonderful, instead of merely bearable.

Larence's monologue broke into her thoughts. ". . . The cross was big—as big as the man who carried it—and painted the brightest, most flawless shade of white. . . ."

She closed her eyes and let the words pour over her, filter through her. The story wound around her, captured her heart and soul. For the first time in her life, she let herself dream. Visions of a beautiful, forbidden city swirled through her mind, fueled her imagination. Gold; she saw a thousand shimmering doubloons of gold. Enough to keep her safe and warm and secure all the days of her life.

Her breathing sped up, her heart beat faster. She began to *believe*. And not just for herself, but for him. For Larence.

Huddling closer beside him, she smiled. It was the first time she could remember wanting something for someone else. It was a good feeling. She planted a kiss on the hard ball of his shoulder.

For the second time since meeting Larence, she had hope for her future.

Hope for her soul.

Larence watched Emmaline brush her hair. Yellowish pink postdawn light wreathed her, turned her hair into a fiery spray of silver and gold. The brush moved slowly through the curled, tangled mass, and with each stroke Larence felt something in his chest tighten.

God, she was beautiful. He knew it was cliché, this image of a woman brushing her hair in the dawn's tenuous light, but what was cliché to other men was new to him. Even now, after spending a night wrapped in the warmth of her embrace, he couldn't believe his good fortune.

If only he could tell her how much he loved her.

He ached to say the words, had ached to say them from the moment she'd first kissed him. But he wasn't stupid; she wouldn't want to hear about his feelings. And she sure as hell wouldn't share them. Oh, she might kiss him, might take him into her bed—for Emma, those were easy things. The one place she kept protected, the one place he'd never be given access to, was the place he most wanted to touch: her heart.

A small, wry smile tugged his lips as he thought of all the women he could have fallen in love with; women who'd long ago given up on love and would gladly take a broken-down, crippled professor into their hearts.

He sighed, feeling suddenly old and lost. He belonged with such a woman.

The irony of the situation struck him, and he smiled in spite of himself. He should have fallen in love with a homeless wren, and instead he'd picked a fairy-tale white swan. He'd almost assured the fact that his grandmother's words would come true.

He, a lonely, inexperienced cripple, had fallen head over heels for a self-confident, independent, breathtakingly beautiful woman who had the face of a Madonna, the brain of a railroad tycoon, and the body of a high-priced whore. A woman who could have any man she wanted—and obviously had.

He sighed again, wishing for one fleeting second that things were different—that *he* were different. That he could be the kind of confident, devil-may-care man who would know how to handle a woman like Emma. That he could be a spray of alcohol to her fire, instead of a cool, calm puddle of rainwater.

Then his hope fled. He wasn't that kind of man; he never had been and he never would be. In truth, he didn't even want to be.

He was lucky to have what he had. Whether it was a night with Emma or a dozen nights. It didn't matter. He'd been given a wonderful, irreplaceable gift. And he intended to make the most of it.

"Look, Larence! It's another one of those black and orange daisies. A big one."

He grinned down at her. "Black-eyed Susan."

Stopping, they slid off their mounts and walked hand in hand to the clump of wild-growing flowers. As they sat side by side on a big, flat rock, Larence pulled out his notebook and began to sketch.

"No, that's not right."

Larence turned to look at her, trying to hold back the smile lurking in the corners of his mouth. "Oh, really?"

She shot a quick glance down to the notebook, then she looked up at him. There was a tentative shyness in her eyes. "May I try?"

Wordlessly he handed her the pen and notebook. She worked at a snail's pace, making sure each line, each stroke, was perfectly drawn. He slid his hand along her tensed shoulder, reveling for a moment in the soft feel of her skin, and even more in his right to touch it. His palm moved slowly from the ball of her shoulder to the curve of her throat and back again.

Idly he glanced around. The earth had changed again since the *Malpais*, and once again they were in a strange new land, except this time there were familiar sights and scents. Green grass, colorful wildflowers, trees. And always the mesas, ancient, wind-twisted earthen mesas cutting through the high-altitude plain like thrusted tableaus of nutmeg-colored rock.

Cibola was just around the corner. As usual, the thought brought a quick surge of excitement. His mind drifted lazily to the images that had sustained him all his life. Golden streets, silver doors, turquoise window-sills. And answers. Glorious, all-important answers.

Soon they'd see the entrance to the box canyon. . . .

Emma jabbed him in the side. "Larence, I'm talking to you."

"Huh? Oh, yeah. What did you say?"

She showed him her drawing. "What do you think?"

Larence suppressed a smile at the pride shining in her eyes. It had finally happened. Emmaline had taken over his notebook. "It's perfect." He planted a long, slow kiss on her mouth. "Just perfect."

By dinnertime, Emma's newly discovered hope for her future had dissipated.

"I don't know," Larence said in a clipped, angry voice she barely recognized. "It should be here."

A headache started behind her tired eyes. She pressed two fingers to the throbbing, pounding hollow of her temple and glanced dully around. They were in a box canyon—*the* box canyon if that damned diary was worth spit. All around them gold-red stone mesas stood like ancient, dour-faced guards, trapped them. Trees stood stiff and motionless; no wind reached the hidden valley. The animals walked freely, their only avenue of escape a thin, twisting passageway that Larence had roped off.

He paced past her, muttering angrily.

"Larence," she said softly, "there's no point in—"

He spun around and speared her with a shriveling, *don't-you-dare-say-it* glare, then he pivoted again and marched toward the nearest mesa. Staring at the huge, fistlike block of golden-red sandstone that jutted up from the grass-and-black-eyed-Susan-carpeted plateau, he snapped the diary shut. The sound echoed feebly in the stone prison. "It should be here, damn it," he yelled at the rock. *"Here."*

Emma took a few halting, hesitant steps toward him. "Larence . . ."

He turned suddenly. Their gazes met and held. She saw the strange burning passion that filled his eyes, and it frightened her. For a single second he was someone else, someone she'd never met before. A zealot.

"Larence . . ." She said his name again. Hopefully. Quietly.

He deflated before her eyes, turned from a towering, angry man to a small, defeated one. His broad shoulders caved downward, and a bleak, desperate darkness clouded his eyes. The zealot's light went out. Emma swallowed thickly. She felt the loss of that fire, that burning passion, as keenly as she'd ever felt any loss in her life.

Her heart wrenched, her steps faltered. She felt helpless and lost and useless.

What could she do or say to ease his heartache? The diary was wrong. *Wrong.*

They'd scoured every inch of this box canyon, and there was no passageway to be found.

Larence tore his defeated gaze away from her and looked once again at the fist of rock. The leather-bound diary slid out of his numb fingers and plopped in the grass.

"Why?" he screamed suddenly. The single word bounced off the silent rock, vibrated through the grassy sanctuary, and threaded through the pine needles before the silence snuffed it out. Then, quieter. "Why . . ."

He dropped to his knees beside the fire. Emma walked over to him, and the moment she saw him, she knew he could just as easily have dropped into the flames. He was staring into space with the glassy-eyed look of a drunkard with no bourbon. His eyes saw nothing save the city that had called him all his life.

Except there was no city. His life's work, his life's dream, had been a lie.

The enormity of the situation struck her. Cibola wasn't here. Larence hadn't found his city, and she hadn't found her treasure. She was broke. Flat broke.

She had no fortune, no future. She'd return to New York as penniless as she'd left it. Rosare Court rose in her mind like an evil specter. A chill slithered icelike down her spine.

No. She forced the image away. Now wasn't the time to think about her own paltry loss. In truth she'd lost nothing; she'd never really believed in Cibola anyway. Larence had lost everything. And she was afraid—more afraid than she liked to admit—that he'd also lost his spark. His soul.

She stood a few feet away from him, staring at his hunched back. Raw, agonizing indecision consumed her. She wanted to go to him, to take him in her arms and tell him everything would be all right.

And yet even as the thought surfaced, she shoved it

away. Tell him what? her practical businesswoman's mind railed. That he'd find another life's work tomorrow?

She lifted her gaze from his hunched, defeated body and stared silently, angrily, at the stone walls. The diary had led them to this hidden canyon's secret center and then deserted them. Far above, the barest hint of a breeze rustled through the treetops, and the sound was hideously akin to human laughter. . . .

Unexpectedly, Pa-lo-wah-ti's words returned to her. *You are meant to seek, but not to find. Leave now. While you still can.*

Still can . . . still can . . .

She snapped out of it. She had to do something. Now. If she didn't, she would go quietly mad. . . .

She walked to the canyon's small, spring-fed pond. Diablo and the pack mule were lazily drinking the crystal-clear water, and Tashee was nearby, munching greedily on the shin-high green grass. Emma leaned against the burro's dusty rump, listening with half an ear to the continual snap of grass being ripped from the earth and the slow, grinding chomp of Tashee's teeth.

What could she do to help?

Maybe someday I'll get lucky and you'll make real stew.

Larence's joking words came back to her. She latched on to them; they weren't much, but they were *something*.

She hurried over to the pile of supplies and dug through the overfilled saddlebags for Larence's *Guide to Edible Plants and Herbs in the American Southwest*. Finding it, she dropped cross-legged on the hot grass and began flipping through the sketches of edible plants.

When she knew what she was looking for, she tucked the book under her arm and headed out.

An hour later, Emma was humming an almost happy tune. Tucked in her waistband was a small bag filled with bitterroot bulbs, common camas bulbs, wild mustard leaves, and shepherd's purse leaves (which supposedly tasted like cabbage, although Emma had her doubts). All she needed now were a few wild potatoes—and the guide assured her they were here to be found.

She moved one step at a time, her nose bent to the ground like a prized Labrador. The grass crinkled beneath her feet, let off a fresh, familiar scent. Dozens of wildflowers and black-eyed Susans fluttered alongside her skirts. Tiny burrs leapt from their waving stalks and stuck to her skirt.

She saw something. Her step slowed. She bent farther down. Up ahead, winding through a crack in the red-gold sandstone wall, was a forest green plant with large, arrow-shaped leaves. Dotted throughout the leaves were long, spiraled, unborn blossoms.

Emma's breath caught. She surged toward the plant and dropped to her knees. Opening the book, she flipped to the page marked *wild potatoes* and studied the black line drawing of the plant and its tuber. Then she looked at the plant huddled alongside the sandstone wall. It looked the same. . . .

She clawed furiously through the dry, red-hued dirt for the plant's root. Her fingers closed around something hard and egg-shaped. She let out a quick yelp of joy and wrenched the root free. It was as big as her palm!

She looked at the root, then at the plant, then at the book. It looked the same. Not *identical*, but as much the same as a man-made ink drawing can look. She'd learned from Larence that it was impossible to capture every single nuance.

She'd found her wild potato. Her mouth watered in anticipation of something *fresh*. With a grin, she brushed the potato off, jammed it in her small leather pouch, and headed back to the campsite.

Emma peeled off the potato's harsh outer skin and cut the tuber into four equal pieces. Plopping the bits into the slowly boiling water, she added a generous dollop of beef extract, some salt and pepper, a few dried onions and a can of evaporated carrots, and the shepherd's purse leaves. Gradually the water began to darken, turn a rich, mouth-watering brown. She added a tablespoon or so of flour and stirred the stew until the broth thickened.

Beef-scented steam wafted her way, and her stomach grumbled in anticipation. Emma inhaled deeply, savoring the comforting smell of homemade stew.

Then she sat back on her heels and laid the spoon on the rock beside her. She glanced over at Larence, who was still pacing back and forth along the sandstone wall like an injured tiger who'd been caged. Every now and then she heard him mutter, "It has to be here. It *has* to be . . ."

She let the stew simmer for two silent, nail-biting hours, then she called to him. "Supper's ready."

Larence turned slowly toward her, and the expression on his face made her heart wrench anew. His eyes, normally so full of life, were the dull, lifeless green of dying weeds. His face was pale, almost gray, and his mouth was drawn into a colorless line. He tossed the diary down, barely noticing where it landed in the grass, and rammed his hands into his pockets.

He tried to smile, and the effort almost broke Emma's heart. "Sure," he said. "I'm starving."

Emma got to her feet and met him halfway. She slipped her hand into his; they walked wordlessly to the small fire and sat down side by side. Emma spooned a healthy portion of stew into his tin bowl and handed it to him.

"Fresh stew," he whispered with a dry, near soundless laugh. "I guess I got lucky after all."

Emma couldn't believe that now, in the midst of his pain, he remembered.

He stirred his stew, staring silently at the tin fork as it swirled round and round. The dull, scratchy sound of tin on tin filled the air. Then, finally, he looked up again and met her gaze. "I let you down, Em. There's nothing for you here. . . ."

She swallowed thickly. Tears stung her eyes. They stared at each other for a long, quiet moment.

Emma longed to say it didn't matter, that money didn't mean a damn thing to her. But she couldn't do it; the words would be a lie, and she couldn't lie to him. Not now, not after everything. He'd know, and the knowledge of her deception would hurt him more than the truth of her silence.

She wished she didn't care, wished it with all her heart. But the sad, sorry truth was that she *did* care. She cared desperately. She had changed, grown on this trip, but not that much. She'd never change that much. The thought of being poor again made her almost sick to her stomach. She might change enough to allow love into her life, but she'd never put the need for money out of it. . . .

"I'm sorry, Em."

"Me, too," she answered quietly. "Now, eat."

She broke eye contact first, then he looked away. Silently, staring into their bowls, they began to eat.

Emma took a small sip of the broth. It burned all the way down her throat and landed like a hot coal in her stomach. Then a foul, bitter aftertaste filled her mouth.

Frowning, she raised the spoon to her lips again and blew on it until the steam was gone. Then, hesitantly, she tried another bite. It burned as badly as the first; not a hot burn, a spicy one. She winced in pain, almost gagging as the bitter aftertaste flooded her mouth again.

Larence grimaced. "It tastes sort of . . ."

"I know." She took another bite, wincing at the sharp, burning taste of it. She hadn't put *that* much pepper in it. "Maybe it's the bitterroot."

Larence tried again. "Yeah. Maybe," he agreed doubtfully.

Emma felt a giggle start. She tried to stifle it, knowing this was no time to laugh, but she couldn't help herself. It spilled out. "I . . . I'm so . . . rry," she managed between giggles. "But I *told* you I'd kill us if I tried to cook."

A reluctant smile tugged at Larence's lips and crept into his eyes. "I should have known you're never wrong."

She smiled back, then took a sip of coffee. The hot, familiar liquid slid down her throat with comforting ease, banishing the memory of the stew's aftertaste. She leaned lazily backward, resting on her elbows, and stared at the shadow-darkened mesas that ringed them.

After a moment or two, she noticed something odd. Her heart was beating too fast. A hot flush crept up her cheeks, leaving a fiery trail. She pressed a hand to her cheeks, relaxing for a moment at the cool feel of her own flesh.

A headache started. Slow, thudding, hitting behind her eyes and at the back of her skull with mallet-hard force. She winced at the sudden pain of it. She pressed two shaking fingers to her temples, wishing she had some Foley's Family pills.

She stared across the fire at Larence. He was frowning at her. *Frowning*. The unexpected expression made her heart pound even faster, made her headache intensify. She reached shakily for the coffeepot.

"Would you like so—" The word *some* turned thick and muddy. She swallowed—at least she *tried* to swallow. But it was a feeble attempt. Her mouth was as dry as cold ash.

A wave of nausea tickled her stomach, then punched it. She clamped a hand over her roiling midsection. "Larence . . . I . . . feel thick, er—" she concentrated, trying to remember the right word, and then, once she'd remembered it, trying to force it off her huge, heavy tongue "—sick."

Her fingers started to shake. She stared at them in rising panic. The bowl fell into her lap, and hot stew splashed across her skirt. The gooey fabric stuck to her thighs and burned. "Owww . . ."

Larence flung his bowl away. It landed with a thunk and a clang that vibrated in Emma's ears. She clamped her hands over her ears, but still the ringing persisted, grew louder. She heard the heavy, marching *clang*, *clang*, *clang* over and over again; the sound matched the rapid-fire beat of her heart, thudded in her ears.

The din was huge, crashing in on her from all sides. She screamed to be heard above it. *"Larence!"*

He tried to crawl toward her. She could see how hard

he was working, see the concentration it took for him to move. Panting, wheezing breaths shot from his pursed lips and added to the cacophony of sounds battering Emma's ears. Each desperate, clawing movement of his hands gained less than a hair breadth of ground. He'd never reach her. Never.

Panic swelled up from the bowels of her soul, swamped her, pulled her into its black, whirling eddy. The world tilted, spun, became a foreign, frightening blur of brown and black and green. The stars overhead blurred, melted into the ebony-hued night sky and disappeared, plunging her into a lightless void.

A frightened cry lodged in her throat and vibrated there. She was losing control of everything, her mind, her body, her senses. . . .

She clasped her shaking hand to her throat and tried to focus on something. Anything. But the world was a shifting, dancing kaleidoscope of evil shadows and impossible movement. Mesas swayed in the twilight's thickening darkness and crept toward her. Trees whispered loudly among themselves and inched closer to the fire. Far away—or maybe right beside her—a hawk screeched loudly. Then came the sounds of a dozen nocturnal animals: the distant hoot of an owl, the whisper-soft whirring of bat wings, the hollow rattle of a snake's tail. For one crazy second, Emma even thought she could hear the padding of cat paws as a cougar crept through the grass toward them.

Suddenly a hand broke through the darkness. She stared at it with a mixture of horror and awe. It was a platter-sized blob of canary yellow. Each finger vibrated, swelled, throbbed to the rabbit-fast pattering of her heart.

"Emmaline . . ." The word echoed through the long,

dark tunnel of her mind and landed in her lap like a lifeline.

She reached for him. The hand turned into a trailing, violet haze and dissipated.

She screamed.

"Emmaline . . ."

She concentrated, tried to think of a single word. None came. Her throat was closed up, her tongue a dead thing wedged in her mouth.

"It's okay . . . Em . . . don't fight it. . . ."

Then she remembered his name. "La . . . re . . . nce . . ." The word seeped past her huge lips in near soundless pants of breath. His fingers threaded hers and closed tight, giving her an anchor in the lurching world. A great, heaving sob of relief burst up from her chest. She clung to him desperately, crying. Each tear felt like a trail of fire down her cheek. The taste of salt was thick on her tongue.

He sidled up beside her, took her in his arms. "It's . . . okay." His voice sounded far away and pained. His breath came in racking, wheezing pants. "There was . . . something . . . in the stew."

Laughter swelled and died in her bone-dry throat. *No kidding.*

"Datura root . . . jimsonweed . . . looks like . . . wild potato." He held her close and helped her to her feet, tucking her protectively under his arm. Together they stood up. Alone against the crazy, illogical world around them. "Relax . . . enjoy . . . adventure . . . ancient . . . Indian . . . ritual."

They clung to each other. Overhead, the stars reappeared, danced. Streaks of colorful light shot up from the swaying treetops, flittered across the shadowy night sky.

Then Emma saw them: the cobras. Huge, terrifying, they rose up, hooded. Dozens of lidless black eyes focused on her. Forked tongues spit through reptilian mouths. Hissing filled the quiet air. The cobras swayed left and right with the wind, then slid inexorably toward them. The hissing grew louder.

A scream swelled in Emma's chest, writhing in the pit of her stomach like the deadly snakes gliding toward her. She opened her mouth and set it free. The high, shrill sound bounded off the sandstone walls, echoed through the canyon.

"Hang on, Em." Larence's words filtered through the shriek, reached her pounding ears. "You're . . . hallucinating."

Hallucinating. Yes. She clung to the word that made the unreal real. Her teeth came together with an audible click.

She glared at the snakes. *"You're not real."*

They disappeared, leaving in their stead an army of silent, swaying trees.

She started to shake again. Her headache intensified, brought a stab of nausea so sharp, she staggered from the force of it. Clinging to Larence like a drowning woman, more frightened than she'd ever been in her life, she said the words over and over again like a litany. "It's not real. None of this is real. . . ."

She didn't know how long she stood there with him, her arms wrapped around his waist, her face buried in the soft cotton of his shirt. But it seemed like forever. Longer.

Gradually her headache diminished. The rapid beating of her heart subsided. Even the shaking in her fingers melted away.

"Emma?"

She looked up into his comforting green eyes and felt an overwhelming surge of relief. They'd made it through; whatever she'd done to them, they'd survived it. Together.

Her hands slid up the warmed, bumpy fabric of his shirt and anchored around his neck. He pulled her close, his laced fingers settling possessively in the hollow at the base of her spine.

He leaned down. She pressed up onto her tiptoes and met him more than halfway for a kiss. Slowly, reluctantly, they pulled apart.

A soft night breeze whistled through the treetops above their heads, and the small fire crackled and hissed, as if in celebration of their victory. Sparks fluttered upward from the fire and gilded the darkness. Moonlight broke through the thick, charcoal-hued clouds and shone down on them like the finest Waterford chandelier. Shards of sparkling light touched their faces.

Larence took her face in his hands, holding her as if she were wrought from the finest Sèvres china. She blinked up into his eyes and saw something she hadn't seen in years. Something she'd long ago stopped believing in. Love.

Something hot and iron-strong coiled around her throat and squeezed. She felt a surge of something light and wonderful and pure. An emotion so huge, so magical, she was afraid to name it.

"Emmaline, I love you."

She watched his mouth move. The slow, sensual opening and closing of his lips sent a vibration through the private regions of her body. It took a moment for his words to register, and when they did, her mouth fell open in shock.

Her? He loved *her*, Emmaline Hatter?

She shook her head in denial and opened her mouth to correct him. To tell him it was the drug speaking, or the passion. No one loved her. "I—"

A loud *crack* split the silence. The grass shuddered and the earth beneath their feet rumbled. A sound like the grinding together of rusty gears echoed through the box canyon.

"Oh, God," Emma cried, "not again . . ."

"No," Larence said quickly. "This is real."

They spun toward the sound. As they did, a blue-white lightning bolt snaked out of the midnight black sky and struck the sandstone wall. Sparks flew everywhere. A giant schism zigzagged down the rock face, splitting the stone. The smell of smoke was strong.

The grinding sound intensified; the earth rattled and shook beneath their feet. Grass shuddered in fear. Dirt rained down from the mesa's top.

Then it was over.

They stared in awe at the huge, gaping gash in the sandstone wall.

Larence let go of her hand and moved toward the crack, his hand outstretched.

"Cibola." The word floated back to Emma's ears, terrifying her more than the hallucination had. He wasn't going to go *in* there? *Oh, God* . . .

"Don't move!" she shrieked.

He didn't listen to her; he just kept moving forward like a sleepwalker.

She raced after him and grabbed his sleeve, spinning him around. "You can't go in there. It might close up on you."

He looked down at her, and there was a certainty in

his eyes that made her dizzy with fear all over again. "It's Cibola."

She shook her head. "No." The word squeaked past her lips in a frightened whimper. "You don't know that. Please . . ."

"Come with me, Em, and be my love . . ."

She tried to pull away. He held her tight. The thought of him walking into that darkness filled her with unreasoning fear. The rock could close as quickly as it had opened, and then he'd be gone. Gone.

She protested. "The animals—"

"Will be fine. They can't get out of the canyon, and there's plenty of food and water in here. Come with me."

Emma blinked up at him, clinging to his sleeve like a frightened, fretful child. Afraid. Uncertain.

He gave her hand a squeeze. All the love in the world filled his eyes. "Come on, Em. It may never open again. Come with me. Please. I love you. . . ."

There was only one thing she could do. With a deep, shuddering breath, she shoved her fear aside and did what she'd never done in her life. She trusted.

Together, hand in hand, they walked into the jet black opening.

Chapter Twenty-two

It was a darkness unlike anything she'd ever known. Like being buried alive.

"Emma?"

Larence's voice came to her from the blackness, disembodied yet comforting. She squeezed his hand tighter, trying to quell the infinitesimal shaking in her fingers. But whether she was afraid or excited, she couldn't honestly say.

He let go of her hand. She heard him rustling around beside her, picking up something from the ground. Then came the hissing *rip* of cotton being wrenched apart, and the scratchy sound of a match being lit.

The match flared brightly, and Emma immediately noticed that Larence's left sleeve was missing. The next thing she noticed was the makeshift torch in his hand. He grinned at her look of surprise. "Another gem from Diamond Dick."

He touched the match to the cotton wrapped around the stick's top. It took hold and flared brightly, sending golden fingers zipping through the blackness. The cave funneled into a thin strip of black. A passageway.

"Cibola."

Larence said the word at the exact moment she

thought it. Her heart sped up; sweat dampened her palms, turned them cold and clammy. *Cibola.*

Excitement wedded with fear and made her breath quicken. The harsh tenor of it echoed loudly in the confined space.

Together, holding hands, they felt their way along the cool, gritty sandstone walls. The torch created a kaleidoscope of twisting, dancing light. Golden-hued spirits writhed on the floor in front of them and leapt on the curved walls.

After about fifty feet the tunnel wedged into a corridor no wider than Larence's shoulders. The fecund scent of ancient dirt seeped out of the opening.

He let go of her hand. "I'll go first. Stay right behind me."

She grabbed hold of the warm cotton of his shirttail and followed. Darkness pressed in on her. She couldn't see anything beyond the light-wreathed silhouette of Larence's head. The temperature dropped. She wrapped her free hand around her waist in an attempt to keep warm. Her fingers curled tightly around the shirttail. The cotton became her lifeline.

The constant shuffling whisper of their footsteps mingled with the quickened march of their breathing and echoed in the tunnel.

Shuffle, pant, shuffle, pant. Then, unexpectedly, Larence's heel hit something and clicked.

He stopped. Emma rammed into his back.

"We're standing on something," he said, and she could hear the excitement in his voice. "Move back."

When she had backed up, he shoved the torch at her, and dropped to his knees. She gripped it in fingers that couldn't seem to stop shaking. Light slipped in bumping streaks down the sandstone wall and puddled on the shadowy floor. Beneath the layer of long-dry dirt, an almost invisible network of lines appeared.

She went weak with hope and excitement, and kneeled. Cold dampness seeped into her bones and plastered her skirt to her knees, but she didn't notice the discomfort. All she could think about was *maybe*. Sweet God, maybe there really *was* a Cibola. A treasure.

"What is it?" she breathed.

Larence bent supplicantlike to the floor and blew. A tiny stream of dirt fluttered onto Emma's skirts.

"Tiles. Move the light closer."

She did, and saw what he saw. Two large, perfectly cut stone tiles made a two-foot square on the floor. One tile was raised slightly, as if it had been lifted long ago and never set right again.

Larence began carefully to lift the tiles. They scratched against one another, sounded like nail-sharp fingernails clawing on brick.

Beneath the tiles lay another tunnel.

Emma moved the torch. Light splashed through the opening and landed on a human skeleton a few feet below. She screamed and scuttled backward. The torch wobbled in her hands, and light vibrated haphazardly across the arched walls.

"Don't be afraid, Em. They're just bones."

Just bones. Calming herself, she inched back up to the hole and peered into the pit.

Pale, gray-white bones lay atop the brown soil. A jawless skull sat cheekbone-deep in the soft, dry dirt. Empty, eyeless sockets stared up at her, as if daring her to come forward. To come into *his* realm.

"It's just a grave," she told herself, trying to remain calm. "Just a damn grave."

"I don't think so." Larence leaned over the hole to better study the skeleton. "See the way his arms are crossed across his chest? And see that marking above his head? That's the ancient symbol for danger. The same one Ka-Neek left us." He sat back on his knees, rubbing his fingers along the coarse day's growth of beard that darkened his cheeks and chin. "No, I think he's—he *was*—a guard."

Her heart missed a beat. "Really?"

"I think so." He grinned at her. "Let's find out what he's guarding."

Emma felt an unexpected hesitation. She glanced down at the bones. A strong sense of premonition made her skin tingle. Perhaps they weren't meant to be here. Pa-lo-wah-ti's words came back to her with blinding force. *Leave. Now. While you still can . . .*

"Em?"

She tried to smile. He reached out and took her hand in his. Squeezing gently, he whispered. "Believe, Em. Believe."

Before she had time to answer, he took the torch from her and was gone. Down the hole. His boots hit the dirt with a muffled thump, and a second later the thick aroma of disturbed earth wafted up to her nostrils.

Emma leaned over, watching him. A strange sound, like the muted rattle of a baby's toy, reached her ears. *Shucka-shucka-shucka.*

Straddling the skeleton, he examined the blood-brown marking on the wall. "Emma, I—"

They saw the snake at the same time. Its small head shot out from the tangle of grayed ribs. Beady, lidless eyes dominated the scaly head. The rattling intensified, filled the hole with terrifying, throbbing sound.

"Shit!" Larence lurched up and back at the same

time. His skull cracked into the wall, and dirt rained down on his head. Scrambling backward amid the terrible snap of breaking bones, he flung the torch at the snake. It hit the reptile hard between the eyes. The rattler jerked back and retreated into the relative safety of the skeleton's rib cage. Larence waited a moment, then bent down and plucked up the torch.

"Give me your skirt," he rasped.

Emma peeled out of her muslin skirt and dropped it into the hole. Larence threw the billowing garment over the rib cage and tucked the fabric under each and every bone. "That should give us time. Come on down."

She didn't move. She couldn't. All she could do was stare into the black, bone-ridden hole and wait for the sandpaper-soft shaking of the snake's rattle.

Larence's hand appeared before her. She stared at it in horror, knowing the second she saw it what she would do. What she had to do. "Oh, God," she groaned, "not snakes . . ."

Words drifted up to her: "Believe, Em. Believe."

Lord, how she was beginning to hate that word. No doubt it would appear on her tombstone. *Emmaline Amanda Hatter. She believed—and it killed her.*

"Emma, the snake won't be covered forever."

She grabbed hold of his hand, squeezed her eyes shut, and dropped into his waiting arms.

"See, now," he said, "that wasn't so—"

"Get me out of here!" Her words bounced off the walls and rang back at her.

He carried her toward the grave's narrow opening and set her down. They stood side by side, their eyes glued to the pale pile of bones. Larence leaned down and wrenched the skirt away from the skeleton. Emma's breath jammed in her throat.

Nothing. No sound, no movement.

Her breath whooshed from her lungs in a hot, painful sigh of relief. She quickly donned her skirt, then offered Larence her hand.

Together, slowly, they began their journey down the dark, dank, winding passageway. Into the bowels of the earth itself.

Sometime later—and Emma had long since given up the idea of calculating time—she began to hear something besides the shuffling whisper of their shoes on the sandy floor.

It began as a soft sound, like the fall of a single drop of rain into an overfull barrel, and had gradually intensified into the echoing roar of falling water.

At first she hadn't believed her ears. It wasn't possible, these sounds of a waterfall in the dry, arid intestines of the New Mexican desert, two hundred or more feet below the earth's surface. And yet, against all odds, the sound had continued. With each step it grew louder, closer.

Then came something even more unexpected. More impossible.

Light. It began as a pinprick at the end of the corridor, but with each step the unbelievable light strengthened. The circle of its whiteness grew larger, and then larger still, until there was no longer a circle at all. There was simply light. Everywhere, filling every nook and cranny and giving the harsh, cold sandstone a gold-like brilliance.

Larence picked up his pace, limping ahead as fast as his bad ankle allowed. Emma clung to his hand and kept up.

As they neared the corridor's end, things changed

subtly. Gone was the musty smell of earth too long in the shade; now she smelled fresh water, sunshine, piñon needles, and late spring grass. Beside them was a light-gilded lip of sandstone. Beyond it, who knew?

And suddenly, Emma knew that it—whatever *it* was—lay just around the corner. She knew just as completely that it only existed if she believed it did.

She stopped, yanking Larence to a halt beside her.

"What are you doing? It's right around the—"

"I know." She half turned, closed the infinitesimal gap between them. "I want you to know I believe it's there. I *want* it to be there. For you."

"I love you."

An emotion so pure, so *big* it made her knees weaken, swelled in her heart. Her toes and fingers tingled in its wake, her throat closed up. It was an emotion the likes of which she hadn't seen in years, had long since stopped expecting. Perhaps even stopped believing in.

It was—

Before the word solidified in her mind, he led her around the corner.

Larence turned the corner and gasped. It was grander, bigger, richer, than anything he'd ever expected. Ever imagined.

"Oh, my God," Emma breathed beside him.

The passageway emptied out onto a huge, circular plain. Velvety soft, dun-colored sand stretched from one mesa wall to the next like an expensive blanket of the finest chamois. The warm, dry perfume of it scented the air. Nutmeg red canyon walls arched high into the sky, their time-smoothed blocks curled upward like the fingers of a carefully cupped hand. Slabs of rock formed a towering circle around them, without entrance or exit,

beginning or end. Overhead a fist-shaped blotch of cobalt blue sky stood in stark contrast to the reddish gold
walls.

In the center of the plain was an oval-shaped pool the
pale green of fine Oriental jade. Cattails limned the
water's edge, swaying softly as water lapped their stems.
From somewhere high in the mesa's cracks and cre-
vasses, white, foamy water tumbled gaily downward,
splashing noisily on the pool's glassy surface and sending ripples of silver-green from shore to shore.

Larence stared in awe at the beauty of it. Everything
was quiet, and muted, and old. So very, very old . . .

In his mind's eye he could *see* the Ancient Ones mill-
ing quietly about the square, or squatting in the doorways to grind corn into meal. The high-pitched giggle
of playing children echoed in his mind, and though he
knew the children of this place had not laughed in a
very long time, he heard them still. Saw them still.

He was so caught up in the exquisite loveliness of the
place that it took him a moment to notice the gold.
When he did, his mouth dropped open.

They were standing on a street paved in bricks of
gold. Thirty feet wide, it spilled down the sand-hued
plain, skirted the cattail-edged pool, and then rose
gently again to the row of stone-carved doorways beyond. Sunlight turned the street into a twisting, blinding river of molten gold. Excitement pounded in his
chest. It was exactly the way he'd always seen it in his
dreams. *Exactly.*

Images bombarded him, hurled him from one place
to another with exhilarating velocity. Silver and turquoise doorways winked at him, reminded him of every
dream he'd ever had. He stared in breathless wonder at

the row of elaborately decorated silver arches carved into the mesas' rock walls.

Instinctively he reached for his notebook. Then stopped. Now was the time to see, to experience the place that had called to him for a quarter of a century; later was the time to capture it.

Slow down, Lare. Slow down.

Emma threw herself into his arms. "You did it! You did it!"

He twirled her around, barely noticing the pain in his ankle at the movement. Their laughter merged, floated upward, and vibrated through the stone-ringed canyon.

"*We* did it."

She looked up at him. Adoration brightened her eyes, bathed him in its unfamiliar light, and something in his chest tightened. He felt special. Extraordinary, even.

And there was something else in her eyes. Something that filled him with longing. Something he wanted so badly, it made his stomach twist into knots.

Love.

He licked his paper-dry lips and prayed his desperation didn't show. It was getting harder and harder to be in love alone.

He loosened his hold, and she slid down the length of his body. Her heels clicked softly onto the golden bricks.

She giggled playfully and grabbed his hand. "Let's go."

Laughing, they raced down the twisting golden street to the pool.

"Last one in's a cow chip," Emma called out, already squatting to remove her serge Congress gaitors.

"Emma, let's—"

Her shoe sailed past his head and thumped in the dirt behind him.

He tried to remember that he was a scientist and that this was his life's work. "There's plenty of time for swimming. I want—"

Her other shoe hit the dirt at his knee. Still grinning, she crawled over and grabbed him by the shirt collar, yanking him toward her.

Bright blue eyes impaled him, and there was something in her eyes that made his gut clench. An honesty, an intensity that spoke of passion shared, passion promised.

Remember, her eyes said. *Remember.*

It worked. Images of last night tumbled through his brain, shot through his blood, and landed in his groin. The buttons on his Levi's suddenly seemed too tight.

He swallowed. Every word he'd ever known vanished from his head; he had trouble remembering what his life's work was. All he could think about was her; her lips, her touch, her fire . . .

She let go of him so suddenly, he plopped on his backside in the sand. Then she slipped out of her clothes and ran, naked and laughing, into the water.

Larence lurched to his feet and started fumbling with the buttons of his jeans. Tossing his clothes in a heap alongside the cattails, he hurried after her. Water curled around his legs, lapped gently against his inner thighs, reminding him forcibly of her touch. Her tongue.

He dove into the water and came up effortlessly beneath the waterfall. The foamy white spray engulfed him. He thew his head back and let the water pummel his desert-dry flesh.

"Larence?"

He heard her voice through the pounding roar of the

water. He stepped backward, letting the water form a silvery curtain through which he could see but she could not.

She was standing about twenty feet away, looking for him. He could tell she was perturbed, by the small frown that tugged at the edges of her mouth.

"Larence, this isn't funny."

He smiled, almost *hearing* the underwater tap-tap-tap of her foot. Grinning in anticipation, he dove under the waterfall and headed her way.

Emma didn't notice a movement in the water. Then suddenly there he was, rising from the glassy pool like Triton emerging from his watery world. Naked, waist-deep in water, he walked toward her. Sunlight shone from the slot overhead and gave his skin a pale golden glow. Silver-bright water droplets clung to his dark brown lashes; one by one falling lazily down his cheeks and plopping silently onto the hard, muscular squares of his chest. His fingertips trailed sensuously in the silver-green surface, sending snakelike ripples fanning out behind him.

Anxiety fluttered in her stomach. There was a raw, unveiled passion in his eyes she'd never seen before. An almost animallike intensity that stole her ability to breathe. As if he wanted more than her touch, more than her kiss, more even than access to the secret passageway of her body. As if he wanted her soul.

The fire in his gaze burned hotter than she'd ever seen it. She felt singed by its heat, branded as a possession.

Their roles had reversed. She was no longer the huntress; she was the hunted. The realization sent a white-hot bolt of desire careening through her body.

Real desire; not the regular, familiar passion she'd

known for Eugene, but something more. Something dark and wild and forbidden.

She licked her lips nervously.

A strand of breeze murmured through the trees stationed at the bank and ran cool, invisible fingers along her breasts. Gooseflesh popped out along her arms and turned her nipples into pointed, puckered peaks. Instinctively she raised a hand to her throat, feeling the rapid, rabbitlike dancing of her pulse.

It took a supreme act of will to remain motionless. Her heartbeat sped up. She swallowed dryly. Waiting. Wanting to stand here and be touched by him, and at the same time wanting desperately never to have met him at all.

She felt suddenly as if she were standing on the edge of a great cliff, and that all he had to do was hold his hands out and she would jump. Into the black void of a need she couldn't control, a desire she was powerless to deny.

She shivered again and closed her eyes. Waiting.

And then he was touching her. His warm, damp palms cupped her shoulders and squeezed lightly, resting there for a heartbeat before gliding down the length of her arms and letting go. "Come on."

She blinked sleepily, surprised.

He cocked his head to the left, where a huge, flat rock lay tilted half-in and half-out of the pool. Its wet, red-brown surface glowed like polished copper. A huge old cedar tree stood guard behind the rock, its long, needle-studded branches arched downward to taste the slowly moving water.

She stared at him blankly. "You want to show me the rock? Now?"

He nodded.

"I was thinking we mi—"

"Don't."

She frowned. "Don't what?"

"Don't think." Before she could stutter a reply, he swept her into his arms and carried her toward the rock. Water splashed up from his moving legs and dappled her naked body. She felt every droplet like a bead of fire.

The rock felt cool and mirror-slick beneath her bare back. He grabbed her wrists, and forced her hands over her head. When her arms were dangling limply amid the tangle of her own hair, he let go.

She didn't move, didn't breathe, as his gaze moved slowly down her body. She lay there, naked, pinned to the rock like a prize butterfly, and let him study her

Desire uncoiled deep in her body, sent burning feelers sliding through her blood. Restlessly she shifted her position on the rock. Her heart thumped hard in her chest; her pulse throbbed.

"You're so beautiful," he whispered, planting a kiss on her right nipple.

Emma gasped at the unexpected contact. Her body went cold, then hot. Her breathing sped up.

He pulled back. Cool air immediately rushed in, mingled with the moisture from his kiss, and turned her nipples pebble-hard. She stared up at him, mesmerized by the hungry passion in his eyes. A dull ache settled between her legs.

His hands slid down her sides, formed to the flesh of her thighs, and gently urged her legs to part. Moving between her knees, he leaned closer.

She strained forward for his kiss. His mouth slanted possessively over hers and forced her back onto the rock. She shoved aside the tangle of her own hair and clutched his shoulders.

He settled possessively between her legs. Naked flesh pressed naked flesh. She felt the thudding of his heart against her breast. Water beaded between them, turned hot, and then zigzagged down their sides and plunked into the pool.

His hardness probed the wetness between her legs, rubbed against her in a fluid, circular motion that made her whole body throb and tremble and *need*.

Oh, God, the need . . .

Her hands slid down his dew-sprayed back and clutched his buttocks. The ache between her legs turned into a fiery, almost painful throbbing. "Now, Larence. Now."

An unmistakable laugh slipped from his mouth to hers. "Patience," he drawled against her lips.

She shoved his chest hard. He straightened, peered down at her. Suppressed laughter crinkled the corners of his eyes, twitched his lips. "Yes, Emma?"

She stared up at him, breathing hard. "I want you to—"

He shook his head. At the movement, a dozen droplets of water sprayed her face.

She frowned. "But I think—"

"I told you not to think." His lips formed to hers as if God had made them as a matched set, and moved in a gentle, sensual rhythm that restoked the fire in her body.

After an eternity, he moved on. His kisses trailed down her throat, each one like a spark of fire burning along her exposed flesh. Down the pale curve of her throat, along her collarbone, past the swell of her breast to her nipple.

She felt the flick of his tongue and gasped. Her back bowed above the wet rock, strained for the feel of his tongue. Her breath came in hot, harsh gasps.

The licking intensified, turned into a gentle laving. Then a not so gentle one. The sensations set her on fire. She trembled, quivered, arched. Her fingers clawed, dug into the muscular flesh of his upper arms. Need washed through her body in waves.

"Now, Larence," she whimpered. *"Now."*

Still sucking her nipple, he let his hands slide down the length of her body. Gently but firmly he eased her hands away from his arms and pushed them back above her head.

"Grab hold." The words were spoken in a voice so thick and raw, she barely recognized it.

Without hesitation she grabbed hold of the branch above her head. The knotty bark felt foreign and erotic beneath her fingers. She pulled herself higher up the rock, and at the movement, the limb groaned. Needles rained down on her face and breasts.

She moved higher; Larence moved lower. His hands and mouth inched with a scientist's precision down her tingling, burning flesh. One by one he plucked the pine needles from her goosefleshed skin and tossed them aside.

He touched her in places she'd never thought sensitive, and yet beneath his inquisitive fingers, her skin vibrated, grew hot and damp. His mouth trailed slow, sensual kisses over her breasts, down the flat, quivering expanse of her stomach, and still downward.

When he reached his goal, Emma sucked in her breath and stiffened. "Wait!"

He looked up.

She suddenly felt awkward, unsure. She swallowed

thickly. "Don't do that." Her voice came out breathy and hesitant.

He smiled. One eyebrow cocked upward. "Do what?"

"You know. *That*."

"Don't worry, love," he drawled. "What I lack in technique, I make up for in patience."

"No. I don't want either one of us to be patient. I want—"

He lowered his head. His tongue touched her, and the wet tip sent a spasm of pleasure through her body. She groaned and closed her eyes as his tongue began to move in a slow, circular motion. She clung to the tree limb, her palms slick with sweat, her hands shaking. The sounds of her heart and the waterfall mingled, roared together in her mind until she couldn't hear anything, couldn't *see* anything. All she could do was feel, and oh, God, what she could feel. . . .

The motion intensified, turned fast and fevered. She moaned his name over and over again, whimpered. The pressure between her legs doubled, tripled, turned hot and hard and demanding. She felt as if she were flailing toward something, desperate to touch it, and yet the closer she came, the faster it spiraled out of her grasp.

Her breath came in hot, aching gasps. Her body went taut, then slack, then taut again. Mindlessly, desperate for release, she writhed on the rock. "Please," she said, near weeping. "It hurts. Oh, God, it hurts. . . ."

"Let go of the tree."

Trembling, she slid down the rock's slick face into Larence's lap. Shamelessly, aching with need, she opened her legs and straddled him.

He guided her onto his hardness. She coiled her arms and legs around him and buried her face in the warm, water-dappled crook of his neck. She clung to him as he rose out of the water and pressed her against the slick rock. The cool stone touched her flesh and she shivered uncontrollably.

His hardness slipped inside her. She gasped at the pleasure of it and clung to his sweaty body. He moved harder. Faster.

Her knees slid up and down the sweat-and-water-slicked muscles of his sides. Her fingers clawed and raked his back. She moved up and down, matching him thrust for thrust. The heat in her loins turned from a slow-burning fire to a liquified inferno of desperation and need.

"Oh, God, Larence. Oh, God, oh God, oh God . . ."

Her body went bow-string-taut, quivered. She strained forward, panting with need, aching; her nails sank into his back. She was almost there, almost there. . . .

Release blasted through her body like a tidal wave. A white-hot volcano of pleasure so pure, so elemental, she cried out. Tears stung her eyes, blurred her vision. She bit down hard on her lower lip to keep from screaming as spasm after spasm throbbed through her body.

She was dimly aware of Larence as he plunged inside her one more time, deep and hard. He buried his face in the crook of her neck. She felt his strangled, bitten-off cry as a blast of hot breath against her flesh.

When Emma finally summoned the energy to open her eyes, she found Larence staring down at her. He was looking at her with love, and caring, and a hint of laughter. The way a man should look at his wife and so rarely did. God help her, it made her want him all over again.

She smiled, realizing she'd been wrong all these years. Sex wasn't work. It wasn't an asset, or a way to get to the top. It was fun. And somehow Larence—the virgin—had known it all along.

Laughter sparkled in his eyes. "So, Em," he drawled. "It last long enough for you this time?"

Grinning, she pushed a lock of wet hair out of his face. Her hand was still trembling from the aftermath of their passion. "Not quite, Doc. But perhaps with a bit more practice . . ."

Chapter Twenty-three

Larence carried Emma toward the shore. Her body felt warm and solid and *right* curled against his chest. The whisper-soft caress of her breath fluttered in the crook of his neck; it sent a shiver scurrying across his flesh.

At the pool's edge he lay her down. Like a cat she stretched out, burrowed a warm place for herself in the gilded sand.

He stared down at her, mesmerized. Her bare skin looked like pale peach silk against the dun-colored sand. A waterfall of drying blond hair cascaded around her shoulders and formed a pool of perfect silver-gold behind her elbows. A riot of uncontrollable wisps curled across her brow, and longer strands, gilded by sunlight, crisscrossed her bare breasts and clung to the damp flesh of her stomach. Sand peppered her skin like flecks of gold dust.

Something in his chest tightened. He dropped to his knees beside her, and plucked a lock of hair from her breast. It coiled around his forefinger, strong and yet easily broken. Like the new, tenuous connection they'd made.

If only she would love me.

It wasn't a new wish, this wanting of love; it was one

he'd had all his life. Even now he could remember the agony of wanting his granny's love so fervently, so desperately, he would have done anything for a morsel of her grim approval. For years he'd tried and failed and tried again. Until finally he'd given up. And he'd never tried again; not with Granny or with anyone. Friends and acquaintances he had by the double dozens, but a real lover—emotional, spiritual, or physical—he'd never known.

Until Emmaline. Something in her—he thought perhaps it was the pain he'd seen in her eyes from the very beginning—had drawn him like a moth to a flame. And like a moth, he'd beaten his wings, closer and closer to the heat, battering himself on the golden walls of it, wanting to be warmed for even a moment.

He'd tried to tell himself it didn't matter that she didn't love him, that she'd never love him. But he wasn't a man given to lying—to himself or to others. It mattered. More than anything had ever mattered in his long, lonely life.

He didn't know what to do, how to make her fall in love with him. He'd given her everything he had to give. Everything. If it wasn't enough . . .

"Larence?" she said his name softly. "What is it?"

"Nothing." The word came out cracked and dry. Aching.

She reached out, touched him. Her finger glided lovingly down his cheek. "Lie down with me."

He forced a smile. "Greedy wench."

She laughed. The bright, clear sound of it filled him anew with longing. God help him, he wanted to hear that laughter every day of his life for as long as he lived.

He stretched out beside her, curling an arm around her shoulders and drawing her close. She snuggled against his side, casually easing her bent leg across his thighs. Holding her close, he stared up at the patch of cerulean blue sky. Sunlight streamed like Heaven's Gates through the opening and cast them in a halo of golden warmth.

It took Larence a full minute to realize he hadn't limped when he carried Emma from the pool.

At the realization, he sat bolt-upright. Emma rolled off of him and plopped on her back in the sand.

She tented a hand against the sunlight and blinked up at him. "What are you doing?"

The magnitude of it stunned him. He studied the golden city with new respect. Magic curled around him, became a breathing, tangible force.

He saw the concern in Emma's eyes and lay back down, drawing her close once more. Warmed by the feel of her body against his, he stared up at the bright blue sky, feeling as if he'd been given a fragile gift. He held it in trembling, uncertain hands, afraid that a single breath would blow it all away and he'd be left again with empty hands.

Hands. An image shot through his brain, brought a shudder of remembered pain. Hands, small and pink and perfectly still, pressed against cold glass. Hands that ached to reach for the doorknob, to wave to the boys playing ball in the park outside.

But the hands had remained pressed to the window. Separated from the other children not only by glass, but by a firm belief that he was unwanted.

Larence squeezed his eyes shut, and found that for once, it was easy to forget. All he had to do was think about walking from the pool, pain-free, and the terrible memories of his boyhood vanished like smoke.

His breath escaped in a disbelieving sigh. He'd waited

forever for this moment, prayed for it, believed in it. Somehow he'd known that Cibola was his compensation for being crippled, but never, not in his wildest boyhood fantasies, had he dreamed that the city would cure him.

"Larence, you're trembling."

"My limp is gone."

Emma sat upright. Twisting around, she rested her hands on his chest and studied him. Her blue eyes were huge and earnest as she said quietly, "Gone?"

"I can't believe it, either."

She didn't blink, didn't move or smile or frown. She simply sat there, staring at him through eyes that were clouded with uncertainty. For once, he couldn't tell what she was thinking, but he had the distinct impression that she was on the verge of saying something she thought perhaps she shouldn't say.

He knew precisely the moment she made her decision. The uncertainty in her eyes evaporated.

"How did it happen?"

Larence's breath caught. She was asking about his life, about his past. It wasn't much perhaps; in another woman it might be nothing more than idle chitchat. But not from Emma. Emma didn't engage in polite conversation. She was reaching out, admittedly with frightened, tentative fingers, but she *was* reaching out.

He could see her nervousness; it showed in the way her teeth nipped at her lower lip. Instinctively he knew that if he denied her now, she'd never ask again. Never reach out again.

Don't be afraid, he told himself. Talk about it. Give her everything you've got, and pray it'll be enough. . . . Let her know what it means to share. He took a deep breath. "Carriage accident. My ankle was crushed."

She sat perfectly still, staring at him. Waiting.

"I see you've learned patience," he said dryly.

"It was one of my favorite lessons." She gave him a soft, beguiling smile that warmed the cold spots in his soul. "Now, how did it happen?"

Don't be afraid. Give her everything, and make it be enough. . . . For Emma, he opened the door that had been closed for thirty years. Memories hurtled through his mind, one after another. He grimaced, squeezed his eyes shut.

Suddenly it was 1863 again, and he was a four-year-old boy on his way home from the theater.

The carriage tilted. A woman screamed. Larence flew out of his mother's arms and slammed into the wooden door. Pain exploded in his foot, he screamed in agony. A barrage of sounds battered his ears: the terrified shriek of a falling horse, metal-shod hooves sliding on slick cobblestone, the crack-thud of the carriage door hitting the hard road.

And then it was over. Silent.

Crying, he crawled through the darkness of the overturned carriage, his tiny, trembling hands feeling their way. "Mama? Mama?"

"Larence?"

Emma's voice yanked him out of the past. Startled, he glanced up at her and saw something in her eyes he'd never seen before. Compassion. Understanding. As if she knew what it felt like to be lost and alone and utterly, utterly afraid.

Her silent understanding wrapped around him like a warm blanket, soothing and comforting him, giving him the strength to explain. "We were coming home from the theater, and my dad lost control of the horses. The carriage overturned, and my folks were killed. I . . . I waited a long time to be rescued.''

A long time? he thought dully. A lifetime.

"Mama? Where are you?"

Dark, black nothingness closed in on him, made it difficult to breathe. He fought girlish tears, tried desperately to be strong and make his daddy proud of him.

"Lare?" came his mother's weak, tired voice.

He crawled toward her, dragging his useless, aching foot behind him. Crossing his legs, he pulled her head into his tiny lap. Something warm and sticky seeped through his pant legs and chilled his flesh. "Mama?"

"I love you, baby," she whispered brokenly. "Be strong."

"But, Mama . . . Mama . . ."

Larence couldn't believe that even now, thirty years later, the memories still hurt so much. God knew a man should grow up sooner or later.

But he'd never been able to forget. Every time he came close, something would remind him of the hours he spent locked in that overturned carriage, his dead mother's head in his small lap, her blood seeping through his clothing. Waiting in the terrifying darkness for a father who was already dead.

He'd tried so hard to be strong. To be grown-up. But he'd been so scared. . . .

Emma felt as if she were being strangled. Hot, sharp tears stung her eyes, slipped unchecked down her face. Her heart ached for the little boy sitting alone in the dark, waiting, praying to a God who didn't listen. No wonder he still had nightmares about the dark. "It must have been awful. . . .''

He squeezed her tightly and stroked her naked back.

It was a second before she realized that *he* was comforting *her*.

"I was lucky, I guess, to have a grandmother alive to raise me."

Emma heard the lie in his voice, saw it in the almost undetectable flinching of flesh at the corners of his eyes. A few weeks ago she wouldn't have heard it, wouldn't have cared enough to hear it. But now things were different, *she* was different. "Yes, lucky," she said evenly.

"She tried so hard to take care of me, to keep me safe."

Emma took a chance. "Too hard, maybe?"

Pain twisted his face. "Maybe." The word slipped out as a quiet groan.

Emma's heart twisted again. Instinctively she knew she'd never get him to say more, never get him to admit the hurts of his childhood, the loneliness. For Larence there was no going back. He'd refashioned his pain into something he could live with: a dream. From the darkness of despair, he'd found hope.

No, not found it, she corrected, he'd created it. Within himself.

She stared down at him with a respect that was almost awe. How had he done it? If she had lived his life, she'd be bitter and angry and isolated.

Exactly as she was.

The realization stunned, then shamed Emma. She *had* allowed herself to become angry and mean-spirited. She not only remembered her past, she wallowed in the pain of it until the memories had twisted and crippled her soul.

Where Larence had found strength and optimism and hope, she had found only darkness and despair and anger.

He'd been orphaned, crippled, and raised by a woman who obviously didn't want him. Didn't love him. And yet still he'd had the strength of character to rise above it all. To believe that the world was a wonderful place. To make it a wonderful place.

She drew a deep, shaky breath. For years she'd railed about the injustice of her own childhood, worn her injury like a chain-mail mantle around her shoulders. Used the horrible darkness of her past to keep the sunlight at bay.

But now she wanted that light, wanted to wrap that warmth around her soul and let it heat the cold, dark edges. She wanted to find optimism and joy in her life, the reality that Larence had so carefully constructed.

Remember the good times; forget the bad. His words came back to her, and this time they held new meaning. New promise.

Consciously she tried to remember the good times of her childhood. They floated to the surface of her mind with surprising ease. Hugs. Kisses. Laughter.

She thought about their last Christmas together. For years she'd remembered it only as a morning when they'd huddled, cold and hungry, around a bare tree. But now she saw a glimmer of something else, a remembrance of lightness and love. Instead of remembering the chill of the darkened tenement, she remembered the warmth of her father's touch. The love in her mother's gaze.

She had suppressed so much, forgotten so much. Suddenly she felt young and free and happy. Ready to begin anew. Joy and hope filled her. Smiling, she threw her arms around Larence and hugged him with all her might.

"Hey," he said, stroking her naked back, "what's that for?"

She swallowed the lump in her throat and pulled back enough to look at him. Their gazes locked, and in the green depths of his eyes she saw a love so pure, so honest, it made her want to cry again. "I love you, Larence."

He paled. "Don't say that unless you mean it, Em." His voice cracked. "Anything but that . . ."

She caressed his cheek. "I mean it. All my life I've thought about money. Only money. You've changed that, changed me." She laughed quietly at herself and added, "Now I think about money and *you*."

"Marry me."

Her smile froze in place. Fear collided with happiness.

"Emma? Don't tell me you're speechless?"

She stared at him, feeling dazed. His words were like a bright, hot light, offering her the warmth she'd sought all her life and never expected to find.

She wanted to throw caution to the wind and say yes—to shout it at the top of her lungs. But she was deeply, desperately afraid. What if it was all a lie? What if she'd only changed a little bit, and tomorrow she turned cold and hard again? She couldn't live with herself if she hurt Larence.

"Marry me. Now."

"I . . . I can't."

His hands cupped her face. "Marry me."

She tried to shake her head no, but his hands refused to let her move. "I'm afraid." The hated words crept out of her mouth. Barely heard.

"Don't be."

"I'm not nice. Really, I—"

"Then change."

"What if I can't?"

He smiled softly. "Emma, you already have."

Her heart stopped beating. Her gaze sharpened, probed the truth in his eyes. She saw his faith in their love, and his certainty gave her the strength to believe in herself. "Do you really think—"

"Emma, I *know*. Now, say you'll marry me. I'll only ask another twenty-two times, so start thinking."

Nervously she ran her tongue along her bottom lip. She *had* changed; he was right about that. Maybe not all the way, maybe not about everything, but too much to go back to her old life. Now that she knew what it meant to be in love, to be loved, she couldn't go back to being alone and lonely.

Larence had been right about so many things. Maybe— *please God, maybe*—he was right about her. About them.

For once in her life, she had to make a leap of faith. Had to really believe she was capable of love. She swallowed dryly, wishing she had a snifter of brandy to calm her shaking nerves. "Okay," she whispered. "I'll marry you."

The minute the words left her mouth, she felt an almost unbelievable sense of freedom, of coming home.

"Are you sure?"

She raised a hand to his face, felt the bristly plane of his cheek beneath her palm. Their gazes locked; his unblinking and yet afraid, as if he'd just glimpsed the Holy Grail and expected it to vanish at his touch, hers watery and filled with the most profound sense of love, of *peace*, she'd ever experienced. Ever imagined. "I'm sure."

Chapter Twenty-four

※〜　　　　〜※

Emma had agreed to marry him.

Every fifteen minutes or so that sentence flashed through Larence's mind and filled him anew with wonder.

"Look, Larence!"

She let go of his hand and bounded ahead. Her *camisa* slid alluringly off one shoulder as she ran. Streamers of white-blond hair fluttered out behind her, bounced gaily against her back. Her bare feet made a muffled, thumping sound atop the golden bricks.

"Hurry up," she hollered, laughing.

He watched her with an almost unbearable sense of pride. She ran nimbly, so sure of herself and what she wanted. Always so sure. The lilting, happy strains of her laughter floated back to him, and he had a sudden urge to race up and grab her . . . to scoop her into his arms and rip the dress from her body, then lay her out on the sun-warmed bricks and kiss every inch of her body. . . .

"Come *on* . . ."

He pushed aside the delicious fantasy and sped after her, marveling again at his ability to *run*. Catching up to her in a few strides, he grabbed her hand and spun her around to face him.

She blinked up at him, surprised. Her eyes seemed huge and incredibly blue against the sun-darkened oval of her face. Strands of hair clung to her parted lips, her nose, her lashes. Her rapid breathing made the moonlight-pale curtain flutter gently against her face.

In that split second he fell in love with her all over again. He smoothed the hair from her face and tucked it behind her ear. "Do you know how much I love you?"

"How much?" she demanded with a cocky toss of her head.

He grinned. "More than you deserve."

She grinned back. "There was never any doubt about *that*."

He curled his arm around her shoulder and drew her close, thinking again how good it was to be alive on this beautiful spring day. She slipped her hand around his waist and rested her head against his shoulder. Together, more slowly this time, they walked down the street. There was no sense of urgency, of being rushed. They had all the time in the world, and they both knew it. They were young, they were in love, and the city of their dreams lay sprawled all around them.

Larence smiled. It was amazing how he'd almost forgotten about the city. He'd found it, his life's dream, and yet, now that he was here, it paled in comparison to the love he'd found so accidentally.

They turned a corner and came upon the first dwelling. Stopping, they stared at the entrance in silent amazement. The arched doorway was wrought of polished sterling silver decorated with turquoise stones.

Faded remnants of a once red blanket hung limply across the doorway's opening.

"It's beautiful," Emma breathed.

Wordlessly he took her hand, and together they stepped up the low earthen step. The frayed edges of the rotting blanket fluttered across Larence's brow, and wreathed him for a moment with the scent of old, cobwebby wool. He inhaled deeply, savoring the smell as he pushed past the blanket.

What he saw inside brought him to a dead stop. *This* was what he'd waited a lifetime to see; not the golden streets or silver doorways or turquoise carvings, but this: everyday life in Cibola. The smell of dry sandstone, centuries-old leather, and rotting wood filled his nostrils. And something else, something he could almost identify and yet not quite . . .

Corn, he realized suddenly. He could smell the faint, distant memory of corn.

Sandstone walls formed a rounded, cozy home. Two glazed, circular openings in either wall served as windows, allowing twin mote-thickened wedges of sunlight to slant across the floor and create a perfect X in the shadowy interior.

X marks the spot. . . .

Beside him, Emma sneezed. "I can't see much. . . ."

Larence let go of her hand and moved into the light to better see the riches spread out before him. Against the back wall was a square, rock-flanked fire pit. A flagstone flue cut the pale stone wall in half. Between the fire pit and the mealing trough, an even dozen *metlatls*, grinding mills, were slanted precisely in a stone trench.

A skinned pole hung suspended from the ceiling, and

he could almost *see* the blankets and articles of clothing that had once fluttered gently from its knotty surface. Antelope-horn pegs studded the right wall, housing countless quivers, bows, war clubs, disks of haliotis shells, rabbit sticks, and other ornaments.

In the far corner, peeking out from behind the long, low-slung adobe bench that hugged the wall, were several exquisite water jugs and a half dozen black earthen cooking pots.

Even from this distance he could see the artistry of the pots. He hurried to the corner and dropped to one knee in front of the treasures. Reaching out, he touched the gritty, intricately decorated surface of the water jug. It was the most perfect example of Anasazi craftsmanship he'd ever seen.

Emma kneeled silently beside him on the hard stone floor.

He grinned, thinking how wonderful it was to have her here right now. It would have been so much less rewarding a discovery if he'd made it alone. . . .

An image came to him, as clear as day, crowding out every other thought in his mind. He saw himself and Emma, old, gray-haired, bent over a paper-strewn table. They were working on something—a book perhaps—about another faraway place. Working together.

A team, he thought with pride, that's what they'd be for the rest of their lives. Together they could do anything.

If only—

He tried to stop the thought, but couldn't. There was only one thing that stood between them. Only one thing that could wrench them apart. Money.

He had to ask, had—finally—to know her answer. His

hands curled into nervous, clammy fists. Turning to her, he said, "It belongs in a museum. . . ."

She looked confused by his words. "Of course it does."

Relief rushed through him. He touched her face, gently cupped her chin in his palm, and looked deeply into her eyes. In their vibrant blue depths he saw his future, his life. He'd given her his soul days ago, trusted her with his love long before he should have, and now she'd vindicated that trust. His love, his soul, his dream—they'd all be safe in her hands.

"I love you," he said, realizing for the first time how woefully inadequate the words were. How small in comparison to the feeling they expressed.

She smiled, and he marveled again at how beautiful her eyes were now that the coldness had disappeared. "Go ahead," she said, "get out the notebook."

He grinned at how well she knew him. Turning back for one last look at the pot, he placed his hands on his knees and started to push to his feet. Then something blue caught his eye.

He reached for it. The pottery wobbled, clanked together as he slid his hand through the opening between two pots. His fingers closed around something cold and hard, and gently drew back. He opened his hand, and in his palm lay a shining heap of turquoise and silver.

Emma gasped.

The necklace caught the sun and glowed with blue-green life. In the midst of the perfectly polished stones was a saucer-sized circlet of smaller beads set in intricately scrolled silver.

"Oh, Larence . . ."

He uncoiled the necklace, and as he did, a small, unadorned gold band fell to the ground with a thump.

He flicked a glance at it, grinned, and then raised the necklace to Emma's throat.

"F-For me?"

"For now at least," he said, placing the treasure around her neck. She sat as motionless as the marble statue he'd often compared her to. The square turquoise beads wreathed her throat with color, and the circlet settled in the valley between her breasts.

God, she was beautiful. And she was his. *His.*

Larence's chest suddenly felt too small for his heart. Never had he known love could be like this, could *feel* like this. It was the fulfillment of every wish he'd ever held, every prayer he'd ever been too afraid to utter. The long, lonely years spiraled away, washed away like flecks of dirt beneath the cleansing water of her love.

He thought of a poem by Cartwright he'd read long ago. The words had moved him then and stayed with him, hovering in the back of his mind. Waiting, he knew now; they'd been waiting for this moment.

"Emma?"

She looked up, gazed unblinkingly into his eyes.

"Give me your hand."

She did. Still on one knee, he took her left hand in his. Staring deeply into her eyes, he began to recite the words he'd waited a lifetime to use: *"There are two births; the one when light first strikes the new awaken'd sense, the other when two souls unite. And we must count our life from thence. When you loved me and I loved you, then both of us were born anew."*

"Poetry," she murmured. There was wonder in her voice, as if no one had ever given her a greater gift. Tears flooded her eyes, but she didn't look away. Her breasts rose and fell in shallow, emotion-filled breaths.

"Emmaline Amanda Hatter, will you marry me?"

Tears slid down her cheeks and plopped onto the turquoise necklace. "I—I will."

"Then, Em, in the face of God and history and all that I hold sacred and holy, I vow to love you and care for you and cherish you all the days of my life."

She dashed the tears from her cheeks. "La-Larence . . ." She frowned in thought. "What's your—"

"Alexander."

She gave him a wobbly smile. "Larence Alexander Digby, in the face of God and . . . gold and all that I hold sacred and holy, I vow to love you and care for you and cherish you all the days of my life."

He slipped the plain gold band on her finger. Her hand lowered a fraction of an inch, as if the precious metal weighed it down. They stared at the ring for a long, silent moment, both lost in their own thoughts.

"Is it legal?" she asked suddenly.

A slow, sensual smile curved his lips. "Not yet. There's the matter of the consummation. . . ."

He grabbed her by the waist and pulled her toward him. They toppled hard, landing in a tangled heap of elbows and knees on the hard stone floor. Laughing, Larence rolled her beneath him.

"Here?" she said breathlessly.

His fingers worked deftly to unbutton her *camisa*. "I doubt it'll be the first time someone's done it on this floor."

She smiled seductively and met him more than halfway for a kiss. "Just don't make it the last."

Night crept in to steal the daylight from the rounded windows. The X had wavered for half an hour or so, then gradually disappeared. Now the only light in the chamber emanated from the fire in the pit. Bright orange-red flames sputtered and hissed and sent shifting, dancing shadows across the curved walls.

Emma sat back on her heels and leaned tiredly against Larence's shoulder. She closed her eyes for a moment, taking a brief respite, then let her gaze wander back to the pad of paper in his lap. The largest water jug was just beginning to take shape beneath his skilled pen.

He sketched the intricate design with sure, steady strokes. The calm in and out of their breathing echoed in the shadowy room, gave the long-deserted place a new heartbeat of life.

"That band should be darker," Emma said automatically.

"Right you are," he answered, planting a kiss on the top of her head. "You're shaping up to be a great professor's wife."

Emma smiled, thinking about how much she'd changed in the last few days, how much Larence—and love—had changed her. Two weeks ago she'd have cold-cocked anyone daft enough to call her a great professor's wife. Now she found the compliment endearing.

Wife. Her heart swelled until it felt heavy and almost painfully full. For most of her life she'd been alone, a loner. Nothing had reached her soul or touched her heart, and she'd moved blindly, obsessively forward toward her goals, never allowing herself to want too much, need too much from anyone.

She'd done it because she had to, because it was the only way to survive in the cold, dark slums of New York. In that environment she'd become diamond-hard and ice-cold, and those traits had kept her fed. Kept her alive. She'd kept herself sheltered from all human contact, because she'd learned the hard way that love—unlike money—didn't last.

Never once had she allowed herself to believe that she could have more than simple monetary security. That she could have it all: a home, a husband who loved her, children, *and* financial security.

Larence had changed her self-centered path; he'd offered her a bright, searingly hot beam of hope that blasted through the darkness of her solitude. And now, as she sat beside him, leaning lovingly against his side like a loyal wife, she couldn't help believing in that light, in that hope. She felt an almost boundless sense of happiness and security because he was right. She could have it all.

She already did.

Closing her eyes again with a contented sigh, she rested her cheek against his shoulder and fingered the circlet of turquoise that hung heavily between her breasts. The stone felt cool and mirror-smooth. Whoever had crafted it had—

She froze. Her head jerked up. *Whoever had crafted it.*

"Larence!" She lurched to her feet.

Without her support, he tumbled sideways. And kept drawing. "Yes?" he said without looking up.

"Something's wrong."

"Uh-huh."

Emma crossed her arms across her chest to ward off a chill. Nervously she studied the chamber. What moments before had seemed warm and cozy and benign, seemed all of a sudden cold and vaguely malevolent. Her foot started tapping nervously. "Where are the people?"

The pen stopped. He cocked his head toward her and grinned. "They've been dead for hundreds of years."

"I know *that*. But where are their bones? Or their graves?"

For a single heartbeat, Larence looked at her with no expression on his face whatsoever. Then he jumped to his feet. The notebook fell to the floor with a muffled thud. "Shit!"

There was a moment of stunned silence, then Larence pulled Emma against him and lifted her off her feet in an exuberant bear hug. He twirled her around until she was breathless and laughing.

As their laughter dwindled, his hold loosened. She slid down the long, hard length of his body. Her bare feet plopped on the cold stone floor. And still they stared at each other.

He kissed her, a long, slow kiss that spoke of love and caring and promises. "Pa-lo-wah-ti was wrong, love," he murmured against her lips. "You *are* part of this quest. Now let's find the burial grounds."

Three hours later, they came to the end of the road. There they found a five-foot circle made up of polished, palm-sized pieces of jade. In the center of the circle, propped against the sandstone wall, was a gnarled walking stick decorated with what had once been ostrich feathers and beads.

Larence stared at the stick with bulging, glassy eyes. Fumbling in his breast pocket, he pulled out the diary, and flipped through the pages with shaking fingers. After a few seconds, he did a quick, professorial jump and thumped his forefinger against one of the open pages. "Aha! Proof positive."

Emma waited patiently for enlightenment as to the particular meaning of *aha* accompanied by a hop and a thump. When none came, she said, "Aha, what?"

"This is Esteban's walking stick. Here, look."

He flashed the drawing at her so quickly, she barely had time to ascertain that it was, in fact, a walking stick before he yanked it back and buried his nose in it. He stared at the drawing, studying it from first one way, then another. "Still, it's strange. . . ."

She peered at the picture and decided immediately that he was right: they were both sticks. "Looks pretty ordinary to me."

"What?" he answered distractedly. "Oh, yes, the stick itself is normal. It's just . . ."

"Just what?" she prompted.

He tugged on his chin, frowned. "Esteban never went anywhere without his stick. It was a sort of a . . . talisman, I guess you'd call it. Why would he leave it behind?"

He jotted something down, then frowned again. "Of course, an equally intriguing question is, where did they get the jade?" He shot her a knowing glance. "It's not indigenous, you know."

Emma restrained the urge to roll her eyes. Perhaps she wasn't such a great professor's wife after all. It required a good deal more patience than she possessed. "Larence," she said pointedly, "the more intriguing question is, where are the graves? Or the bones? Except for the guard, there isn't a body in the place. Not one."

She hugged herself tightly and glanced around. Gold and silver and turquoise glinted at her from every corner. But for once, it wasn't the treasures that captured her imagination, it was the city itself. The magic of the place seemed stronger, an almost tangible presence, as obvious and unconquerable as the sandstone walls.

"No one would build a place like this and then walk

away," she said, as much to herself as to Larence. *"So, what happened?"*

Far away, a hawk screeched. The vibrating, scratchy sound floated on the wisp of a morning breeze and then disappeared.

Larence woke slowly, unconsciously drawing Emma's languid, still-sleeping body closer to him. "Morning, wife."

She blinked awake. "Morning, husband."

They lay together for a long, quiet moment, staring up at the robin's-egg patch of sky. Beneath them, the soft, chamois-colored sand warmed to their bodies.

Emma ran her hand through the curling brown hair that darkened Larence's chest. It was such a warm, cozy feeling to waken in his arms. A small, contented sigh escaped her, fluttered through his chest hair.

It had freed her, this business of falling in love. Made her feel whole, and happy, and confident.

She thought of all the dreams she'd suppressed throughout the years, all the desires and hopes and prayers she'd buried beneath an icy layer of ambition. There were a hundred of them. A thousand.

And yet there was only one. Hesitantly, wistfully, she touched her stomach. Her hand roved up and down the flat, naked surface. Inside her, deep, something fluttered. She knew it was only nerves, or the cold, or just a plain old twitch, but for one heart-stopping moment, she thought it was a life.

Larence covered her hand with his. "I want a baby, too," he whispered.

Emma gasped. Immediately she was swept up in thoughts of *maybe*, of *someday*. For years she'd been afraid to let herself even *want* a child. And yet, no matter how hard she'd tried to control her thoughts, when she'd lie alone in her big, four-poster bed, the yearning had surfaced. Strong. Aching.

Familiar images ran through her mind: her holding a baby, singing a lullaby, kissing a tiny, downy-haired head. Only, this time the pictures made her smile. Made her *believe*.

She began to smile, then stopped. Fast on the heels of hope came doubt. Crushing, aching doubt. Eugene's words stabbed through her brain: *You just aren't exactly the woman I'd choose to raise my children.*

"Don't even think it," Larence said sharply. "You'll make a wonderful, loving mother."

Tears stung her eyes at his quiet confidence. Fear melted into manageable proportions. Yes, she was afraid; she'd probably be afraid until the day she gave birth and for every year of her child's life thereafter. But she had Larence beside her, and that would make all the difference.

She offered him a shaky smile. Maybe, she thought, please God *maybe*, if Larence believed in her, she could find the strength to believe in herself. *You can have it all.* She repeated the words again, making herself believe. "And you'll make a great father."

"I hope so."

Like a fire that starts as a single flame, the dream took hold and built into a raging inferno of hope. Emma nodded fervently. "Our baby will have only the best. The very best."

She tried to make the vow sound casual, and failed miserably. Her voice held all the desperation of her past, all the fear of the child still alive within her. God help her, but even now, with Larence's arms around her, she couldn't forget what it meant to be poor. Her child would never know that horror, never know what it meant to be hungry or cold or desperate. She'd rather remain childless and lonely all the days of her life than to raise a child in poverty.

She remembered the baby she'd seen at Rosare Court, and shuddered. Emma would rather die than ever, ever hear her child cough like that. . . .

"She'll have hot food, clean clothes, good water to drink, and a bedroom filled with white eyelet and Hamburg lace."

"All the things you didn't have?"

She thought instinctively of lying, of covering up her past as she'd always done. Then she remembered: It was Larence. A small, hesitant "Yes" slipped past her lips.

"She'll have all that and more," he said. "She'll have confidence, and love, and light."

The fantasy grabbed hold of Emma's heart. Secret, hidden hopes bubbled to the surface of her soul, demanding for once to be released into the light of day. "When we get back I'm going to donate money to Columbia College for a building or something. I'll make sure they name it Digby Hall. Then our little girl—or boy," she amended with a carefree laugh, "will know her daddy's dreams mattered. That they meant something. She'll know from the very beginning it's okay to believe in love and dreams."

Emma waited for Larence to answer, but he said nothing. The silence turned thick, almost palpable. Surprised, she turned to look at him. He was staring at her with an odd, unreadable expression in his eyes. "Larence? What is it?"

"Michael Jameson said you'd lost everything in the

crash." His voice was quiet, almost strangled. "I thought that's why you came with me."

She laughed. "I left New York with fifty dollars to my name. And I had to sell my last possessions to get that."

"Then where are you going to get the money to finance Digby Hall?"

"From Cibola, of course."

Larence yanked his arm out from behind her head and snapped to his feet.

Her head thumped backward. "Hey," she said, rubbing the back of her head. "What's the matter?"

"What's the matter?" He grabbed his jeans and stabbed his feet into the pant legs. "What's the matter?"

She regarded him with sudden wariness. Levering to a sit, she plucked up her *camisa* and held it to her naked breasts. The Wall Street facade slid cautiously into place. "Yes, Larence, that's the question on the table. What's the matter with you?"

He wrenched the last metal button through the buttonhole and slammed his hands on his hips. "How can you ask me that? You said those water jugs belonged in a museum."

She frowned in confusion. He was obviously angry, but why at her? What had she done? "Yes, and I meant it. All the artifacts belong in museums—for the Indian children."

"Unbelievable," he muttered, shaking his head. "You really don't understand."

"No, I—"

"Just tell me this: Where are you going to get the money to donate to the college?"

"From the street. I'll just take a couple of hundred

feet of it.'' She noticed he'd gone pale, and she frowned. "Is there a problem with that?"

"A problem with that?" He stared at her in obvious disbelief. "Is there a goddamn *problem* with that?"

She flinched at the loudness of his voice. "Larence, you're scaring me."

He surged toward her and jerked her to her feet. "Good," he yelled in her face. "Because you're scaring me, too."

"Let's just—"

"I won't let you have the gold. Not one brick."

Emma felt as if she'd been slapped. The color in her cheeks evaporated. "But our deal—"

"Screw the deal! Jesus, Emma, we're *married*."

She stared up at him dumbly, unable to move or think or even respond. Everything began to crumble. All the hopes, the dreams he'd made her believe in, the new prayers, edged beyond her grasp. Panic widened her eyes.

She tried to back away. His fingers tightened on her upper arm and held her in place. "No, Emma. You can't run from this one."

Their gazes locked, fused. She felt the harsh, angry pelts of his breathing against her face, saw the raw pain in his eyes.

He was asking her to give up the money, the security. He was asking her to be poor.

She wet her trembling lower lip and looked up at him. Tears blurred her vision. "Don't ask this of me, Larence. Anything but this. I . . . grew up poor—not 'gosh I need a dime for the train poor,' but really poor. I lost my virginity to an apple vendor for the price of a few half-eaten cores. Don't . . ." Her voice broke, but she refused to look away. "Don't ask me to go back."

"I'm not asking you to go anywhere," he said quietly. "I'm asking you to stay. With me. Please . . ."

She heard him ask her to stay, heard the raw, aching need in his voice that matched her own. The words were clear. *Stay.* But so was the truth. *Good-bye.*

You can't have it all, you fool, and you always knew it. A small sob escaped her. It was all a lie. She couldn't have it all. She had to choose. Love or money.

The choice she'd been running from all her life had caught up with her. It had waited all these years, patiently, waited for her to begin to believe in love. To weaken. Then it had struck, and struck hard.

"My God, Em, it's *stealing.*" His voice vibrated with emotion. "And not from me, but from the world. From the Indian children who need this memory a hell of a lot more than you need another fur coat or some diamond tiara."

She snapped her chin up. How dare he judge her? When had he slept in the gutter or eaten other people's leftover table scraps? Had he held his mother's hand as she died of poverty, or cleaned up the mess of a father's suicide? What right did he have to tell her what was *right*? She yanked out of his grasp and glared up at him. "Sure!" she spat. "Go ahead and lecture me, Larence. But you're getting what *you* want out of this city. Everything will go in your precious museum. It's only me—*me*—who's left out in the cold."

He grabbed her by the shoulders. "Don't you see, Em? Don't you understand? There won't be a museum for Cibola. This place is special . . . magical. It's to be seen, recorded, written about, shared. But it's not to be . . . robbed."

He shook her until she looked at him. The pain in his eyes hit her like a blow. Her righteous anger dissipated. Without it she felt hollow and frighteningly alone. "Oh, Larence." His name slipped from her lips in a sigh of defeat. They saw the world so differently. Not even their concept of right and wrong matched. Oh, deep down, Emma knew that technically, Larence was "right." It was wrong to take the golden bricks from the city. A nice person wouldn't do it.

But she wasn't nice. *Nice* didn't get one very far in life. Once, long ago, she'd been as nice as nice could be. Until the day she'd had to sidle up to the fat, greasy apple merchant and beg for a few half-eaten cores.

The memory charged through her, made her feel dirty and alone all over again. Trembling, she closed her eyes. The moment she did, she saw her mum's blanket-wrapped body slipping off the wagon and hitting the pile of other dead bodies with a muffled thump. Heard the driver's practical condolences: *Too bad you dint have more money, kid. These paupers' graves ain't a pretty sight.*

Then came the image of her father, slumped over the kitchen table. Dead. His blood dripping down the—

She shook her head to clear it and wrenched her eyes open. Larence's eyes stared into hers. In their unblinking green depths she saw so very much. Love, laughter, joy, hope. So much. And so little.

Pain closed around her heart and throat, made breathing difficult. Maybe someday she could have done as he asked. Maybe, after years of living in the safe, happy glow of his love, she'd have begun to believe in princes on white horses and happy endings. But a few days wasn't enough time; it was too early. She had a lifetime worth of fear and pain as experience—and less than a weeks' worth of love. She couldn't turn her back on her whole life, on everything she'd ever wanted or worked for. She couldn't make herself really, truly believe that love alone was enough, that it kept you warm or fed you.

Not yet. Maybe never. He'd asked the one thing of her she couldn't—wouldn't—give. God help her, she couldn't go back to being poor.

"Y-You said you loved me," she whispered. Each word twisted her heart and broke off a piece of her soul.

Pain blazed in his eyes, turned them glassy and over-bright. "I *do* love you, Em. So help me God, it'll be my curse. When you tear the last gold brick out of this magical city, I'll love you still. But it won't be enough—not if you destroy this city. I'd never respect you."

There it was. Finished.

Emma's breath expelled in a sharp gust of pain. She felt small and cornered and afraid, as if a great, heaving beast were tracking her. Closing in for the kill.

Silence stretched around them, cocooned them. The world shrunk to just the two of them, standing face-to-face in the center of a magical city. Together, less than a breath apart, and yet each frighteningly alone.

He gave her a look so sad, it sliced right through her. "I love you."

The words filled Emma with an ache so big, a need so mammoth, she had to clamp her lips together to keep from crying out. At her sides, her hands curled into tight, white fists. He was right; this feeling, this *need*, would be their curse.

She reached up, laid a hand to his cheek. He stiffened, as if jolted by the contact.

"I love you, too," she said in a voice like the rustling of long-dead leaves. Her hand dropped to her side, and immediately her palm went cold. She fisted her hand, as if in doing so, she could maintain at least the memory of his warmth. His touch.

Shaking, she gathered her clothes and dressed in aching silence. Then she grabbed the torch and walked away.

Not looking back was the hardest thing she ever did.

Chapter Twenty-five

Larence stood rooted to the golden bricks. His whole body was shaking, his hands were curled into tight fists. The muffled patter of her bare feet striking the street hit him like a rapid fire series of rabbit punches to the gut.

She was leaving him. She'd chosen the gold.

At the thought, his face crumpled. His legs buckled, started to give way. Only sheer determination kept him from collapsing in a useless heap on the floor.

No, he thought grimly, it wasn't determination that kept him upright. It was practice. Years and years of practice. He'd been fighting pain for as long as he could remember, and he fought it now.

All his life he'd been alone, an outsider. A crippled little boy with his nose pressed to the glass, watching the other kids play. Too shy to make friends easily, he'd waited for the other boys to approach him, and, of course, they never had.

He'd long ago stopped waiting, long ago given up hope. And then, when he'd least expected it, God had answered his prayers.

Emmaline. Her name washed through his mind like a relaxant, bringing a bright, shining moment of peace and then plunging him back into the darkness of despair. She'd come into his life like a ray of the purest sunlight, warming and lighting the cold, dark, lonely parts of his soul—the parts he'd buried and tried to forget. With little more than a smile, she'd swept him off his clumsy feet and made him fall in love. Irrevocably. Completely.

He took a deep, shuddering breath and stared blindly at the pale green pool. The glistening surface of the rock caught his eye. Her laughter rang out in his mind. Memories from last night slammed through him, bringing knife-hot stabs of pain. He jerked his gaze away from the cool, inviting water.

He'd always thought love would solve it all, that in love he'd finally find the invitation he'd never had. That someone—*finally*—would ask the crippled, friendless boy behind the pane to play.

And it had happened. Just as he'd always prayed and hoped it would. Love was everything he'd always imagined it to be, and more. So much, much more.

He tightened his fists so hard the nails dug into his palms. He tried to think of something else, tried desperately not to let himself wallow in despair, but this time he wasn't strong enough to dredge up a smile, or a snippet of hope.

He felt weaker, more defeated and alone and abandoned, than ever before. When he'd dreamt about love, it had always been a forever love. Never, in all the long, lonely nights when he'd lie alone in his bed, dreaming about his someday wife, had it occurred to him that love could end. That once invited, he'd be left standing alone.

He squeezed his eyes shut, battling the tide of self-pity and pain. Sweet Jesus above, it hurt. . . .

Go after her.

The thought brought no more than a split second of hope. He knew he couldn't be a party to the destruction of this city. Dreams of this place had always healed him, kept him going, held the darkness of the night at bay. It was here that he'd always run when the realities of life became too harsh. For years the city had given him hope and kept him alive. Now it was his turn to return the favor.

His lips twisted into a grim, self-deprecatory smile as the irony of the situation struck him. He'd asked Emma to choose between love and money, and been devastated when she'd chosen the money.

But what about him? How was he any better? He hadn't chosen love either. He'd chosen his dream over love, and even now, knowing how it felt to be alone, he'd choose history again.

He couldn't rape history and plunder this ancient treasure. Not even to hold on to the only love he'd ever known. If he did, if he threw away everything he believed in for the sake of her love, he'd lose himself in the process.

The tiny, not-yet-beaten voice of his heart piped up again. *Maybe she'll come back to you.*

He latched on to the hope, fraying and ragged as it was, and clung to it.

Maybe . . .

It wasn't much, he knew, but it was all he had, and he refused to give it up.

Emma clenched her fists and pumped her arms, striding purposefully away from the campsite. The gold-bricked road angled across the plain and rose. She moved faster, boot heals thumping on the metal. Her breath came in quick, painful gasps, and a stitch pinched her side. Still she refused to slow down.

With every step she wanted to turn around and run back to him, to fling herself in his loving arms. But years of self-discipline held her in good stead. She kept her lips clamped grimly together and her eyes pinned on the passageway's darkened mouth.

There was no point in turning around, no point in going back. Staying with Larence meant poverty. Gut-wrenching, soul-stealing poverty, and that was too terrifying to even contemplate.

She knew she was exaggerating, knew deep inside she was being irrational, but she couldn't stop herself. Couldn't eradicate a lifetime's worth of fear in a heartbeat of hope. He had a job, nothing more. Her father had had a dozen jobs. Employment wasn't security. Scientific glory wasn't security. Money—cold, hard cash— was security. And God help her, Emma couldn't live without it. Not again.

She loved him, yes. And she'd do anything—*anything*— he asked of her except that. She couldn't be poor for him. She'd lived in that hollow, icy-dark place before, and she couldn't go back. God help her, she couldn't march back into Hell. Not even for Larence.

And he had no right to ask it of her.

The moment she turned in to the passageway, her strength left her. Dank, smelly darkness closed in on her. She thought about lighting her torch, then remembered she had no matches, and flung the stick away. It thwacked against the wall and clattered to the floor.

At the sudden quiet, every bone in her body seemed to dissolve. She leaned tiredly against the cold stone wall and closed her eyes.

It took her a moment to realize she was waiting for

him. Her senses focused with pinpoint precision on the golden world around the corner. She heard the blood-pumping thud of her heart in her ears and the ragged spasms of her breath, and the deadened roar of the waterfall, and . . . and . . .

Nothing else. It hit her like a well-placed fist to the heart. He wasn't coming after her. Larence couldn't give up the city any more than she could give up the gold.

It was really and truly over.

Tears blurred her vision, turned into a thick, twisted lump in her throat. She buried her face in her hands and sank to her knees. Her forehead hit the cold, dark floor with a silent thud.

Memories and images and thoughts spiraled through her mind, merging with hopes and dreams until they became a tangled, useless coil of burning pain. With each thought, each remembrance, her body shuddered harder, tears fell faster, hotter. Her breath came in strangled, watery sobs, and the acrid, fecund scent of old dirt curled around her like a bank of fog.

She cried until she had no tears left to cry; until her soul was parched and dry, and her eyes were puffy and red. And still she lay there, broken and defeated and afraid, her forehead pressed to the cold stone.

Gradually the tears dwindled, leaving in their wake a bone-dry, raw ache. Tiredly she sat back on her heels and wiped the wetness from her cheeks. A headache pounded behind her eyes.

How could he have asked her to give up the gold? He'd said he loved her.

It wasn't love to make someone give up something she'd worked for. Almost died for. Was it?

Goddamn him, he'd made her actually *believe*. He'd

taught her love and given her hope, and made her think that happiness was actually possible. After all the years of darkness and despair and loneliness, he'd held his hand out like a beacon of light, and fool that she was, she'd reached for the warmth with a schoolgirl's eagerness.

Now the light was gone; if, in fact, it had ever been. She was back where she'd always been. Alone.

Alone. Her head seemed to swell to twice its size. Her neck bowed under its weight. The headache became a series of mallet-hard strikes behind her eyes.

Enough. With a ruthlessness born of practice, she set her chin and gritted her teeth. She'd cried enough. Now it was time to go on. She'd made her decision, just as he'd made his, and there was no going back. That was one lesson she'd learned well in her life.

They loved each other, yes. But it was just as she'd always known. Love wasn't enough.

She reached deep in her soul for the inner strength she'd always known. The familiar core of ice was there, buried deep beneath a layer of newly blossomed love and trust and shattered hope. Small, perhaps, and melting, but still intact.

She had known she'd find it: it was what had given her the strength to walk away from him. It was what would keep her from going back.

Curling an arm protectively across her abdomen, she pressed her other hand to the wall and took a step. Then another, and another. Her feet felt like twin bricks, and her head was a pounding mass of pain, but somehow she plodded onward.

One step at a time she felt her way through the blackness. The crashing sound of the waterfall gradually disappeared. The passageway became cold and dark and deathly quiet. And still she stumbled on.

Finally she came to where the passageway narrowed. Cautiously feeling her way through the slit in the stone, she moved forward.

Her toe hit something. Bones clinked.

The guard! She plastered her body against the wall and froze. Her heart thudded against her ribs. Ragged bursts of breath thundered in the quiet. Images of gaped, fanged mouths and rattling tails turned her knees weak.

Calm down. Sliding her sweat-dampened palms down the gritty wall, she unclasped her petticoat and let it fall to a pile at her feet.

Still there was no sound, no rattling. With a silent prayer, she scuttled sideways, yanked up the petticoat, and flung it over the skeleton. Dropping to her knees amid the snapping crunch of old bones, she shoved the cotton beneath the rib cage.

When it was in place, she lurched shakily to her feet. The second her legs quit shaking, she raised her hands.

Shucka-shucka-shucka.

Emma's stomach hit the dirt.

Shucka, shucka, shucka.

She lurched onto her toes and grabbed the hole's hard-packed edges. Dirt rained on her face, sprayed in a hollow-sounding shower on the slack cotton of her petticoat. She clutched the fraying edge and heaved her body upward, flopping face-first on the floor above with a grunt of relief.

She yanked her dangling feet up and lay there, panting for breath.

Gradually she became aware of the change. Something was different. She felt . . . warmth.

She lifted her head and saw a streak of yellow light cutting like a lightning bolt through the pitch blackness of the corridor. She knew she should feel relieved, but all she felt was tired and old and filled with regret.

Wobbling, she clambered to a weak-kneed stand. She took a moment to regroup, then forced her feet to move. With each step her legs grew heavier, her sorrow more intense. She was leaving him. *Leaving him leaving him leaving him leaving—*

Molelike she emerged from the darkness. Sunlight splashed her face and sent warmth careening through her body.

She wobbled. Her legs turned to mush and she sank, shaking and exhausted, to the warm ground. Her knees hit the dirt hard, sending shots of pain into her thighs. Grimacing, she sat back on her heels and bowed her head.

The sunlight wrapped its comforting, soothing fingers around her face and banished the darkness's chill. A shiver wrenched her body; goose bumps popped out on her flesh. She hugged herself, trying to draw some of the sun's heat into the ice-cold regions of her soul. God, the warmth felt good. Almost good enough to make her forget the man she'd left behind.

The man who let you walk away . . .

She forced the painful thought aside. There was no point in rehashing her decision. She'd made the only decision she could live with, and that was that.

Rubbing her aching eyes, she looked up.

In the distance, a lone rider was silhouetted like a spectral vision against the blinding noonday sun. Far above the rider's head, against the brilliant blue sky, a hawk glided in effortless circles. Its abrasive screech echoed off the walls and grated along Emma's spine.

The shadowy rider moved toward her.

Emma suppressed a sharp sting of fear and jerked to her feet, tenting a hand across her bloodshot eyes.

The quiet clip-clop of hooves on sand came toward her. Squinting, she strained to make out the rider's face. When she recognized the man, her fear turned to anger. It was Pa-lo-wah-ti, seated on a small gray-brown ass.

About ten feet away from her, the bent, gnarled old man reined his burro to a stop. His muddy, blind eyes found her with eerie accuracy. *"Hai,"* he said with a solemn wave.

Emma gritted her teeth. She knew it was irrational to be so irritated, but she didn't care. Until now, all she'd felt was betrayal and hopelessness and pain. Anger was a definite improvement; it had always been an emotion she felt comfortable with "What are you doing here?" she demanded, slamming her hands on her hips.

"Your burro is saddled and waiting."

That stopped her. "Why?"

"For your ride to the white man's fort."

She frowned. "Look, I've had a hard—"

"I will ride with you. It is not a long journey." Before she could answer, he whistled, and Tashee—traitor that she'd always been—trotted dutifully to the old man's side.

Emma looked down at her little burro, all saddled and packed and ready to go, and her determination wavered. It *was* sort of frightening to be in the desert alone, without knowing how to read a compass or follow a map. And Pa-lo-wah-ti, eerie as he was, was the only guide available.

"I'm going to Albuquerque," she said sharply.

"The fort is closer, and it is filled with white men."

Emma chewed on her lower lip. She had to admit the

old man made sense. "All right," she said at last. "You may go with me."

"Yes."

Trying to appear calm, she plucked up her skirt and picked her way down the small embankment to Tashee's side.

You shouldn't be going. The sentence reverberated through Emma's brain like a summer rainstorm, fast and hard and thunderously loud. New tears stung her eyes.

Gritting her teeth, she flipped open her saddlebag and wrenched out her pantalets. Stabbing her feet into the frothy cotton undergarments, she buttoned the waistband and flopped on Tashee's back. "Let's go," she said throatily.

"You should not be going," Pa-lo-wah-ti said.

That's what I need right now, she thought with an angry sniff. A goddamn mind reader. She dashed the tears away and glared at him. "What the hell are you doing here, anyway?"

"I said I would find you."

"A month from now," she shot back. "Generally that means thirty days, not three."

"It has been thirty-three days since you left my home."

Emma was speechless. She had no idea how to respond to such absurdity, so she didn't.

She tightened her grip on the reins and turned Tashee toward the box canyon's hidden entrance. Setting her mouth in a grim line, she urged her mount to a plodding walk.

Pa-lo-wah-ti's burro trotted up beside her, then slowed until they were walking side by side. "I was wrong about you. For this I am sorry."

Startled, she glanced sideways. The old man was almost nose to nose with her, studying her face.

"I was wrong." This time the words were spoken softly. The sharp scent of aged teeth and tobacco drifted to Emma's nostrils. "This quest of Larence's vision was yours as well. He alone would have come to the canyon and been defeated. It was you, his other half, who found the jimsonweed and followed the ancient ritual."

Emma's mouth dropped open. How did the old man know that? They had been alone that night. *Except for the hawk.*

She shivered suddenly. The hawk had always been with them on this trip. Watching. Tracking. Could it be that somehow the old man saw through the bird's eyes?

She glanced sharply at Pa-lo-wah-ti's muddy, sightless eyes. No, she told herself firmly. It was ridiculous to even think such a thing. Blind was blind.

"You were wrong, too, I think," he went on. "You thought you were nothing. . . ."

Pa-lo-wah-ti was wrong, my love. You are part of this quest.

Her fingers spasmed around the leather reins. The warm metal of her wedding ring bit into her flesh. She stared down at it.

When I loved you and you loved me, then both of us were born anew. . . .

Tears blurred her vision, ran in searing, white-hot streaks down her face.

Pa-lo-wah-ti squeezed her shoulder. "Stay."

She shook her head. Strands of hair stuck to the moistened sides of her face and further obscured her vision. "I can't," she croaked. "Just lead me away. Please."

His touch disappeared. A long, tired sigh slipped past his seamed lips. "It is as I thought. Follow me."

Pa-lo-wah-ti dismounted slowly and untied the rope that barred the canyon's entrance. Then he remounted and disappeared through the near-invisible opening.

Emma couldn't help herself. She turned to look back, hoping against hope that Larence would be there.

But of course, he wasn't. There was only the circular, grassy plain and the silent towering mesas.

She forced her gaze back to the dusty, stone-walled trail ahead. Every muffled thump of Tashee's hooves hitting the ground vibrated up Emma's slumped spine. She reined the burro to a stop and retied the rope. The hemp scratched her flesh, reminding her with every movement that she was leaving.

It's not too late. Turn back. Turn back.

Her heart was talking—screaming, in fact. But it wasn't that organ that had fed and clothed and housed her in the long, dark years since her parents' deaths. It was her brain that had kept her going.

And her brain was speaking now, too. Not as loud, but in a steel-edged voice that cut through the hysterical ranting of her heart with cold precision.

She wouldn't be poor again. Not for anyone.

The decision had been made.

Almost an hour later, the world began to shake. An avalanche of booming noise echoed through the forest and rattled the trees.

"What's that, Pa-lo-wah-ti?"

He didn't bother to look at her. "The earth quakes as the circle draws to its close."

"But—"

He held up a skeletal hand for silence. "In time."

Emma's frown deepened. She'd read about earthquakes, but she'd never experienced one. Her fingers tightened around the makeshift saddle horn. Absentmindedly she reached up to touch the turquoise necklace at her throat. Her fingertips glided across the ruffled cotton edge of her *camisa* to her throat.

She gasped as realization struck. Adrenaline surged through her body, made her heart beat faster. The earthquake was forgotten.

The necklace had vanished.

Chapter Twenty-six

Larence stood there, alone, for what seemed an eternity. Head bowed, eyes closed, hands fisted, he stood motionless in the city's golden center. Not thinking, not seeing, not even feeling. Just standing. Surviving. Waiting for the agony of her betrayal to pass.

He felt it first as a rumbling beneath his feet. In the depths of his depression it took him a moment to care what was happening, but as the sound grew louder, the shaking more intense, he lifted his tired gaze to the patch of sky overhead.

The whole world was swaying, trembling as if in fear. Dirt showered from the mesatops, scattering across the golden bricks and dappling the jade-hued pool. Sand shifted and danced beneath his feet.

A sound both earthly and unearthly reverberated through the city. The pool's glasslike surface shuddered. Then came the terrible, ear-shattering sound of stone grinding against stone.

The opening! Emma!

Larence whirled around and raced toward the passageway. Legs and arms pumping, he sped into the darkness. His foot hit something and he tripped, sprawling face-first on the cold stone floor. His cheek slammed against a knotty stick of wood. He felt his flesh rip. Warm blood slid down his face.

He crawled to his knees, feeling around for the piece of wood. It was the torch. Tucking it under his arm, he fumbled through his pocket for the matches and lit the stick's cotton-wreathed top. Orange-bright flames sputtered reluctantly to life, and he took off again.

He made it to the guard's grave in no time and crunched thoughtlessly through the pile of bones. Ignoring the rattler's soft *shucka-shucka-shucka*, he leapt upward.

The corridor above was dark and deathly quiet. He pulled himself up and stood. At the tunnel's end he saw the zigzag of light. His knees almost buckled in relief.

The rumbling came again. Louder this time.

Dirt showered all around him, pattering the shadowy floor. Nervously Larence tightened his hold on the torch and picked up his pace.

It came again; that awful, otherworldly wrenching of stone on stone, like the grinding together of planet-sized gears.

The light at the end of the tunnel began to blink.

"NO!" Larence threw the torch aside and surged forward. Breathing hard, he pumped with his arms. The ragged, overworked spurts of his breathing pounded in his ears, mingled with the hammer-strokes of his heart, and drowned out the grinding sound.

He reached the zigzag of light just as it disappeared. The schism in the rock fused, leaving a bloodred curve of sandstone where before there had been an opening.

Larence skidded to a stop. His hands shot out, connected hard with the solid stone wall. Pain ricocheted up his forearms and lodged razor-sharp in his shoulders. Desperately he clawed at the wall. Dirt clogged his nails and stung his eyes. Brown tears snaked down his cheeks.

Stay together in the city.

The words sliced through his brain. Now—too late—he understood them. The magic of Cibola had been in their togetherness.

He clawed until his fingers were bloody and raw. Finally, exhausted, he slowed down and heard something other than the ragged spurts of his breathing. It came from behind him; a sputtering sound. He paused, fingers poised against the sandstone, listening. Then, slowly, he turned around.

The fallen torch lay in a pool of shuddering, throbbing light. Shadows crept up to the torch like feeding jackals. Tentative, hungry.

Light quivered, weakened. The torch gave a final sputtered cry and died. Jet black night consumed the cavern.

Larence's hands fell to his sides. Terror wormed its icy, insidious tentacles through his body.

Dear God, he thought desperately, not this. Anything but this . . .

It was just like before. He squeezed his eyes shut, remembering the dark, overturned coach. How he'd waited, alone and lonely and terrified, for someone to come and help him.

Only this time, no one would be coming for him. This time he'd die. Alone. In the darkness.

Staggering sideways, he hit the sandstone wall and crumpled to his knees. The silence around him was awesome, oppressive. He touched his cheek, but his skin was cold and clammy. The warmth of her last touch was gone. A memory.

She was gone. The words sliced like a rusty blade through his brain.

The hope he'd clung to so tenaciously since she'd chosen the gold vanished. He was left with nothing to reach for, nothing to steady him. For the first time in his life he could find no goodness, no sliver of hope.

A vast, impenetrable emptiness invaded his soul, chilled him to the bone. Without hope, there was nothing. He couldn't lie to himself, couldn't cling to the fabricated belief that Emma would change her mind and come back to him.

There wouldn't be a change of heart, or an apology. Years from now there wouldn't be a bittersweet smile over the antics of their youth.

There would be no years from now. There would be no love or laughter. No wife. No son. No daughter.

He curled his dirty, aching hands into fists and pounded his knees. It was so goddamned unfair. He'd been a good man, lived a good life. He'd never sought more than his share, never complained about having been crippled, never hurt another human being.

He hadn't even asked for much from life. Just someone to be with, and someone to love. He had so much of it to give. So very much . . .

If you loved her so damned much, why didn't you compromise? He thumped his head back against the cold stone and closed his eyes, letting his breath out in a sharp, angry sigh. Why? he demanded of himself again. He'd known how much the money meant to her, so why hadn't he done something—anything—to make her stay?

But he knew why. He'd been so hurt, so angry. He'd wanted—just once—to be chosen. And he'd thought there would be time to correct their mistakes. Time to mend their fences . . .

Time . . .

He cracked the back of his head against the wall. Pain exploded in his skull, but he hardly noticed. It was nothing compared to the agony in his soul.

He slammed his fists onto the cold, dark ground and screamed her name. *"Emmaaaaa . . ."*

The word clung to the shadows for a long, vibrating moment, then disappeared.

Pa-lo-wah-ti stopped at the crest of a small hill. The hawk glided in one last circle overhead and came to a whirring, flapping perch on the nearest tree.

"The white man's fort," he said, nodding toward the cluster of wooden buildings spread out below them in a red sandstone valley.

Emma stared at the small encampment through tired eyes. Reaching down, she ripped another piece of cotton from her hem and tied the small scrap around the nearest tree. Pale blue fabric fluttered in the noontime breeze, marking the trail. The sharp, tangy scents of juniper, piñon, and cedar filled her nostrils.

Beside her, Pa-lo-wah-ti gave a weary sigh. "You remember the night you were taken by Ka-Neek?"

She shot him a sharp glance. He hadn't been there that night. So, how had he—

She looked warily at the hawk. The beady black eyes were fixed on her face. "How do you know about that?"

For once, his sightless eyes remained fixed on the horizon. "We meant you no harm. It was to frighten you so you would give up your search. We watched your every move, tracked your every thought."

"But—"

"We are the guardians of the sacred city. The *Keo-ye-mo-shi*. For generations we have sworn our blood to protect the secrets of our ancestors. For two hundred seasons I have been chief, and never once in all that time have I been . . . confused. . . ."

Emma felt a surge of tangled emotions at the bitter-sweet remembrance. "Until Larence?"

"He saw the city so clearly. With such fire and passion. How could I stop a quest of vision? I am a man only, not a god. Such decisions cannot be mine."

He sighed heavily, shaking his head. The haliotis shells around his neck chinked together. "When I became chief, God took my eyes and taught me to see with my heart." His bony hand touched his chest for emphasis. "Your man was easy to read; his soul was as clear as a mountain stream. He was *ke-hi*, a friend of the spirits

"So I was confused. I was to stop white thieves; but was I to stop a *ke-hi*? Many nights I wrestled with questions, many nights I lay awake, seeking guidance from the gods. But they were silent.

"My heart saw the truth clearly, but my mind, and my son's son, Ka-Neek, called my heart a liar. I lost much sleep.

"Finally I listened to my heart, as I should have from the beginning. Your man had been called here. He was meant to seek. And so I waited."

Listened to my heart. A sick, sinking feeling weighed down Emma's stomach. Shame made her look away. "I-I . . ." she stammered.

"It is not about you, Emmaline. You think it is—you are used to thinking only about yourself—but this is about something . . . greater."

"Larence and I made a deal," she protested weakly. "Half the gold is mine."

He looked at her with infinite sadness. "You would destroy it, then?"

"I'm not destroying it. I'm moving it. Larence will still have his museum." But even to her own ears, the words sounded weak and feeble.

Pa-lo-wah-ti bowed his head. "You have already made a fatal mistake. Do not make another."

She stilled. "Is that a threat?"

He turned to look at her, and the sorrow in his eyes made her stomach knot. "Remember, Emmaline, it takes much gold to fill an empty soul. And only a drop of magic."

Emma reined Tashee to a halt outside the fort's tall, skinned-log gate. She only had a moment to worry about her ragged appearance before a uniformed guard pushed through a door hidden in the spiked wall and headed her way.

She stiffened. Her fingers tightened nervously around the reins. She fought the urge to run a quick hand through the leaf- and twig-entangled mass of her hair.

"Can I help yah, miss?"

She ran her tongue along the chapped surface of her lower lip. "I'm Emmaline Hatter of New York."

The young man's tanned face broke into a bemused smile. He pushed the military hat higher on his head and scratched his pale brow. "I'm Private Henry Snort of Saint Louis. Now that we got that outta the way, what can I do for yah?"

"I'd like to see your commanding officer."

Private Snort didn't bother hiding his surprise. Frowning slightly, he cocked his head and studied her disheveled appearance. It was a slow, take-your-time sort of look that made Emma wish fervently for the petticoat she'd left at the skeleton and the chemise jammed in her saddlebag.

"I dunno, miss," he said, scratching his sweaty forehead, "Cap'n MacEwan's a married man, and I don't think he'd take to no . . ." His words trailed off.

Emma felt a moment of embarrassment, then a flash of anger. "I am a *lady*, sir. A very famous, very *wealthy* lady who has just had a rather . . . unbelievable experience in the desert. So quit gawking like a thirteen-year-old and take me to your captain."

Ten minutes later she was seated on a comfortable leather chair, sipping a cup of tea. The chair felt indescribably wonderful after so many jarring hours on Tashee, and the tea slid through her blood like laudanum.

Suddenly the door banged open. Emma turned. A tall, broad-shouldered bear of a man stood silhouetted in the open doorway. Hot yellow sunlight streamed behind him, but even in the half-light she could see the unruly mushroom of rust red hair that wreathed his head.

He moved purposefully into the dimly lit room, and Emma's first impression was that everything about him was big and red—his hair, his skin, his nose. The floorboards rattled and shook as he walked past her and settled himself behind his desk. Beneath his weight, the leather chair's tired springs twanged. He plopped his elbows on the oaken desk with an audible thunk of bone on wood, then steepled his sausage-thick fingers and studied her through bright, intelligently blue eyes. "So ye say ye're Emmaline Hatter from New York."

"I am."

Thick, stiff-haired red eyebrows drew into a deep, imposing vee. "I dinna believe ye."

Emma was caught off guard. "Why not?"

"I keep up on me readin', ye know. Emmaline Hatter's a famous woman. Call 'er the 'Mad Hatter.' I dinna think a steel-hard, rich-as-God lady'd be dressed like a Mexican whore and wanderin' alone in the desert."

She didn't even flinch at his rudeness. In fact, it relaxed her. She liked people who dealt from positions of strength and didn't pussyfoot around. "Captain MacEwan, you may wire Smitherton Guaranty and Trust. Eugene Cummin, the president, will verify that Emmaline Hatter did indeed travel to New Mexico in search of the legendary Lost City of Cibola."

Captain MacEwan sucked in his breath. It made a sharp, wheezing sound in the quiet office. His ruddy face paled. " 'Tis a big source o' gossip, that. We been speculatin' about it fer years."

Emma considered her next sentence carefully. She had no choice but to tell the captain the truth; it was the only way she'd get his help. Slowly she leaned forward. "Can you keep a secret?"

His blue eyes shone with a firelike intensity as he nodded. "Aye."

"I found it."

He rocked back in his chair. "Holy Mother o' God . . ."

She leaned back, taking a sip of tea. The meeting had just turned around. Now she was in the position she'd always enjoyed, always sought at all costs: the position of ultimate power.

She frowned at the thought, her lips resting against the cup's hot metal rim. Today she felt no joy in the victory. No pleasure or pride. All she felt was a sharp sense of loss.

She pushed the foolish emotion aside and set her cup

down on his desk. "I need a few—two or three—*honest*, reliable men to accompany me to the city to retrieve the gold."

"Is there a lot of it?" he breathed.

"Wagons full. I'll need men in good shape, willing to walk and crawl through the passageway. I'll pay them, and you, very well."

He grinned. "I think we can help ye, Miss Hatter."

A strange sorrow kept her from smiling. It was as if some part of her, deep down and squashed by common sense, had *wanted* to be thwarted. "Yes, Captain MacEwan, I thought perhaps you could."

As he stood to leave, Emma thought of something. It was nothing, really, but for some odd reason, she found herself saying, "Oh, and Captain, what day is it?"

He frowned for a moment. "About the beginnin' o' June."

Emma felt herself go pale. Pa-lo-wah-ti had been right. They'd been in Cibola a month.

The fort bustled with activity. After so many days of restful quiet, Emma felt a little breathless by the hustle and bustle going on around her. Sounds buffeted her ears: boot heels thumping in the hard-packed dirt, squeaking wagon wheels, braying mules and barking dogs, the clanging ring of a blacksmith at work, the muffled chatter of a dozen conversations, and, over-head, the snapping of an American flag in the noontime breeze.

Captain MacEwan led Emma across the dusty mid-section of the camp to a small house. The grayish brown wooden structure looked like all the other buildings clustered inside the protective walls, except for the flowers growing in pots beneath the shuttered windows. Bright spots of pink and green and yellow gave the tiny dwelling a homey, cozy look.

He bounded up the house's low wooden steps. The planks sagged and groaned at each step, then bounced back into place behind him. "Moll, me love," he yelled as he opened the door. "Come 'ere!"

Emma heard the patter of hurrying feet. Self-consciously she straightened the thin cotton *camisa*, wishing—again—that it could be coaxed into covering her sunburnt shoulders.

"What is it, Francis? Is somethin' amiss?" came a bright, happy-sounding voice from behind the door.

Laughter rumbled from his mighty chest. "Nae. Quite the opp'site, in point o' fact. There's a lady here from New York, a Miss Emmaline Hatter. I thought ye might get her a sweet or somethin' whilst I ready her things."

"A lady? Why, ye big oaf, get away from the door and let 'er in!"

MacEwan turned around and offered Emma an easy grin. " 'Tis lonely for female companionship, she be. There's only a few women crazy—"

"In love enough, ye mean," laughed the unseen woman.

"*Crazy* enough to follow a husband to the middle o' nowhere."

Emma swallowed thickly, took a step backward. Suddenly she didn't want to go in, didn't want to see any couple so much in love. "Perhaps, if she's too busy—"

"Nonsense," he answered, holding the door open.

Nervously Emma plucked up her thin cotton skirt and made her way up the stairs. The room she entered was exactly as the flowers promised: cozy and homey.

Honey-colored wood paneled the floor, walls, and ceiling, its uniform color broken by several multicolored braided rugs and crisp white cotton curtains. A blue and white gingham sofa faced the fireplace and cut the room in half. Overturned orange crates flanked either end of the couch, their slatted tops cluttered with pictures and knickknacks. Beside the fireplace was an old, well-used rocking chair with a tired bit of lace draped carefully across its high, curved back.

A sound crept into Emma's subconscious: the whining creak of a rocker as it moved back and forth across a hardwood floor. It was a moment before she recognized the sound as a memory—one she'd long ago suppressed. But now she remembered. Her mother had often held her closely and crooned to her, soft, now bittersweet songs of love designed to help a child sleep.

Emma was surprised to feel the sting of tears. She yanked her gaze to the other side of the room. The only furniture was the dinner table, its round oaken surface brightened by a lard bucket full of fresh spring blossoms. Beside one of the chairs stood a tall, plainly dressed woman, a baby plopped on one hip and a small, redheaded toddler clinging to her hand.

"This is me wife, Molly," MacEwan said. "Moll, this is Emmaline Hatter. Why don't ye have a bit o' tea? I'll be back in about half an' hour."

The door closed behind the captain, and Molly flashed Emma a conspiratorial grin. "Don't ye hate it when they tell ye what to do?"

Emma couldn't help smiling. The woman's easy intimacy and friendly smile made her feel immediately welcome. Molly led Emma to the table and gestured for her to sit down. Then she disappeared into the kitchen for a few moments and returned with a pot of tea and a tin plate layered with homemade tarts.

The two women sat at the dining room table, sipping tea and talking. Molly's two-year-old son, Willie, lay stretched out on the floor beside them, intently stacking and restacking a brightly colored pile of blocks, and the baby, Susan, slept in her mother's arms.

As they talked quietly, Emma watched the gentle swirling motion of Molly's hand on the baby's back, and her heart twisted into a tight, aching knot. The flesh on the back of her hand tingled with the memory of Larence's hand forming to hers. *I want a baby, too. . . .*

Emma's lower lip trembled. She bit down on it, hard, and wrenched her moist gaze away from the baby's head.

"I got to go pee, Mom."

"Aye," Molly answered. Standing, she stepped gingerly over the sprawled toddler and eased the sleeping child away from her breast. "Here, take the wee one, will ye? Young Willie's just learnin', an' I need to help him."

Emma paled. "Oh, I—"

"Thanks," she said, shoving the infant into Emma's arms. "Come on, Will." Taking the boy's hand, she led him out the front door.

Emma was alone with the baby. She screwed up her courage and glanced down. Huge brown eyes blinked up at her from a small, pink face. Tiny, bow-shaped lips pursed into a taut frown.

Emma brought a hand to the child's face and gently stroked the unbelievably soft cheek, the downy white curls.

Regret merged with sadness and twisted her insides. *This* was what she had given up by leaving Cibola. She tore her gaze away from the baby and glanced at the spotlessly clean, welcoming house. Love. A home. Children. That's what she'd walked away from.

Marry me, Em.

When you loved me and I loved you, then both of us were born anew.

Images and words tumbled through her mind, reminding her with blinding force of how good it had felt to be in love. How right. She remembered Larence's gentleness as he stroked her fevered brow and offered her sips of lifesaving water. She remembered his easy laughter, his strength. *It's okay to be afraid.*

And she remembered his touch. Oh, God, she thought, biting her lower lip, his *touch.*

Don't worry, love, what I lack in technique, I make up for in patience. . . .

Tears burned behind her eyes, slipped silently down her cheeks. The flowers blurred into a colorful smear, and she yanked her gaze away. Through the window she saw Captain MacEwan supervising the loading of the wagon, and the pain in her chest trebled. Fear and regret and longing churned in her stomach, made her feel nauseous and headachy. The noose of irrevocability and remorse tightened around her neck, made it difficult to breathe.

How could something be right if it caused so much pain?

For the first time she allowed herself to question her decision. Really question it.

She glanced around, and this time she noticed things she hadn't noticed the first time, like the chipped spout of the china teapot and the ragged, oft-resewn hem of the curtains.

A spark of something dangerously akin to hope slid

through her blood. Tightening her hold on Susan, she stood up and moved toward the slatted box at the couch's arm. The knickknacks were hand-carved bits of wood, as were the frames.

The MacEwans were poor.

Emma stiffened in shock. She'd never thought about the difference between being poor and having limited money. Why? she wondered. Why hadn't her razor-sharp mind probed the obvious question?

Perhaps the question itself was too rooted in darkness; perhaps deep down, her mind had thought to protect her soul. She didn't know. She knew only that for her, it had always been all or nothing. A person was either rich or poor, secure or at risk.

She'd spent a lifetime running from the horrible specter of her childhood, running headlong into anything and everything that appeared to keep the icy chill of poverty at bay. But she'd started running at a tender age, and from her first step, she'd run hard and fast and never looked back.

Blind, naked ambition. It had started her moving and kept her moving. But somehow her mind had never quite caught up with her body. Like a child, she'd fixed a face on poverty; to her it had always been the lightless, soulless facade of Rosare Court. Never once had she considered that she might have been . . . immature. That poverty might sometimes wear a gentler face.

Now, looking around the cozy MacEwan home, she considered that and more. Much, much more. With each realization, her heart lightened. She felt like a woman coming out of a long-term coma, seeing a new world for the first time.

Her room in Rosare Court had once looked like this. True, it had been nothing but a sagging old tenement room, but her mother had filled it with flowers and laughter and bits of tired lace. It had been a *home*. And they had been a loving, happy family.

Poor but happy. As a child, she hadn't needed money to be happy. All she'd needed was her parents and the warm, protective cloak of their love. It wasn't until *after* their deaths that the poverty had become unbearable. . . .

And maybe that wasn't even the complete truth. Maybe it wasn't the poverty, but the lack of love that had been so bloody awful.

God, how had she forgotten? Why had her child's mind focused so completely on the negative and completely suppressed the positive?

Molly and Willie swept into the room on a cloud of laughter, followed closely by Francis. When the big man slammed the door shut, the windows and floorboards rattled.

"I went pee all by myself!" Willie yelled.

Francis dropped to one knee and opened his arms. Willie spun around and hurled himself into his daddy's beefy embrace. "Did ye now, Wee Willie?" he said gruffly, rubbing his son's curly hair. "I'm proud o' ye."

"Thanks for watching our Susiepins," Molly said, taking the baby back in her arms.

Emma stared at her now empty arms. She could still feel the warmth of the baby's skin, still hear the quiet, regular cadence of her breathing. The scent of cotton diapers and talcum powder lingered on her sleeves.

Lifting her gaze, she saw the MacEwan family, standing huddled together like a Christmas photograph. Their smiles and quiet laughter filled the small, sparsely decorated room and gave it a richness Emma had never seen before. The knickknacks on the tables glowed like the finest gold.

And that's when she knew. She'd been wrong to choose the money. Wrong to leave Larence and the only chance for happiness she'd ever had. Nothing, no amount of money or security or gold, was worth the single moment she'd held that baby, or the second it had taken Larence to whisper the words *I love you.*

The realization lifted a thousand-pound weight off her shoulders. Suddenly she felt light enough to fly.

She'd made a grave mistake, but it wasn't too late to fix it. She'd go back to him, tell him how much she loved him, how desperately sorry she was to have left. She'd do anything to make things right with him. Anything.

And she'd never, ever leave him again.

She straightened, tilted her chin. She was just about to tell MacEwan her claims about Cibola had all been a hoax when she glanced out the window and saw the men loading dynamite on the wagon.

"*What the—*" She barreled past the MacEwan family and burst out the front door.

"What are you doing?" she yelled to the young man organizing the crates on the planked bed.

Startled, he looked up.

She marched down the creaking steps and across the yard. Twigs and rocks crackled beneath her punishing steps. "Who's in charge here?" she demanded when she reached the wagon.

A grizzled, hump-backed little man spat a wad of tobacco and thumped himself on the chest. "I am, ma'am. Drake's the name."

"Why are you loading dynamite onto my wagon?"

He spat again, a huge, brown-gray blob that hit the

sandy dirt near her bare feet and splattered upward. "Well, ma'am," I ain't gonna crawl through no hole like a goddamn snake. We'll just set a few blasts, then walk in an' grab the gold easy as Christmas candy."

Shock rooted Emma to the spot. It was a moment before she could find the words to speak. "W-What about the artifacts?"

"Arti-whats?"

"You know, the baskets, the water jugs, the bows and arrows."

The look in his eyes changed. He studied her as if she were a foreign object of questionable value. Or no value at all. "Who cares about a bunch of jugs?"

"*I* care," Emma answered instinctively. The words stunned her. She rocked back on her heels, her eyes widening as she realized it was true. She *did* care about the baskets and the jugs and history of the place. She cared deeply.

"Well, I'll be . . ." she muttered, shaking her head.

Drake took a step backward. "What's that, ma'am? You okay?"

She flashed him a bright, white grin. "Yes, Mr. Drake. I believe I finally am."

"You want me 'n the boys to—"

"No, sir, I do not." She skipped over to where Tashee was tied to the wagon. Quickly checking to see that her canteen was filled and her bedroll was intact, she untied the little burro and began leading her toward the gate.

"Hey, Miss Hatter!" Captain MacEwan's voice boomed across the yard. "Where ye goin'?"

Turning, she held up her left hand. The wide Cibolan wedding band glinted in the afternoon sun. And suddenly she knew why the necklace had disappeared but the ring had not. The marriage, if nothing else, was meant to last. "You were right, Captain, I lied. I'm not Emmaline Hatter. I'm Mrs. Larence Digby. And there is no Cibola. I made it all up."

A loud string of curses followed her blithely uttered statement, but Emma paid the disgruntled men no mind.

Humming a happy tune, she mounted up and headed out.

She was going back to her husband.

Chapter Twenty-seven

"Whoa, girl," Emma said, reining Tashee to a stop. Leaning sideways, she plucked the last marker from the piñon tree's branch. The pencil-sized bit of pale blue cotton fluttered in her palm. Lovingly she ran her forefinger along the trembling cotton. Someone these scraps would hold a place of honor in her home. On the mantel, or next to their bed, in a cut-glass or pottery bowl. Where other women would display fresh-cut roses or dried violets, Emma would showcase these ragged pieces of fabric.

She'd show them to their children, time and again. Bring them out at Christmas and on the anniversary of their wedding in Cibola, and tell the children about how foolish their mother had once been. And about how she had changed. She would use these little bits of cloth to teach the power of love.

She tucked it in her pocket, along with the other markers she'd collected since leaving the fort.

"Okay, Tash, let's go."

The burro pricked up her ears and began plodding forward. Emma tented a hand over her eyes and stared ahead. Dawn was just breaking across the sky in a profusion of pink and gold. Ahead, a huge slab of rock jutted into the still-darkened sky, its black face silhouetted by tenuous strands of magenta light.

Emma's breath caught. They were almost there. Anticipation surged through her blood.

God, she felt good. Better than she had in years. She finally understood what real, honest-to-God hope felt like, and she couldn't imagine how she'd lived her whole life without it. Having hope for the future and something to look forward to made her feel buoyant. Lighter than air.

Almost there. The thought came again, brought a renewed smile to her lips. Soon, she thought. Soon the horrible mistake she'd made in leaving Larence would be behind her, forgotten. She'd do anything—anything—to make him forgive her. And she'd spend the rest of her life proving to him that she was worthy of the love he'd bestowed on her.

She strained forward in her seat and urged Tashee to a trot.

Half an hour later the bouncing duo came to the box canyon's secret entrance. Emma reined Tashee to a circumspect walk. The burro picked her way through the thin, twisting slit of a path. Reddish gold sandstone hemmed them in and reached to the robin's-egg ribbon of sky overhead. The crunching impact of each step reverberated through the confined space.

They came to the end of the trail, and Emma slid off Tashee and ran, stumbling on the loose rocks, to the makeshift rope barrier. Untying the big knot, she flung the coil aside and raced into the box canyon. Tashee trotted past her and barreled toward the pond.

Bright yellow-orange black-eyed Susans blurred before her eyes as she tore through the knee-high grass.

Burrs clung to her skirt, tugged at her hem, but she wrenched the fabric free and kept running.

"Larence!" she yelled, laughing, at the top of her lungs. His name bounced off the silent stone walls and echoed back at her.

Diablo jerked up his head and looked at her. Beside the horse, alongside the small green pool, was the pile of Larence's supplies. Some distance away the pack mule was busily munching on the choice grass.

Emma felt a surge of joy. Everything was exactly as she'd left it. *Exactly.* God, in His infinite wisdom, had believed in her even when she'd stopped believing in Him. And He'd given her a second chance. For once, He'd answered her prayers.

She wouldn't botch it this time. Emma might not be the brightest flame in the fire, but she learned fast. And she never made the same mistake twice.

"Hi, Diablo," she shouted with a wave as she ran past the big sorrel and headed for the plain's center.

Panting, heaving for breath, she clutched her side. Lord, but she was out of shape. Wheezing, she bent over for a moment—only a moment, for she didn't have a second to spare—and tried to calm her breathing. A dozen slim spears of grass tickled her nose.

She smiled and started to brush the grass away. Then she stopped, and inhaled deeply. The rich, springtime-fresh scent of grass and flowers and good earth filled her nostrils.

Slowly she straightened. Bright yellow sunlight beat down on her, and for the first time she noticed how hot it had become. A few vagrant drops of sweat popped out along her hairline and itched across her brow. The flesh between her breasts grew moist.

Standing tall amid the grass, she tented a hand against the sun and squinted toward the opening to Cibola.

The smile slid off her face.

The crack was gone.

It took Emma a moment to react. *Noooooo* . . .

With a strangled cry, she snatched up her skirt and started running. Ahead, the wall of sandstone was a blurry wash of brown. No matter how much she blinked, or how hard she focused, she couldn't see anything except the wall. No crack, no opening.

Pain jabbed her side, but still she kept running. Now and then she swiped at the sheen of tears and dust in her eyes, but the moisture returned almost immediately. Dust puffed up from her punishing steps and formed a gray-brown cloud around her. Tears blurred her vision, turned the world into a shifting, incomprehensible mist of rust and blue. Her breath came in serrated gasps.

She clambered up the escarpment. Her skirts tangled in her feet, and she hit the dirt hard. Coughing, she got back to her feet, and ran blindly through the cloud of dust.

She crashed into the rock wall, and staggered backward. Her breath expelled in a pain-sharpened groan.

Where was the opening? Where was the goddamn opening?

Sick fear and panic sluiced through her. Desperately she searched. Her fingers scoured the rock, probed every hairline crack and indentation. "Please, oh please, oh please, oh please . . ."

There was nothing. Not even a hint that there had ever been an opening.

Fear and horror and panic coiled in her stomach, twisted her insides into a fiery knot. She pressed a shaking hand to her midsection and pressed hard, hoping to stop the vomit she felt rising to her throat.

A bleakness unlike any she'd ever known pulled her into a black pit of hopelessness and despair. Tears welled in her eyes and then dried up, became a bone-dry ache too deep, too raw, for tears.

A kaleidoscope of images and pictures tumbled end over end through her mind. Larence. The home they would have built. The children they would have had . . .

In agony she screamed, a high banshee wail that bounced off the mesa's walls and rang back at her, taunting her.

"I'm sorry," she screamed to God. "*I'm sorry. Don't do this to* him because of me. Please." Her voice cracked. "Please," she said with a sob, "be just. Take me instead. I want to die. . . ."

"Emma?"

The word came to her as a thought. A loving memory.

Oh, God . . . She'd spend the rest of her life hearing his voice in the whispering of wind, feeling his touch in the brushing of every breeze. She slumped forward, rested her forehead against the warm, gritty rock. The feel of it reminded her of resting her brow on Larence's bristly chin, and a new wave of pain washed through her. *It's okay to be afraid. I'll take care of you. . . .*

"Emma, are you out there?"

She jerked upright and stared at the rock in horror. It couldn't be. She had to be going insane. That couldn't be Larence's voice, coming from *behind* the rock. Could it?

She stepped closer, pressed her fingertips against the rock. "Larence?"

"Emma," he yelled, "is that you?"

It *was* Larence. He was behind the rock, buried alive. *In the dark* . . .

She hurled herself at the rock and started clawing. "Open, damn you!" Sobbing, she beat her fists against the wall and clawed at the solid rock face until her fingernails were ripped and bleeding and her hands were coated with blood. Every blow surged up her arm and lodged like fire in her shoulder, but still she persisted. Screaming, crying, pounding.

"Emma." His voice came to her, jolted her out of her frenzy. "It's not your fault."

Exhausted, hollow, she sank to her knees. Her fingers scraped down the sandstone wall and fell in a useless heap in her lap. He was wrong. It *was* her fault.

She wanted to die. *Ached* to die.

This time the tears did come, great, wracking sobs that wrenched her soul and scalded her eyes.

Emmaline had come back for him. Larence couldn't believe it. He felt the pain of the last few hours melt away. She *did* love him. Somehow that made all the difference. At least now he could die happy, knowing he'd been loved.

If only he could see her again, touch her one last time. He huddled close to the jet black stone, trying to draw some remnant of her scent through the rock, trying to feel some hint of her warmth in the cold darkness around him. The muffled sounds of her sobbing reached through the rock and coiled around his heart.

"Ah, Em," he said in a ragged whisper of despair, "don't cry . . ."

"I love you so much, Larence. I came back to—to say I was wrong. Only, it's too late. I'm so sorry."

"It's my fault, too," he choked out. "I was wrong, too, Em. You're my dream. *You*, not some city."

"Oh, Larence . . ."

He could hear the sadness in her voice, feel her hopelessness.

Stay together in the city. The words came back to Larence, mocked him. He'd ignored the Indian, and in anger and hurt, had let her go. Now they were both alone, both frightened and afraid and vulnerable. And Cibola, the glorious city of his dreams, had become not his refuge, but his tomb.

"I should have listened to Pa-lo-wah-ti," he said dully.

Larence's tired voice seeped through the stone. It was a moment before the words registered.

Pa-lo-wah-ti! Emma surged to her feet. Hiking up her skirt, she scrambled down the escarpment and ran pell mell through the tall grass. By the time she reached the plain's center, she was wheezing and out of breath. Gasping, she doubled over and concentrated on each breath until her breathing normalized. Then she straightened and looked around.

"We watched your every move. Tracked your every thought."

Tall, silent mesas stared back at her. Overhead, the sky was a bright cobalt blue.

She cupped her hands around her mouth and screamed as loudly as she could: "Pa-lo-wah-ti!"

The word vibrated in the hot air for a long moment, then evaporated.

Emma's narrowed gaze scoured the heavens and the mesatops. She listened intently, tried to hear something besides the thumping of her own heart and the restless sigh of breeze through the grass.

Nothing. No movement, no sound, no answer.

She yelled his name again. And again and again and again, until her voice was ragged and hoarse and tears were streaming down her face.

And still there was no answer.

Finally, defeated, she dropped to her knees and bowed her head. "Help us," she said in a cracked, pitiful voice.

"Emmaline."

She jerked her head up. Pa-lo-wah-ti and Ka-Neek and another man stood before her. Proud, solemn.

"Pa-lo-wah-ti! Oh, God," she whispered, crawling on her knees toward him. "I was wrong. Please help us. Please . . ."

His muddy blue eyes fixed unerringly on her face. "Sometimes choices are made too late."

Emma knew that somehow he could see her. She held her gaze steady on his, refused to look away. Directly overhead the hawk banked right and swooped closer. She felt the soft whirring of displaced air against her cheek. Still she didn't look away. "And sometimes they are not."

A glimmer of respect flickered in the sightless blue eyes. One ash gray eyebrow pulled upward, and Emma knew he was waiting for something else.

"I came back alone," she said quietly.

"Why?"

"For the drop of magic."

She thought for a moment that he would smile, but he did not. He just continued to stare down at her through light, muddy, soul-searching eyes. "And what do you seek of me?"

She swallowed thickly. "I want you to open the doorway to Cibola."

"Why?"

"Larence is in there. Alive."

Pa-lo-wah-ti said nothing. His gaze cut to the seamless rock face. Long minutes passed. Emma felt the thudding of her heart. The sound pounded in her ears like repeated hammerblows on hardwood.

Please God, please God, please God . . . The formless prayer cycled through her brain in dizzying repetition. She remained on her knees, her hands clasped in her lap. It was all she could do to keep from standing up and yelling at Pa-lo-wah-ti to do something, but she held herself in steely control.

For Larence, she'd remain on her knees a lifetime.

"There is a price," Pa-lo-wah-ti said at last.

Emma uncoiled her fingers and forced them to her sides. "There always is."

"You must walk away from this place—both of you. And you must never tell a soul what you have found."

Emma gasped. Her eyes rounded with horror.

"I know," he said quietly, and there was a wealth of compassion in his voice. "You have cost him much."

Emma squeezed her eyes shut. Tears seeped past her seamed lashes and fell in hot streaks down her cheeks. Not much, she thought dismally. Everything. She'd taken everything from him. Fame, fortune, peer respect. His dream. By leaving him alone in Cibola, she'd stripped him of every dream he'd ever had.

"Your answer?" Pa-lo-wah-ti asked solemnly.

She winced at the sound of his gravelly voice. What answer could she give? It was too late to salvage some remnant of Larence's life's work. She'd taken it all from him. All she could do was give him back his life, and pray to God it would be enough. Pray he could someday forgive her.

God knew she could never forgive herself.

Dully she opened her eyes. "Yes." The word felt as if it had been ripped from the depths of her soul.

Pa-lo-wah-ti laid his skeletal hand on her shoulder. Warmth seeped from his flesh to hers. Emma looked up, met his gaze. For endless seconds they stared at each other, and she knew he saw her every fear.

"You have chosen well. The magic will fill your soul. Now close your eyes."

She did as she was told, and immediately she felt the change. Shadows fell across her downcast face; the sky overhead darkened. The ground rattled and shook. Dirt rained down from the mesatops and pattered the earth. The air turned cold. Wind swept through the canyon, whistling through the tree limbs. Grass slapped across her lap and lay shivering.

The scent of burning rock mingled with the sharp tang of magic and filled the small valley like a cloud.

Thunder rumbled before a flash of unearthly light. Something hit the rock with a resounding *crack*. The vibrating grind of shifting rock echoed through the valley.

And then it was quiet.

When Emma found the courage to open her eyes, the sky was a bright blue. The sun was strong and hot.

She looked around. Pa-lo-wah-ti and the other men were gone, and there wasn't so much as a bent blade of grass to hint that they'd ever been here.

"Emma!"

Her gaze shot to the sandstone wall. Larence was standing inside the gaped zigzag entrance to Cibola.

She lurched to her feet and started to run toward him. Then she remembered the vow she'd made to Pa-lo-wah-ti, and her steps faltered. Uncertainty gnawed a hole in her heart. How could anyone—even Larence—forgive what she'd done?

He started running. When he crossed into the sunlight, he tripped, stumbled. He regained his balance quickly, and kept running, but this time he moved unevenly. Awkwardly.

The magic was gone. His limp had returned. Emma felt an overwhelming sense of sadness and regret and self-loathing. God, hadn't her greed cost him enough?

He scooped her into his arms and twirled her around. She wrapped her arms around his neck and clung to him, knowing that the moment she told him that her greed had cost him his life's work, it would all end.

Gradually his hold loosened, and she slid down the long, hard length of his body. Looking up at him, she lifted her hand to his face and stroked his cheek. She memorized every line of his face, every detail so that years from now, when she was old and alone and lonely, she could remember this moment, this man who was everything she'd ever wanted and more. Every dream she'd ever suppressed, every prayer she'd ever bitten back.

This man who was her love.

"Emma, I—"

"Wait! Before you say anything, I have to tell you something. I—" She looked away, chewed nervously on her lower lip. "I . . . I had to promise we'd never say a word about the city."

He touched her chin and forced her to look up at him. "Emmaline Amanda Hatter, in the face of God and all that I hold sacred and holy, I promise to love, honor, and cherish you all the days of my life."

"Oh, Larence . . ."

Tears formed in his eyes, slid silently down his cheeks. "Mrs. Digby, do you love me?"

Emma was crying so hard, it was impossible to speak. All she could do was nod.

Then he did the most amazing thing. He kissed her. Emma felt his lips form to hers, felt the whisper-soft touch of his tongue against her tear-dampened mouth, and hope filled her heart to bursting.

She blinked up at him.

"I love you, wife," he said simply.

She was afraid she'd misheard. "But your dream—"

"*You're* my dream. I may be an absentminded professor, but I never make the same mistake twice."

"But, Larence, I—"

"You never did know when to shut up," he said, kissing the moisture from her eyes. "Don't you know by now that I'm a man of many dreams? Have you heard of Atlantis?"

"Of course, but that's just a legend. . . ."

He kissed her again, a slow, gentle, loving kiss that set her heart and soul afire. When their lips parted, Emma thought she felt a whir of breath against her mouth, thought she heard him whisper: "So was Cibola."

And that's when Emma knew: The adventure of her life had just begun.